THE
BROKEN
ROAD

B.R.COLLINS

BLOOMSBURY

LONDON · BERLIN · NEW YORK · SYDNEY

Bloomsbury Publishing, London, Berlin, New York and Sydney

First published in Great Britain in February 2012 by Bloomsbury Publishing Plc
50 Bedford Square, London, WC1B 3DP

A CIP catalogue record for this book is available from the British Library

ISBN 978 1 4088 0649 4

Typeset by Hewer Text UK Ltd, Edinburgh
Printed in Great Britain by Clays Ltd, St Ives Plc, Bungay, Suffolk

1 3 5 7 9 10 8 6 4 2

www.bloomsbury.com

For everyone I met on the Camino de Santiago de Compostela

– *What is life?*
– *A delight to the blessed, a grief to the unhappy, an experience of waiting for death.*
– *What is death?*
– *An inevitable happening, an uncertain journey, the tears of the living, the confirmation of the testament, the thief of man.*
– *What is a human being?*
– *A slave to death, a traveller passing through, a stranger in the place.*

From *The Debate between the Noble and Princely Youth Pippin and Alcuin the Scholar* by Alcuin of York (c. 735–804)

PART I

*An inevitable
happening*

I

You're high up, so high up you can see the edge of the world, the sun sinking on the western rim. Below you the earth is spread out like a shield, a wide circle of land like hands cupped round a sea, the tiny heart of Jerusalem in the centre where they meet. From up here, if you didn't know already, there'd be no way of telling who held the Holy Land: true believer, infidel, barbarian . . . There'd be no way of knowing whose feet dirtied the sacred places, whose lips opened on prayers, or whose eyes rose, distracted, to the sunset reddening the bones of the hills, the harsh, impersonal glamour of the sky. From up here it's hard to see why you'd care one way or the other. Men are men, after all; to you, so high up, we must all look the same, more or less.

But you're not watching Jerusalem, not now. Your gaze has turned north, to Europe – a colder, soggier continent altogether, where the men are paler and dirtier, still wary of forests, dark places, ravens and one-eyed men, where the old battle-gods aren't quite forgotten. Slowly you drift downwards, circling, until your eye catches the details you've been searching for. A city, at first so far away no one else could see it, until it blooms, expands into a knot of roofs and walls, a patch of smoke over a

3

nest of sewers, taking up more and more of your field of vision. It swells on the bank of the river, the new, sleek city wall fattening as you drift closer, the gates expanding, throwing themselves open like seed-pods. The pimples of churches rise, the scab of the cathedral hardens and darkens. But no, it isn't that, whatever you're looking for . . . You circle, riding the edge of the breeze, your gaze moving sideways, a fraction east, a fraction south . . . You're sinking faster now, side-slipping so smoothly it's as if the ground is rising at your command. Closer and closer, and you're still looking . . .

The meadows outside the city wall. One particular meadow, where a path emerges from the trees into the glassy spring evening. A curve of a brook – a drooping plume of willow – two figures coming from the shadow of the trees, the one in front a greybeard, whistling tunelessly, the other –

And you say: *Mine*.

You stoop to him, straight down, talons outstretched. You dive like an arrow, with such violence, such quiet speed that even if he's heard you there's no time to look up, no time to step aside, before you're on him like a handful of knives. Your eyes stare into his and he cries out, clutching at himself. You tighten your grip until you feel the flesh give way, the bravado of bone start to crack, the heart ready to drop like fruit from the branch. He falls to his knees, still crying out – as if he thinks you'll listen – flinching from the beat of wings, your vicious strength.

The older man stops and turns to look over his shoulder, then heaves a deep breath and sits, leaning against his pack. He plucks a stem of grass and rolls it between his fingers. From time to time he glances over at the

4

boy – half proud, half bored – then idly presses his thumbs together over the blade of grass and blows. The grass squeaks, squeals, twitters, like an imitation of bird-song. The man puts his hands behind his head and closes his eyes.

The boy is quieter now, shuddering from your attack. His hands start to move again as if he could push you away; then he holds them still, face resolutely lifted towards you. His eyes are open and unblinking a few inches from yours. He's breathing shallowly to manage the pain. You tighten your hold, just to see him tremble. He waits, as if he knows that one false move will cost him an eye, a face, a soul. When, at last, you let him go, he bites his lower lip. He follows your flight with his gaze, the brief ungainly moment as you leave him behind, the final disappearance into a clear sky. He stands up and carries on walking, towards the city walls.

The older man drags himself back to his feet and catches him up, the interrupted tune back on his lips as if nothing has happened. He starts to sing, half-swallowing the notes between the consonants, scratching the bites on his neck in time to the melody. He sings, 'And now they lie in hell together . . .' He adds, 'Hey, Nick, nasty one, was it, this time?' but the boy doesn't answer, and after a while the man starts to sing again. 'Long their "ah" and long their "oh", long their misery, long their woe!' These seem to be the only lines he knows, because he sings them again and then stops. They walk quietly for a few paces, until he clears his throat and begins another song: 'Sweet leman, my cods ache with desire –' but the boy glances in his direction and he falls silent.

They reach the shadow of the city walls. There's a gate ahead, and beyond that they can see the towers and roofs

5

of the stinking city, hear the bells and shouts and animals. The boy was walking with his head turned to stare into the setting sun, as if he's already a saint, hungry for suffering; but now he looks straight ahead, at the track in front of them, the first door he needs to pass.

He nods in a curious, dismissive way, as if he's the master here, and the older man walks on without waiting. Then the boy turns to look back the way he's come, eyes sliding from side to side, lips moving as if he's reading, pausing on the meadow where he saw you. He almost smiles.

Then, in a language only you can hear, he says, *Yes*.

Or, at least, that's how I imagine it. I wasn't there, of course. Perhaps it wasn't like that at all. Who knows?

Perhaps it wasn't even Nick you were interested in. Perhaps it was his father – that's right, he's Nick's father, the old man, although I didn't know that yet, didn't know *anything*, was probably, at that moment, sitting in a stinking garderobe with other things firmly on my mind – his father who interested you, who brought you stooping to his level, claws outstretched. After all, fathers and sons are your speciality, aren't they? Abraham and Isaac. David and Absalom. Nick's father, who loved him – or might have done, maybe; and mine, who didn't. Perhaps Nick was never even the one you were after.

But either way, I think you were there. You were watching, waiting, lured by the promise of meat, soon, the scent of carrion that Nick didn't even know he exuded. Oh yes, you were there. You wouldn't have missed it for the world, not a moment that beautiful, that peaceful, the calm before your tempest. You would have watched them go up to that muddy twelve-gated city with your blank golden eyes, following every move.

And all the time . . . while Nick and his father were tramping along that trail to the city gates, Nick seized by ecstasy and dropping to his knees to pray – or not, depending on which of my versions you like better . . . all the time that was going on, I was in a privy.

Watch. This *did* happen.

Engelgerus leans forward to see the ring my father's showing him. He takes it between his finger and thumb, tilts it as if he's feeling the weight, then gives it back. 'Hmmm.'

'The intaglio is my own work,' my father says. 'Gold and Baltic amber.'

'Ye-es . . .' Engelgerus coughs, then takes a deep breath, the air whistling in his nose. 'Your own work . . . I'd've thought it was one of your journeymen . . . or an apprentice.'

I glance at my father's face and away. Wings of unease beat in my guts.

Engelgerus coughs again, spits into the rushes, and picks the ring out of my father's hand like a bird pecking at a worm. He turns it so that the design catches the light. 'Of course, goldsmiths aren't what they used to be. I've seen gold . . . the stuff I took to England – now *that* was fine work. Cologne gold for English wool, and they got the better side of the deal.'

My father follows Engelgerus's movements with his eyes. 'An emerald? Or I have a sapphire *en cabochon* . . .'

'Yes, I'd like a sapphire,' Paul says, as if being Engelgerus's son gives him the right to demand whatever he wants without even saying *please*.

My father says, 'Rufus, go and get the sapphire ring.'

I nod and go to the back of the workshop, making for the armoire where my father keeps the finished pieces. The noise rises around me: a hot wall of hammering and wheezing bellows, tapping, rasping, the whole world ringing like beaten metal. If heat made a noise, it would be the sound of my father's workshop. Sweat starts out on my forehead and upper lip. No one looks at me as I squeeze past the workbench, trying not to knock the files off the walls. I have to step over the new apprentice, who's struggling with the cross-shaped lever and drawplate, but he's sniffling and blinking miserable, sweaty tears out of his eyes and doesn't seem to notice. In a few months that'll be me, but I'm not going to think about that now.

I unlock the armoire and take out the ring. I put it on my finger but it's too big, so I close my fist to stop it sliding while I turn the key in the lock again. The metal nudges at the bones in my hand like something's broken. I feel sick: hungry and dizzy with the smell of hot wax and molten gold. I don't want to go back to my father, Engelgerus and Paul. But I do.

Engelgerus is scratching his beard with his left hand and turning a cameo clasp over and over in his right. 'The reliquary of Saint James . . . now *that* was good, by all accounts. Not that we'd know, after the blasted English stole it.' He sniffs, venomously, as if he can smell them from here.

Paul says, 'But – isn't Saint James's body in Compostela –?'

'His hand, boy, his *hand*.' Engelgerus's knuckles stand out against the clasp like ivory. 'That drunken, perverted Saracen-lover of an English king took it and never gave it back.'

My father's face tightens. They say the English king could have taken the Holy City, and chose not to. 'A fine sardonyx,' he says, his eyes on the clasp. 'And an apt symbol for a young man to wear.'

I peer closer, trying not to make it too obvious. Joined hands, pale on a brown-red background, like dried blood. The emblem of prayer and piety. I glance at Paul's face and want to laugh.

Paul catches my eye as if he's seen what I'm thinking. For a moment it looks as if he's going to smile too. Then he clenches his jaw and stares at me until I look away. He says, 'Let me see the sapphire.'

My father jerks his head at me and I hold the ring out, but Engelgerus reaches past me and takes it before Paul can. He clears his throat, rubbing his thumb over the smooth curve of the stone. 'Not much better, this one . . . the setting isn't quite right . . . another of yours, Johannes?' But he doesn't give my father time to answer. 'It makes me sick, to know they've got our relics. The damned English . . . drunkards, every last one of them.'

'And they have tails, don't they? Englishmen?' Paul says, but no one except me seems to hear.

'And what's worse, he let the infidels keep Jerusalem,' Engelgerus goes on, and spits a gob of phlegm into the rushes without bothering to cover his mouth. 'That English sodomite. Sent *presents* to Saladin. And those heathen barbarians have still got the True Cross. It's shameful.'

Suddenly there's silence. Even Paul looks down, nudging at the wrinkled hose over his ankle with his other foot.

My father is frowning, deeply, so that looking at his face I can't quite recognise him. He says, 'Well, we still have the bodies of the Three Kings in the shrine here. We must thank God for that.'

Engelgerus snorts and shakes his head. He slips the ring on to the middle joint of his finger and taps it with his fingernail. 'The Rood, Johannes. The very wood on which our Lord was crucified . . . in the hands of those filthy, decadent unbelievers. And so is the Holy Land . . . God is reminding us of our sins.'

For the first time, my father's voice is taut. 'No doubt.'

'I don't think this sapphire will do, I'm afraid. Shoddy workmanship.' Engelgerus hands it back to my father and adds, with a casual sniff of disdain, 'How much would you take for it?'

My father doesn't bat an eyelid, but suddenly I can sense that he's relaxed a little bit. 'Twenty-five marks.'

'Oh, Johannes . . .' Engelgerus smiles, his voice indulgent, as if he's talking to a child. 'You know it isn't worth that.'

My father meets his eyes and smiles back. This is an old game; they know how it works. 'It's worth rather more, in fact. But as you're a friend . . .'

Engelgerus plucks at his beard, tugging at each separate hair. He's forgotten about the True Cross, apparently, and so has my father. 'Come now. I'll give you twenty, if you throw in the cameo as well.'

There's a gust of fetid air from the street outside, a sudden ripple of louder noise, the splash of a chamber pot being emptied past our window. I feel a warm draught on my face, smelling of piss and sour sweetmeats from Paul's breath.

'I'd be cheating myself, Engelgerus, and you know it. If you want both, you can pay me forty and call yourself a thief.'

I lean back, slowly, until I'm almost but not quite off-balance, pretending I'm not really here. There's a shout from the workshop, a cut-off yelp of pain that means someone's got burnt. Daniel, probably, who's got the shakes. He's too clumsy to carve the gems any more; soon he'll be too clumsy to do anything. There's a dull chorus of sympathy and irritation from the other journeymen, and someone yells at the new apprentice to clean up the mercury and help Daniel start again. I glance at my father, but he doesn't react.

Engelgerus grins, showing his last few teeth. 'You drive a hard bargain, Johannes. Thirty for the pair.'

The noise from the workshop dies down, back to the constant pounding of metal on metal and the drag of someone's stool over the floor as they get back to work. It's never quiet in there – or anywhere, come to think of it. And when I'm a man I'll work in there with the others, learning from my father, sweating and cursing and gathering tiny burns on my hands like flea-bites. I narrow my eyes and concentrate on what my father's saying.

'Thirty-five. You won't find better work anywhere in Cologne.'

'Seventeen for just the sapphire, then.'

Paul frowns. He wants both, now. But my father sighs and says, 'Twenty,' with a peculiar softness that means he'll give in to Engelgerus's next bid.

'Eighteen.'

'Done.' My father smiles, and I realise he's got more than he expected – more than the ring's worth. Something says a prayer of relief in my head: *Thank God, thank God* . . . But it gives me a funny surge of shame, too, to see him suddenly triumphant. 'You're robbing me,

Engelgerus. You take that to England and you'll get double what you've paid for it here.'

Engelgerus shakes his head good-humouredly and starts to get the money out of his purse.

Paul says, 'I want the clasp too.'

Engelgerus glances at him, and then carries on counting the silver. 'And if I come to you for Katerin's wedding ornaments, I want an *honest* price,' he says to my father.

Paul clenches his jaw. He looks very young, suddenly. Everything in his body is saying, *I want, I want*. One of his hands is pulling the fabric of his cotte into a spiral knot, twisting and twisting. He says, 'Father . . .'

Engelgerus takes the ring from my father and turns, ignoring me. 'Don't be greedy, Paul. Or I shan't give you the ring.'

Paul's face doesn't change. I can't believe it. His father is giving him a *sapphire* – and whatever Engelgerus says, it's good work, it's the best in Cologne – and Paul is still looking mutinous, lagging behind as his father leaves the shop. I feel a strange, astonished laugh trying to break out of me, the muscles in my cheeks tightening. I swallow, digging my nails into my hands, but suddenly my throat tightens and I hear a kind of squeak, like a hiccup.

Paul shoots me a glance over his shoulder. I hold his gaze for a fraction of a second and then look round, as if I'm wondering what he's looking at. But another gulp of laughter is surfacing, swelling as it rises, like a bubble. It's not that funny, really; I'm just so relieved that my father got what he wanted after all.

He pauses, checks that my father isn't listening, then whispers, 'What's so amusing, Red? Do you like seeing your pappy cheat honest men?'

12

I shake my head, so determined not to make a sound that I don't care what he's saying.

'He's a stingy man, your father. And his work is rubbish. Everyone says so. We only come here because it's cheap.' He looks round again. Engelgerus is at the door, cursing a cart that's got stuck in the quagmire of the street outside. No one's listening to Paul except me. 'So shut your face, Red.'

I hold his stare for just long enough.

He pushes his chin forward, screwing his mouth into a mulish knot like a cat's bunghole. 'You smarmy skite.' Then he steps towards me and stamps down on my ankle with his foot.

He's wearing pattens, and for a second there's only the sound of the wood hitting the bone, the tiny fizz of the rough edges catching on my hose. The impact jars right up my leg, but it's like a burn – for a second I don't feel it. Then it hurts. It really *hurts*. I stagger and hiss with pain.

'Serves you right.' And he glances – quickly, as if it's automatic – at Engelgerus.

I can't help myself. I kick back.

I'm only wearing my turnshoes, and they're soft, and it doesn't hurt him much; but I don't think he cares about the pain one way or another. It's the fact that I'm fighting back at all. He catches my shoulder and tilts me backwards, so even though I'm as tall as he is, I'm looking up into his face, smelling his breath, as he kicks my shins swiftly, one foot after another. Something inside me registers the new pain, spilling over the old one like fresh solder, but I'm not listening to it. I curse, in spite of myself, and draw my hand back to swing a punch.

Someone grabs me, pulling me sharply away, and then

the world jumps and rocks and goes black for an instant. When I can see clearly again my face is burning and my father still has his hand raised to me. There's quiet; somehow, even now, I have room to realise that the journeymen are hammering more softly so that they can hear what's going on. *How childish*, I think, and blink the involuntary tears away.

Engelgerus is back in the room. He looks from Paul to me and back again. Nothing shows on his face.

My father says, 'Say you're sorry. *Say you're sorry.*'

'He kicked me,' I say. 'He started it.'

Paul opens his mouth to disagree. Then he shuts his mouth again and crosses his arms over his chest, posing with all his weight on one leg like a troubadour in a picture. All he needs is a lute.

'Say you're sorry,' my father says.

My knees feel as if they're filling with something cold and wet. Now I can feel the pain in my shins. The wool over my ankle is sticky; I don't dare to look down but it feels like the skin's broken. I say, 'I'm sorry.' It's a lie, but I don't have any choice.

Engelgerus nods and turns away. 'Paul,' he says, and the tone of his voice doesn't give anything away. He walks out without looking to see if Paul follows him.

Paul gives me a final look – a tight, furious smile – and trails after Engelgerus.

I don't want them to leave. I stand where I am, looking out into the street, trying to hold on to the sound of their footsteps through the mess of other noise, but it's no good. They've gone, and I'm alone with my father.

He says something, but when I turn and try to look him in the eye I realise I wasn't listening and I don't know what the words were. I feel the familiar weakness in my stomach, the melting sensation like my insides have turned to tallow. I say, 'I'm sorry, Father.'

'Come with me.' He's so gentle. I wish he'd be angry; I wish he'd punish me as if he *wanted* to, at least. But it's always for my own good, and he never lets me forget it.

He takes the bunch of willow sticks from the hook on the wall and leads me upstairs, into the sleeping-room above the passage, next to the solar where my mother will be sewing or praying.

I say, 'It was Paul. He was insulting you and all I did was smile at him – honestly. He kicked me, he stamped on my foot – look, I'm bleeding . . .' I even call him *Papa*. But it's no good.

For the first few strokes I'm thinking, *It's not fair, it's not fair*. Then I'm not really thinking anything.

II

Afterwards, I stand up and thank him and he goes back down to the workshop. I take deep breaths, not ignoring the pain, not pushing it away, but not exactly welcoming it either. After a little while it fades and there's room in my head for other things.

And it's not fair. It's not *fair*. I shut my eyes and Paul is looking back at me, sneering and arrogant. But it isn't Paul I'm angry with. My father must have seen what happened – he must have known – and he punished me, he punished *me* . . .

The door opens. I spin round, wincing, but it isn't one of the apprentices; it's my aunt Lena. She looks at me with her head on one side, her pale eyelashes blinking slowly.

'Poor Rufus.'

'It's all right,' I say, because she doesn't like it when I'm beaten.

'Poor Rufus. Poor, poor Rufus.' She tilts her head even more, so that her veil swings out to the side; then, distracted, she starts to fiddle with it, surprised that it doesn't hurt when she pulls. Her wimple slides slowly out of place and a wisp of hair uncurls on her forehead.

'It's all right,' I say again. It's the only thing I can say,

16

and it's a lie. I hear my own voice in my head: *Thank you, Father*.

'A dog, a wife, and a walnut tree,' she replies, smiling up at me unexpectedly as if it's the answer to a question. 'The harder you hit them the better they be.'

I nod, trying to smile back.

'But you're not, are you?' She adds, 'Woof. Rrrff. Grrrr. Woof, woof.' There's a silence, and she sways a little, as if she's thinking about trees. Then she says, unexpectedly, 'Our Lord was whipped. He didn't deserve it either.'

I can't help laughing, and that helps, a bit.

'He *didn't*,' she says, as if she thinks I'm disputing what she's said. 'In my heart's eye ever it must be, that hard, knotty Rood tree . . .' She nods at me, and whispers, 'For us. Dead. Dead done, for us.'

'I know.'

'Think on it,' she says, suddenly stern. She probably isn't trying to mimic my father, but it's uncanny. 'Think on it.'

I nod, taking a deep breath. I'm knackered. Lena's so hard to follow – not what she says but how she's got there. She drifts and circles like a bird of prey, but she never actually catches anything.

My mother's voice says, 'Lena.'

Lena flinches. She reaches for my hand. I step back, gritting my teeth. In a very small, panicky voice she says, 'Rufus . . . ?'

My mother flings the door open. It hits the wall and the floor shakes at the impact. 'Lena! What are you doing? Come back this instant.'

Lena's mouth moves but no sound comes out. I imagine my name sitting in the air between us, silent as an egg.

My mother grabs Lena's wrist, wrenching, and she

squeaks and stumbles, treading on her hem. 'Come *back*. How dare you go wandering! You stay where you're told, you understand?'

I look down, pressing my toes into the rushes. There's a heavy, muffled sort of thud, and I hear Lena start to cry.

'And what are you doing in here, Rufus?'

'Getting something for Father.' Technically that's a lie, but we all know what I mean.

'Go back to the workshop. I've told you before not to encourage her.' My mother gives me a look that isn't quite angry: more sort of hopeless. Then she turns to Lena and pulls her towards the door. 'And you – we'll have to tie you up if you don't behave. Now come on, we'll go on with our nice sewing. You'll like that, won't you? That's right . . .'

Lena gives me a final desperate look – as if she's got mixed up and she thinks *I'm* our Lord and I can save her. There's spit swinging off her chin. She looks round, tears welling in her eyes, then opens her mouth and starts to wail, fighting my mother's grip.

I stay where I am. The door closes again.

And then, for the first time, I feel the burning under my eyes that means I'm going to cry.

I make it to the privy. Just. Then I put my head on my knees, tasting the skit-heavy air, and sob like a baby. It's not the pain I care about. It's not even Lena's face, the familiar shine of tears on her cheeks, the terrified way she tried to catch hold of my hand. I'm sobbing with fury because it isn't *fair*.

And as I'm sitting there, crying into my hands, choking on the stench of other people's bowels, Nick's coming through St Severinus' Gate, stating his business. At least, I like to think so. Just as I'm cursing my father, and my mother, and every worldly despicable adult in Cologne; just as I'm calling for a judgement on them, in my childish, vindictive sort of way . . .

I don't know it yet, but at that moment, less than a mile away, Nick's coming into the city.

I like to imagine you roosting on the roof of the inn where Nick stays that night, your head tucked underneath your wing. But that's wrong, isn't it? You don't sleep; you sit on the windowsill of the room where he's sleeping, blinking your round nocturnal eyes. He's exhausted from the journey, so he sleeps well, even though the air's thick with the scent of humanity and the night watchmen call out every hour. He's not going anywhere. But even so, you won't let him out of your sight. None of his bed-mates would notice you – you don't touch him, not this time – but he knows you're there. He's used to it.

And when they wake up, Nick and his father, they join the flow of pilgrims that push through the city streets, and you follow them. This isn't Jerusalem, but it's a shoddier version of it: the city with its twelve gates, the shrine at the centre, the hordes of pilgrims. You must relish this, at least a little bit: the peasants looking round at the houses that push one another out of place like crowded teeth, their frowns as they follow the right-angled Roman-built streets, their deep breaths when they catch sight of the cathedral. They think they're coming closer to you, poor fools. They think that massive, half-finished gold shrine holds a piece of you – no, not even that – something that's been near to you, once, a long time ago. They think that's a good thing.

Nick's never seen the cathedral before either. But he doesn't even blink.

His father is stumbling along behind him, bleary-eyed. He shouts, 'Nick – hey, Nick, wait for me –'

Nick grins and speeds up, sliding deftly between the footsore pilgrims. He's as tired as any of them, but he's used to pain; his blisters don't even register. He shouts, 'Come on, Dad, we're nearly there,' spinning round to laugh in his father's face, running backwards.

And goes straight into something.

The breath goes out of him. His first instinct – the terrified reflex you've taught him – is to stay still, freezing at the impact like a mouse caught by a hawk; but then he remembers he's human. He turns and he's looking up at another boy, only a few fingers' width away. He has a thin, spiky face, with eyes set too far apart, pale skin that looks like it would bruise at a breath, a few dark flecks that could be freckles or mud thrown up from the gutter. But the first thing Nick sees – the first thing anyone would see – is the hair, blazing so red even a winter's build-up of grime can't dull it, fox-red, red as a sow's udders. The kind of red that earns you nicknames, or insults, or jokes shouted from doorways. The kind of red that makes polite people wonder what colour your beard would be, if you had one. And makes everyone else speculate loudly about the hair on your testicles.

But Nick doesn't think that. Of course not. Nick thinks of Pentecost, and the flames that marked the apostles.

I say, 'Look where you're *going*, can't you.'

He blinks, and he stops staring at my hair and meets my eyes instead. He gives me a long, straight, intimate look that somehow doesn't belong in this street. Then he says, 'Who are you?'

20

I want to push him aside, whoever he is, this skinny peasant boy with odd dreamy eyes. But I don't. I say, 'Who are *you*?'

'I . . .' He interrupts himself, as if he's forgotten his name or it'll take too long to say it. 'I'm going to see the Kings.'

It's funny, the way he looks at me – as if he thinks I'll know why he's telling me. If he wasn't a peasant I'd almost think he was ordering me to go with him.

I ought to walk on. I'm supposed to be fetching wax for my father and I'm in a hurry. And it's difficult to stand still because of all the people elbowing me, pushing, shouting over my head to each other . . . but I stay where I am. I say, 'I'm Rufus.'

'Yes, I can see *that*,' he says.

I look at him, daring him to laugh. I'll hit him if he laughs.

And he does laugh.

But something happens. Something odd happens as he laughs at me. I don't know what it is – a touch, light as a feather, an invisible net settling on my skin – but whatever it is, it happens, and he's grinning at me and I laugh too, and from that moment I'd follow him into hell if he asked me. Not that I know it yet. It's like a sickness; the symptoms take a while to develop.

I shake my head, grinning. 'Go scrape,' I say, and walk on.

But he doesn't let me get very far. He spins round and dives after me, making his way miraculously through the crowd like it's parting to let him through. Someone swears, but they're swearing at the man who's struggling to run after us. I notice him and wonder who he is, but then Nick grabs me. He says, 'Come to the cathedral. Please.'

If he was someone I knew, I'd explain that I can't, I'm running an errand for my father. If he was someone I didn't know, I'd tell him to let go of me and get stuffed. It's because he's something in between that I say, 'Now?'

'Yes. Now. I'll see you there.' He laughs, no doubt with delight – his first disciple; who would have thought it would be so easy? – and then turns away as if he's done with me.

'But,' I say. 'What? Who – Why?' I feel a bit queasy, lopsided, like one of my legs is longer than the other.

Nick doesn't answer me. But the older man elbows his way past the nuncheon-seller and a child with a pig on a rope, and leans towards me, panting wetly. 'Touched by God, he is – my son,' he says. 'Give us a couple of marks for our dinner.'

I recoil, catch my breath, and feel the blood mounting to my face as surely as if my father was watching. A beggar and his son, and I almost thought – I don't know what. I say, 'Get lost,' and try to get past. But there are too many people; there's nowhere to go.

'No, he is,' the man says. 'God's own chosen. Really.'

'Leave me alone.' My father's voice, out of my own mouth: cold, urban, tight as his purse. I try to turn away, but I can't get past the pig rootling round my ankles. I say to the child, 'Get your blasted pig out of the way!'

'Alms, sir . . . Pennies, then, for the love of God.'

I glare at him, watching the way his accent pulls his mouth into a strange shape. A money-grabbing grown-up, like all the men in this city. And suddenly it makes sense that my father's money should end up in this man's grubby grasping hands. I feel such a wave of anger that I dig in my purse, pulling out the first coin my fingers touch. It's a silver mark. At least a week's worth of dinners for them both. I drop it in front of him and he dives to catch it before it disappears into the slurry. The pig looks round, outraged, as he leans on its back to get up again.

He says, 'Thanks, many thanks, bless you, young sir.'

My tongue is sticky with disdain. I say, 'For the love of God,' and I don't know if I'm mocking him or myself.

Then Nick turns back. His father slips the filthy coin into his mouth, slotting it into his cheek to keep it safe. Nick sees that and he frowns, just a little. He looks straight at me, and says, 'Thank you.' Then he looks at the older man and holds out his hand.

Slowly the man bares his teeth, grinning mechanically until the coin slides back out into his cupped hand. He passes it to Nick.

Nick looks at it, as if he's calculating how many hours of not-being-hungry it would buy, how many nights in an inn, how many cups of hypocras. Then he looks around, waiting for a gap in the crowd.

The man says, 'No –'

And then the coin flips up and away in a low arc. A woman jerks her head round, reaching out as it goes past her nose, but it's too late, because it's already hit the ground. It drops like a beetle into the mud in front of a beggar. A long pocked hand appears out of a tatter-ragged sleeve and scrapes it up.

Nick says, 'I don't want your money.'

It sounds like an insult, but it isn't. He means: *Money isn't enough. Not from you.* And he's right. Money is easy; money comes out of contempt, not charity.

The man says, 'For God's sake – !' But he stops himself, as if he's afraid.

I don't say anything. I stand still while Nick walks

away, and the older man follows him. Someone knocks against me and curses and I feel the crowd thicken, nearly lifting me off my feet. There's something inside me, like talons. Like being held too hard by someone you love.

I fight my way to the side of the street, the mucky corner where the beggar's sitting. It's wearing a hood and its head is bent, hiding the face, so I can't even tell whether it's a man or a woman. If I were a saint I'd kiss it. But I'm not.

I take my purse and empty all my father's coins into its hand.

I don't even know Nick's name.

I haven't bought the wax my father wanted, and I've just given away all the money I had, so I can't go home even if I want to. Which means there's nothing to stop me going straight to the cathedral – letting the flow of people carry me to it, or even hurrying through them so that I catch up with Nick before he gets there. But I dawdle, not wanting to be too eager, and then it occurs to me all at once that I'm hungry and I'll be in trouble when I *do* go home and why am I going to the cathedral anyway? Or rather, why is *he* going to the cathedral, and why does he want me to go too? If he's just a pilgrim, then it's not as if he needs me there to watch him kneel to the Magi. He's not a cripple, he doesn't need a leg-up to touch the shrine.

I don't know what I'm doing. I wish he'd just grabbed my sleeve and not let go. I don't like having a choice.

I turn sideways into a quieter street. Everything feels wrong. I've never disobeyed my father – on purpose, anyway. There's no good reason to do it now.

Someone shouts, 'Hey, Rufus!'

A bundle of rags tied together with strips of leather lands squelchily at my feet. I kick it at random, just in time, and a knot of youths pelts past me, grunting with exertion and pain as they punch and duck and trip each other up. One of them slides sideways out of the others' reach and nods to me, adjusting his tabard. Lucas, who was never exactly a friend even before he was apprenticed. I wish I had a master who'd let me play football on the street; my father would whip his apprentices for that.

'Nice kick,' he says, watching the other boys chase the ball on to the dungheap on the corner. They're up to their ankles in muck. He laughs. 'Straight on to the mixen. You always had a good aim.'

I nod and smile, although nothing feels quite real. 'Long time ago,' I say.

'You all right, then?' he adds, still watching the game, although they're just scrapping now and the ball's almost irrelevant. 'Playing truant? Shouldn't you be helping your papa cheat honest men out of their money?'

'I'm going to the cathedral,' I say. 'Want to come?'

As soon as it's out of my mouth I wish I hadn't said it. I don't know why I did. Neither does Lucas; he turns and squints at me, then pretends to press his hand to my forehead to check for fever. Then he laughs. 'Don't tell me he wants riches in heaven as well. It's not going to happen. Camels and needles, you know.'

'Go scrape, Lucas.'

'What for, then?'

They go all the time to laugh at the pilgrims, to see if there's anyone good preaching, to check out the girls; but I don't trust myself to say any of those convincingly. I say, 'I don't have anywhere else to go.' It isn't a lie exactly, but

25

it feels like one. As if I have a small glowing secret in a pocket just over my stomach.

'Wow, so you *are* playing truant. Rather you than me when you get home . . . Yes, all right,' he says. He shouts to his mates, 'Hey, you lot! I'm going to the cathedral. If anyone asks, one of the journeymen sent me out for a left-handed hammer.'

The group's separated, clutching bits of themselves, swearing at one another without malice. The ball is forgotten, balanced stickily on the side of the dungheap.

'Right, because old Carpenter'll notice you've gone,' one of them says.

His neighbour adjusts his cotte, glancing ruefully at a tear in his sleeve. 'Let's all go.'

'Yeah, see if he notices *then*.' They swap looks and laugh. The carpenter's apprentices are notorious; he can't keep them in order.

I say, 'Wait – Lucas, I only meant –' but nobody takes any notice. Suddenly everything seems real again. This is all wrong. I wanted to turn up with a friend, looking casual, in case Nick (whose name I don't know yet) isn't there or doesn't remember me – not with a rowdy crowd of apprentices who'll scoff at the preachers and imitate the cripples.

It's too late. Lucas gives me a quick beckoning punch and now I'm at the edge of a straggling, shouting group, following them helplessly. I'm furious with myself, still a bit shaky, not knowing why I'm being so pathetic.

It takes a while to get to the cathedral – because of the crowds, and the pie-sellers, and the juggler, and the fact that the apprentices can't walk past a chicken without trying to kick it, as a matter of pride – but in the end we get there. And unexpectedly I feel like a pilgrim trying to swallow my disappointment, because in front of the shrine of the Magi there are all the usual deformities and tears, smells and coughs and noblewomen drawing their skirts away from the fleas and muddy crutch-ends. And there's nothing I haven't seen hundreds of times before, except the skinny peasant boy with odd dreamy eyes.

And he's doing the worst preaching I have ever heard.

It's not even *loud*. He's speaking almost under his breath, to himself, like someone talking in their sleep. The old man is shifting from foot to foot behind him, staring fixedly at one pilgrim after another, and no one else is listening.

It hurts. I don't know why, but it makes me angry, like a broken promise. I thought something special was going to happen. But he's just a skinny inarticulate kid like me, and I can see that any moment now the old man will try to wheedle some money out of that noble lady over there, the one in the red dress with warts on her knuckles between the rings.

Lucas is next to me, giggling at something. He splutters and wipes his mouth with his sleeve. He follows my gaze. 'Hey! Speak up!'

Nick – the boy whose name I don't know – carries on muttering, his tone low and level.

A few heads turn. Eyes stare at us, and then at Nick. A couple of people look surprised – someone preaching, and they hadn't even *realised* . . . A man leans across to another, portlier man, and says something. They both snigger.

One of Lucas's friends limps over to us, kicking one leg out in front of him. He winks at Lucas and shouts, 'We can't hear you, mate!'

They all look round, then – the whole group of

27

apprentices – stopping dead in the middle of their silly walks, distracted. They weren't getting enough attention anyway. Their faces light up at the prospect of new sport. Someone says, 'You preaching or confessing, kid?'

Nick falters in the middle of a sentence, swallows, goes silent. His cheeks flash red, as if someone invisible has slapped them.

The man behind him – I know now he's his father – hisses, 'Go on. Go *on*. I thought you wanted –'

Nick says, quite clearly, 'I can't.'

Someone whistles. Someone else snorts and blows his nose noisily. Someone laughs. But I can't look away from Nick. Every shaft of summer sunlight coming through the windows is pointing at me like a finger. I know he's going to glance up and see me. And he does.

He frowns, narrowing his eyes, and the dreamy look goes out of them.

His father says, 'Go on. We've come this blasted far. I thought you said God would speak through you –'

He says it far too loudly. Someone shouts, 'Well, I wish he'd speak up!'

Nick turns his head swiftly. 'Try *listening*,' he says. His voice has changed; he's not mumbling any more. There's a subtle loosening in the air, like laughter, and now it's on his side.

He looks straight at me, and he says, 'I'm going to take Jerusalem.'

There's a tiny pause, like a trap; then it snaps shut.

It could be the punchline to a joke. The apprentices draw their breath in as one; then they whoop and collapse with mirth, slapping each other on the back, repeating it: *Jerusalem . . . he's going to take Jerusalem . . .* Someone says, through a mouthful of giggles, 'What, from behind?'

Oh God. He's still watching me, looking at me, as if I'm the only person in the whole cathedral . . . I take a feeble step sideways, away from Lucas, trying to pretend I'm on my own.

But the laughter fades, and in the new quiet I realise something's changed. More people are listening. They're not taking him seriously, but . . . well, they're not taking him seriously *yet*. At least he's not preaching in that desperate, ignorable undertone.

'God's calling you,' he says, and it's still as if he's talking to me, personal and direct as an insult. 'God's calling you. Because you understand what it means, that Jerusalem is in the hands of the infidel. The places where our Lord walked and prayed and died – the very cross he died on – are in the hands of people who don't even know his name.'

Lucas has the same expression on his face that's on mine – and so does the portly man, and the woman in the red dress. They all think he's talking to *them*. The apprentices shuffle a bit, half sheepish, half waiting for a moment to heckle.

'They've tried to get it back – the nobles, the soldiers, the big people – and they've failed. They failed because God wasn't on their side. He looked at their riches and their sins and their pride and he decided they weren't worthy. And he was right.'

A couple of people swap glances. Someone says, loudly, 'Hey – what do you mean? You better be careful what you –'

Nick laughs, easily, and flicks him a look. 'Unless you think God *wasn't* right?' He carries on, like an archer who doesn't even wait to see his arrow hit the butt. 'The people who will win the Holy Land back are those closest to God's heart. Not the nobles, not the crusaders who despoil Christian cities and come home with cartloads of loot, not the kings who steal relics from each other and lie with the heathen –'

A murmur of something like support.

'– but the innocent, the pure in heart, the poor.' A beat; he takes a breath and we stand, silent, watching him. 'Children.'

Children? We wait for him to explain. It's a metaphor, presumably, or one of those gimmicks that preachers use to get your attention. He's certainly got ours.

But he just stands there. And then the strange authority drops off him like a surcoat and he shrugs, grins with embarrassment, glances over his shoulder at his father.

'*Children?*'

I don't know who says it, but it's a woman's voice, husky and breathless, with a peasant's accent. I don't know why it makes me think of my mother.

Nick nods, hunching his shoulders, and suddenly everyone remembers that he's only a child himself. The hilarity starts to seep back into the air like smoke. Any moment now it'll be an even bigger joke than taking Jerusalem from behind.

Lucas gives an unexpected, joyous giggle. 'That's *right*!'

The portly man looks round at him, disapproving, and Lucas laughs again, freer this time, and puts his hands on his hips. 'You keep out of this, master, you're too old – and too fat, probably . . . You lot have tried and failed – so now it's up to us.'

Nick blinks, suddenly a spectator.

Another apprentice breaks suddenly out of stillness, like a poppet on a string, slashing at the air with an invisible sword. 'Yes! Why shouldn't we take back the Holy Land? If God's angry with anyone it isn't us. *We* didn't sack Constople, we weren't even born . . .'

'Con*stantin*ople,' the portly man says. 'You arrogant little –'

'I can take on the infidel, easy. What with being innocent and pure in heart and really good at fighting –'

'We won't fight them – we'll *convert* them – no killing –' Nick says, but his voice has subsided back into a murmur that no one listens to.

The noise builds and breaks like a wave. The apprentices pretend to fight each other, one of them keening, 'Ellellellellella!' in a high falsetto, because that's what infidels do. Then someone kicks a bit too hard and they start fighting for real.

Nick stands there with his mouth a tiny bit open, like someone who's thrown a stone at a wasps' nest without actually expecting anything to happen.

The grown-ups don't look at each other, but they start to move away from the shrine – except the cripples, obviously, who'll stay there until they get better.

Nick's father says, 'Give 'em a bit more. Hurry up. They're *leaving*!'

But Nick stays silent, his face so blank he looks like my aunt Lena. And before his father can say anything else, a skeletal man in a long grimy gown appears from nowhere, takes a big breath and then starts to rattle off something about hellfire. Nick flinches. No one's paying attention to him any more; the last of his strange magic has gone. The people who haven't left relax and settle down to listen to the new preacher – because, after all, hellfire is something they can understand.

The squirming, anarchic knot of apprentices works its

way out into the street again. Lucas doesn't seem to notice that I'm not with them; or if he does, he doesn't care. I stand where I am, looking at the shrine of the Magi. It looks back at me, not letting me into its secrets. I'm only a few feet away from bones that were only a few feet away from God, and I don't feel *anything*.

Nick drops into a crouch, rubbing his face with his hands. His father walks in a little circle, bouncing impatiently, muttering things I'm too far away to hear. In the end Nick gets up and walks towards the great door in a straight, unseeing line.

At least I think it's unseeing. Then he walks past me and stops.

'Thank you.'

'I'm sorry,' I say, so hastily I garble the words. 'Really, I didn't mean to, I wanted to come on my own, it just happened, I'm sorry, really –'

He frowns, and then his face clears as if he can't be bothered to wonder what I'm talking about. He says again, 'Thank you,' and this time I realise that he means it. 'You brought people to listen.'

'They jeered at you. I'm sorry.'

He smiles a small, brief smile. 'But they listened. And you . . . It was only when I saw you'd come – that you had faith – that I could say anything. It helped.'

I feel scorched on the outside and cold on the inside, like a half-cooked capon. I shake my head. 'They weren't my friends,' I say. 'They were just . . . people I know.'

He shrugs. He looks like he doesn't care.

I say, 'It wasn't that bad.'

It's the worst possible thing I could have said. Nick bites his lip and then catches my eye. We stare at each other, hearing the lie swell until we can't ignore it. The chill spreads outwards from my gut, sapping the warmth from my skin.

He says, 'It wasn't exactly the Sermon on the Mount.'

'It wasn't exactly the Crucifixion, either,' I say.

He blinks. Then, suddenly, he laughs. He looks older when he laughs. It catches me off-guard and makes me feel like a kid: dizzy, hero-worshipping.

'Come and have a drink,' I say. As soon as I say it I remember I don't have any money.

Nick's father looks happier immediately. 'Don't mind if we do,' he says. He pats Nick's shoulder awkwardly. 'Might as well, right? Make the most of the city, while we're still here.'

Nick gives him a look that I can't read. Then he nods. He gives one last glance towards the Magi. There's an odd, secret expression on his face, as if he's thinking about someone he knows. I feel a surge of something that isn't quite jealousy.

Then we go to the Bird and Tree.

III

There are pilgrims everywhere. In the Bird and Tree
tavern they take off their hats and coats, but you can still
tell they're pilgrims from the smell; they don't smell
worse than everyone else, just different. Clusters of staves
lean drunkenly in corners. Every so often someone slips
round the door, checks them over to find one he likes, and
slips back out again, taking it with him. The pilgrims will
notice tomorrow, when they don't have anything to
defend themselves with, but today they're too celebra-
tory, or too drunk. Some of them are singing drunken
songs that could be psalms or something ribald, so
distorted I can't tell which. Possibly the people singing
don't know either. But they're happy, most of them:
they've done it, they've got here. They've earned themselves a few lapses before they die. Not that they say that,
even to themselves, but it's definitely some kind of
bargain. A completed pilgrimage gets them a bit of leni-
ency on your part come the Last Trump. You – the love of
you, I mean, love of you for what you *are*, apart from
judgement and hellfire – well . . . I doubt you come into
it, really. I doubt you come into it at all.

Nick looks around. He wasn't impressed by the
cathedral – he knows what holiness is like, he always has

done – but this is different. This is humanity – a packed, belching, sweaty mass of humanity, in a warm been-here-since-Terce fug – and he doesn't know what to do with it. His mouth opens, just a little bit, and then shuts again.

I follow his gaze. But for once I'm not paying much attention to Nick; I'm worrying about not having any money, and what possessed me to bring them here.

And Nick's father . . . But I don't know what Nick's father is thinking. Not about you, certainly, or Nick. He's probably wondering how good the ale is.

I say, 'Maybe we should . . .' and I stop because I don't know whether I'm going to say 'sit down' or 'leave'.

Nick nods, as if I've made a decision, and squeezes himself on to the end of the nearest bench. His father turns in a slow circle, smiling, then hovers opposite him, waiting for someone to let him sit down. People shifted up a bit to make room for Nick, but they ignore his father. And me, naturally.

Nick's father looks at me expectantly, then cranes to find the nearest serving girl. My insides writhe. I can't explain that I gave all my money to Nick's beggar. I just can't. I pray for the ale to have run out, or for a fire to break out, or for Nick's neighbour suddenly to reveal that he's a leper by dropping one of his fingers into someone else's tankard – anything that will get us out of here . . . but there's no answer. The serving girl comes over and I cringe.

Nick's father says, 'Three of us. Ale. Please.'

She looks at him with the sort of obsequious-insolent look we all reserve for peasants, and gives a heavy blink that could be meant as a nod. Then she turns round and goes to draw the ale.

35

Nick is still staring at the crowds of pilgrims, marvelling, half frowning, looking like one of my cousins from Mainz the first time she saw piglets. I wish he'd stop; people have started to notice.

I look around helplessly. Everything hits me at once. I've given all my father's money away, and I didn't go home with the wax he wanted, and he doesn't even know where I am. I brought the apprentices to the cathedral and ruined Nick's preaching. And I'm here, with no money, and Nick – this boy who, for some reason, I want to impress – is now gazing down at the table, digging at the grain with a fingernail like he's trying to get gilt off a sheet of vellum, and I don't even know his name.

He looks up at me then, as if he's heard me thinking about him. He says, 'I'm thirsty.' I don't think it's meant to be a hint: he's just telling the truth.

I can't hold his look. Instead I glare resolutely at the nearest pilgrim, a man with a dark chaperon hanging off his shoulders. He's either got a tonsure or very bad ringworm. In the end he wriggles sideways and I sit down. Nick's father is still standing, looking over my shoulder. I ignore him.

A fat drab-woolsey-sleeved arm dumps two tankards on the board in front of me. I look up and see another tankard emerging from a drab-woolsey-cyclased bosom and have time to duck away from the splashes of froth. The serving girl says, 'Three cups of ale.'

I say, 'Thank you,' but it's not courtesy, just playing for time. Any moment now she'll ask for the money. I stare down at my lap and feel my cheeks already going hot. My neighbour shifts his weight and his purse flops against my leg. Then he sighs and collapses face-down on to his hands. His eyes are closed. He's a pilgrim, of course, exhausted by the journey and the emotion. One of God's favourites.

My hands are almost completely steady as I unloose his purse-strings, take out a couple of coins and pay for the ale.

Nick smiles at me. I should feel ashamed, but I don't. All of a sudden I feel like I'm giving off light.

Nick drinks in a strange, childish way, pushing his lips out like he's kissing someone. He wipes his mouth and says, 'Thank you, Rufus.'

'My pleasure,' I say.

Nick's father picks up his ale and goes to sit somewhere else. Nick and I grin at each other. I still don't know his name, and I don't care. It's enough that we're both here. The space between us is singing, too high-pitched to hear.

We sit in the tavern for hours. It gets to Vespers time. The air fills with bells. Then they stop, and we're still there.

Nick is talking. I don't say much, but he doesn't seem to mind. He murmurs down at the board, drawing patterns in the spilt ale, so that I feel like I'm eavesdropping. It's like watching my father make something in the workshop, when he knows I'm there but it doesn't make any difference to him, the way his fingers create something beautiful and he doesn't look up.

'And I can't explain,' Nick says, 'only I know I have to do it, and it matters, like it's a door and through it there's everything, shining, like the brightest fire in the world, and it hurts even to look at it but I have to, I have to get to it, and the door isn't real, but if it was real it would be in Jerusalem . . .'

He glances up and I say, 'Jerusalem,' back to him, because I want him to know I'm listening.

'We'll do it, Rufus. We have to. Because he couldn't – God couldn't be so cruel, to take everything away from us – the Holy Land, the True Cross. Not for ever. We have to get them back.'

I say, 'We?' but I'm agreeing. Not *I*, but *we* . . .

'It's so simple. Children. Innocents.' He laughs. 'Like the answer to a riddle – it was there all the time . . . I know it sounds crazy, but what's wrong with that anyway? Let's go mad for the love of God. And with God on our side we can do anything. *He* can do anything.'

Part of me knows that Jerusalem is a big place a long way away, and the infidel are really good fighters. But that part of me keeps its mouth shut.

Nick says, 'We have to. Because . . . Even to know it's *there* . . . we can't ever really understand, but it's so . . . there's a place, a *real place*, where God actually . . . he did all the things that people do, he slept and snored and – and ate and drank and –'

'And the food came out the other end.'

It's the first thing I've said that he really *hears*. And from the expression on his face I think I've blown it. It's like the world's gone dark and I can see something burning in his eyes.

Then something flickers. The sunlight floods back and he's human again. He splutters with sudden mirth, laughing properly, like a kid. Through his giggles he says, 'Yes – that's exactly – that's – *yes* –'

'I didn't mean to be –'

'No, but you're right – that's *exactly* . . .' He shakes his head as if he's trying to get water out of his ears. 'That's *it*, though. It came out the other end. Of *God*. That's the amazing thing. He was human.' A smile tugs at his mouth and then fades again. He looks as if he's listening to

38

something I can't hear. 'That's why it matters. The Holy Land. Everywhere else, God is just God. *There*, he was one of us.'

'All right,' I say. 'I agree. I mean, everyone would. But you don't seriously mean that all the children in Cologne should just up sticks and –'

'Of course I do,' he says. He tilts his head to one side, as if I've got something so wrong he can't understand how it happened. 'Why not?'

I know there are hundreds of reasons. Common sense. Because it's a *bad idea*.

I say, 'Oh. Well . . .'

And then we're both laughing, because he's right, he's so right. With God on our side we can do anything.

I don't know how long we carry on. All I know is that I stop giggling with a jolt, because I need to get home before the curfew. I've got a few sweaty coins clenched in my fist, sticky with ale. I open my palm and look at them and the world rocks gently. I say, 'I have to go.'

Nick looks up, his face glistening, and rubs his eyes. Then he looks around. There aren't as many people as there were. His father is nowhere to be seen.

I stand up and I realise how drunk I am. I can feel the acid slosh of all the beer I've drunk in my gut. Nick stands up too, steadying himself on the edge of the board, and we grin sickly at each other.

Outside . . . Oh dear. Outside it's late. The air is cool, full of shadows, and the sky between the roofs is deep blue, not giving any light. I lean against the tavern wall, staring up at the sign swinging in the breeze, too dizzy to move.

Nick says, 'I'll see you tomorrow.'

Maybe it's a question, but that doesn't occur to me. I say, 'Will you? Oh.'

'Thank you. For coming to the cathedral. And the drinks,' he adds.

'I stole the money,' I say. At least, I think I say it. But he doesn't seem to hear.

'God bless you.' He gives me the kiss of peace. His lips are wet and unyielding and leave the taste of beer behind. My head is reeling. I close my eyes and open them again hurriedly, because everything's peeling upwards at the corners. I try to kiss him back but it's too late, he's already moved away.

'Goodnight,' I say. I always thought peasants couldn't hold their drink, but his steps are surprisingly steady as he walks away.

I shout after him, 'What's your name?'

He laughs, but he doesn't turn round. I hear him say, 'Nick. Nicholas.' Then he turns the corner and he's gone.

'Nick,' I say. 'Good old Nick. Good . . . old . . . Nick . . .'

I'm so happy I feel like I'm going to die of it. The laughter surfaces again, bubbling up uncontrollably into my throat. I feel young and raw, like something newly hatched, bald and wormy and still tacky with egg-white. I lick my lips and taste yeast and earth. I can still smell the peasanty scent of Nick's clothes, so different from my own. The talons tighten round my heart, squeezing.

I stare up at the sign to keep my head from spinning. A bird, grey with grime, above a two-branched tree. A raven and an ash tree . . . or a dove and an olive tree . . .

My grin hurts my face. I'm going to Jerusalem, with Nick.

The sign swings to and fro. Raven, dove, raven, dove . . . And suddenly I remember. I'm not going anywhere. I ruined everything. If it hadn't been for me, the people in the cathedral might have listened. There might have been a crusade. But now . . . And then I stole money to pay for our ale. And I can't go home.

I drop to my knees and puke.

There is nothing as dark as a city at night. There are little lights here and there: forbidden tapers lighting people to bed after the curfew, little votive lamps left burning on street corners in front of statues, flecks of moonlight caught in puddles between the shadows of the overhanging eaves. But all that makes it harder to see, not easier. Only owls can see properly; owls and gods.

So you can see me, while I drag myself to my drunken feet and stagger away, but I can't see a damned thing. I know where I'm trying to go, but that doesn't help much. I'm not used to being out after the curfew, and I'm scared as well as legless. It's so dark anything could jump out at me, and if I knock myself out on something I might get eaten by a pig before I wake up. But I'm not going home, because the doors will be locked – I know that, I'm not stupid – and I'm just sober enough to count the turnings to the inn near the cathedral where Lucas said there's a loose plank in the back of the stable wall. As I walk I can't help remembering the last time I was there, months – no, years – ago. My father thought I was sliding on the ice with my cousins, and actually I was watching Lucas's bare arse bob up and down as he swived a girl I didn't know in the straw. It was boring; I'd rather have been sliding on the ice.

I'm less giddy than I was. I can feel my stomach settling down, although I've still got a kind of icy chill when I breathe in, like I'm scared. Well, I *am* scared. But there's

41

something else: excitement and happiness and nausea, and what I'm scared of isn't just being alone on the streets after the curfew bell. I can't remember any of what Nick said, but that doesn't stop me carrying on the conversation. I say deep witty things that impress him. Then I go knee-deep in a puddle of something that smells sharp and stale, like the dyers' yards. I force myself to concentrate on finding my way in the dark.

I go further than I need to, wandering round in circles in the dark. There aren't many people around, but noises come out of the houses I pass: snoring, praying, children crying, the animal noises of men and women in bed together. But in the end I find the place I'm looking for. I sneak into the stable – well, crawl, that is, fairly quietly – through the triangle of splintery hole in the wall. Then I sit in the nearest corner.

And I pray. I say a paternoster of thanks to you for guiding me through the city. I'd have said two if it hadn't been for that puddle of piss.

I don't know if gods laugh. But if they do, you must be laughing at me at that moment, because I think one paternoster is enough to pay my debts. A muttered prayer that lasts for a few breaths . . . It's like trying to pay my father with stalks of straw.

And you're laughing at me, maybe, because when I fall asleep I dream about love, and I think I'm dreaming about Nick.

I wake up and the bells are ringing for Mass. I don't know where I am. I try to turn over, rolling sideways to where the edge of the bed should be, the way I always do, because if I kick Daniel by mistake he always kicks back . . . But there isn't an edge, just a wall and something gritty coming off on my face. I open my eyes and remember where I am.

It's still early, before sunrise, but there are a few spots and streaks of sky showing through the top corners of the eaves. I wince, screwing up my eyes, and then I lean sideways and retch into the straw. Then I feel better.

It's noisy outside. As well as the bells there are voices, people bustling past, all on their way to Mass . . . but there's something different, something odd, about the sounds . . . I don't have time to wonder about it, though, because I have to sneak out of here before anyone sees me. I pull myself up to standing and peer through the murk to find the hole where I got in last night. It's so narrow I can hardly believe it's the same one, except that I've left a scrap of brown-green hose on one of the splinters. I get back down on my hands and knees and wriggle through into the street. The smell of horses wafts through after me and fades.

Automatically I turn towards the cathedral and start walking. I'm not thinking properly, but as my head starts to clear I realise I might as well go to Mass. I almost wish I still went to school, just to delay the moment when I have to go home.

And as I'm walking I realise why something seemed different.

The streets are full of people. Not just the merchants and goldsmiths, the respectable guildsmen that go to Mass every morning, but apprentices too, shoemakers and fishmongers who don't always have the time. And children. Children younger than me, children carrying smaller children, children leading toddlers on strings and holding babies in their arms. I don't normally feel small, but now I feel like a giant. I look around, feeling queasy again. What's going on? It's like the children of Israel leaving Egypt, like they can all hear something I can't.

And then I do hear it.

A chant, rising through a cacophony of shouts, too indistinct to make out. The voices are rough and tuneless, men and boys – or even women, maybe, or girls. I screw up my eyes as if that'll help me listen.

And above that, the noise of a pipe. Four notes, like four syllables; and then a melody, fluttering around them like a bird circling a perch, never resting but never taking flight. It makes my heart beat quicker, as if it's trying to keep the same rhythm. I walk faster, holding my hands at waist-height to stop the littlest kids cannoning into me. I can't tell if it's the music that draws me or the shouts; and as I turn down the streets, running faster now, swerving round turds and offal in the gutters, I realise they're the same thing. *Jerusalem*, they're saying. *Jerusalem* . . . and the pipe plays like a lapwing, flapping to keep our attention.

Call me stupid. But it's only then that I connect it with Nick.

I stop worrying about what I'm treading in and start to run.

I weave in and out of the current of people, go east, then north. I stand in the square in front of the cathedral and stare at the crowds. Not that crowds are anything unusual here, but so many of them are children . . .

Then I see Lucas. He's with the other apprentices in a spiky kind of circle, and they're shouting. And beside them there are other youths I don't recognise – apprentice dyers, by the look of their hands – and next to them more apprentices, hundreds of them, and hovering on the sidelines there are boys I used to know from school before my father stopped me going. One of them sees me somehow, and waves. I raise my hand to wave back but I'm too distracted to do it very convincingly.

What on earth is going on? Someone pushes me and I start to stumble towards the cathedral, still watching Lucas and his mates. They're yelling to each other, chanting like spectators at a joust. One of them is sharing out bits of pie. It's like a festival – any minute now a fight'll break out. That pipe is still going, shrill and catchy. In the corner of my eye two girls are swinging round in a circle, arms linked, in a kind of jig.

I keep walking towards the cathedral, because it's the only thing I can think of. I just don't get it. If this is something to do with Nick . . . well, it has to be. But – yesterday they were all laughing at him and now . . . It's a miracle.

A group of pilgrims trundles towards the door, fighting its way doggedly through the crowd. One of them, a girl, is lagging behind the others, tilting her head to look up at the cathedral, and one of Lucas's friends catches her by the arm as she tries to get past. She can't be much older than me, and she looks around for help, panicking, but her mother's fussing over a little lame boy – probably her brother – and doesn't notice. The apprentice leans towards her and says something, gesturing at the people surrounding them. Then he grins, drags her sideways, thrusting a bit of pie into her hands, and the others lean in to give her the kiss of peace. She looks scared, but she takes the pie. Lucas says something, and as she turns to answer I catch sight of her lips moving and I can see what she says. *Jerusalem . . . ?*

They were *serious*. The apprentices, yesterday, when

45

they said they wanted to go on Nick's crusade. Dear God, they were serious.

I start to laugh. If every apprentice in the city joined the crusade – if *half* the apprentices joined the crusade . . . The sheer scale of it goes to my head, like wine. I still don't quite believe it, though.

I get closer to Lucas and his friends than I mean to, and he sees me. He shouts, 'Rufus!' The pilgrim girl turns to look, calmer now, digging her fingers into her bit of pie.

'What are you . . . ?' But the rest of the question doesn't even make it to my mouth. They've got crosses on their coats – some sewn on, some splashed on with dye, some drawn on with charcoal – and bundles of food. They've got staves and gourds, like pilgrims. They're all ready to go.

'You're coming, right?' But Lucas doesn't give me time to answer. 'We're leaving tomorrow. To Jerusalem.'

'Yes . . . I gathered,' I say, but no one hears except the girl. She catches my eye and grins, so suddenly and briefly it's gone by the time I start to smile back.

'They can't stop us, you know. When God calls, no one can tell us not to go.'

I look down, noting the splashes of mud on my hose. It's true what he says, but it doesn't sound quite right the way he says it.

The girl says, 'So you think he's a real prophet, this boy?'

Lucas frowns at her, looking from her face to her bit of pie and back again.

'You think he's the voice of God?' Her voice is very clean, like polished metal.

'Sure.'

'Then where is he?'

Lucas glances over his shoulder at the cathedral. 'Inside, I suppose.'

'Then I shall go and listen to him preach,' she says, dropping the words neatly, like a magpie that's stolen a ring. 'Coming?'

She says it to me. I could tell her I already know Nick, that I've already heard him preach, that what matters about him isn't what he says. But I shrug and go with her because I want to see him. And because of her voice – how clear it is, like water.

She lets me walk in front of her, and I slide through the gaps in the crowd. Words float around me like jetsam: *crusade. Jerusalem. Hungry. Cross.* I turn my head. Someone says, 'I'm *not* cross, I just meant . . .' and I laugh. The girl behind me gives me an odd look but she doesn't say anything. I think I might still be drunk.

And then we go into the cathedral and I *know* I'm still drunk.

It's like flying. This is what flying must be like: like swifts in the air, heady, giddy, buoyed up by emptiness, swooping from current to current. The crowd murmurs – like wings, like the wind – and the floor seems to disappear under my feet. And in front of them there's only Nick's voice – Nick, of course, there with his father, but really it's only his voice that matters, lulling and commanding and –

There are so many people listening his voice seems to echo and echo. They're like birds too. Like birds, silent before a storm. And it's not that Nick's different from before; it's the crowd, listening.

I stagger sideways and the girl catches my elbow and

forces me back the other way. I'd smile and thank her but that bit of my mind doesn't seem to be working.

'The lemons and oranges, the damask, the pepper and canelle and comyn, the medicine . . .' Nick draws in a breath and we wait. 'But that's only the shadow of the Holy Land. The *real* Jerusalem waits for us beyond a different sea – and we can earn our places in it. It doesn't matter if we fail. To die on crusade is the greatest gift God can give us. Martyrdom –'

The girl next to me makes a little noise that could be a scoff or a sob. I look at her, but all I can see is her hair in a golden crespine and the curve of her cheek. I turn back, trying to concentrate on what Nick's saying.

My father is in the crowd. I close my eyes, squeezing them shut, but when I open them again he's still there.

'No purgatory – no hell. To die for God . . .'

It's quiet while we all stand in front of what he's said, trying to take in the size of it. Of course we all want to die for God. Of course we do. It dwarfs everything else; real life is the size of an ant next to it. For a moment none of us can even remember what it's like to be an ant at all.

The girl next to me makes that noise again. She's clearing her throat like a priest before a prayer. She whispers something and it takes me a moment before I hear the words. 'The glory,' she says. 'Think of the glory of it . . .'

I try to catch a glimpse of her face, or my father's. But neither of them is looking at me. Everyone's staring at Nick as if they can't help it.

I want to ask Nick what's happened. I want to ask how he got here from the Bird and Tree. How I'm still drunk and dry-mouthed and he's here, in the hands of

God, catching souls like a net. But I couldn't speak if I wanted to.

'Tomorrow we leave,' Nick says. 'Tomorrow. And the sea will open up before us, like the Red Sea parted for Moses, and all those who want to come with me can.'

IV

I look at my father, listening steady-eyed in the middle of the crowd, and I think I'm going to be sick.

I turn and get to the door somehow, and stand outside in the square taking deep breaths of the new morning, willing my heart to slow down.

'Are you all right?' It's as if there's an angel behind me: bemused, faintly pitying.

I don't look round. 'Yes.'

A sigh. The angel knows lying is a sin. 'Well, I'm hungry. Fancy a bit of pie?'

Suddenly I am hungry. 'Yes.' And then I have to look at her.

She glances round and then makes for a barrel that someone's left against a wall, stepping over the puddles of beer that reflect the sky. She sits sideways, so there's room for me too, but I lean on the wall a few feet away.

'Are you *drunk*?'

'Possibly,' I say.

She nods, but narrows her eyes. 'What happened? You pushed me right out of the way.' She adds, 'You don't look strong enough,' but it isn't an insult.

'Nothing.' And then, because I've just been in church, I try to get as close to the truth as I can. 'My father was there. I was scared.'

'Oh.' She thinks she understands, but she doesn't. She breaks the pie into two bits and holds the bigger one out. 'Here.'

I take it and we sit, chewing silently, watching the people go in and out of the cathedral. It's like a dance: one goes in, one comes out . . . because, after all, this is Cologne, where boats are unloading boxes and fish are going bad on the quay, where molten gold won't stay hot indefinitely. God may be talking to them in the cathedral, but the townspeople have better things to do, most of them, than stand around listening to him all day. So even though they're impressed with Nick – even though some of them say magnanimously that the boy isn't bad, for a peasant – the adults edge out of the door and go home. The muddy, sunshining streets fill with people and new rubbish and nothing is much out of the ordinary. Not for them, anyway.

My father doesn't come out, though.

I'm starving. The girl finishes her bit of pie and then watches me eat, but she doesn't say anything until I've wiped my mouth and flicked the crust away.

'I'm Sophie.'

'Hello, Sophie,' I say.

She grins. Her barbette has slipped sideways, giving her a rakish look. I almost reach out to adjust it, the way I would if it were my aunt Lena's, but I catch myself in time.

'And your name is . . . ?' she says.

'Rufus.'

'Real name? Or nickname?' She glances at my hair.

'Real name,' I say, shrugging. 'It's been this colour since before I was baptised.'

She nods. We watch a group of little kids running

around, squealing and dribbling with excitement. One of them falls over and starts to cry. I wait for Sophie to go over and help him up, but she doesn't move.

'Are you going to go?'

'Go where?' I say, like a lover pretending he doesn't know his mistress's name.

She slips me a sideways smile that makes me feel as if I've known her for much longer than a few hours. 'Canterbury.'

'Oh, *Jerusalem*,' I say.

'Oh, *Jerusalem*,' she repeats, mimicking me.

'Shouldn't you be with your family?' I say, because it's suddenly occurred to me that she's on her own with me. I don't even know where she's from. Not Cologne, but she's not a peasant. And she's a girl in a strange city.

'I don't know where they went.' She links her fingers and looks down at them. 'We're staying at the Three Crowns. They'll be there tonight.'

I nod, because there's something about the expression on her face that I recognise.

'I don't know,' I say. 'I mean . . .' I search for words, but none of them are big enough to hold what I want to say. I thought I knew last night; I could feel Jerusalem in front of me, ripe as an apple, ready to fall into my hands. But last night it was just me and Nick, and I was drunk. Now it's different. It's complicated. I say, 'All those people . . .'

'Yes,' she says. 'Wasn't it wonderful? All of us, listening.'

That wasn't what I meant.

'I'm going. They can't stop me.' She laughs, like she's been looking for something that was there all the time.

'All those people – *yes* – we know, now, we know what we have to do, like a gift –'

I say, 'I'm not sure.'

She looks at me. I say, 'We're not innocent. I mean, Nick said we'd take Jerusalem because we're innocent, we're not like the other crusaders, but . . . the apprentices aren't exactly . . .'

I say, 'And if . . . we're supposed to obey our parents – they might not want us to go . . . if they don't want us to go . . .'

She's still looking at me.

I say, 'Yes. *Yes*, I'm going.' And I stare down at my hands, gripping each other so hard the skin's the colour of teeth.

She gives me a look that makes me think of Nick's kiss last night. Only I don't know why, because it's not the same at all. She says, 'Me too. It's scary.'

We laugh, and now I do reach out to adjust her barbette. She looks surprised but she doesn't move away. I grin, because it's just like helping Lena with her wimple.

She says, 'What? Have I got crumbs round my mouth?'

She glances up, over my shoulder, and I see a tiny dark shape reflected in the apples of her eyes.

'Rufus.'

My father. I feel his voice like claws, lifting me off the ground. The world sways and drops away under my feet, like it did inside the cathedral, but this time it makes me feel sick. I turn to look at him.

He doesn't say, *Where have you been?* He doesn't ask me where I was yesterday, or what I'm doing here. He only says, 'You'd better come with me.'

I stand up and go with him. I don't look at Sophie, or even back at the cathedral, because in my father's world no one else exists. Nick and Sophie are figments of my imagination. Even Jesus Christ is a myth. The only person who'd die for me is me.

There's a funny kind of quiet in the workshop. At first I think it's because the journeymen want to hear what my father says to me. Then I realise it's because Daniel's not there. And the new apprentice isn't there either. It makes the room feel uneasy, like an open door anyone might come through.

My father makes me walk through the doorway ahead of him. I feel the heat of the furnaces on my face. I don't turn round until he says my name.

Then he says, 'I forgive you.'

There's a clink and a choked-off curse from behind me. Someone's hit their thumb with a hammer.

'You're young,' he says. 'I understand. Boys will be boys.'

I blink. It's like watching a juggler drop his balls deliberately one by one into the dirt. I don't know what to say.

'When I was your age I played truant too. You'll start your apprenticeship soon. You want to let off steam.'

It's as if he's learnt it by rote, like a lesson.

'You went to a tavern, didn't you?'

'I . . . yes,' I say. I don't know what's going on, but lying won't help. Well, it *might* help, but I don't have the guts to risk it.

My father's face goes rigid and blank and I take a tiny, instinctive step away. Then he says, 'Do you have any money left?'

'No.'

He nods. 'I'm going to give you some more,' he says. 'And you're going to go out and buy me the wax I need, and you'll come straight back here without talking to anyone. And then you will spend the rest of the day with your mother, practising your reading, and we won't mention this again.'

I try to keep my face neutral but I know I'm squinting, like I'm trying to find something in the dark. I say, 'What?'

But he doesn't answer straight away. He gets his purse, and instead of counting the money out he gives the whole thing to me. His hand falters as I take it, as if he's wondering whether to hit me, but I look at his eyes and it's not that at all. He says, 'And mind you come straight home.'

He's scared. My father's *scared*.

I say, 'Father . . .'

I don't know what I'm going to say. It doesn't matter anyway, because he doesn't let me finish. He turns his back on me, as if the conversation's over.

I stay where I am, waiting. He brushes his sleeve with his hand, over and over again, like a bird fussing at a broken wing.

There are voices outside; then Daniel comes past the window, calling to someone out of sight. Then he comes in and walks straight past my father, towards the back of the workshop. Work stutters to a halt.

My father says, 'I didn't give you permission to go out.'

Daniel picks up the chaperon that's draped over his stool. He's shaking, but then he always does. He wipes the wetness away from his mouth, goes over to the journeymen one by one and gives them the kiss of peace. They sit, silent, not meeting his eyes. Then he faces my father and says, 'Thank you for everything, Master.'

'*I didn't give you permission to go out.*'

'I'll come back if I can,' Daniel says, and spit glistens and overflows from the corner of his lips. 'I'm sorry I have to leave like this. My uncle will give you something to compensate.' He says it like it's a gift.

'You're not going anywhere.'

'Only to Jerusalem,' Daniel says. He smirks but he can't hold my father's look.

My father stares round at the journeymen, and then he seems to relax a little bit. He snorts. 'You idiot, Daniel. You think you'll get to Jerusalem when you can't even hold a bowl without spilling it? Look at yourself. You can hardly remember your own name.'

Daniel shakes his head and flecks of sweat drip on the floor. He looks like he's melting. He says, 'I will – they're preaching a crusade in the cathedral – *our* crusade, not yours – there are little children going, cripples, girls . . . I'll get as far as anyone –'

'My God,' my father says. 'You can't even finish a sentence.'

Daniel keeps shaking his head, compulsively, like a goldfinch in a cage. 'I'm going. And you can't stop me.'

One of the journeymen mutters, 'So *there* . . .' and there's an inaudible ripple of laughter.

My father gives Daniel a long look. Then he steps back, holding his arms out. 'Very well, then. Light a candle for me in Jerusalem.' The mockery is so subtle I'm not sure it's there.

Daniel's eyes widen and he glances at me. I recognise that look; it's how I felt when my father said he'd forgiven me. But he doesn't stick around to work out what's going on. He bolts outside and a few seconds later we hear him going up the stairs.

My father says, 'Back to work, please.'

I say, 'Father . . .' I hate the way I keep saying it, as if it's the only word I know.

'Yes?'

'You heard the preaching in the cathedral, didn't you?' Silence. 'Most people left after a bit, but you stayed to listen. You stayed for ages.'

My father looks as if he's trying to read something on the opposite wall.

I say, 'I was there too. And I –'

'Be quiet,' he says.

'But – you heard what it was like – Nick's preaching – and you didn't leave, you really *listened*. You weren't like the others.' I breathe in, trying not to move, like a mouse in the shadow of a kestrel. 'And – Father, I thought – you understood, didn't you? There was – *God* –'

Another sentence I don't know how to finish. A split second while he looks at me and I search for words.

And then the floor swings up like a stoolball bat and smacks me. The wood hits my skull, shoulder, hip and the side of my kneecap all at the same time, and I ought to be flying through the air, except that I'm already on the ground.

There's something digging into my gums like a husk of wheat. I push at it with my tongue and it resists, then gives way. Suddenly my mouth is full of saliva, tasting of metal. I feel it creeping out of the side of my mouth and try to wipe it away.

Then it hurts. It hurts so much I want to be sick. I realise I'm spitting blood. A tooth – I've lost a tooth . . . My whole left side aches fiercely where I hit the ground, but it's my gum that hurts the most, the new tender hole full of blood. And my cheek, for some reason, on the other side . . .

I try to look up. I can't focus because my eyes are full of water but from the odd, skewed quiet in the air I know the journeymen are stock-still, hardly even breathing.

My father hit me. That's what happened. My father hit me so hard I fell and knocked out a tooth.

I cough and splutter and a knot of bloody saliva lands in the rushes in front of my face. The way I ought to feel is circling a long way away, too high up to touch me.

'Don't you *dare* say that to me,' my father says.

I can't even remember what I said. Something about God, wasn't it?

Someone says, very low, 'Johannes . . .'

'Don't you *dare* – you disobedient little ne'er-do-well –'

I look up at him. He still has his hand up, like the wind's changed and he got stuck like that. I want to laugh.

He kicks me.

There's a gasp that could be me or the journeymen. Then there are big racking gulps that are definitely me, as I fight for air, sobbing with the shock. Hitting me is one thing, but my father *kicking* me, like a kid having a tantrum? I push myself up to all fours, feeling the ground tremble and moisten under my hands. I retch and spit, and morsels of half-digested pie drop into the rushes. There are strands of blood mixed in with the eel and curdled egg.

'Johannes. That's enough. Let the boy get up.'

There's someone between me and my father. I watch two pairs of legs scuffle. I think whoever's closer to me is winning, until his boots stagger to the side and my father grabs my arm and drags me to my feet.

He leans close to me. 'That boy is a blasphemer. I stayed to listen because of the sheer evil of what he was saying – tempting children away from their rightful homes – don't you *dare* mention God and that devil of a boy in one breath –'

'Johannes . . .'

'Do you understand?'

I can't speak. I shake my head and try to swallow the slick of blood that fills my mouth.

'*Do you understand?*'

'He's not evil. He's not a blasphemer.' The consonants don't come out right. Something warm runs down my chin and I wipe it away with my hand.

'You foolish little –'

'For God's sake, Johannes!' A pause while my father turns, his hand still drawn back. The journeyman says, 'Come on. He's just a kid. They're all just kids. He hasn't done anything wrong. So he listened to this crazy preaching, but so what? He's not like Daniel. He's not going anywhere.'

My father turns to look at me.

'He's *not going anywhere*,' the journeyman says again. Then he meets my eyes, and the expression on his face could break my heart. 'Are you, Rufus?'

I say, 'I'm sorry.'

The journeyman stares at me. Then he shakes his head, clenching his jaw, and goes back to the workbench. For a few moments there's the sound of him tapping at a cameo.

My father says, 'He's right. You're not going anywhere.'

'That's what you said to Daniel,' I say. 'And you let *him –*'

He takes hold of me and swings me round in front of him – roughly, so I yelp with pain – and pushes me forward, out of the door and up the steps towards the living quarters. My face stings and throbs with the movement. It hurts, oh God, it hurts . . . but it's funny too, the way my knees hit the stairs so I'm almost crawling, staggering clumsily to my feet and falling again. It's so strange. I wouldn't recognise either of us.

He slams the door of the bedchamber and I'm kneeling on the floor, my shoulder blades tingling because he's behind me.

But he doesn't hit me. Not yet. He puts his hand on my shoulder, very gently.

'Rufus . . . don't do this,' he says. 'We all get things wrong. What you heard was the Devil. He wants you to be deceived.'

I shake my head.

'You're being very foolish.'

'You heard it. You heard him preach,' I say. 'Papa, you *heard* him.'

'I forbid you to go. Disobeying me is a sin.'

'Disobeying God is worse,' I say. But it isn't logic that makes me say it; it's the thought of Nick.

He takes a sharp breath in and I flinch. But all he does is take his hand off my shoulder and move away. 'You are an ignorant, blasphemous boy.' His voice sounds tight, like a bowstring. 'But I'm not going to punish you. I'm going to lock you in here, for your own sake, until you can learn to distinguish between good and evil.'

I spin round. A split second while we stare at each other. Then I make a dash for the door but he moves too, faster than me, and it slams shut. I'm staring at the grain of the wood a few inches from my face, and he's on the other side. I try to pull it open, but it stays closed, and I hear the noise of the lock.

'You can't. You *can't*!' I pound on the door with my fists. The impact jolts my jaw and sends twinges of pain into my stomach. 'Please – please let me out – you can't keep me here – please – Papa –'

There's no answer. I keep shouting until I have to stop for breath. Then I hear raised voices – my mother, and then a sudden desolate wail that must be my aunt Lena – and my father replying, but I can't make out the words. Then there's silence again. I keep hitting the door, throwing myself against it. I call out, 'He's locked me in! Please let me out – Mama – *please* . . .' I know there's someone there because there's a shadow under the door, but when I stop and listen again there's silence.

I keep on until my voice is worn ragged. Then I lean my forehead against the door and breathe, listening to life going on without me. There's noise from the workshop, the bustle of the street, the honks and hisses of the geese in the yard behind our house. And somewhere, high and commanding, just on the edge of hearing, there's the sound of a pipe. The melody flares out suddenly, like a peacock·showing its tail.

'I'm going to Jerusalem,' I say to the shadow under the door, just in case it's my father's.

No answer. I say it again, hoping there's someone listening. Then I sit against the nearest bed with my knees up, watching the sliver of dark to see if it moves. It doesn't. Maybe there isn't anyone there after all.

My head aches. I open my mouth and dig at my gum with my finger, exploring the damage. It hurts but there aren't any bits of bone left, so at least it came out cleanly. But when I close my eyes I see the floor coming up to meet me, swinging up to vertical, clouting me across the temple . . . I lick my finger and wipe the corner of my mouth where the blood has dried, stiffening the skin. My fingertip tastes of iron.

That pipe plays on and on, shrill as birdsong. It's calling me – us . . . I wonder where Nick is. He must be getting ready to leave, drunk with success, still not quite believing his good fortune. No, that's not right. He always knew God was on his side; he knew he'd go back to the cathedral, day after day, until the miracle happened and people started to listen. He was just lucky that it happened so soon.

That was my doing. I brought the apprentices yesterday.

And now I'm here, locked in, and they'll all leave without me.

V

I don't think my father was trying to be kind, locking me in the bedchamber – and I don't know what he's planning to do, come bedtime – but all the same I'm grateful, kind of. I curl up in the middle of the bed I share – shared – with Daniel, and watch the way the light changes on the parchment over the windows. It's hard to measure time. I drowse a little and when I'm awake again I'm hungry. That pie was all I've had today, and most of that ended up on the workshop floor. I must have missed dinner again. But no one brings me any food. Even the shadow outside the door has gone.

There are the bells for Vespers. The window glows and blazes.

I say in my head, *Please, please, please.*

Are you listening? You're not answering, but then you never do.

I say, *Please. If you want me to go on crusade, you have to help. I'm only a kid. I can't do it on my own. If this is what you want . . .*

Even if it isn't. Please.

The bells jangle together, discordant, all the churches disagreeing with one another. Then, one by one, they stop. I stare at the window and can't think of anything else to say. You know it all anyway.

I close my eyes. I whisper a paternoster under my breath, trying to mean it. *Pater noster, qui es in caelis* . . . but my throat tightens on *pater*. The sunlight glares on the window, red as fire. The streets are quieter now; the pipe has stopped playing.

And very faintly – for a moment I think I'm imagining it – I hear a girl shrieking, and a dull knocking sound like someone banging on our door. I kneel up, my heart beating. If it's a fire – if there's a fire and I'm locked in –

Martyrdom, I think.

And then there's a bustle of other voices, older and deeper, men, a woman . . . and I realise. They've locked her in. Like me. I listen until her voice gives out and there's just the banging. I think about joining in, but it's enough just to listen. I'd shout to her if I thought I could do it loud enough.

And further away, towards the west, I can hear more of the same. More fists pounding on walls and doors, more young voices yelling to be let out, more parents losing their tempers, shouting back. No, maybe not. Maybe I can't actually *hear* them. But I know they're there. And suddenly I'm frowning, running my tongue over the blood-tasting gap in my gums, trying to think. *Please, Lord, please* . . . The light dies out of the window.

The paternoster tells itself over and over in my head, like someone else saying it. It's a kind of background while I struggle for ideas. What can I do? There must be something.

I can hear something else. A high note in the air – not the pipe, but something similar, dipping and swerving into something that isn't quite a tune. It's in time with the banging, but it's not coming from the same direction. And it has words, or vowels, at least . . . vowels that I follow unconsciously until suddenly I know it's my aunt Lena. She's singing an old song, her favourite: *The bitter withy that causes me to smart, to smart . . .*

'Lena. *Lena!*'

Quiet. A scuffling as she drags her feet towards my voice. Then she says, 'Ooo-oo?'

I *think* she's saying 'Rufus'. I say very precisely, spitting the consonants, 'Come here. Please. Come and talk to me.'

A pause. I hear a knocking sound and I wince, because she might be trying to push through the wall. Even if my mother hasn't tied her to the rail, Lena isn't very good at working out where to go. But then I hear a door open, and steps on the floor outside. I take a deep breath.

'Help me to get out. Please, Lena. I need you to help me. Only you can do it.'

A rustling noise and her voice murmuring from note to note, closer to me now, as if she's sitting on the floor.

'My mother has a spare key. It'll be in the solar,' I say, softly but as clearly as I can manage. 'It'll be in the chest against the wall.' I hope I'm right; I hope my mother isn't wearing the keys on a bunch on her belt, the way she sometimes does. Lena might be able to get the keys from the chest, and maybe – just maybe – she'll be able to find the right one; but she couldn't nab them from under my mother's nose.

Still the same song. I swallow my frustration. 'Lena? Are you listening?'

A little pause, the length of a hiccup. Then the melody again, but a little firmer, more confident.

I lean my head back against the wall and mouth what I want to say. *Come on, you silly sow, please stop messing around, just do it* . . . I lick my gum until the taste of iron fills my mouth. 'Lena . . . please. I haven't done anything wrong. My father locked me in because I have to go away and he –'

'Go away?' For the first time I'm sure of the consonants.

'There's going to be a crusade. A boy came to the cathedral and preached. He's going to lead a crusade of children. And we'll take Jerusalem because we're innocent, we're closer to God. We'll be soldiers for Christ.' I can't get the words to say what I mean; I want to explain the way I felt when Nick gave me the kiss of peace, the sky-silence in the cathedral as the crowd listened, the disbelief when I realised it was really going to *happen*. But it's like trying to explain the way the sunset blazed on the window.

'Me too?'

'I . . .' Oh no. 'Lena . . .' Of course she can't go. But if I tell her so . . . She's the only one who can help me.

I shut my eyes and think of the call I felt – still feel – in my blood, surging like a tide, my whole body aching to obey. I think of Jerusalem and the True Cross; I think of Nick's voice. And I say, 'Yes, you too, Lena.'

There's a little squeak. I wish I could see her face.

Then silence. I take a deep breath. 'You can come too, Lena. You can be a soldier too, for God.' I lean closer to the door, keeping my voice low and gentle. 'And now, if you let me out . . . it'll be like the angel rescuing Saint Peter. You've always wanted to do

66

something for our Lord, haven't you? Well, you can now. Please.' That bit is the truth. But it feels like a lie, all the same.

I wait. Any minute now she'll scuttle away and back, turning the key in the lock . . . but I don't hear any movement. She's thinking, that's all, and it takes her longer than it takes most people.

'You should see Jerusalem, Lena. All the rich things the merchants sell are from Jerusalem. The spices, and fruit, and silks and perfumes. The city smells like heaven . . . and the holy places, they're beautiful. We'll go there together. I'll take you there. I'll look after you. But I have to get out first – you have to get me out . . . Please.'

If Lena were really a child – or if she were talking to anyone else – she'd say, 'Promise?' But she trusts me; I've never lied to her. I've never needed to. Her hand creeps towards the door, her fingertips just visible under it.

I say, 'Think of Jesus, Lena. Think how pleased he'll be with you.'

Her fingernails go pale as she presses on the floor. I hold my breath, but I'm smiling. This is going to work. It has to; God's on my side.

Then she gets up and leaves.

I wait. There's the noise of the door opening and closing. I wait for the clunk as she lifts the lid of the chest against the wall, but it doesn't come. A few footsteps; a double thump, like the heartbeat of the house, or someone dropping to their knees. Then the rise and fall of Lena's voice, the meaningless sighs that she thinks are praying. I clench my hands, wondering what she's doing. I want to batter myself against the walls like a bird trying to escape.

It's getting cold. There are raised voices from below me. My parents. I almost smile, because I can imagine what my mother is saying. She may not be on my side, but she's bound to ask my father where they're supposed to sleep tonight.

Then the voices fade. Even Lena's dies away.

I shiver, wrapping my arms round my knees, rocking a little with impatience. I try to pray but my whole skin is tingling with urgency. Come on, Lena. Where *is* she?

I wait. It's not as if there's anything else I can do. The air has gone chill and damp and even the banging from my fellow prisoner has stopped. Slowly the light fades.

It takes a long time for me to realise that Lena isn't coming.

I wake feeling like the end of a bonfire: grey, brittle, half dead with cold. My mouth tastes of ash. It's not quite dawn. I feel as if something woke me, but the house is quiet.

I get up. Something in my body takes me through the triple sign of the cross and pulls on my hose and shirt as if this is an ordinary morning. My gum is throbbing, and there are bruises on my shoulder and hip that make it hard to move normally. My eyes are sticky and the skin on my cheeks is stiff with dried tears. I lick my finger and run it over my eyelids. I start to reach automatically for the pot of salt on the board, but my mouth's too sore to clean my teeth, and anyway it'd only make me thirsty.

Where did everyone else sleep? It's so strange to be alone I want to laugh, but it's creepy too. I feel like I'm the only person alive in the world. And . . . if my father would rather stop everyone else going to bed than let me out . . . I blink and shake my head. I wish I was still angry, but instead I just feel empty and a little bit scared.

Slowly I ease myself down until I'm kneeling on the floor, leaning sideways so I don't press too hard on the bruise on my knee. I don't say anything, because I feel like I'm praying already. This emptiness, this dead, quiet emptiness feels closer to prayer than any number of paternosters. I stay still, listening, not really caring if I get an answer. The only words I can think of are, *I'm here*. But right now that seems like it's enough.

There's food on the floor next to the door.

I don't move immediately. I look at the sheen on the bowl, the grey dawn light following the curve of the pottery. I breathe in, and I'm almost sure I can smell something – spices, or the rich comfort of milk. My mouth floods with saliva and suddenly I'm sick with hunger. I make myself stay where I am, counting my heartbeat. Ten. Eleven. Twelve.

Then I stand up, a bit giddy, and walk over to it. A mug of small beer, a bowl of frumenty warming my hands through the pottery, a hunk of bread and a little bowl of honey.

It tastes like – well, like heaven; even though it hurts to chew, it tastes so good it's *holy*. I bolt it, swallowing so fast I can feel the food sliding down into my stomach, saying a kind of wordless grace in my head. I take a gulp of beer, and another, and suddenly my mouth is full of beer and not blood, and it's wonderful, it's the best thing in the world. I leave the honey till last. Then I eat it slowly with my fingers, smearing it over my gum, working it deeper into the wound with my tongue. Honey is for healing; whoever left it here knew about my tooth. If I didn't feel so good I'd cry with gratitude.

I sit back. I feel stronger, but sleepy too. For a moment I'm glad I'm locked in. I can curl up again on the bed, sleep for . . . sleep for *hours*, sleep until Prime or Terce . . . Maybe someone will bring me more food. And if I'm locked in – well, no one could blame me for not going on the crusade, could they? It's the will of God. Not even Nick could argue with that.

Nick. Nick'll be waiting for me; he'll think I've changed my mind.

Or maybe he won't wait for me.

I stand up and look at the door. I take a deep breath. Then I slam the soft part of my hands into the wood, as hard as I can, not knowing if I'm trying to hurt the door or myself.

And it opens.

It swings slowly, inert, until I'm staring into the empty corridor, and the scent of cooling metal and the kitchen hearth fills the air.

Lena. She did it. She left me food and unlocked the door.

I give a tiny sob of joy and fear and disbelief. I can hear Nick's crusade calling me as clearly as a melody, and the obstacle's gone, like a miracle, like the walls of Jericho falling into dust at the sound of a pipe . . . I'm alone. The door's open.

I ought to take things with me. A spare set of clothes. A spare knife. A bundle of surcotte, mug, bowl – even my clay horse or soldiers-on-strings that I'm nearly too old for. But they're too far below me – shrunk to the size of pinheads, as if something's lifted me away from the earth and I'm airborne.

I walk out of the door. I go down the steps. I can smell the workshop and the street. I can hear the geese outside waking up.

The door to the workshop is ajar. As I go past it I hear someone speaking. I pause to listen, in case it's my father, in case he's talking about me. And it *is* my father, and he *is* talking about me. But it isn't what I expected.

He's praying. 'Into your hands, O Lord . . .' He says my name, as if God wouldn't understand otherwise. A murmur of something too quiet for me to hear. I lean closer to the edge of the door.

'I'm sorry,' he says. 'I'm sorry. I don't know what to do. It can't be right. Please don't let this happen. Don't take him away. He's my son. Don't take him away.' He says it as if he means it, and he probably does. After all, who else is going to look after him when he gets old?

'Please. He's only a child. He doesn't know . . . You can't be calling him, not really. You can't . . . I don't know what you want me to do, I don't *know* – please . . .' His voice trails away again. He sounds soft, uncertain, in pain. I peer through the crack in the door to make sure it's really him.

'*Please* . . .' And in the silence I hear the weight of my father's fear. I hear the look on his face when he was listening to Nick. I hear what made him hit me.

I ought to go in to him, kneel for his pardon and blessing, give up Nick and the crusade. What a sacrifice that would be: to give up God for my father. Would that be

71

perfect love or perfect stupidity? But it doesn't matter, because I know already that I won't do it.

I walk out of the house and turn towards the cathedral.

The sun's rising. The streets are still murky, full of shadows, the roofs reaching out to each other over my head. But the sky's lighter, and the bells are starting to ring: St Ursula and St Gereon to the north, St Cecilia to the west, St Pantaleon to the south . . . And somewhere, calling me, there's the catchy, maddening noise of a pipe.

My heart lifts, like a weight falling off my shoulders, because I'm on my way. I don't have any will of my own. I've surrendered. It feels better than anything I've ever known.

In a few hours – a few moments – the streets will fill with other children, apprentices, servants, girls, the occasional grown-up who doesn't have anything better to do. And they'll all flock to the cathedral, with bundles of clothes and food, staves they've bought or stolen from the exhausted pilgrims, all ready for the big adventure. People will watch and scoff, drawing back their clothes in case we're contagious. They'll laugh and marvel, speculate about us in the taverns, not understanding. We won't understand either, any more than they do, but that won't stop us. We'll set off like a procession, a parody of a crusade, like the Feast of Misrule has come half a year early. Like fools and idiots, like children . . .

But I don't think about that. I pause, leaning on a wall, and peer up at the lightening sky, and I know you're there. I can't see you, but you're there. When I step forward the new sunlight slants down in a sudden line, thin as a blade,

72

sliding between houses, straight into my eyes. I blink and see the flicker of wings: white, dazzling, covering my whole field of vision.

And by the time I get to the cathedral the sun's risen above the roofs, and the light spreads itself out over the sky like fire, like something being born out of ashes.

PART II

An uncertain journey

VI

A little while ago the darkness beyond the fire was shining lustrous blue, like enamel; but now it's flat and thick, dark as fur, dropped as neatly as a cloak between the flames and the world behind. It would take sharper eyes than mine – hunter's eyes, like yours – to make out the sleeping children, the trees and humps of long grass, the debris of crusts and pastry and apple cores. It would take your eyes to see that some of them are already tossing and turning, reaching out for comforting grown-up hands that aren't there; it would take your eyes to see that some of them are already bewildered, searching in their sleep for the path that brought them here, so they can go home. And if you're here . . . well, if you *are*, we can't see you; you're slinking through the shadows, head tilted away from the fire so we don't catch your eyes glinting in the flickering light. You tread delicately between the bodies, feeling the tiny wind of their breath, watching their dreams jump behind their eyelids. You sit and watch, baring your teeth. You don't mind waiting.

You're hungry, though. It won't be long.

'Where's Nick?'

I don't know what it is that wakes me. Perhaps it's my own voice, speaking out of a dream; or the dream itself, catching at me like a claw. I sit up, sweating, and the question's there, in the air, before I realise I'm awake.

Sophie murmurs and rolls over, groaning. 'What?'

I don't answer. I stare into the fire. Someone's put some more wood on it, but it's damp, smoking and spitting like it's trying to keep us at a distance.

Sophie drags her hair out of her face and peers at me through the dark. 'What did you say?' Her voice is deep and blurred with sleep. 'Rufus?'

What was the dream? It clings to me like moulted hair. Something about my father, something about someone's father. I shiver, feeling the sweat evaporate off my arms and forehead. I lean sideways, trying to see past the fire to the place where Nick knelt at sunset, on a little bit of raised ground, so we could follow his prayers. That's where he ate while the littlest kids stared at him; that's where he slept. It's where he ought to be now.

'He isn't there,' I say. I sound lost and small. I clear my throat.

'Who . . . ? Oh,' Sophie says. 'Don't worry, I expect he's . . . gone for a . . .' She yawns too widely to finish the sentence, and gestures drowsily towards the trees.

I nod, but the sticky feeling of the dream doesn't go away.

'Go back to sleep. There's a long way to go tomorrow.' She reaches out a warm hand and squeezes my leg. I don't think she meant it to be my leg particularly – it's dark, after all – but I shift my weight and she draws back.

I say, 'Yes, I will,' and listen to the rustling of her settling back down. I count my breaths, sitting still until the fire has subsided into embers and the darkness has thinned a little. Then I get up and walk towards the river.

Once I get further away from the fire it's easier. There's a half-swollen moon and enough light to see by. The quiet makes me uneasy, because of the way it magnifies all the smallest sounds, the tiny noises of nocturnal things hiding in the grass. I feel like something's watching me, padding alongside me silently. I think I see the glimmer of eyes staring from the edge of the water. It makes me speed up, even though I don't know where I'm going.

There's a cry.

My heart jumps so hard I feel it hit the roof of my mouth. My pulse stutters and slides. I'm breathless. I stumble forward. There's the smell of river mist and mud, thick summer warmth, the woodsmoke that's got into my hair. Another cry – and this time it trails off into a sob, so that I know it's someone, not a fox or wolf, not one of those almost-human cries that animals make at night as they hunt, no, but someone in pain . . .

I say, *Please, God, please, please* . . .

There's a little clearing next to the water, where the trees knot together overhead like hands so that only spots and rosettes of moonlight can get through. But in the splashes of white I can see fragments of a person: a wrist, a cheekbone, a bare kneecap. The river gurgles round the tree roots, talking to itself, unconcerned. There's another sound, another sort of gurgling, but I don't have time to work out what it is before the cry comes again, ending on a kind of sob. An eye and forehead slide into the light and out again; the toes of a bare foot dig into the earth.

I stand perfectly still. *Please, please* . . . but I don't know what I'm praying for.

I stay there for as long as I can. When he moves again I can see more of his face and I know it's Nick.

I feel sick and hot. My face and hands and armpits are soaked; there are drips crawling on my skin, like tiny tongues. I crouch down near him and reach out, but he doesn't seem to see me, and when I try to pat his shoulder he goes rigid. I take my hand away and he breathes in with a great gasp, as if he was holding his breath. I don't know what to do. I wait for him to speak, but he doesn't. I want to go back to Sophie, but I can't just leave him here.

I kneel in front of him, and because I can't hold his hands I clasp my own together, twisting my fingers until they hurt. It's as if he can see something I can't. He looks into my face and past me, his breathing very quick and shallow.

I say, 'Are you ill? Nick . . . is there anything I can do?' Of course he doesn't answer – of course – but the sound of my own voice comforts me a little. 'Shall I get Sophie? Or anyone else? Does anyone – will anyone know what to do?'

His eyes flicker and focus. Somewhere, hoarsely, his voice digs up the word, 'No.'

'Should I . . . ?' I struggle to my feet. Of course . . . 'I'll get your father –'

He shakes his head with an odd, stiff movement, like an injured animal. 'No.'

It occurs to me, then, that I haven't seen his father since we left Cologne. Slowly I kneel down again.

'Just – stay. Will you? Stay.'

'All right.' I'm so glad he's talking I can't help grinning. I must look like a skull in the moonlight, all pale cheeks and teeth.

'Talk to me.'

'What about?'

'Anything. Just talk.'

There's a silence. No one's ever wanted me to talk before. Not with my own words. I lick my lips and run my tongue over the hole where my tooth used to be.

Nick says, 'Sometimes I think that's why God does terrible things to us. He just wants us to talk to him. He'd rather we hated him than ignored him.'

Another pause.

'Just *talk*. Please. Just give me something to listen to. To drown out –' He stops.

So I clench my eyes shut and try to think of something to say. I struggle for words, but my head fills with a kind of helpless silence. I want to help him; I want to give him lots of little soft words to bandage the pain, to cover the places where you've been too rough with him. But I can't think of anything. Everything I can think of – *It's all right* or *I'm here* or *We all love you* – is clumsy, just a version of the voice he's trying to drown out.

I don't know how long I've been quiet. When I sneak a glance at Nick he's very still, eyes lowered, patient as stone.

I clear my throat. I know if I try to tell him how I feel . . . well, it won't work, that's all. Words are so little. It's like trying to give someone a river in thimblefuls.

But I have to say *something*.

Suddenly I can hear Nick's own voice in my head. *Thou shalt not be afraid for the terror by night; nor for the arrow that flieth by day . . . Thou shalt tread upon the lion and adder . . .*

I take a deep breath.

'When I was small – really small,' I say, 'my mother used to tie me to the end of our bed while they went to

Mass. They used to go out and leave me, not for very long, but I used to hate it. I used to try and try to get loose. And when I was tiny I couldn't undo the knots, but one day I managed it. It took a really long time, but I did it. I was really pleased with myself. And I was running around in the bedchamber, and I got all the blankets and furs out of the chest and put them on the big bed, and I . . . I made a big mess. I didn't mean to, but I was playing. And the lid of the chest fell down on my fingers and it really, *really* hurt and I started to cry. I didn't hear my parents coming back, but my father came in and he looked at the mess I'd made, and he looked at the strap he'd used to tie me to the bed, and he looked at me. I tried to stop crying but I couldn't. In the end he asked me why I was crying, and I told him I'd hurt my hand. And he crouched down and looked at my hand and asked me how I'd hurt it, so I told him. And he untied the other end of the strap and looked sort of stern and asked me was I sure, and I said yes. And then he nodded and turned to look at the chest, and he said, 'Don't you ever bite my son again, do you understand?' And he hit the chest with the strap, and he kept telling it how naughty it had been, and how if he ever caught it hurting me again he'd take it into the yard and have a big bonfire.'

There's a pause. I feel the blood rushing into my cheeks.

Then Nick laughs. The sound goes straight to my heart, cutting through a knot I hadn't realised was there.

'It's stupid,' I say. 'I just . . . I know it's stupid.'

'No,' Nick says.

'He's not like that normally. When my grandfather

died and my aunt came to live with us . . .' But that's too long a story for the middle of the night. Even if I wanted to tell it. My gum starts to throb, stabbing deep into my jaw. 'It doesn't matter.' I hiss my breath out through my teeth. 'I don't know why I thought of that.'

'I think I do.'

The moon has shifted like a huge eye, trying to get a better view of us. Now the moonlight streams sideways through the trees, turning us to alabaster. I can see all of Nick – crumpled shirt and bare legs, hands linked over his knees, his hair all over his face. He looks up, meets my gaze, and smiles. I hold out my hand and he takes it and we stand up together, balancing the weight between us.

I say, 'Um . . . the rest of your clothes . . . ?'

He glances down at his legs. 'Oh, *cods*.'

'Yes,' I say. 'Exactly.'

'I left them . . . I was sleeping like this, and then when I . . . I think I was asleep. I had to get away, I knew I was . . .' He screws his face up, shaking his head.

'I'll go and get them.'

'Thank you.'

'You're all right?' I say, in a rush. 'I mean –'

'Yes. It's over. Don't worry.'

I want to ask him what happened; what those cries meant, whether there really was something ripping him apart, how often it happens . . . but his face is very watchful and I know he won't tell me.

I nod and go back along the river to the dying light of the fire. Nick's things are in a bundle in the flattened grass where he slept. I take them and pick my way through the sleeping children, trying not to wake anyone. But as I get to the edge of the group, one of them sits up and I see the reddish glint of blinking eyes. For a sickening moment I think it's a hunchback, one of the cripples Nick seems to attract; but then I see it's a little girl with her hood hanging off her shoulder. She says, 'Why are you stealing his clothes?'

'Nick asked me to. He's –' But I don't know what to say. 'He left them behind.'

'Where did he go?'

'He's just over there, in the trees,' I say. 'He wanted to go off on his own.'

'To pray?'

'Yes. Go to sleep,' I say. 'You'll wake everyone else.'

'Why did he leave his clothes?'

'He was . . .' I bend my knees so that we're eye to eye. 'Like Jacob. Wrestling with an angel.'

'With an *angel*?'

'Yes. Now go to sleep.'

She flops down quickly and lies motionless, as if she's playing sleeping lions. But she doesn't close her eyes. I look back at her once as I make my way back to Nick and I see the fire reflecting in her pupils.

And when Nick and I come out of the trees there's a whole line of little faces watching, a whole line of eyes catching the light from the glowing coals. He smiles when he sees them, but it makes me uneasy. Their mouths are open and they don't move, like rabbits that have been hypnotised by a dancing stoat.

Nick puts some of his weight on a forked, T-shaped branch that I broke off a dead tree, but he's very straight-backed as he walks back to where he was sleeping. He doesn't say anything to the kids, but they reach out and trail their fingers along his legs as he passes.

I watch him settle down quietly. Then I go back to

where I was sleeping before. Sophie's turned her back on the space I left, curling towards a dark shape that might be Lucas, or Otto, or one of the others.

I lie awake for a long time, thinking.

VII

It's only yesterday – less than a day and night ago – that I left my father. Now I shut my eyes against the dark and I can see myself.

I'm hurrying through the streets and even though I'm not exactly scared my heart's going hard and quick, like someone hammering gold. I know when we leave the city I'll have to duck sideways into doorways or lower my head behind other people so that my father can't find me and lock me in again.

But then I get to the cathedral and it isn't like that.

There are so many people. There are so many *people*. Not all of them are children – there are youths, apprentices too – but most of them are. The average height is about six inches smaller than me. And the noise . . . I can't hear myself think. There's a shrill, discordant psalm coming from somewhere, and still the music from that pipe . . .

Someone's made a platform from a couple of planks and barrels, and there's Nick. His face reminds me of the window, last night, flaming with the last of the sunlight. But next to him –

The boy next to him is a little hunchbacked cripple, in clothes that could be motley or just so patched they look like it. He's the one playing the pipe. As I stare, he leans his head sideways and rubs it against Nick's shoulder, like a cat, without losing the melody. I grit my teeth and my face goes hot, although I don't know why.

I look away, deliberately sizing up the crowd. Most of the kids are poor, ragged and drab, clutching bits of bread for the journey. As I watch, a woman in a stained cyclas lets go of her son's hand and kisses his forehead. Then she turns and goes back the way she came. The little boy frowns and his mouth knots up, but an older girl grabs him and pulls him into the throng. The last I see is her hand making a cross on his tunic with a bit of charcoal, then putting his bit of bread into her bundle.

'Rufus! Rufus –'

Sophie. She's waving from a corner, half-hidden by a group of apprentices. I walk over, slowly, because people keep on getting in my way.

'What happened?'

I'd forgotten about my bruises. I shrug.

'I didn't go home at all,' she says. 'There were so many people on the streets last night . . . Everywhere. They were talking and preaching and there were people praying, all night. I drew a cross on my dress, look, and people kept giving me money . . .'

I say, 'My father locked me in.'

'Oh.' Her eyes slide over my face and she looks away. 'But you're here now.'

'Yes.'

'I should have been going home today,' she says. 'I'm supposed to be getting married in the winter.'

'I'm supposed to be starting my apprenticeship in the winter.'

We grin at each other. And suddenly it doesn't matter about anything else. She takes my hand, and no one's looking at us. I say, 'I wonder what Jerusalem will be like.'

'Wonderful.'

'Well, *obviously*,' I say. We both laugh. If I don't look at Nick on his platform I can be perfectly happy.

In the end the crowd starts to move. There's a commotion as someone moves the barrels into an oxcart and sets up the platform again on top of them. Then we lose sight of Nick as the cart lurches and stogs its way down the street away from the cathedral, with him on its back. We try to follow, but there are too many people for us to decide where to go. All we can do is hold each other's hand and hope. The crowd carries us forward; people press against me and my feet leave the ground. I have to wriggle and stick my elbows out before I feel myself drop back to earth.

'Oh, God . . .'

I twist to look at Sophie. She's gone pale. I squeeze her hand so hard I can't tell if she's squeezing back. She gives me a funny little smile, as if she's learnt it from a book.

Something hits me in the face. I don't know what it is – something soft, like skin. I look up and there are people in the windows. A woman leans out, her arms outstretched, praying loudly. Something else falls into my eye and I blink. There's no room to try to catch it, but as I turn my head I see more flecks drifting down from the woman's hands. Petals. Red petals, like blood. The people around me are smiling.

Sophie shouts to me, 'It's like going on a *crusa*—' She catches herself in the middle of the word; then she says it, slowly, tasting the syllables as if she's never said it before. 'Like going on a *crusade*.'

'Yes,' I say. '*Exactly* like it.'

I know then that my father won't find me; that he couldn't get through the mob to drag me home, even if he dared to try. I'm free.

I lick my lips and I can taste salt.

It takes hours to get out of the city. We move so slowly we're standing still most of the time. The noise dies down a little bit, but the psalms and the pipe carry on mercilessly. It's hot, and I didn't bring any water. But most of the time I can forget about my thirst, because it's like the best kind of game. We're playing at crusades, and the grown-ups are joining in.

There must be people like my father. There must be people watching silently from their workshops, or from the top of their steps, watching their children go to war. But they don't make any noise, and when I look around it's hard to remember they might be there.

Further out, towards the city walls, the streets broaden and we're walking in pasture or fallow land, where the houses aren't so crammed together. It's a bit quieter; people stand in their doorways to watch us, but it's not like it was further north, in the centre.

And by the time we get out past the city wall the line is straggling and the tune of the psalm is sagging in the middle. The sky arches above us and Sophie and I slow down, tilting our chins to stare up at the blueness of it. Without the roofs it's so *big*.

'We're going towards God,' Sophie says.

'Yes,' I say. Somewhere in front of us there's Nick on his oxcart, the hunchback dancing lopsidedly next to it like a familiar demon. But I look sideways at Sophie instead, and realise I'm still holding her hand. It's wet and sticky, and if I move my fingers I can almost hear the suck between moisture and skin.

I take a deep breath of clean new air and say again, 'Yes.'

By mid-afternoon the littlest kids have fallen behind. We've spread out into a line: oldest kids at the front, apprentices shouting and flicking at one another with long switches, eating and scuffling as they walk; the nearly-grown-ups next, trudging like they've forgotten what an adventure's meant to be like; middling kids after that, struggling to keep up. And then, strung out along the river the way we came, the toddlers, the ones not quite little enough to be carried. Some of them are sitting still, grizzling or screaming, waiting for someone to come back for them; some of them are still putting one foot in front of the other.

Sophie and I are at the front. Neither of us is much used to walking, but we're not tired. If we look back over our shoulders Cologne has disappeared; you can't even see the cathedral or the tower of St Mary-of-the-Steps on the hill. We've wiped it out.

'Rufus! Hey! Rufus!'

Sophie looks round before I do.

It's Paul. He looks as if he's put on all his best clothes. He smiles at Sophie and waves his hand so that the new sapphire on his finger gleams. 'Your daddy let you out of the house, then?' For a moment I think he's saying it to her.

Sophie blinks and then glances at me and away. The look on her face makes me take my hand out of hers, but we're still walking. I say, '*Your* daddy wanted to get rid of you as quickly as possible, did he?'

Sophie says, 'Does it matter? We're here now, aren't we —'

Paul says, 'Don't you talk about my father like that, you skinny little —' He looks at Sophie and his face slides back into that smile. He stops where he is, in his musician pose, and ignores me when I stumble, trying not to walk into him. 'My name's Paul. My father's a mercer.'

'Hello, Paul,' she says. 'Hello, my-father's-a-mercer.'

'Are you one of Rufus's cousins?'

'No. I'm one of his friends.'

I look as surprised as Paul does. I can feel it on my face. I try to get rid of it, but the grin spreads across my cheeks like a stain that won't budge.

Paul looks at her for longer than he should. Then he skips sideways to look at me. 'God's truth! You've got a *friend*, Red?'

I don't answer.

'Or should that be "Purple"? Or "Blue"? Because, let's face it, you're looking a bit . . .' He licks his lips, screwing one side of his mouth into a tight little knot. 'You're looking a bit . . . *damaged*. He doesn't care what he does to you, does he? Not like one of his precious bits of metal. Oh no. He'll hit his little babby as hard as he damn' well —'

'Shut up,' I say, so quietly I don't expect him to hear.

'He doesn't care if he breaks *you*, does he? Hasn't learnt his lesson?'

'Shut up.'

He laughs. Sophie is looking down at her feet, as if she's counting her steps. 'You'd think he'd be a bit more careful. He may not love you — well, let's face it, who would? — but, well, looks to me like he doesn't give a —'

'Stop it, please.' Sophie, this time. I can't speak.

'I guess you're pretty scared of him, right? Because if you don't do what he says you might end up like your drooling idiot aunt.'

I draw my hand back to swing a punch. And this time there's no one to stop me.

I smash my fist into his mouth. His lips open and I feel his teeth, the bare bone and wetness on my skin. It hurts my knuckles. I hear myself yelp with surprise. Paul staggers backwards. Sophie says, '*Rufus* –'

'Don't you ever say that about – don't you *ever* –'

Paul makes a grab for me. Somewhere, distantly, there are the sounds of kids crowding round or moving out of the way, grumbling or egging us on, a lone nearly-adult voice saying, 'Oh, for God's sake . . .'

I look down at Paul's hand on my elbow, pulling me into a better position for him to hit me back.

This is the moment when my father would step in. This is as far as it would get, at home. But we're not at home.

I throw myself at him. I'm scratching at his face, kicking his shins, jerking my knee up into his groin, all at once. I'm not used to fighting, but he's not used to being fought. He cries out and forgets to defend himself. He scrabbles at me, shouting, and manages to land a couple of punches, but I don't stop. He slaps my face, and my gum oozes the taste of metal. I grasp a handful of his hair and twist it until I feel the roots yield. He said my father – he said, about Lena –

A voice says, on a high note, 'Please, *stop*.'

I swing my elbow straight up, into his jawbone. The impact is strangely quiet, but it goes down the whole length of my body. Paul grunts, like someone waking up, and then drops to his knees. I kick him. I'm going to kick him again but there's someone holding me back.

'For the love of Christ!'

'But he –' I say. 'He said – he called Lena a – he said my father –'

'Yes. I know. I heard. Now *stop*.'

There are tears running off my chin. I brush them away with my sleeve.

'I thought you were going to kill him.' It's Sophie. The other voice wasn't, but this one is. She sounds detached, mildly curious, but when I look at her she's gone white.

Whoever is holding my arms lets go of me, slowly. I don't want to turn round, but I can't help it. It's a man, just young enough to be an apprentice. He looks at me and shakes his head. 'You little savage.' Then he turns away. 'God help us.'

'I'm not,' I say. 'I'm not . . .'

He's gone. He's not listening. Everyone else drifts away. There's only Sophie, and she doesn't meet my eyes. She kneels down and stares at Paul.

'He'll be fine,' I say. 'Won't he?'

'Yes, I think so. You're bleeding.'

I raise my hand to my face, but I don't know which bit to wipe. I dab at my mouth and my cheeks and my chin, because they're the bits that feel damp. And something *is* bleeding, because it stains the cuff of my shirt.

Sophie gets up, still looking down at Paul. She nudges him with her foot and he gives a grunt of protest. That seems to reassure her.

'I didn't knock him *out*,' I say. 'He's just being wet.'

Sophie gives me a very swift glance and doesn't say anything.

Paul says, 'Jesus Christ our Saviour . . .' There's no

way of knowing whether he's cursing or praying. It could be both. He struggles to his knees, swaying. 'Holy Mary, Mother of God . . .'

Sophie takes my wrist. It's not the way she held it before, like we were friends; now it feels as if she's trying to stop me getting away. She says, 'Come on, Rufus.' She starts to walk again. I follow her, because I don't have a choice. Some of the apprentices are looking at me. I can't read their expressions.

I say, 'He asked for it.'

'He wasn't a model of Christian courtesy,' Sophie says. I don't know whether she's agreeing with me or not.

'He thought, just because my father always – he thought I wouldn't . . .' But I can't explain what I mean. I can't tell her how it feels to be able to fight for myself, how the world is suddenly a better place. I say, 'He won't pick a fight with me again.'

'No,' Sophie says. 'No, he probably won't.'

At last she smiles at me. Her grip on my wrist loosens and slides down until our fingers are laced together.

We walk in silence, then. It's a golden afternoon, full of the smell of things growing, river water, the peppery, sweaty smell of bracken. I feel clean and light, as if I've been newly shriven. My sore tooth and face are aching, but not too much. The noise of singing and shouting has deepened and softened to something wordless. I'm not thirsty, but when Sophie passes me a gourd of water I drink mouthful after mouthful. Neither of us says a word until the column bunches and frays, spreading out, and we realise we're stopping. Then Sophie flops down, covering her eyes against the sun, and I sit down next to her. We watch the rest of the crusaders – *the crusaders!* – arrive, grizzling, staggering with fatigue, sucking their thumbs, and she catches my eye and gives me a secret, wicked grin. I try not to smile back, but I can't help it.

Then, on a kind of sudden sigh, she says again, 'I thought you were going to kill him.'

We pray at sunset. We've been praying all day, but this is different. Nick kneels on a patch of high ground, just beyond the pile of wood for the bonfire. He says the paternoster and the Ave Maria and then he sings a psalm. His voice rises high and thin, slightly off-key, the words only just distinguishable. *Out of the mouth of babes and sucklings hast thou ordained strength because of thine enemies, that thou mightest still the enemy and the avenger . . .* I bite my lip, feeling something pushing at my voice box that might be a laugh or a sob. *When I consider thy heavens, the work of thy fingers, the moon and the stars, which thou hast ordained . . .* I turn round. I can't bear to look at Nick, who's spread his arms like a cross, throwing a long shadow. I stare at the sunset. *What is man, that thou art mindful of him?* The words fill me up like water; if I move I'll spill. The sun flares like a rose.

Later they light the bonfire. We don't really need it for warmth, but it keeps the dusk away, and the littlest kids quarrel about who gets to sleep nearest to it. We sit further back and stare into the flames, watching tiny fortresses of gold form and collapse in the heart of the fire. Lucas and his friends have got a gourd of braggett, which they share with us in return for some of Sophie's bread and fruit. It's sweet and fierce and strong, and before long we're laughing and talking loudly about what it'll be like in Jerusalem. No one listens to what anyone else is saying, but we smile at each other and laugh at our own jokes and we're all friends. In the end there's a game of football in the bumpy meadow on the other side of the fire from the river. Sophie plays too, tying her skirts up. She doesn't know how to tackle or kick the ball, but she's a fast runner. Her hair comes out of its crespine and hangs down her back like a tail. When it finally gets too dark we all lie in the grass and look at the stars, and Lucas lies beside Sophie and tells her how she's too pretty to be good at boys' games. I grin to myself, half amused, half uneasy, because I've heard that tone before. But all Sophie does is laugh. She props herself up on her elbows and looks from Lucas to me and back again. 'Rufus is prettier than me, and *he*'s good at football,' she says.

Lucas laughs too, for quite a long time; then he yawns, stretching his hands above his head, which means he wasn't really trying. I'm not absolutely sure whether Sophie meant it as a compliment, but I smile anyway in case anyone's looking at me.

'Hey, Rufus,' someone else says, 'you an apprentice yet?'

'Not yet,' I say. It's Otto. He went to school when I did. He has a lazy, gentle sort of voice that I always liked. 'Soon. At least, it was supposed to be soon.'

'Don't hurry back,' he says. 'It's a proper nightmare most of the time.'

'Mmm.' I lean my head on my arm and stare at the white band of the Milky Way, wondering why it leads to Compostela and not to Jerusalem. Beside me, Lucas murmurs something, hiccups and giggles. Sophie laughs and says something in her cool, distant angel voice. I feel a warm hand nestle into mine and it takes a moment to realise it's hers.

And in a sleepy, dreamy, honey-tasting sort of way, it's suddenly real. I might never go back. I don't have to go back.

I close my eyes. I'm too happy to sleep. But I do; until I wake from my nightmare, and Nick's gone.

And now it's nearly dawn, and I'm staring up at the stars again, wondering about Nick, whether he'll be all right, whether he's sleeping now, exhausted from the touch of God, or whether he's lying awake, like me, remembering . . . I wonder what things look like from his eyes. Does he see things the way we do, or are they all blanked out, like colours under a blinding sun?

I remember the sound he made, like an animal caught in a trap. A rabbit, its spine snapped by something bigger, something merciless.

I roll over, breathing in the smell of Sophie's hair, sweat and grass and fresh air. It's a comforting smell: freedom and contentment, the last thing I smelt last night, before I fell asleep.

And then the memory of sleep melts into the real thing.

VIII

In the morning – the second day – it takes an hour of walking in the sun before the dew's dried off us and the early-morning cold has thawed. My muscles are stiff and my feet hurt. There's a blue sky and hot sun overhead, but no one's singing. Someone's saying, 'I'm hungry, I'm hungry, I'm *still* hungry,' over and over again, just loud enough to be annoying.

We've had breakfast, but I saw Sophie's face as she wrapped up the last of the bread, and felt the same expression on mine. She turned her back a little as she did it, so that Lucas couldn't see over her shoulder. They brought food, but most of it got eaten last night, and the leftover salt herrings are starting to smell hot and tired. At least there's the river, for water; it still tastes of downstream-of-Cologne, but after the braggett last night we're grateful for anything that can quench our thirst. I'm tired, and the sun snaps at my eyes like teeth.

We keep walking. Someone starts to sing. *Trust in the Lord, and do good; so shalt thou dwell in the land, and verily thou shalt be fed.*

I've never been this far outside the city. I ought to be looking around, marvelling at the space and light, the fields and pasture and woods, the way it smells of dry grass and clean earth. But it makes me feel dizzy. The city's manageable. The city's human. This is something else. I keep my eyes on the ankles in front of me.

The long crowd of us trudges along the river. When I look back I can't see the end of the line. The littlest kids, right at the back, are just dabs of colour, a herd of tiny charcoal crosses that stand out black against the rest of the world.

'How far is it to Jerusalem anyway?' I'm not sure who said it, but at least it wasn't me.

Sophie says, 'We have to get to the sea first.'

'How far to the sea, then?'

'Miles,' Lucas says, over his shoulder. 'We've got to cross the mountains first.'

'Oh,' the same voice says. It says it with such a mixture of disappointment and awe that I want to laugh. I blink the dust out of my eyes and look round to see who it belongs to. It's the little girl from last night, the one who saw me taking Nick's clothes. She says, 'Will it take a very long time?'

Sophie catches my eye and presses her lips together, trying not to smile. Lucas sees that and slows down until he's next to Sophie, looking down at the little girl. 'Why?' he says. 'Planning to be home for Lammas-tide?'

'No,' she says. 'But . . .' And for the first time I notice she's dragging a little boy along with her and he's limping badly. He's even smaller than she is. 'It would be easier if we knew, that's all.' You can see the strain in her shoulder, as if she's tied to him and trying to get away. She has to take two steps for every one of mine, or Lucas's.

'Why don't you walk slower?' Sophie says. 'You can always catch up.'

'I want to be close to the prophet.'

'To the *who*?' I say. I don't know why I say it, because, after all, I know exactly who she means.

'To the . . .' Her face creases and she looks round at us, then tugs automatically on the little boy's arm. 'Like Moses. Leading us to the Holy Land. And he saw an angel.'

He saw an angel.

The world seems to have gone very quiet, poised silkily, ready to jump, like a leopard. Someone's going to say, 'Really? How do you know?'

But no one does. Sophie says, 'Well, if you can't keep up, you shouldn't be here.' She looks for a strange, long moment at the little girl and the little boy, struggling along together; then she takes my arm and pulls me forwards, faster and faster, until we're pushing through the people in front. It's funny, how her face has set; as if seeing the two little kids hurt her, somewhere. She's lost her immortal look. But I go with her, obediently, because I can still hear those words in my head: *He saw an angel . . .*

It wasn't a lie. It really wasn't. It was . . . a metaphor.

I didn't mean for her to tell anyone.

And finally, inevitably, I hear someone – Otto, not that it matters – say, 'He saw an angel? When? How do you know?'

After a while Sophie lets go of my hand and gives me her bundle. She doesn't say anything, but I know I'm supposed to carry it, not open it. It's not heavy, but I wish I had a scrip, like some of the others, or at least a strap to tie it over my shoulder. I open my mouth but I take one look at Sophie's expression and shut it again.

We're stopping. It's only noon, maybe even earlier, but

people are slowing down, bunching up, and the path is swerving away from the river.

A village. We know we're crossing the boundaries, because there are peasants working the fields around us; they stand up and stare, but no one says anything to welcome or warn us away. I look back, to start with, but I can't hold their gaze. I feel a laugh building in my gut, and when I look at the people walking next to me I can see the same feeling on their faces. It's the wrong way round – the peasants should be laughing at *us* – but it's irresistible. And the slower we walk, the harder it is to keep it squashed down.

Until, finally, one of them calls out.

She's old – her hair is starting to go grey – and her skirts are pinned up around her knees. She's taken her wimple off and it's lying on the ground, and she's got a trowel in one hand and a weed in the other, and dirt on her face. But she stands very tall, and the blue flower in her hand makes her look like a painting. She says, 'Who are you? Where are you going?'

And in the midday silence, a voice says, 'Children of God, going to Jerusalem.'

The workers look at us and now no one wants to laugh. This is how I'll feel when I set eyes on the infidel: this feeling of being naked under the sun, every part of my body aching with tension. They've got trowels and knives, tools I don't recognise that could be weapons.

The same woman says, 'Why?'

'To win it back from the unbelievers.' It's Nick's voice. I wasn't sure, at first.

'*Deus le vult?*' she murmurs. The old battle-cry: *God wills it*.

There's a ripple of movement at the head of the line.

Then I see Nick walk towards her. He pauses at the edge of the field and holds out his hand. There's something formal about it, as if this is a ritual, or a meeting between people who already share secrets.

She has such power in her look. I feel as if I should recognise her – as if any moment –

She bends, slowly, and puts her trowel down. Then, still with her flower, and her hair loose, and her skirts hitched up, she walks straight through the rye to Nick. They look at each other and smile.

And then there's the noise of other tools hitting the ground, and suddenly the blades-on-sticks aren't weapons, they're for weeding, and the peasants don't need them any more. They trample the crops as they come towards us. They don't say anything. They don't even meet our eyes as they join the line: they're already looking ahead.

Slowly we start to move again. It's still very quiet. I find myself treading carefully. It's as if something's happened and no one is quite sure what it was. As if the peasants walking with us could be angels or demons – but something unfamiliar, either way. Not children like us, but not the kind of grown-ups we're used to.

And there's the small, shameful fear in my stomach – maybe not even fear, but dread or resentment – that sooner or later the adults will start to tell us what to do. Why can't they just leave us alone?

We keep walking, and the heat rises off the ground, circling us on little predatory paws.

It's only a little village, but it has a stone church and an open space in front where we stop. By the time Sophie and I get there it's hard to find anywhere to sit down; the only way to get enough room is to crouch on someone's feet until they move them. The air is full of dust and I can smell hot, sweaty wool. Even though we're so squashed together the rest of the column stretches back through the houses.

I pass Sophie her bundle and she starts to open it. Then someone – a girl with black hair – nudges her with her elbow. 'Save it, I would,' she says, and points. 'Look.'

Sophie kneels up, craning to follow the girl's finger. Then her face lights up with a kind of amusement.

I look too. Nick, and a couple of the villagers, with baskets and a barrel . . . As I watch he nods and gestures, and they lower their burdens to the ground. Bread and beer. It must be. They're feeding us.

'That won't feed all of us,' Sophie says. 'Nowhere near.'

'Wait,' the other girl says. 'They're bringing more.'

They are bringing more. I don't know much about farming, but I know July is when the grain stocks are lowest, the hungriest time of the year. It must have been a good harvest if they have all this stuff going spare – three more baskets, two pottery vessels, two or three pitchers that slosh and dribble milk as the peasants put them down. One little kid is dripping wet, holding the corners of his cotte up into a makeshift pocket. He drops something proudly on the ground in front of a woman carrying a basket, and it's only from the way she exclaims and rolls her eyes that I realise he's been fishing – for crayfish, probably. Nick watches everything with an odd, knowing smile.

It isn't a miracle. The food doesn't multiply – in fact, it divides so fast it's almost the opposite of a miracle. But the baskets get passed from hand to hand, and no one takes more than a palmful of anything. I have a couple of mouthfuls of pickled cabbage, dried herring, a broken-off bit of bread, a wrinkled apple, a bit of tough smoked meat. I'm still hungry, but then so is everyone else, presumably. And it's part of that quiet unfamiliarity – the way that no one is being greedy, the way we all pass the pitchers on after one swallow each.

Sophie is talking to the dark-haired girl. I hear one of them laugh. I've lost sight of Lucas and the others. I lean back until I feel someone's knees against my backbone, and close my eyes, bathing in the orange of the sun coming through my eyelids. The wild, unreasoning happiness is back.

O come, let us sing unto the Lord: let us make a joyful noise to the rock of our salvation . . .

I open my eyes and sit up. Nick is standing on the oxcart, the little boss-backed cripple beside him with his pipe at his lips. As Nick's voice rises in a psalm the pipe echoes the notes wordlessly, carrying further in the heavy air, until everyone is looking round and falling silent.

Some of the villagers sit on the barrels; the others subside gently, crouching or kneeling in the dirt.

'My brothers and sisters . . .' Nick says. Unexpectedly, he laughs. It's a laugh of pure delight, like the noise children make when they're winning a game and everything is as it should be. And his face is suddenly a child's too. 'Thank you. Um. You're very kind. Thank you very much.'

Sophie is watching him with her head on one side. I can see her wondering what happened to the low voice that mesmerised half of Cologne, the voice of God.

'We're on our way to Jerusalem,' he says. 'The sea will open before us, the way it did for Moses, and we'll walk dry-shod over the sand, all the way to the Holy Land.'

A murmur from the villagers. I try to imagine it, but all I can think of is the Rhine, and I can't see it opening before anyone.

'And we won't kill the infidel,' Nick says. 'There's no need. God will speak through us. We'll convert them.'

The old woman with the flower is leaning against the side of the cart. She smiles to herself, nodding. But there's a man pushing his way through the people outside the church. He's got a tonsure and a long gown, and his face is pale and wet, like a melting taper. He shouts, 'Who the hell are you?'

Nick looks round, startled, and has to grab the side of the cart to stop himself staggering. 'I'm . . .' He licks his lips and his hand tightens on the wood. 'I'm –'

'What on earth is going on? What are you doing?'

It's someone else, not Nick, who says, 'Preaching a crusade.'

'By whose authority?'

'By God's.'

It makes the priest blink a little, but his mouth tightens and he stares round at the mass of grimy, sweaty children, the quiet villagers, and the ruins and grease of their food. 'Blasphemy,' he says.

'It's not –' someone says, and at the same time someone else says, 'Don't you dare –' and someone else joins in with 'Hey – what do you know about –'

'Look at yourselves,' the priest says, spitting. 'Children, most of you. Go home to your parents. You should know your place. God put you where you were. Who are you to say something different?'

'Father . . .' It's the woman with the blue flower, her voice steady. 'God is calling us.'

'Nonsense.' His face screws up into a bitter little knot.

'You owe a duty to your lord. These children owe a duty to their parents. The world is ordered according to God's law. To leave your place in it is to turn your back on Christ.'

The problem is, he might be right. I can feel Sophie's eyes on my face but I don't dare look at her.

We wait for Nick to argue. But he doesn't say anything.

The priest turns to look at him, softening, as if he can already see us trudging obediently back to Cologne. 'Honestly. How old are you? You probably can't even read. How could you possibly know what God wants?'

A very clear voice says, from somewhere behind me, 'He sees angels.'

Nick looks up, surprised.

'Oh, really,' the priest says. 'Silly me. Of course he does. Well, in that case . . .'

'He *does*,' the little girl says. 'Last night. And it gave him a cross to carry.'

A cross? Then I realise what she means: the T-shaped branch Nick was leaning on, that I gave him . . . It's still in the oxcart, propped against the side. I see the priest register it and start to scowl again.

'Tell him about the angel,' the cripple says. It's the first time I've heard him speak. He has an accent like a nobleman that sets my teeth on edge.

'But I . . .' Nick shuts his eyes. 'Yes, I did – I *do* see angels. They come like lightning, only the flash lasts for an eternity, and they – they hurt . . .'

'Oh, please – this is heresy –'

'And they tell me God's will. They write it in my heart, with fire. They watch and guide and punish and protect. They fill my soul with light. It's like trying to hold the sun in my hands.' He clenches his jaw as if it's hard to

106

speak. 'You're right. I'm nothing. I'm only an instrument. But I know – I do *know* . . .'

The silence around his words is soft. His voice sinks into it like a pillow.

The priest clears his throat and spits again into the dust. He wipes his mouth on the back of his hand and starts to say something.

But suddenly one of the villagers stands up. 'I'd trust an angel over a priest any day,' he says, and although some people laugh I don't think he's trying to be funny. There are loud agreements from every side, drowning out the priest's words.

The woman with the blue flower says, 'The plants know to grow upwards. They know God's will. They don't need books or churches.'

That *is* heresy. But no one seems to notice. I'm on my feet now, and so is everyone else: calling insults to the priest, hoisting their bundles on to their shoulders, pressing forwards to try to touch Nick's sleeve. The priest shuffles backwards to the church door, his face covered in disbelief and outrage.

A jaunty, mocking tune leaps into the air, like a cat after a bird. Grins break out on people's faces. Someone shouts, 'Lead us to Jerusalem!' and slowly Nick's oxcart starts to move. The notes of the pipe jolt and bounce in time.

A couple of the villagers are darting in and out of one of the houses. As the crowd begins to thin I catch sight of a hurdle on the ground, and I realise they're piling it up with food and tying straps to it, ready to drag.

Sophie mutters, 'About time. Otherwise we'd have starved in a week.' She tightens the knots on her bundle and holds out her other hand to me. I'm going to take it, when I realise she's offering me an apple.

I go to grab it, then pull back. 'Didn't you want it?'

'I took a couple of extra ones,' she says.

'But –' I bite my lip. *But that's not fair. But that's stealing.* 'Are you sure?' She nods and I take it, feeling my hunger raise its head inside me like an animal waking up.

We carry on walking. The villagers walk with us, but a little way apart, in groups. They don't talk to us and we don't talk to them. Some of the apprentices squabble, pushing to get to walk behind the hurdle with its haul of precariously piled food, because every so often a morsel of herring or bread jumps out of its basket into the dust. When I look behind there are people trudging in a line for as far as I can see.

The sun is beginning to sink and my feet are aching by the time someone says, 'I think we're stopping.'

Sophie speeds up, weaving her way through the people in front to try and get a place near the fire, or at least not too close to the river. I stay with her. It's only when she's found a little hollow in the grass and spread her cloak out to sit on that I say, 'Sophie?'

'Yes?'

'Do you think he really sees angels?'

She looks at me, with two sudden parallel creases between her eyes. She breathes in, so I think she's going to ask me a question. But in the end all she says is, 'Yes. I think he does. That's why we're here.'

Nick's laughing. The sound carries, even through the other noises – the crackle of the fire, shouts, the gurgle of the river. I hear it as I walk past, trying to find somewhere to be on my own. There are so many people around now. Too many.

I stop in the shadows where no one will see me and watch. He's playing jacks with the cripple and a couple of other kids, bending forward and hissing with concentration before he leans back and laughs, defeated. They've built their own little fire, and the light plays on their faces. When Nick's turn is over he leans back against the wheel of the oxcart, tearing at a rabbit leg with his teeth. Someone says something to him and he nods and grins. I feel a pang of something I don't want to think about. I turn away and walk up the slope, making for the trees as if I'm going for a squat.

I meant to pray, but the words don't come. Instead I sit and listen to the noise of the camp while the darkness grows under the trees, wakes and stretches and comes out to stare at me.

When I walk back the way I came, Nick is the only one awake. He's hugging his knees to his chest, staring into the dying fire. I stand and stare at his back until he looks round and sees me. He has to squint through the dark, but he gets up and comes towards me and I know he's recognised me.

I don't mean to speak, but I can't help it. 'I didn't mean to lie. Honestly. It was just that – I didn't want to say you were ill –'

'What are you talking about, Rufus?'

Something about the way he says my name catches me off-guard. 'It wasn't your fault, it was mine – lying – I said it first, but I wasn't trying to . . .' But the sentence won't form. If I were my old schoolmaster I'd be reaching for my bundle of birch twigs.

'You haven't done anything wrong,' he says, so softly I almost believe him.

'I told them you'd seen an angel.'

Nick glances at me and smiles. 'I thought it might have been you.'

'But I . . .' He doesn't understand what I'm saying. 'I didn't want them to know what really – and then you had to lie – to the priest, and . . .'

'What?'

I don't know how to make it any clearer. 'I lied. And then you had to lie too.'

'You weren't lying.' He laughs, under his breath. 'You thought you were lying?'

'But –'

'I do see angels, Rufus. I did see an angel.' A pause while I struggle not to look at him, and fail. 'No, not the way the priest meant. Not standing in front of me with wings. Not like that.'

'Then –'

'You knew. You didn't *truly* think you were lying.' Another laugh, only this time it's lighter, less painful. 'My prophet, my Saint John . . . You're perfect.'

I don't know what he means, unless it's that I'm his instrument, the way he's God's . . . *You're perfect.*

I say, 'Thank you,' feeling foolish, feeling the heat spread out from my heart to my face.

Silence, while Nick looks back over his shoulder at the fire and I press my hands against my cheeks, trying to cool them.

Then he smiles and puts his hand on my shoulder. I'm taller than him but I feel younger. 'You don't have a cross,' he says. 'A crusader's cross. On your clothes.'

'No, I . . .'

He takes my wrist and pulls me towards the fire. He kneels down and scrabbles carefully at the blackened edge of it, piling ash into his hand. He spits into his palm and stirs the mixture with his finger until it's a dark paste. Then he stands up again. 'Stay still.'

I stand there obediently. He's so close I can feel his breath on my lips. He draws a cross on me with his finger, using the ash-and-spit as ink. It's too dark to see very much but I know it must be blobby and awkward, a bad imitation of a real crusader's cross. His fingertip digs into my breastbone. I feel light-headed, unreal.

'There.' He tries to wipe the remains of the ash from his hand, but he ends up with black spread all over his fingers. He goes to wipe them on his clothes, but hesitates.

'It's a bit . . . home-made,' I say.

He grimaces at me. 'Don't be so ungrateful.'

'Not to mention *messy*,' I say. His eyes glint at me. 'What will my mother say when I –'

And then there's a hand on the back of my neck, holding my head, and another on my face, fingers dragging damply down my cheek, the taste of burning on my tongue. There are stripes of wetness from my temple to my mouth, the smell of ash-and-spit, the tiny crunch of charcoal between my teeth. I splutter and try to push him away and he's laughing – and this time it's because of me and I'm laughing too, and I hook a foot behind his ankle and he trips, grabbing at my shoulder, and when we hit the ground the grass cushions us a bit so even though my bruises hurt I don't mind. And we lie there shaking with laughter and I wipe my face with my hand and then wipe my hand on his face so we're even.

'Ugh,' he says. 'I never liked Ash Wednesday.'

That sets us off again, although it's not very funny.

It's chilly. At first we're lying next to each other because that's how we landed when we fell; then it's because we haven't moved away; and in the end it's because it's cold.

I say, 'What *is* it like, then?'

He knows what I mean. He takes a deep breath, so I feel his ribcage move.

'Like our world tears in half and the real one shows through,' he says.

I nod. I know he can feel me doing it. I don't need to say anything.

He says, 'I'm glad you're here. Will you stay with me?'

'Yes,' I say. I can see the moon rising. 'Yes. Yes.'

IX

It's going to be hot again. When I open my eyes there's a haze from the river hanging over the camp, but up here on the slope the sun has already clawed its way through. I'm on my own. My mouth tastes of burnt wood and something bitter.

There's the newly familiar noise of lots of children waking up, grizzling and arguing, talking with their mouths full. I roll over and sit up, brushing the dew off me, grimacing at the low, glaring sun. Then I stand up and jog down the hill, past the little blackened circle of half-burnt wood that was Nick's fire, towards the place where Sophie should be. By this time yesterday we were already on our way, but today hardly anyone's even standing up. I pass Lucas curled in a sodden heap of wool, and he mutters, 'I'm not moving till I have to.'

Sophie looks at me, then away. I sit on the grass beside her, watching the little kids yawn and scrub at their eyes with their fists. I say, 'Do you have any food left?'

She snorts and kicks her bundle sideways to me. An apple rolls out and I pick it up. I want something a bit heftier, but an apple will have to do. I eat it and flick the core at Lucas. He narrows his eyes at me. Sophie still doesn't say anything.

'Why's it taking so long?' I say. 'It's not like we've all got stuff to pack up.'

'What happened to you last night?' Sophie says.

'Nothing,' I say, surprised.

'I wondered if you'd got into another fight. Got yourself killed.'

'No,' I say.

'So nice of you to come and find us again.'

'Is something wrong?'

'I'm not good enough for her,' Lucas says, screwing his face up against the light. 'All night she kept asking where you were. It was very boring.'

'That's not true,' Sophie says. A blush starts under her chin and opens upwards like a bud. 'Shut up, Lucas. I wasn't . . . I was worried, that's all.'

'I was fine. I'm fine.'

'Good.' She stands up, her hands on her hips, and winces. 'Ouch. My legs hurt.'

Lucas gets heavily to his feet. 'She hardly slept at all,' he says with a wink. 'She missed you, all right. She was tossing and turning and sniffing the air, like a vixen on he—'

Sophie kicks him on the shin, flushing deeper red. Then she takes my arm and pulls me away, so we're walking side by side, towards the front. I can hear the creak of the oxcart and the noise of a pipe.

'Rufus – what he said – I'm not, you know, I was just worried about you . . .'

I look sideways at her, and I can feel the grin trying to take over my face. 'Right. That's all.'

'Yes, because, honestly, when you fought that boy –'

'Paul.'

'Yes, I thought . . .' She swallows, glancing at me.

114

'Don't laugh. I mean it. You were frightening . . .' But she can't stop herself. She smiles. Then she giggles. 'Oh, all right. And because I like you, *relatively* speaking. Relative to Lucas. And that doesn't take much.'

' 'Course. That is, 'course not.'

A pause. We keep walking while the sun gets hotter, filling up the sky, and the river runs beside us like a pet.

'I know why it took so long for us to set out this morning. Because no one was quite sure if we'd be going on today.'

My heart hops and stumbles, trying to catch up with itself. 'What do you mean? You mean, people are giving *up*?' But they can't – they *can't*. I don't know why the idea scares me so much.

'No, idiot. Because it's Sunday.' She laughs and takes my hand, tilting her head back to look at the sky, pearly and opaque with heat. 'The Lord's Day. Some people said we should rest.'

'The Lord's Day . . .' It doesn't feel any different from yesterday. And I think: *Because all the days are the Lord's days*. We've gone beyond that now. The rules don't apply any more.

But maybe it's because it's Sunday that we stop early, with the afternoon only half done. We flop down willy-nilly beside the river, and even though there's nothing different about it but the time of day, it feels like a holiday. We're all glad of the rest; the sky's clouded with heat-haze, and the air holds water like wool. No one's playing football, or wrestling, or building fires.

And some of the children don't even bother to sit down; they go straight into the river, paddling about in the shallows, squeaking at the slippery pebbles underfoot, bending to scoop water up in their hands at first, then dropping to their hands and knees to drink like dogs. More kids are taking off their cottes and hose before they go into the water, because it might be hot but nothing dries instantly and soggy wool still itches like mad. Sophie is sitting beside me, with the last of our gourd of tepid water in her lap, staring unashamedly as the apprentices strip off. When she senses my gaze she looks at me and grins. 'Feel free, Rufus.'

'No, thanks.' I refuse to look away first. 'Anyway, I can't swim.'

'It's not deep enough to matter, here. I bet most of them can't either.'

I smile and shake my head, glancing around to see where Nick is, and Lucas and Otto and Paul . . . I don't know why, except that I feel odd, uneasy, as if Sophie and I are the only people who are really here.

'Look,' she says. 'There's Lucas. Over there. Hmm, it's not very *big*, is it? I'm sure my little brother's –'

I feel my face flare, and I stand up. 'I'm just . . .' I point in a random direction. 'Just, you know . . .' And I'm gone before she has time to ask where.

Downstream it's quieter. The water's deeper and murkier, the green, opaque surface flat as glass, except for occasional rings spreading outwards and the glimmer of fish. The trees are closer to the edge, roots digging into the banks like gnarled paws.

It's so hot, and so still . . . so still that your eyes catch anything that moves. The air is heavy, as if we're in another world.

And you stay immobile, watching, as I pick my way to the edge of the river. I glance over my shoulder once or twice, as if I sense that you're there, but you're hidden in the shade, waiting out the day. You don't need to move; everything you want will come to you. And I shake my head and tell myself that I'm imagining things.

I settle myself at the bottom of a tree and close my eyes. I drift, not quite sleeping, lulled by the sound of the river, the way the heat rubs itself against me, purring.

You watch, and wait.

And finally, as the air thickens, sucking the colour out of things, a little boy comes along the same path that I took, squinting at the ground every time he puts his twisted foot down. He looks round, but he doesn't see you, or me. He strips off, hanging his clothes on a branch. He's very small – maybe six or seven – and if I were awake I'd recognise him and wonder where his sister is; but I'm not. And you, of course, you *know* where his sister is, and – more to the point – you probably don't care. You stretch yourself, the shadows moving and blurring on your back. Maybe you even yawn.

He crouches awkwardly, like a scrawny white frog, holding on to a root that's thicker than his wrist. He dips his bad foot into the water and shudders. For a moment he's still, relaxing into the shock of the cold water. He's been walking all day – he's not sure exactly why, except that Hetty told him to, and wouldn't let go of his hand – and his foot's very bad. It takes longer than it ought for the pain to ease off. But in the end it does, a little, and he takes a long, sobbing breath. Then he grabs a branch with his free hand and manoeuvres himself so he's sitting with both his feet in the river.

There's a flicker of movement from behind him.

He whips his head round, grabbing for his clothes, because he doesn't want anyone to see his leg. His fingers touch wool but the material's snagged on a bit of branch. He drags until the whole branch is bent towards him. It was probably Hetty, following him, but all the same –

Suddenly something gives. The tension goes out of the fabric in his hand and it's wrapped round his fist, flapping, and he's off-balance, thrown sideways. He tightens his other hand on the root, but too fast and too late, and it twists under his fingers and slides, and now he's not holding on to anything, and all he's got is handholds of air –

The splash is what makes me open my eyes.

You slink back into the shade, satisfied.

I don't know where I am, at first. A drop of water hangs off a lock of hair over my eyes, then falls. There's an arc of moisture staining the wool across my chest.

There's a noise like . . . someone doing laundry, beating wet linen. I roll my head sideways. A patch of the river is churning and bubbling. There are drab flags of material flapping and billowing on the surface. As I watch they subside, filling with water, and there's a flash of something white, like a thin bald fish, rising and sinking again. A tangled brown-mossy sphere bobs up and rolls, until I see the other side of it, and it has a face. An open mouth, glazed eyes. Dear God, a *face* . . .

He's drowning. There are bubbles spewing out of him as he sinks again. For a second his hands are out of the water, clawing upwards, climbing an invisible ladder. Then they're gone too, as if something beneath him is pulling him down.

I can't swim. And I don't know how deep it is.

I'm standing up, tugging at the nearest branch where it

meets the tree, ripping downwards so it comes away in a gash of white wood. My hands are sticky and shaking and I'm clumsy. I wedge my foot into a clump of roots and lean across the water, waving the stick like a madman. 'Come on – get hold of it – there's a branch, just grab the *branch* –'

A swirl of water, a white gaping grimace, and the river shuts over him again like a lid.

I dig the end of the branch into the water, fishing for him, jabbing too hard in my panic. I hit something and freeze, praying I'll feel some resistance, some weight, as he grabs it and pulls himself to the surface. But there's nothing, only the wood twanging and relaxing in my hand. He's there. I hold myself still. He'll find the branch with his hands – now he knows it's there – he'll grab –

Nothing.

A string of bubbles bursts. Fragments of colour slide and lurch over the water, moving less and less until they form into my own face. It trembles, but stays where it is.

He'll come up again. Any moment now. I slash at my reflection, stirring the water with my stick. Where has he gone? He can't have sunk like that, not that quickly, not . . .

He's drowning. He's probably dead already.

Oh God. I should – I have to – oh *God* –

I take my shoes off. I know that much. Shoes and cotte but there's no time for anything else. I look round for a big bit of wood – something big enough to bear my weight – but there's nothing. *Dear God, let it not be deep. Dear God, oh God, oh my God* . . .

But I'm not stupid enough to jump. I lower myself down, careful of the mud, which is slippery now with the splashing. I take hold of a root that's poking out in a loop like the handle of a tankard, and *then* I push myself into the water, and I don't let go.

It's cold, and the current is nosing at me, and I can't feel the bottom. I stretch my foot sideways, then back, desperate for the feel of something solid, but there's only water.

I twist, ignoring the pain in my shoulder as my muscles protest. Where is he? There's nothing breaking the surface any more. He could be anywhere – swept downstream already, or stuck in the mud a hand's span away from me. I sweep my hand back and forth underwater, and the greenness fractures, reflecting the sky. A scholarly, irrelevant little voice in my head tells me that the patron saint of drowning is St Radegund. I don't know if it's true but I pray to her anyway: *Please, don't let him die, please, please . . .*

Then I catch sight of something, deep in the water.

I don't even know if it's him. Perhaps it was a fish, or a water rat, or a bit of weed. All I saw was something moving, something darker than the water around it. I don't know what's in the river; for all I know, there could be nixies or loreleis or wodneks . . .

I push myself further out from the bank, stretching as far as I can, and kick, sweeping the water. For a second I'm sure I can feel scaly, icy fingers closing round my ankle; but I'm imagining it. There's nothing. There's – no, wait –

My foot hits something hard, something hard and soft at the same time, the way only something alive can be. Or something that was alive, a few minutes ago . . . He's there.

What do I do now?

I can't swim. So it would be suicide to let go of this

root. I'm not stupid; I don't want to die here, floundering ingloriously in the Rhine, thousands of miles from Jerusalem, dragged down into the mud and surfacing again bloated and blue . . . No one would even know I was here. Sophie would think I'd got into another fight; Nick would think I'd deserted . . .

This root is the only thing between me and watery death. There is no way I am letting go of it. My mind is very clear on this point.

Into your hands, O God, I say. And I let go.

In the same movement I launch myself backwards into the river. I flail with my hands, resisting the panic, trying to work out how to stay afloat. There's a lot of splashing but my mouth is gasping in air. So far so –

There he is. A hand, rising, beckoning languidly at the surface, as if he's suggesting I join him on the riverbed. And I'm only an arm's length away. I flounder in his direction, sinking, trying to push myself up and the water down, running out of strength. Nearly there . . . I won't take my eyes away from where I saw him, because I can't dive, I'm *not* putting my head under, I can't . . .

I get hold of his arm. For a split second I'm triumphant, full of relief to be touching something solid. But he's cold and slippery and worst of all he's *heavy*, heavier than anything I've ever known. I can't hold him. I try to drag him back towards the bank but it's all I can do to keep my own head above the water. It's not fair – it's hopeless, ludicrous – like trying to fly by flapping your arms – what idiot, what skit-brained blasted *idiot* thought this was possible? I'm going to drown, I'm going to *drown* . . .

But I won't let go of him.

I make a last effort. I know it's going to be my last

because my lungs are bursting and the whole river's shaking from my heartbeat. This is it. I splash furiously with my free hand, frantically, in a kind of prayer. *Save me, save me*.

No good. The water comes up over my face, clapping and sucking at my ears, so I'm lost in a storm of bubbles and rushing murk. I fall forwards, burning for a breath, stumbling . . .

Stumbling. My feet have found something solid.

I stand up, sucking in great desperate gouts of air, and heave on the boy's arm. Now I'm on firm ground I can lift him. Out of the water he's light, skinny, easy to sling over my shoulder like a burden. He's not breathing, though. There's a trickle of new, chilly wetness running down my back. For a moment I think he's coughing up water, but it's from his hair.

Carefully, feeling in front of me before every step, I carry him towards the side of the river. I can't go back the way I came, and for a long way as I go upstream there's still that hidden depth in the shadow of the bank, so I can't get out of the water. In the end I round a curve and I'm looking at the children paddling in the sudden shallows, the water sleek as oil under the glazed sky. I feel gravel, not mud, under my feet, and suddenly I realise I've left my shoes and cotte back downstream. The kids turn to look at me as I wade to the bank and let the boy flop off my shoulder on to the grass.

I look at him for a moment and everything goes very still and clear.

He's dead.

I sit down, shivering, even though it's hot and I'm already starting to dry off. Someone looks up at me and I look back. I'm invisible. I'm not really here.

Other people see him staring at me. They're like a herd of sheep, all looking round at the same time. They move awkwardly, leaping to their feet and running towards me. I could tell them there's no point, but they wouldn't hear me anyway, because I'm not really here. They say stupid things. They call for help and ask what happened and whether he's my brother. It takes a while before I realise they're talking to me. I shrug and wrap my arms round myself to try to stop the shaking. The noise spreads outwards like ripples from a stone.

There's a voice, getting nearer. 'Eric? Eric – that's my brother, he just wandered off, I was looking after him, I *was*, really, but I had to go and – is he – what happened, what *happened*, I told him not to go anywhere –'

I don't look round but she's there in front of me, wringing her hands like a grown-up, not even crying yet. The little girl I told that Nick had seen an angel. This time I don't trust myself to open my mouth. He was only little, and he was *lame*. What kind of sister would let him swim by himself?

'He's – he's, is he *dead*,' she says, and it would be a question if she didn't already know the answer.

People crowd round. They make a rough circle, with us in the centre. I don't like being so close to them but I can't move. The boy who was kneeling next to the body stands up, wiping his hand on his leg, over and over again. The hubbub dies down into silence. Then it swells again, only now it sounds different: quieter, harsher, shriller. The faces that look from me to the body and back again aren't sympathetic any more.

'What *happened*?' the little girl asks, her voice cracking, as if she thinks knowing the answer would bring her brother back to life.

If I open my mouth nothing will come out but river-water and weed. I shake my head. Drips trace lines on my back like cunning little fingers.

All of a sudden her face alters. It's like watching the wind change: you can't see what's different, exactly, but you know something is. I feel my breath pause in my chest, cupping itself round my heart like a hand.

She opens her mouth and a sound comes out like an animal, a howl in the depths of winter, so raw and cold that I start shivering again. She drops into the grass next to her brother's body and curls over, butting his chest with her forehead. A few people step backwards; a few others step forward, ready to comfort her. But when someone reaches out she snarls and shrugs them off, blind with grief. She's holding the little boy's shoulders and her knuckles are whiter than his skin; she's not letting go, now or ever. She shakes him. His ankles flop from side to side, pale and asymmetrical. I watch the way the heels jump in the grass.

'Let me through.'

The extra light falling on my face makes me look up. The children have stepped aside for him. Nick.

'Move back.' Strange, how it's his voice but not his voice, how it carries the commands easily, as if they don't weigh anything.

The circle of people moves back. It takes a lot of pushing and shoving and whispered insults, but in a few moments Nick and the little girl are alone with the body – and me, of course. The crowd of children is still there; everyone is now – apprentices, peasants, the adults pushing vainly to get to the front – but we can pretend we're alone, in this bare little space under a blank sky.

Nick doesn't look at me, but I know he's seen me. He kneels beside the little girl as if he's about to put his arm round her, but he doesn't touch her. He just waits.

She seems to sense him there. When she looks up she jolts upright, wiping the snot away from her top lip, as if it's bad manners to cry in front of him. She can't help it – the tears still run down her face, and she coughs and hiccups – but it's as if his presence is helping, somehow.

He says, 'I'm Nick. What's your name?'

Her eyes go a different shape. 'Hetty.'

'Is that your brother?'

'Ye—' She can't finish the word. She breaks it off like a twig, cleanly, but the tears spill out of her eyes and drip onto her collarbone.

'What's his name?'

'Eric – he –'

For God's sake, Nick, I want to say. *For God's sake . . .*

'What happened to him?'

'He –' But it's too much. She shakes her head and her whole body convulses silently. Then the sobs start to rip themselves out of her again.

I wait for something from Nick: some kind of compassion, a gesture . . . but there's nothing. His face, as he looks at the little boy, is neutral, utterly unmoved. His hand reaches out, but it stops before it touches anything. He turns to look at me. There's silence, until I realise he's waiting for me to answer the question.

'He drowned,' I say.

'I can see that.' So cold. Why is he so *cold*?

'I was –' *asleep* – 'praying. I had my eyes shut. I only saw him . . . he was already underwater when I saw him. I tried to save him but it was too late.'

125

'No one should swim on his own. Is that understood?' He raises his voice, so that the ranks of children realise he's talking to them. Some of them nod; some only keep staring. He adds, more softly, 'And someone should stay here, with Hetty. Get her to eat something if you can.' He stands up.

'Is that *all*?'

My own voice. I'm not sure I would have known, if it wasn't for everyone looking at me, and the way I'm suddenly short of breath.

'What do you mean?'

'Is that all you have to say? *Don't swim alone? Make sure Hetty eats something?* He's *dead*.'

'What do you want me to do about it?' He means it; he's really asking. His face is still stony, but his voice has a bend in it, like ice. And I see, too late, that he's trembling as badly as I am.

I'd take it back, except that everyone's listening. I make myself look at the space between Nick's eyes. 'He's *dead* . . .' I say again, as if that's all it'll take, and once Nick really understands he'll be able to . . . 'I don't know. Can't you – *do* something . . . ?' It's a child's voice, asking his papa why we have to have winter every year.

Hetty is kneeling up, gazing at Nick with an odd, expectant expression.

'Do what?' Nick says. 'Cry?'

That would be something. But I don't say it.

And in the silence Hetty cries out again, and this time it's not an animal so much as a little girl *wanting* to be an animal, and it's much, much worse. It sounds as if her throat will tear itself open, only it doesn't, and the noise goes on. She gasps for breath and screams again, clenching her fists. There's such a ferocious, furious look in her eyes that I glance instinctively at Nick, expecting him to step away from her.

But it isn't Nick that she attacks.

And it's not me either. She throws herself forward, grabbing at her brother; but this time she's not shaking him, trying to wake him up. This time she's punching him, landing blows that make his body jerk and thrash about as if he's still alive. The noise of it is bad enough – those howls, and the thud of her hands against skinny flesh – but it's her face, and his, that get to me. It makes my throat tighten until I think I'm going to throw up.

I try to say, 'Stop – someone stop her . . .' but Nick says it first.

No one moves.

Maybe they haven't heard. Maybe they're as angry as I was a minute ago. Maybe they're wondering what the hell gives him the right to order them around.

Nick hisses something under his breath. It could be, 'Oh, for God's sake . . .' or it could be a prayer. There's still that dreadful noise, the corpse bouncing as Hetty hits it, everyone watching in silence. Then it's as if Nick's patience snaps, and he moves swiftly towards her, bending and grabbing at her arm, pulling her off Eric's body. I see his hand, flat on Eric's bare chest, the other on Hetty's shoulder – nearly her throat – and the tendons in his arms standing out as he tries to drag her away. She's screaming into his face now, her eyes focused and sane and enraged. She claws at him like a cat, going for his eyes, and he jerks his head back. He doesn't say anything, but there's a kind of violence in the way he swings her sideways, away from her brother, that sends a pang of shock into my belly. He slips his foot precisely behind her ankle and yanks, and they both drop to the ground, with him on top, holding her hands flat above her head.

She yells at him. 'You skite, you – *fake*, you – it's your fault, you brought us here – you said we'd be – you *fake* –'

He just looks at her, his face blank and concentrated.

And Eric coughs.

X

At first I'm the only one who notices. And I can't move; I feel prickles of heat running along my arms and legs, paralysing me, like a dream.

Eric gurgles and coughs again, the breath rasping in and out. Then he turns his head to the side and vomits. There's the noise of river-water splashing into the grass, a helpless little hiccup and a deep, hoarse breath as finally he gets as much air as he needs. His ribcage convulses as he starts to cough again, but he's sounding better. He only sounds ill, not recently dead.

And now everyone's looking, all rooted to the spot, as still as I am. Even Nick.

Someone says, softly, 'Sweet Jesus . . .'

Someone else says, 'Holy Mary, full of grace . . .'

A pause. A deeper, gruffer voice says, 'God's *armpit* . . .'

Nick gets up, slowly, as if he's scared he's broken something. Hetty sits up, but she only watches him as he goes over to Eric and bends towards him.

'Eric?'

He opens his eyes and turns to look at Nick. Then his face changes and he retches again, rolling sideways, trying to prop himself up on his elbow. The vomit swings in strands from his chin. He tries to wipe it away but he misses.

Nick crouches over him, staring and staring, with that closed, unreadable look on his face. Then suddenly he pulls his cotte over his head and holds it out. He doesn't have a shirt on underneath, and his back is wet, the curve of his spine gleaming, his bones picked out by the glare of the sky.

Eric doesn't seem to understand. He lets his head drop back into the grass, exhausted, as if he needs every muscle in his body just to help him breathe.

Nick bites his lip and spreads his cotte over Eric, tucking him in, as if he's putting him to bed. It covers him all the way down to his knees, he's so small.

Hetty says, 'You . . .'

I remember Nick's hand, spread out on Eric's chest, over his heart. And I know what she's going to say.

'You *brought him back to life*.'

Nick says, 'I was . . . I was only trying to stop you hitting him . . .' He sounds lost, bewildered, as if he's done something wrong.

'It was a *miracle*.'

There's nowhere for an echo to come from, but something whispers *miracle* over and over again, brushing against our ears like the wind. The crowd ripples and sways.

'He might not have been dead,' Nick says.

'He was,' I say. 'He was dead.'

'Oh,' Nick says.

Hetty says, 'Thank you.'

I laugh. I can't help it. I put my face in my hands and giggle incontinently.

Nick's feet move; he's standing up. He says, 'Well, you'd better look after him. Keep him warm. And . . . things.'

'Yes . . . Lord.'

I take my hands off my eyes and look up. *Lord . . . ?*

Nick says, 'Are you – ? Don't call me that.'

'But –'

'*Don't call me that.*' He turns away from her, glances down at me, and pulls the shoulder of my shirt. 'Come on, Rufus.'

I clamber to my feet. He doesn't let go of my shirt and the wet linen cuts into the underside of my arm. Suddenly I notice how hot it is. The air is heavy and still, ready and waiting.

He waits for the people in front of us to move. A few kids, the ones closest to us, try to step sideways. But there are others behind them, blocking our way. The dyers' apprentices with their stained hands, grimy street-children who all look the same, toddlers on tiptoes who are still only waist-height and finally – clumped and uneasy, trying to pretend they're in charge – there are the grown-ups. They stare at the ground when Nick looks at them.

Until his gaze lands on the woman from the village. She's not holding a flower any more, of course, but all the same I can see it in her hands – part of her, like St Margaret's daisy. She doesn't look away; she stares at Nick with a hungry, humble look on her face, like she's seeing God.

Nick says, loudly, 'Excuse me. Let me through.'

They shuffle to both sides, clearing a narrow, reluctant path for him. He has to turn sideways to get through.

The woman is the only person who hasn't moved. And she doesn't, even when Nick is only an arm's length away. Instead, she drops to her knees.

Nick flinches. He says, 'Please . . .'

She bends forward, touching her forehead to the

ground, and her fingers creep towards his feet. Nick watches, mouth half open, as she grazes the toes of his turnshoes with her fingertips. Then, under her breath, she starts to sing the *Nunc dimittis*. Nick freezes, closing his eyes.

Lord, now lettest thou thy servant depart in peace, according to thy word, for mine eyes have seen thy salvation . . .

She's not the only one kneeling either. More and more people are copying her, lowering themselves to their knees, echoing her words. I look around, panicking, because sooner or later I'm going to be the only one still standing. Except Nick, of course.

He's got his eyes tight shut, like a kid trying to make himself invisible. His lips are moving but I can't tell what the words are.

And then I realise what I should do.

I press his shoulder, pushing downwards until he opens his eyes and looks at me. I hiss, 'Kneel down. *Pray*.'

His eyes widen. Then he understands, and drops to his knees, tilting his face to the sky, joining in with her prayer: *A light to lighten the Gentiles . . .* And then I can kneel too, and so can everyone who isn't already. And we're not kneeling to Nick; we're not kneeling to anyone but God.

I close my eyes. I'm not really trying to pray – I'm too distracted by Nick kneeling beside me, his bare shoulders hunched as he clasps his hands – but all the same a prayer forms itself in my head. *My soul doth magnify the Lord . . .*

We think we're thanking you: *Glory to God . . .* but under all that, we're scared. The world isn't obeying its own rules; what we thought was real is only the curtain.

We know, now, that you're with us. We can feel your breath; we look up from our prayers, suddenly uneasy, feeling your eyes on us.

You stretch out under the tarnishing sky, flexing your claws, satisfied.

But Nick can't stop people kneeling to him as he walks by, and they do. By the time we've got to his oxcart he's gone bright red, and the blush spreads all the way down to his ribs. He wraps his arms round his chest and mutters to himself, refusing to look up. Even though everyone offers him their spare shirt, or their spare blanket, or the shirt they're wearing . . . I say, 'No, thanks,' for him, and wonder why I don't just accept. I could sell them on and make a fortune.

He crouches beside the oxcart and links his hands together, stretching the fingers until – finally – the shaking stops. Then he looks up, straight into my eyes.

'Was he really dead?'

'Yes.'

His lips say, 'Oh,' but no sound comes out. He turns his hand over and back again, staring at the skin, as if there's still something miraculous clinging to it.

'Do you want me to get you a shirt?'

'I'm not cold.'

'You might be, later.'

He doesn't seem to hear. 'Where's Timo?'

'Who?'

'Timo . . . he plays a pipe – he makes jokes.'

'The hunchback?'

He frowns and nods. 'He went off somewhere.'

'I don't know.' And I don't care either, but I manage not to say that. 'What do you want him for?'

'Never mind. It doesn't matter.' He's gone back to looking at his hands, half awed, half horrified.

'Nick . . . Are you all right?'

He tilts his head a little bit, as if he's thinking about it. Then he looks up and smiles. And the smile says he's more than all right. It says he's blessed, and he knows it. 'Will you do something for me?'

'Anything.'

'Go away, will you?' He reaches up, taking my hand, before I have time to feel the sting of it. 'Go and pray, or bathe, or eat, or . . . whatever you want. Stop thinking about me.'

'But . . . don't you . . . I —'

'I want to be on my own for a while.' He says it quite gently, but I can feel the blood rising in my face.

'All right.' I turn away, but he still has my hand in his, and he doesn't let go.

'Rufus . . . love doesn't stop. You can do other things at the same time, you know.' He bites his lip, but he's smiling. 'Otherwise how would anyone do anything?'

He pulls my hand towards him and kisses it, a brief, matter-of-fact touch of his lips on my knuckles. 'Now shove off, will you?'

I laugh and pull my hand away. And as I turn my back on him I feel the rich, storm-heavy air buoying me up, happiness fizzing on my skin like a premonition of rain.

I wander, without worrying about where I'm going. There are so many *people* . . . hundreds, maybe thousands, more than I can take in. There are faces I'd swear I'd never seen. There are miles of us. Anyone could be here.

After a while I find myself walking along the river. It's shining, like pewter, lighter than the sky. I can still taste the river-water, and feel the current lacing itself between my fingers like rope. But I can see Eric too – the way the colour came back into his face, how death let go of him. What must that have been like, to drown and come back to life? Did it hurt? Was there a shock, like lightning, when he felt Nick's hand on his chest, jolting him awake?

'Hey, Red!'

I glance round. It's Paul – of course, who else calls me 'Red'? – but he looks friendly enough, or at least not hostile. He says, 'Sophie was looking for you.'

'Oh. Thanks.'

'And Red –'

'Yes?'

'They're saying . . . these kids were saying . . . he brought someone back from the dead. And that you were there . . .'

'Yes,' I say. I look into his eyes and smile, and from that moment I know that he'll never fight me again. This is it. I've won. 'Yes, he did, and yes, I was there.'

Paul blinks, and steps backwards, nodding, like a peasant stepping aside for a nobleman. I walk too close to him as I go past, to see what he does; and he doesn't do anything.

I'm not particularly trying to find Sophie, but she's there, shouting my name as I walk downstream. She waves, and then runs after me, holding her skirts up, still calling. In the end I stand still and wait for her.

'Rufus! Why didn't you *stop* – didn't you hear me –'

'I did stop. Look.'

She rolls her eyes and grins. 'So, tell me everything.'

'What?'

'Everyone's saying there was a *miracle*.' She says it the

way the apprentices would talk about the carnival: excited, laughing, ready to be scornful if anyone else is.

I swing round so that we're eye to eye. I say, very steadily, 'You don't believe them?'

'I –'

'You believe the saints could bring people back to life? That our Lord could? Of course you do, because otherwise you'd be a heretic. But you think it's ridiculous, the idea that someone like *Nick* could. A skinny peasant boy like Nick? Of course not. Here and now? No, silly me. Miracles are for people who are *really* touched by God.'

She stares at me. 'I didn't say –'

'Any of that. No, I know. But you thought it, didn't you?'

'You saw it. They said you saw it.' I nod, and she nods back, slowly. 'Then – I believe you.'

I swallow. My mouth is full of the dank taste of the Rhine. I gather a knot of saliva in my mouth and spit.

'What was it like?'

'As miracles go,' I say, 'it was really mundane.'

She looks at me with her mouth a little bit open, as if she doesn't know if she's allowed to laugh. And then we both start to giggle. She hauls on my arm and we follow the river downstream, clutching at each other to keep upright.

We go to find my clothes. I'm glad she's with me; the air is still and ominous, and the shade under the trees is deeper than it should be. When I look at the river I can see flickers of pale flesh rising and falling in the water. I know they're not there, but I can still see them, clear as daylight.

Sophie is ahead of me. She picks up my cotte, brushes

it off, and folds it up carefully. I crouch and put my turn-shoes on again. Their soles are already wearing thin.

'It's going to storm, I think.'

I nod. She's silhouetted against the water, and with my cotte in her arms she reminds me, suddenly, of my mother. I'm so tired I could die.

'Maybe we should stay here. In case it rains.'

'It will rain.' But my voice comes out oddly, high and hoarse, and she turns to look at me.

'Are you – ?' she starts to say, but then she stops herself and only says, 'Rufus . . .'

'I'm so happy,' I say.

'Yes, I can tell,' she says, with a smile that's almost mocking but not quite.

I smile back at her, but I can feel my throat closing, the tension spreading into my jaw. I *am* happy. I'm happier than I've ever been. I don't know why I feel like this.

'What if . . .' I say. The words spill out, without my even trying. 'What if we can only love so much? What if loving one person means you've got less to spare on some-one else?'

She raises her eyebrows, but she turns her mouth down as if she's thinking. The hand that's holding my cotte drops to her side and it falls out of its folds.

'I think,' she says, 'that would mean we'd have to be very careful about who we chose to love.'

The ache in my neck fades a little. It's a good answer; or, at least, it *is* an answer.

She sits down, near me but not next to me, and bunches my cotte up under her chin, rubbing it against her face. Silence.

'I've got a little brother too,' she says. 'Like the boy who nearly – who drowned. He broke his leg when he was really small and it never got right. That's why we were in Cologne, because my mother wanted to take him to the shrine. I don't know what happened. I don't know if he got healed.'

I know, somehow, that I mustn't say anything.

'I didn't even tell my parents I was leaving them. I didn't even . . . Because . . . it doesn't matter, now, does it? I mean, we've left it all behind us. We're God's now. We don't belong to anyone but Jesus.' She takes a long breath in, burying her face in the wool in her hands. 'We can't be happy with earthly love any more, because now . . . now there's only perfect love, and one of the things he asks is . . .'

I wait and wait, but she doesn't finish her sentence.

'Rufus . . . That's what you meant, isn't it? About not having enough love for God *and* . . . About sacrifice?'

Not exactly. Not at all. I say, 'Yes.'

She nods. She's still clutching my cotte, hugging it to her. It must stink, but she doesn't seem to notice. Her eyes are shiny.

I can feel my heart beating in my fingertips. I reach out, and touch her shoulder, very gently, so that if she moves away I can pretend it was a mistake. But she sniffs, smiles at the river and leans towards me, pushing into my palm like a cat.

I shuffle sideways so that I can put my arm round her properly. She blinks and wipes her cheek without looking at me, and rests her head on my shoulder. We're about the same height but it's surprisingly comfortable.

She says, 'It must be very lonely to be Nick.'

Then she raises her head and kisses me.

I'm used to the kiss of peace, but this is different; her mouth opens, deliberately, inviting mine to do the same, and our tongues meet. It's uncomfortable, shocking, wonderful . . . Her hand presses the back of my head, keeping me there, asking for more. A part of me I never knew existed slides my hand round her waist and then up. I can feel the solidity of her back with my fingers, the softness of her breast against my forearm. It's getting hard to breathe.

She pulls away, so we're nose to nose. I have to try hard to focus on her face.

'Rufus . . . I wasn't being – when I said about earthly love, I didn't mean –'

I kiss her, partly to shut her up and partly because I want to.

I feel her giggle – disconcertingly, delightfully – and she kneels up, without breaking the kiss, and puts her hands on my shoulders.

The storm breaks.

In the space behind her shoulder the lightning cracks like a whip, a tree of light unfurling and dying again in a second. And there's a noise like the hounds of heaven being let loose, thunder and the wind rising and the hiss of the sky opening.

The rain pours through the branches above us, filling the air with spray, beating mud up from the ground until I can feel it on my lips. The water's warm, running down into my shirt, pounding on the back of my neck as if it's trying to get me clean.

Sophie laughs. She looks round, too late to catch sight of the lightning, and then turns back to me.

'My clothes were almost *dry*,' I say, but I'm laughing too.

'Poor Rufus,' she says, and pulls at my sodden shirt. I feel it peeling off me like skin, leaving me raw and wet and new. She kisses the hollow in my collarbone. I stroke her hair, feeling the wet tangles cling to my fingers.

And the storm roars above us, unleashed and deafening, louder even than our breath, the great hunt of heaven howling for its quarry.

PART III
The tears of the living

XI

It rains and rains. It rains all night, all day, until the sky goes gaunt and pale and the clouds are stretched so white and thin they look like they have to break up. In the evening the rain drifts like a veil, ragged, almost worn out. Then, somehow, the clouds fatten and sink again, and the rain goes on, with redoubled determination. It won't give up *that* easily.

We go west, through the noise and stink of Trier and on, trudging through mud, blinking rainwater out of our eyes, feeling more water soak through our clothes. It's nearly impossible to get a fire going because the wood's too damp. The soles of my feet go white and wrinkled and blisters swell and pop between my toes. Sophie gets a cluster of them on her heel, blisters on blisters on blisters, and they turn dark red and black, and grime gets into the flaps of broken skin. We walk – limp – in silence, because no one has the energy to speak. Everything we wanted and hoped for is washed away, slowly, by the rain.

Two nights, three . . . and it's only then, that night, in relentless rain, as Sophie and I settle wordlessly under a tree, that something gets through the numb cold in my head and makes me look around. I'm not sure what it is until I understand what I'm looking at.

I can see all of us. I can see the furthest children, huddled miserably in wet surcottes, and the dark beyond the few feeble fires. Back the way we came there are little groups of people, bigger ones where someone's actually managed to get something to burn. There are hundreds of soggy bodies, clenched jaws, hands pulling wool tighter than it wants to go. It's already almost dark because of the lowering clouds, but there's just enough light to see the pale faces, the flash here and there of a white foot where someone's letting the rain wash the dirt off his blisters. There are so many of us – so many . . . too many to feed properly, too many to look after, too many for anyone to notice if the woods claim one or two of the littler ones . . .

Too many. But nowhere near as many as there were.

Instinctively I glance at Sophie. *She's* still here. But the others . . . Lucas – yes, he's there, bargaining loudly with a girl I don't recognise – and there's Paul . . . I know where Nick is without having to look. And his companions – Margareta, the woman from the village, Timo, the other kids, all with sanctimonious expressions on their faces even though they've probably never even spoken to him on their own . . . Eric and Hetty are on the outskirts of the largest group, pushing vainly for a place nearer the fire. But . . . Otto. Where's Otto? Or . . . in my head I run over the faces I've got used to, the fragments of people that serve for names. Where's the fat boy with the hood that comes down too far over his eyes? Or the girl with black hair who talked to Sophie? Or the dyer's apprentices with their stained hands? The crowd of odd-accented, energetic children who joined us at Trier?

'What's happened? Where's everyone else?'

Sophie's dabbing at her blistered heel, her jaw set, but she looks up as if she knew I was about to say something. 'Don't tell me *you* wouldn't go home if someone gave you a palfrey and a picnic and a purse.'

'Of course not – why, would *you* . . .' But she stares at me until I think it's better not to finish my question. 'You're telling me someone gave them palfreys and picnics and –'

'It's just a manner of speaking, Rufus.' She prods her sore heel again, draws her breath in sharply, and reaches for her shoe. It's wearing thin. Soon it won't be worth wearing at all. She grimaces as she puts it back on. 'New shoes in Jerusalem . . .' she mutters, but it doesn't sound like a joke.

I look over at Nick. He's too far away for me to see his expression even if he sensed my gaze and turned to look back at me. The light from his fire – someone's lit a fire for him, of course – plays over his clothes. His new cotte is a deep, expensive blue, spattered with mud, that looks strange on him.

I hunch my shoulders and say to Sophie, 'They all went *home*?'

'Or just stopped. Or . . .' Suddenly she hisses through her teeth. 'For Jesus' sake, Rufus! Where do you think they've gone? Hurrying ahead, to be the first to find the True Cross?'

The sarcasm stings, like a bruise on frozen skin. I shrug and don't answer.

She rolls her ankle, glaring at her foot as if she's daring it to hurt. Her face doesn't change, but she reaches for my hand and takes it in hers. Her fingers are hard and warm – the first bit of warmth I've felt all day – and a shiver goes down my spine. When I look at her she's squeezing her eyes shut. Water slides down her face and catches the last of the light.

I say, 'Sophie . . .'

She opens her eyes and whatever I was going to say dissolves, like salt. I stand up and try to shake the wetness out of my hair. She says, 'Going somewhere?'

I don't answer, because I want to get away from her and she knows it.

'Get some food, will you?'

'I'll do my best.'

I don't know where I'm going but I walk away as if I do. I think about pushing my way to the side of a fire, but it's not worth the trouble. Or I could go and find Nick . . .

I turn and go the other way, following the edge of our makeshift camp. I'm shivering. I force myself to relax into the cold, standing straight in the rain as if it's not there, and that helps a bit. I can hardly believe that we bathed in the river and it was too hot to sleep; it seems so long ago. It's hard to remember what the storm was like, the exhilaration of those first few moments of rain. And . . .

I know the words for what happened – no, what I did – with Sophie. I've heard my father's apprentices tell bawdy stories about priests hiding in cupboards and young wives sticking their bare backsides out of windows and drunkards stumbling into the wrong bed. I know the expression that comes over my father's face when he overhears them. I've even heard my mother talking to Lena about the words she mustn't use when my father or I are there. But none of that helps; it's like a map of the wrong place. I want to know why now it's so hard to look at Sophie, and so irresistible. I want to know how it – *that* – could be a sin, and what Nick would say, and why I despise myself for it, and when we can do it again. I want to know how to do it better.

I'm walking blindly, eyes on the ground, only dodging trees at the last moment. It's almost dark. If I had any sense I'd turn round and go back.

I smile to myself, remembering Lena's voice. *So I can't say quim, or titties, or quent . . .* It was a holiday, and my father was away from home with some men from the Guild; so I could put my head round the door and say guilelessly, 'What about cods? Can she say cods? Or would cullions be better?' and my mother bit her lip and told me to go away, trying not to smile. And then I heard Lena spluttering with laughter . . . *Cullions! Rufus said cullions . . .*

I can hear her now. *Dugs, belly, boobies, bum . . .* her voice lilting, intent, as she tried to memorise them. It didn't work, of course; the next time she saw my father they all spilt out of her horrified mouth in what he thought was a deliberate stream of vulgarity. *Swive, felter, jape . . .*

I really *can* hear her now. Not swearing, but praying. I can hear –

This ae night, this ae night, every night and all, fire and fleet and candle-light, and Christ receive thy soul . . .

I take a step closer to the huddled shapes ahead of me, as the thin, high melody tugs at me like a fishing line.

A deep, male voice says, 'Jesus God! Will you shut up?' There's a wetness about the consonants that makes my skin prickle.

When thou from hence away art past . . .

'I'm warning you. I've had enough. If you don't shut your mouth I'll shut it for you, you stupid cow.'

I close my eyes. It's Daniel. And there's such

tiredness in his voice I almost don't blame him. We've all wanted to hit Lena. Most of us *have* hit her. Just not me.

There's a movement in the darkness, and a soft noise like a clap. Lena's slapped her hand over her own mouth, trying to be obedient. But she's never got the hang of stopping a song halfway through, and the melody goes on, muffled, a little uncertain.

When you know she's not doing it on purpose, it's almost funny. But Daniel probably thinks she's poking fun at him. There's a thud and a whimper.

I stand very still. My hand is on a tree trunk and my fingers memorise the wet rough shapes in the bark. So she did come, after all. And she's with Daniel, who hits her. All the time I've been with Sophie, or Nick . . . So many people. There were so many people I never even knew she was here . . .

But what the hell is she *doing*? It's not like she's going to be much use in Jerusalem. She ought to know that. Oh, *damn* her, how could she have thought – ? She should never have come. She should go home. Someone should take her home.

After a long time she says, in the confused-little-girl voice that means she knows she's done something wrong but isn't sure what, 'Daniel . . . ?'

'What?'

'Will you tell me about the Holy City?'

Daniel sucks in his spit loudly, and lies down, wrapping his cloak tighter round his shaking shoulders. I can't see, of course, but I know he's drenched from the inside as well as the outside, as wet with sweat as he is with rain. My father's right; he won't last till Jerusalem.

'With the . . . the spices? And rich things?'

'Lena, I swear if you make one more sound I'll rip you apart and eat the pieces.'

'Oh –' She cuts the vowel off suddenly, as if she believes him.

Silence.

I imagine myself sitting down beside her, putting my arm round her shoulders. Then I muster the words in my head. I line them up ready for her, like toy soldiers. *Well, it's got twelve gates, like Cologne; only every one of them is a pearl, and the streets are paved with gold and ivory, and everywhere there are towers and bells. And the air is full of the scent of lemons, and canelle and comyn, the smell of pepper and orange, and everyone wears silk and damask and muslin in wonderful colours. There are huge churches, high as the hills, in the shade of the sun, and everyone who comes out is healed and happy and shining with holiness, and they'll give you the kiss of peace as soon as look at you. And no one is crippled or miserable or sinful or foolish.*

I stand there for ages, not moving, not quite praying. Then I make my way back to Sophie.

Paul's there. He was crouching, but he stands up when he sees me. He's covered in mud; the only thing that still looks good is the sapphire on his finger.

'Food?' Sophie says.

I shrug.

'I can get you some,' Paul says. He glances at me. Sophie follows his gaze, but when I meet her eyes she looks away. Her skin is bright and glittering with rain.

'Go on then,' I say. I smile at him, pushing it. 'Something hot would be good.'

He opens his mouth and then closes it again. Then he nods and walks away.

Sophie says, 'You didn't have to come back if you didn't want to, you know.'

'Didn't you want me to?'

'I think you should please yourself.'

'I did.'

She almost smiles, then. 'Where did you go?'

'Nowhere.' I look over at Paul, watching him make his way towards one of the fires. 'What does he want, anyway?'

'Don't you know?'

I think of the way he looked at me when I told him I'd seen Nick's miracle. As if sanctity rubs off, spreading from hand to hand like gold dust. I laugh, although it's not exactly funny. 'He's got a hope . . . What a dizzard.'

Sophie gives me a strange look – sharp and warm at the same time, like a new-forged edge – and takes my arm, squeezing the muscles above my elbow till I yelp. 'He's getting us food, so you can shut up and not cause any trouble,' she says.

'Yes, my lady,' I say. 'Whatever you say, my lady.'

And then that odd, miraculous thing happens to her face, and she kisses me, hard, so I stagger sideways, trying to steady myself without breaking the kiss. It's only afterwards, when we separate, breathless, that I realise she was pushing me on purpose and now we're out of sight behind a tree. I look round, surprised, and she catches my eye and laughs. I say, 'You sly little *eel*.' She pulls my face to hers again, still laughing, and this time I let my hands go where they want, and she shifts so that nothing gets in their way. The taste of her – the taste of the storm, and happiness, and river-water – fills my mouth.

God, I'm so hungry. My stomach gurgles and protests. Sophie pulls away, shaking her head. 'You don't want me at all, do you? If you had to choose between me and a bowl of soup you'd choose the soup.'

'Yes, but I'd choose you next,' I say. She rolls her eyes.

'Sophie?' It's Paul. We turn round. Sophie takes a little step away from me.

He's got a bundle of something. He crouches down and unwraps it. Charred brown meat, enough – maybe more than enough – for three of us. 'It's a rabbit. One of the peasant kids got it with a stone.'

'You *genius*,' Sophie says. 'You *angel*.'

He grins at her and then starts to pull it into pieces, hacking at the joints with his knife. He holds a bit out to Sophie, then one to me. I take it and say, 'Thanks,' but his gaze slides over me without stopping.

'Everyone's run out of food. Someone ate mushrooms and got sick.'

'So how did you find this, then?' I say, with my mouth full. 'What did you do? Hit someone until they gave it to you?'

'Swapped it for my ring,' Paul says.

Sophie's eyes drop to his hand and she bites her lip.

I say, 'You swapped a *sapphire* for a *rabbit*?'

'We need to eat.'

'Thank you,' Sophie says. 'That's . . . thank you.'

I nod. I wish I wasn't so hungry. If I could give it back . . . but I can't. I say, 'Yes. Thank you.'

Paul looks at me properly then. 'That's all right, Red.' He smiles. I look away, into the shadows, and hear his voice: *Your drooling idiot aunt . . .*

I stand up, with my portion of meat still dripping juice into my hand. Sophie and Paul follow me with their eyes, then glance sideways at each other. Sophie says, 'Where are you off to now?'

'This is mine, right?' I grip the bone tightly between my fingers.

'Yes,' Paul says. 'If you want it. Otherwise I'm sure one of us would be happy to take it off your hands.'

'Yes, I want it. See you in a minute.'

I turn my back on them and walk away. I blink at the gathering dark, trying to make out the shapes of people's backs and faces against the dodging firelight. I know I'm looking in the right direction but I can't work out which one is Nick. I stand still, staring at the figures one by one, until I can name them to myself. Margareta. Timo, huddled and sad, for once not playing his pipe. A couple of little kids, already slumped and asleep. For a strange, disorientating moment I can't see Nick at all.

Then he leans forward, dragging a stick through the embers, and I see the flames leap in his eyes. He blinks and stretches his other hand towards the heat. I stare and stare, willing him to notice and look round. In the end he does. The meat in my hand has gone rain-wet and clammy.

He doesn't move, at first. But I stand there and wait until he pushes himself gracelessly to his feet and comes over to me.

'What do you want?'

I hold the meat out to him, silently. His eyes narrow and he frowns, his gaze flicking over my face. I say, 'It's rabbit. A third of a sapphire's worth.'

He blinks. 'Aren't you hungry?'

'Aren't you?'

'I . . .' He hesitates.

'Forget it,' I say. I'm so stupid. Every single person on the crusade has probably offered him their dinner.

'No, I am, I am hungry,' he says. 'If you really don't, if

you're sure – I thought someone would provide, I thought – and no one did,' he adds, on the edge of a laugh. 'Until you, I mean. Thank you.'

He takes it. I can tell from the way he rips at it with his teeth that he's even hungrier than I was. My stomach growls again as I watch him, and I cross my arms over my gut and press. I catch his eye and look away, feeling the heat rise in my face.

He spits, searches in his mouth with his fingers, and wipes a fragment of something on the sleeve of his new cotte. Then he goes back to eating, with such concentration I feel like I shouldn't be watching.

Finally he sucks the bone, crunching the end between his teeth. Then he throws it to one side. It's finished. He wipes his mouth, looking at me over his hand.

'Come on, then,' he says, as if he's answering a question. He walks past me, picking his way through the trees.

I follow him. After a while my eyes adjust and I can see that he's leading me to higher ground, away from the path. It might have been better to make camp up here – the ground might be drier, for one thing – but no one wanted to walk further than they had to. I pause to catch my breath, bouncing my foot to ease the ache in my calf, and look down at the fires and the shadows that surround them. There's the sound of crying from somewhere. I shiver.

'Why don't you ask me where we're going?'

'Not enough breath,' I say, and scramble to catch him up. He watches me climb the last steep little stretch, his face unreadable in the dark. There's a breeze rising, but the sky is still heavy with cloud. The rain spatters and slackens.

He takes a few more steps, and stops. We stand silently in a gap between trees. From here you can see almost the whole camp, half-hidden by the trees and undergrowth, the small, pathetic fires and shapeless bundled people. From here the grown-ups look like giants, grotesque and out of place.

Nick says, 'Go home, Rufus.'

My breath sticks in my throat, as though I've swallowed a hook.

'Go home,' he says again. 'Why don't you? Look at us. *Go home*.'

I swallow. 'Do you want me to?'

'Everyone else has.' A pause. 'Nearly everyone. The villagers went home as soon as the rain started. The apprentices got hungry and went off to find food. The littlest ones stopped to squat in the woods and got left behind.'

'Not all of them,' I say. The words have unexpectedly rough edges in my mouth.

'You remember what people said about us in Cologne. In Trier, too. About me. I'm mad. I'm stupid. How can I lead these – lead you to Jerusalem? It's blasphemy even to suggest it.'

'Nick,' I say, and stop.

'Timo . . . Margareta . . . They think I haven't noticed. They sing psalms and think I won't realise they're the only ones still singing. They pretend they're not hungry so I won't ask for food.'

'We're still here, Nick. Look. Hundreds of us.'

'And tomorrow there'll be twenty less. And fifty less the day after that.'

'Yes,' I say. 'Perhaps.'

'So why don't you go home? No one will blame you.' He turns to look at me, and a thin disc of moon dances in his eyes. For a moment the world behind him goes silver. 'I'll come with you.'

What? I think I've said it aloud, but I haven't.

'We could leave now. Find a better place to shelter from the rain. Let them work out what to do, when they wake up tomorrow and I'm gone.'

The clouds swallow the moon again and his eyes go back to black.

I say, 'You can't.'

'But suppose I do. Will you come with me?'

Yes, I will. I'll go anywhere you want. I'll do anything you ask. I —

Something rises inside me, just in time. Something in my head flickers like a fish, breaks the surface, shows its teeth. I lick my lips, buying myself time, and stare at Nick's eyes. They're so dark I don't know how I know what I'm seeing, but I do. Not quite a lie — but —

'No,' I say. 'I came for God, and Jerusalem. Not you.'

A pause.

'Good,' he says. 'That was a good answer.'

I breathe out and turn away from him, because if I can read his face then he can read mine. 'What would you have done if I'd said yes?'

'Chucked the whole thing over.' I spin back to him and he laughs. 'No. Not really.'

'You couldn't. You can't. God — I mean, it's not your choice, is it? That's what you said before — about having to do it, being called by —'

'I *am* called by God, Rufus.' There's sudden cold in his voice. 'You know that. Of all people, *you* should know —'

'Yes,' I say. 'I do know that.'

Silence. I look over my shoulder and the clouds have torn themselves into strips, unravelling across the blank curve of the moon. An aging moon, the colour of old ivory.

'You're right,' Nick says. 'I can't leave. I can't go home. I have to get to Jerusalem. I've been called, and I have to obey. I could be alone or sick or dead and I'd have to keep going.'

'Not if you were *dead*,' I say, trying to laugh.

'Pray with me.'

'What? Now? But –'

He ignores me and drops to his knees, already praying. His voice is low and monotonous, repeating the paternosters over and over. He sounds crazy.

I'm aching all over. My thighs, calves and ankles protest as I kneel down and I feel my knees sink into wet leaf mould. I shut my eyes and try to pray, but the tiredness swirls in my head like a whirlpool. I have to tilt my head back and look at the moon before the dizziness eases. Maybe that's it; maybe God is only darkness and a giddy emptiness, the end of a long, long day . . .

Where are you? I think. Our father . . . my father . . . look after Lena, and Sophie, and, yes, I suppose so, Paul . . . Lucas and Otto, wherever he is. And me, of course, but I'm too tired to go into that now . . . Nick . . .

Nick's crying.

I almost pretend I haven't noticed. I want to slump sideways and go to sleep. Let him and God sort it out between them. I'm so knackered I could cry myself.

I say, 'Nick . . . ?'

He shakes his head. His hands are bunched into fists, digging at his face like a little boy. But he reminds me of – of my father, strangely enough.

I put a hand on his shoulder. He doesn't even notice. That makes me braver, somehow. I lean closer and rub his back, the way my mother does when I'm ill. I say, 'It's all right.'

'I'm scared,' he says.

'It's all right —'

'I'm so frightened, Rufus. What if everyone goes? What if . . . I don't have any choice. Everyone else has a choice, but I don't.'

'Nick —'

'You can all fail. You can all go home or give up or lie down by the side of the path and die — but I can't. I have to go on, whatever happens. I'm not even human any more. When I brought that boy back to life —'

'For heaven's sake! Don't be so arrogant. You're not the only one who doesn't have a choice.'

The surprise shuts him up, which was what I wanted.

I shift myself round in the mud until we're face to face. 'If God's calling you, he's calling everyone. All of us. Anyone who's gone home . . . well, they just weren't called, that's all. We're *still here*. So stop snivelling and trust us, the way we have to trust you.'

Nick says, very quietly, 'I worked a miracle. I can't get it out of my head.'

I shrug. The anger gutters and goes out.

'Promise you'll stay.'

'I already did, Nick.'

'Swear it in the presence of God. The crusader's oath.'

'I — Nick, this is — I've already taken the cross, you drew it on my cotte — and I already promised to stay with you —'

'Then *promise again*.'

I can't help glancing down towards the camp. He's right: tomorrow there will be twenty fewer, and fifty fewer the day after that.

I say, 'I promise to liberate the Holy Land or die trying. So help me God.'

'Good,' Nick says.

There's a moment when I think he's going to say something else. I can feel the muscles in his back relaxing, as if I've taken a burden from his shoulders. I can almost feel it settling on my own.

'Good,' he says again, and bends his head, until his forehead is only a finger's-width from my mouth.

Then he stands up and walks back the way we came, leaving me there.

XII

Morning is a ghost of itself, the light filtering down through the clouds like we're underwater. We *are* underwater; there's only enough space between the raindrops to breathe. It started again at dawn and woke us all into wet, freezing misery. It takes hours for everyone to start moving, and when we do, eventually, I look behind us and there's a ragged tail of children walking the other way. More than twenty. Leaving. I look around, trying to comfort myself: there are so many of us still, what does it matter if we lose twenty or fifty or a hundred? What does it matter if they fail when we're still here, still struggling on? We're the faithful ones.

Paul is walking beside me. Every time he lifts his feet it flicks mud on to my clothes. Stamp, suck, splat. He says, 'I wish I was a fish.'

'So do I,' Sophie says. 'Then we could eat you.'

'If I were a trout you could tickle me.'

'You'd be a carp,' I say. 'Or a bleak. A lamprey.'

'A charr,' Sophie adds.

'A stickleback,' Paul and I say at the same time. We look at each other. I open my mouth to say something else and he opens his and we watch each other, waiting. I can't read his gaze. He could be about to laugh, or he could be squaring up for a fight.

'A weatherfish,' Sophie says. 'Stop staring at each other, you'll turn to stone.'

He looks away first. He slips a quick smile to Sophie, and she smiles back. No, not a stickleback, a leech. He blinks the rain out of his eyes and hunches his shoulders, looking around.

I lower my head and watch the mud go past. I'm so sick of walking. I'd be sick of it even if it didn't hurt, and I wasn't hungry and freezing my cods off. How can it be this cold in July?

'Hey, Red,' Paul says, and suddenly there's a new note in his voice. 'That looks like – isn't that your aunt?'

'No.'

'You didn't even look,' Sophie says.

I clench my back teeth together, biting down. Then I turn to look where Paul's pointing. I say, 'She's too far away. It could be anyone.'

But it couldn't be anyone but Lena. She's facing away from us, moving like she's drunk, swaying from foot to foot, one hand over her mouth. As I watch she tugs helplessly at the air with the other, glances in our direction, then hitches her skirts up and blunders away.

'Are you sure, Red?'

'She's going the wrong way,' Sophie says.

'Probably just going for a squat in the trees,' I say. 'Anyway, it's not my aunt. You think my father would let her leave?'

Paul shrugs. 'Maybe. Maybe he hoped she'd never come home.'

Sophie says, 'Paul.'

I narrow my eyes, frowning, so there's no room for

anything else on my face. 'Just because that's what *your* father would do . . .'

Paul snorts, but he catches Sophie's eye and doesn't answer.

I look over at Lena as if I don't really care. She's weaving from side to side, confused, her skirts trailing now. I don't understand how anyone could get that muddy, even here and now. She looks as if she's been rolling in it. When she takes her hand away from her face there's a huge brown smear across her mouth and chin.

'She's been eating dirt, Red,' Paul says very, very softly.

'I said it's *not her*.' I look him full in the face and roll my eyes. 'Saint Peter's cock! Stop crowing and grow *up*.'

He almost believes it. I almost manage it.

But I look back at Lena. Her turnshoes are trodden down at the heel, thick with dark clay, but she's still lifting her feet up carefully, trying to walk like a good girl.

And my body betrays me. I twist sideways, ducking between the kids behind, keeping my elbows in so I don't hit anyone's face by mistake. I hear Sophie say, 'Rufus? Where are you going?' but I don't bother to turn back. I scramble across the churned-up path, ankle-deep in a cloggy, clinging pottage of mud. A new gust of rain sprays into my face.

Lena doesn't see me. She's still meandering in more or less the same direction, keening a little disjointed tune under her breath. Long lank locks of hair swing next to her face where they've escaped from her veil. A twig bounces next to her ear.

I grab her by the elbow and haul her round to face me. 'What the hell are you doing here, Lena, you stupid mare? For God's sake! What the hell do you think you're doing?'

She says, 'Johannes.'

'Rufus. You idiot mewling jenny, I'm *Rufus*!'

'Ye-es,' she says. 'Little Johannes.'

'Shut up.' I want to slap her, but I don't. I watch my hand peel itself off her sleeve. I take a long, deep breath. 'What's wrong, Lena?'

Her lips move, echoing the question silently. There are flecks of leaf mould around her mouth, clear streaks on her chin where the drool has washed the mud away. It looks obscene. She says, 'Danny. Danny's gone. He promised to take me with him to Jerusalem. He *promised* . . .' Her voice rises into a wail.

I look round. The column's still moving. I can't see Sophie or Paul. They haven't bothered to wait for me.

'He's over there – he's going – hurry, hurry, he's going . . .'

I wrench my eyes away from the miserable tide of children and follow her finger. She's plucking at the air as if it's a string.

Yes. A shaky, uncoordinated figure, picking its way back the way we came. It wipes its face with the back of its hand. I've seen that gesture so often I hardly notice it any more. Trembling, sweaty Daniel, crawling back to Cologne, just like my father said he would; leaving me with Lena, who should never have come. For a moment I remember what it was like to share a bed with him: how in the morning the whole pallet would be damp, how the straw on Daniel's side of the bed would be in wet, prickly clumps. He said it only came on – the sweating, the sickness – after he started working for my father, but the journeymen teased him anyway. Some of them were merciless. I wish now I'd joined in.

'You'd better go with him, Lena,' I say. 'Come on.' And

I take her cold, rain-slick hand and pull her after me. 'Daniel! *Daniel!*'

He looks round.

Lena makes a wordless, reluctant noise, opening her mouth like a fish.

'Daniel! Will you stop – for God's sake – !'

He slows to a walk, still looking back over his shoulder; then his foot catches in something and he trips. I feel a tight, satisfied smile on my face as his hands splay out, sinking into the mud as if he's trying to dig himself back to his feet.

I let go of Lena and run properly, so that by the time Daniel's on his knees I'm there in front of him. I squash an impulse to tread on his fingers. I say, 'Daniel.'

'Rufus,' he says, the sibilants blurred and liquid. 'What do you want?'

'You brought Lena,' I say. 'You came on the crusade and you *brought Lena.*'

He frowns and shakes his head. 'Met her in front of the cathedral. She was looking for you.'

'You should have sent her home.' I'm trying to stay angry, but it's like trying to keep a candle alight in the rain.

'You should have stopped her getting out in the first place. If you're so bothered.' He coughs and spits. His skin looks grey.

'Are you going home?'

He shrugs. His hands jerk and twitch.

'Take her with you.'

Lena says, 'No-oooo . . .'

'She won't come,' Daniel says. There's something in his eyes that makes me want to look away. 'I'm exhausted, and I'm hungry, and I'm sick. I can't go on. I'm going

163

back because your damned father was right about me. But Lena . . .'

'Danny?' She thinks he's talking to her.

'There's nothing to stop Lena getting to Jerusalem with the rest of you.'

'I can't look after her,' I say. 'She's like a child, Dan—'

'Yes,' he says, and even though his head is trembling his gaze is steady as the rain. 'Innocent and close to God and *in case you haven't noticed*, Rufus, you selfish, arrogant git, most of you are children. She's got as much right to be here as you have.'

'But – I . . .' I look at Lena. We all look bedraggled; we all have mud and bits of tree in our hair; we all smell musty and feral. But . . . I hear Paul's voice again, clear and unwelcome: *your idiot aunt* . . . 'I can't look after her. I –'

'Then don't. Leave her in God's hands.'

Lena says, 'Rufus? I think I need to . . .'

I ignore her. 'Come on, Dan . . . please . . .'

'I'll give your love to your father, shall I?'

'You won't get home,' I say in a flood of malice. 'You won't last another night. Look at you. You're a mess.' Then I realise it's true.

'Pray for me then.' He pushes himself to his feet and looks into my face. He's still shaking, but there's something still and new in his expression, like a shaft of sunlight. He looks like someone on the last leg of a journey: as if he can see Jerusalem a day's walk away. As if Jerusalem is in the other direction . . . Then he blinks water out of his eyes and it's gone. He walks past me, his shoulders hunched against the rain.

I watch him go. Another wave of fury floods into me, but after a few seconds it drains away, leaving nothing but a tidemark of grime. I look round for Lena.

164

She's only just visible, making her way through the trees. Her wimple's come off; it dangles flatly from a dripping branch, like it's been filleted. I make myself follow her before I have time to think. For someone who can't walk in a straight line, she moves surprisingly fast. By the time I catch up she's squatting, holding her skirts clear of her knees. When she sees me she says, 'Rufus! Go away – naughty –'

I turn aside, my face going hot, and kick at the wadded leaves. I know I shouldn't let her out of my sight, but I can't bear to stay. I walk deeper into the woods, until her murmurs are only just audible and I'm alone. Or nearly. As alone as I'll ever be, now that I've got her to look after. I could *kill* Daniel.

I hear distant voices coming through the trees. Somehow Lena's wanderings have brought us round in a circle, curving round towards the path again. In the little sloping hollow in front of me I can see the debris from a night's camping: a sodden black pimple where the fire was, a strip of jagged fabric flapping from a bramble, a tiny, sad pile of bone and apple-core and crust. I feel odd, as if time has slipped and I'm looking at something impossibly old; or like a hunter, examining tracks, calculating how far away his prey is, how fast, how easy . . . For the first time in days I feel your presence: half-seen, mysterious, breathing a different element from us. *This is where you led them*, I think. *This is what you gave them. Mud and a supper that wouldn't have fed a baby*.

But it's a trial. I know that. We all know that. The kingdom of heaven isn't achieved by doing something *easy*. And to suffer for love is the greatest glory of all.

Love . . . I close my eyes and listen – to my own

breathing, to the sounds beyond it – and feel the wetness running down the back of my neck, the chilly clumps of hair clinging to my forehead. I feel the air on my skin and it's as if I'm in another world: like a fish, hoicked up into the harsh daylight, flapping. Everything is alien, demanding, almost impossible. But . . . now I realise I can still breathe. This is the sacrifice you're letting me make; and you're the fisherman, the net, you won't let me drown. When I open my eyes I hold on to the way it feels and everything is transformed: grey to silver, raindrops to jewels, misery to determination. I'm still hungry, but now I can glory in it. I'm where I'm meant to be, and so is Lena, so are we all. The children who slept here, squabbling over bones and that tiny apple, are in your hands. Whatever happens to them . . . it doesn't matter. Nothing matters more than God, the True Cross, Jerusalem. Love. An oath, a promise . . .

Lena says, 'Rufus? Can you wake him up?'

I don't know what she means. I turn to look and she's pointing at a pale off-white sack, a dim triangle of pigskin that I can only just see among the tree trunks. A gust of wind buffets a bush and the leaves reach out like fingers and draw back. I catch a sudden glimpse of a curve of whitish barehide, smeared with mud, at knee-height. I can't tell whether it's moving. It must be a pig, rootling in the muck that's been left in the trees. Who the hell would bring their pig with them on crusade? But it makes sense, in a way. I say, 'He's not ours, Lena. And be careful –' because she's walking towards it, her mouth open, her hair sticking to the bark of a tree as she goes past. 'Lena – if it's hungry it might hurt you –'

'*Him*,' she says. 'I don't think he'll hurt me. Can we take him with us?'

'No-oo . . .' I say, and then wonder. Meat.

'They've forgotten him, Rufus,' she says, from behind the bush. 'They've just left him here.'

Is it wrong to take it, if they've left it behind? If we could catch it . . . There's no sound from Lena, though, so it's not running away. Perhaps it's tied up. All we'd have to do would be to take it, easy as a hornbook. Pigs are messy things to kill, but I've seen it done, and I'd do it if I had to. And someone would help, one of the peasants, perhaps. And . . . I imagine us stopping early, building a fire big enough to roast a whole pig, the grease dripping into the flames . . . and Nick, his mouth shiny with fat, tearing at it with his teeth, that private, intense look on his face. I can't help smiling. I say, 'I don't know . . . maybe we could share it . . .'

'Share it?'

'The meat. Cook him tonight –' I interrupt myself, because Lena's never really understood the difference between people and animals. When we ate our pig, Joseph . . . She's never liked food that used to have a name. I say, more gently, 'We need to eat, don't we?'

'Like our Lord,' she says.

'Yes. Exactly. He knew food was important.' I almost laugh, but I don't want to upset her. And anyway, she's right.

'This is my body,' she says.

'Yes,' I say, although I'm not listening. 'All right. Let's take him with us. Let's –'

She makes a *hoop* noise as she picks him up. I see a flash of mud and tallow-coloured skin.

And then she comes out from behind the bush, holding him in her arms, and he's not a pig. He's a little boy. And he's dead.

167

I turn away. My stomach swells like a bubble about to burst.

All I can think is, *Why?* Why am I so stupid? I can't believe I'm so thoughtless, so narrow-hearted, so – hungry . . . A child. A boy with thin, mud-plastered hair, head curled on to his chest at a sharp angle, fingers pointing down at the ground. And I caught a glimpse – only a glimpse – of flesh, and all I thought was: *food*.

Because he was naked, I suppose. Why would a child be lying there, stripped to the skin, not even wearing a shirt? No one would think it was a person – not immediately, not until they got closer. They'd think – like I did – they'd think: worn white leather, kidskin, animal carcass . . .

Lena says, 'I don't think I want to eat him . . .'

'Shut your mouth,' I say. 'Put him down. We won't –' but my stomach squeezes a trace of bile on to the back of my tongue and I can't even say, *eat him*. Dear God. I want to run away. I want to leave Lena here, frozen, like a statue in painted wood. An idiot woman cradling a bony corpse.

'Why isn't he wearing any clothes?'

I can't speak; I don't know what to say. Because – because . . . Then I understand. I say, 'I expect the other children took them. After he –'

But my body takes over before I can finish the sentence. My gut lurches and the bile floods into my mouth, and I'm retching, my hands on my knees. It's like being at the mercy of something bigger than me; like being jerked on the end of a line, gasping for breath. I cough up emptiness, as if that's all I've got left. I pray for it to stop.

'Rufus?'

I nod, wiping the bitter spit off my chin. Rain sprays into my face and I blink, grateful for the clean water. 'It's all right,' I say.

'Won't he get cold?'

'I don't think he minds any more.' She's older than my mother, for God's sake! I don't want to be the grown-up all the time. I don't want to be gentle.

'I did try to wake him up,' she says, as if it's her fault he's dead.

'I know,' I say. He's definitely dead; his lips are tinged with blue, and the birds have been getting at one eye. And the body's stiffened, so his head is cocked, defying gravity, as if he's peering at his feet or his splayed hand. If I tried to bend one of those accusatory fingers I'd break the bone before the muscle gave way. I say, 'Put him down and we'll try again.'

She nods, her face softening with hope. I don't know why I said that – except that I was scared she might never let go of him if I didn't let her think there was a chance . . . I take a step towards the body and hate the way it lies there, curled into a hollow that doesn't exist. It's disgusting, despicable. What kind of God leaves us like this?

Lena says, 'Shall we take him to the prophet?'

At first the word doesn't make sense; I hear it in my father's voice, *profit*, and wonder what she means. And then I hear myself say, 'Nick?'

'He can bring people back from the dead.'

Yes. Yes, he can. But . . . it was different, before. If this boy came back to life . . . well, for one thing, he'd be blind in one eye. Unless Nick could heal that too.

'We should go back to the others,' I say. 'We'll get left behind.'

'But shall we take him to the –'

'No,' I say. 'No. Leave him where he is. We can say a prayer or something. Then we should hurry to catch up.'

Lena's mouth stays open, her jaw moving as if she's chewing. 'But –'

I say, loudly, 'Anyway, I expect the other kids said a prayer already. Before they left this morning.'

'After they stole his clothes?'

'Come *on*, Lena.' I can't bear it any more. I want to be back with the others, in the noise, unable to see further than the person in front – not here, with only Lena and the corpse and the trees. 'Let's go. Forget you found him.'

'But –'

'And if you say *but* one more time I'll smack you so hard you'll never open your mouth again.' I turn on my heel, sliding in the mud, and duck through the branches towards the path. Lena's breathing heavily and I can hear that she's not following me. My nose is running and I sniff, hard, and swallow the slug of phlegm in my throat. How did this happen? Only a few days ago I was walking with Sophie, in the sun . . . Only a few days ago Nick brought Eric back to life; death didn't exist – it was some-thing that only happened to grown-ups, in the world we'd left behind . . .

And worse than that, in a shameful, slimy kind of way, I can't help wondering what Sophie will think when she sees Lena tagging along behind me in her dress that's all torn and smeared and stained where she's wet herself. What will Paul say? What would *Nick* – ?

I say, in my head, *I can't do this. I can't. You're asking too much.*

I should wait for Lena, but I don't. Now that I've found the path again I can't stop myself hurrying, wondering if Sophie and Paul are laughing about me, and imagining Paul's voice: *Red and his idiot aunt . . . his father hit her when she was small, you know, so hard he knocked all*

170

the sense out . . . I'm surprised Red can still string two words together . . . I don't care if Lena doesn't catch up with me at all. I've done my duty. If she won't come with me, well, it's hardly my fault, is it? Let her stay there with the body – let her get confused and follow the path back to Cologne – let her starve. Anything, as long as she stays away from Nick.

She calls out, 'Rufus?'

I take a deep breath and stop where I am. I don't turn round, but I say, 'If you don't hurry up we won't ever get to Jerusalem,' and I hear twigs cracking and the mud smacking its lips as she makes her way towards me.

'I want to take him with us, to –'

'*No.* No, no, *no.*' I swing round; she's there, at my shoulder, and I grab her arm and start to walk, ignoring her yelp of pain. It's the first time I've ever hurt her on purpose.

'Why not?' She rubs her face with her free hand, as if the grime on it is what's making me angry.

'Because . . .' Why not? Because I wish we'd never found him. Because I'm not sure Nick could bring him back to life; because I'm scared he *could* . . . 'Please, Lena . . . trust me on this one. He's with God now. It would be wrong to bring him back.'

'Would it?' She wipes her sleeve over her forehead, leaving it muddier than before. 'But . . .'

'And promise me you won't say anything to anyone.' I stop and stare into her eyes until I'm sure she's listening. 'We never found him, all right?'

She looks back at me, wide-eyed, until she has to blink. 'All right.'

'Remember,' I say. 'Like that blue jug you broke. It's a secret. Remember the jug you broke?'

'What jug,' she says, and giggles.

'Exactly. So – the boy we found . . .' I raise my eyebrows, prompting her.

'What boy,' she says, but this time she looks worried. 'What boy . . . Rufus . . . ?'

'Exactly. Don't tell anyone.' And I walk away, relieved, as if death is our little guilty secret, something no one else knows about yet.

She murmurs again, 'What boy . . . ?' Then she comes after me, slipping her warm, wet hand into mine, and we trudge silently after the others.

XIII

It's past midday when we catch up with Sophie and Paul. It's not like before, when everyone was hurrying to get to the front for a sight of Nick, pushing and shoulder-to-shoulder like cattle, but all the same it's hard to get Lena through the gaps between people, and to get her to walk fast enough. I don't tell her about Sophie; I don't know what to say.

'I'm hungry,' she says.

I ignore her. I can see Paul's head in front of us, the beginning of a boil on his neck half-hidden by his hair. I'm sure it's him because the dull gold head beside him is Sophie. Seeing her like this, like a stranger, I notice the way the rain slicks her hair into a flat tangle and the shape of her skull shows through.

Lena starts to wail, so that the children around us stare, half disdainful, half horrified. 'I'm *hungry* and why won't you *talk* to me and –'

I turn on my heel, grab her, and pull her backwards before Sophie and Paul look round. 'Shut up – shut *up* –'

But it's too late. When you're walking, anything that breaks the boredom is a godsend; now the girl between me and Paul turns her head, then her companion, then –

'*Red*,' Paul says. 'Goodness me. And isn't that your —'

Sophie says, 'Where did you *go*?' She stops, letting people walk round her, like a fish staying still against the current. 'You just ran off — Paul said you'd gone home . . .'

Thank you, Paul. I hold tight to Lena's wrist and pray for her to shut up.

'And . . .' Sophie pauses, taking Lena in. She takes a step towards us, then sideways, so no one walks into her. She says, 'Hello.' From the tone of her voice I know she's not talking to me.

Lena is still keening and hiccupping under her breath, but she blinks at Sophie and her mouth echoes the word silently. *Hello . . .*

Paul darts a swift glance at Lena, at Sophie, then at me. Then he comes to stand beside Sophie — casually, as if he's hardly noticed she's there — and says, in a low, gentle voice, 'It's Lena, isn't it? Rufus's aunt? I'm Paul. This is Sophie. Are you all right?'

I stare at him. I catch Sophie's eye and try to wipe the disbelief off my face, but it's too late, she's already seen it. She rolls her eyes. Then Paul winks at me — a tiny, mocking flicker of his eyelid — and put his hand on Sophie's shoulder. She doesn't look at him, but she doesn't move away.

'We'd better get going,' Paul says. 'Jerusalem's waiting . . .' He smiles at me. 'I think you're very good, Red. Saintly, even. Looking after your aunt . . .'

He slides his hand downwards to take Sophie's, and she still doesn't react. Then he turns, pulling her with him, and we set off again.

They walk in front, together, and after an hour or so they've left us behind.

*   *   *

The rain stops. I ought to be grateful but it only makes the air feel colder. We go on, and on, and on. We don't stop until Vespers-time. For a moment it's a relief not to have to put one foot in front of the other, and then I start to wish we were walking again, in a trance of hunger and monotony. Once we're sitting on the damp ground, resting, we come alive again. It's like the blood coming back into a cramped limb; it's painful.

We've come out from the trees into a wide field corded with old furrow-lines but fallow. Everyone is already settling in little circles, each with its own smoking attempt at a fire. I rest with my eyes closed, crouching at the side of the field under the last dripping trees, too tired to move, until Lena says, 'The nice boy . . .'

I look up and follow her finger and realise she means Paul. Stiffly I get to my feet again, take her hand, and lead her towards where Sophie and Paul are sitting. They're just close enough to be together, but it makes my heart lift to see that they're not hand in hand or even smiling. Lena says, ' 'M hungry.'

Sophie glances up and away again. She says, 'Rufus, why don't you go and find some wood?'

'Nothing'll burn,' I say. 'Everything's too wet.'

'Well, there's nothing to eat,' Paul says.

'But I'm *hungry*,' Lena says. She's used to wanting food and not getting it, but not when she hasn't eaten for a whole day, not when she's really *hungry* . . . She doesn't understand; she thinks we're punishing her for something.

'So are we,' I say. 'There just isn't any food.'

'But I'll *starve*.'

'So will we,' I say. 'We'll wake up tomorrow and we'll be dead.' The words come out, glib, before I think about them. I see Lena wince.

Sophie says, 'Or we'll freeze. Or both. When they come to plough this field they'll find thousands of sweet little skeletons.'

Paul says, 'Oh, in the name of God!' and stands up. 'I'll try and find some wood. Coming, Red?'

I don't know why he asks me, unless it's to gloat or show me up in front of Sophie, but I say, 'All right.' I want to get away from Lena.

Paul nods and leads the way back into the trees. He's a city boy like me, but already he seems to know where to look, in the thickest parts of the forest where the leaves have kept the rain off the fallen branches, the logs that have been eaten away into holes like wooden lungs, light and almost dry. I follow him wordlessly and he piles firewood into my arms. Green bark-bloom comes off on my hands and his. Both of us are damp and shaking with cold. We can't even be sure that this stuff will burn.

I'm waiting for him to say something – a casual snipe about Lena, a smooth mention of Sophie, even a curse under his breath – but he doesn't. He loads me up like a packhorse. When he piles the last twigs on top and then juggles another few branches in his own arms he smiles, impersonally, and I feel a sudden relief, a breath of warmth.

No one says anything as he builds the fire and takes a cowering, fragile flame from the apprentices on the other side of the field. No one wonders aloud why we don't all make one big bonfire together, the way we did on the first night. We just watch as Paul struggles, cursing, to coax a spitting, reluctant flame into life. We drowse and pull our cottes tighter round us, and we're exhausted, so we sleep, eventually, even though the fire goes out in a last damp sputter.

*   *   *

When I wake up it's because someone's shouting.

I'm so stiff and cold I can hardly move, and for a stupid moment I'm almost sure I *have* died in the night. When I sit up, painfully, my head spins and little black-and-white flecks twinkle in the corners of my eyes. The grass beside me is flattened but I can't see the others. They've left me behind – no – I turn my head and they're standing there, staring into the sun. The sun! I'm so glad the sun's back. I feel the dew rolling down my face and dare to hope that I'll be warm again later.

Paul says, 'What the hell's going on?' From here he looks huge, a black giant against the light.

I struggle to my feet, seasick. Lena is nowhere to be seen. Sophie glances round at me and smiles. Things are going to be better today. The sun, Sophie smiling . . .

I follow the direction of Paul's gaze. A huddle of people around the biggest fire, or the ashes of it, anyway. There's Nick, of course. Outlined like that, against the sunrise, he makes me think of an angel – makes me remember how I felt the first time I saw him, the world-shaking touch of God . . . A wild, euphoric rush of gratitude wells up in me. *Praise ye him, sun and moon: praise him, all ye stars of light* . . .

I move towards them. I can't help it. And as I get closer I see more of what's going on, although I'm still partly blinded by the light. My eyes water and I squint into the bright sky.

There's a strange, spidery figure half-surrounded by children, a bulging silhouette with extra, trailing limbs . . . The shape reminds me of something, but I don't know what. People are staring at it, recoiling, moving away, and I realise that it's making the high thin note I can hear. The noise is halfway between a scream and a pleading, helpless warble. I feel as if I've heard it before.

Someone – Timo, I think, although the sunlight behind him makes him look wasted and knobbly like an insect – takes Nick's arm and tries to pull him away.

That voice . . . it's saying, 'Please, please . . .'

And I know what the shape is. A flat black cut-out of Lena, carrying that boy's body . . . the weight in her arms, the drooping legs, the little skull. But it's on a smaller scale: not Lena but someone else, someone whose voice I know . . .

Hetty. The little girl whose brother –

I'm close enough to see properly now. I peer through the dazzle of the new sun and I already know what I'll see.

It is Hetty. And she's holding Eric in her arms, curved and stiff with cold, his twisted leg at a funny angle. She's saying, 'Please – you brought him back – please . . .'

Nick turns to talk to her, but Timo is still trying to drag him away. They pull against each other for a moment, balanced, like a dance; then Nick jerks his arm back and kicks out in a sudden vicious movement. Timo falls awkwardly. The noise carries through the clear air. No one moves. Nick shouts, 'For God's sake – what are you trying to – let me *talk* to her –'

Hetty gulps and drops to her knees, bending forward to let Eric sag on to the ground. She says, 'I found him like this when I woke up, he isn't breathing, but he'll be all right if you help, please, just touch him . . .'

The old woman, Margareta, helps Timo to his feet. She says, 'Nick . . .' But the warning in her voice comes too late. Nick doesn't even look at her. He takes a few steps until he's in front of Hetty and Eric, and then goes down on his knees.

In the silence, someone says, 'Nick, can't you see he's *dead*?'

Nick turns his head sharply, but whoever said it doesn't say anything else. Nick says, 'What?'

No answer. Or at least no answer that I can hear, only the unspoken one hanging in the air: *This time he's* really *dead* . . .

Nick shakes his head and turns back to Eric. He puts his hand out and carefully lays it on Eric's chest. There's a noise as if everyone's breathing in at once – because we do believe, even if we don't believe, we *do* . . .

I watch and watch. Everyone does. There's no movement at all, from anywhere. Even the kids at the furthest corner of the field are staring. My eyes start to water from the light, the rising sun that glares at me from behind Nick's head. In the end I have to close them. I look at the orange of my eyelids and listen for the moment when God intervenes.

We wait. We wait, in a kind of eternity that feels like prayer. We're like anglers, waiting for the fish that *will* bite, eventually . . . And we're so still, so sure, that we could stay there for ever, frozen. We're content, almost. We're so full of faith we can welcome this silence, the icy pause that comes before a miracle . . . No one has to break it.

Except Nick. After hours, minutes, seconds . . . after the sun's risen above his head and warmed us through and Eric still hasn't moved.

Nick says, 'I'm sorry.'

No one says, *What kind of prophet are you, anyway?* No one says, *If you can't do it now, maybe it wasn't real then* . . . No one says, *You fake.*

Hetty stands up, very quiet and straight, and walks away.

Nick says again, 'I'm sorry.'

Margareta bends and helps him up, very gently. Timo fiddles with the pipe in his belt. The other children trickle away, not saying anything, not meeting Nick's eyes. Something's broken, but it doesn't show yet.

Nick says, 'But I thought I could – why, *why* can't I do it? It's not pride, really it isn't, he's *dead*, I only want to help –'

Margareta says, 'Hush.'

'But –' He whirls, suddenly, catching her with his shoulder, and she stumbles back. 'You didn't think I could do it! You knew I couldn't – that's why you tried to stop me –'

'You can't tempt God,' she says. I hate her for sounding so mild, so logical. 'He gave you one sign. Isn't that enough?'

'But the kid – Eric – he's *dead*, he died because he was here, that's not –' Nick sounds like a kid.

'Martyrdom,' Margareta says, and the word is sharp and clean, like a pike snapping its jaws. 'Who are you to deny that to him?'

Nick stares at her and he doesn't have an answer. He looks away and water swells in his eyes but doesn't fall.

Then someone says, 'Why should that kid be any different anyway?'

Margareta and Timo look round for the voice, but we all glance over our shoulders or down at our feet – as if it wasn't anyone, or as if it was all of us.

Nick says, 'Different? Different from who?'

'The other ones,' it says in that harsh, clear tone. 'The other ones who've died. What about *them*?'

'What – other – ones – ?' Nick blinks and tears slide

down his cheeks, but he doesn't seem to notice. '*What* other ones who've died?'

He doesn't know. It's as if a crack has opened in the earth between Nick and everyone else, and as we watch it gapes and trembles, spitting dust. There's a pause that runs through us like a tremor – through Margareta and Timo too – and then we're still again, looking at Nick across the gap.

The quiet goes on and on. I think no one's going to say anything. I think we're all going to leave, without a word. I wait for someone to start moving.

And then Lena says, 'We found a dead boy today.'

'Some of the little ones got too tired,' another voice says. 'They just sat down and never got up.'

'It's been so cold. And we've been walking so far every day –'

'You look back and you can see them on the path, the corpses –'

'We haven't had any *food* for days –'

It's like a dam bursting. The wave rises, dragging at us; suddenly there are more and more voices – 'My little sister –' 'I had to leave him –' 'A ravine, when he went for a squat –' 'If we'd had a proper fire, maybe she wouldn't have –' and even though I know there can't be hundreds, or even fifty, twenty, ten, it sounds like the whole world is joining in. Most people just went home – most people just gave up and went back – but if you heard us now you'd think everyone's sister or brother or cousin was dead. It's stupid. I want to laugh and cry and tell Nick it isn't as bad as it sounds, but I can't. Through the noise I hear Lena say, 'And he was all *stiff* and Rufus said to eat him . . .'

Nick says, 'But – this isn't true – I'd have *known* –'

This time it's an older, deeper voice that answers him: a grown-up. 'You're at the front, aren't you? You're leading the way. Why would you know who got left behind unless someone told you?'

Nick looks at the man who spoke, and he gives him a grateful, miserable smile. He says, to no one in particular, 'Why *didn't* you tell me?'

Silence again. No one dares to meet his eyes. I stare down at my shoes, my muddied hose, and realise how dirty I am and how far from home.

Lena says, 'Rufus told me not to.'

If only it wasn't so quiet. If only her voice didn't carry . . . but it does, and everyone looks round. Lena opens her mouth like a fish, gaping at all the eyes, horrified and helpless, and says, 'He said not to tell you. He said it was our secret.' Then she adds, bewildered, 'He didn't have any *clothes* on . . .'

I'm the only one who knows what she means. To everyone else, it must sound as if she means me, that *I* wasn't wearing any –

And someone snorts, and starts to laugh.

A group of apprentices – not as many as there were, but still enough – join in, the laughter fizzing out of them like aqua regia, dissolving the tension. Someone says, in a too-loud undertone, 'Oops! Who let *her* out of the cattle shed?'

'Hey, lovely,' another one murmurs, 'bet you liked that, didn't you? Little Rufus with no clothes on?'

Oh, *hell*. I daren't look up in case I see Sophie or Paul . . . But thank God most people don't know who I am – thank God it's just a name to them . . . I shift my weight, shuffling backwards, praying to get away before someone notices my blush, or my hair, and makes the connection . . .

But Nick isn't laughing. And he looks straight at me. 'What's she talking about, Rufus?'

I feel the breath go out of me as if I've been punched. I can feel the eyes turn towards me, all at once. How could he – can't he *see* – ? Everyone's looking at me now, eager for more entertainment, glad that there's something to laugh about. Now they can forget Eric's body at Nick's feet.

Someone wolf-whistles. Someone says, 'Damn, someone with *his* looks stripped off and we missed it!' Someone else – a girl – says, 'I wonder if his hair's as red down *there* . . .'

Jesus Christ. Oh, sweet Jesus Christ, our Lord . . .

Nick ignores them. He says, 'Why did you tell her not to tell me?'

I say, 'She means the boy – the dead boy, someone had taken his clothes – he was naked, not me, she's just confused –' My mouth sticks to itself like a dried herring.

Nick shakes his head. 'Yes,' he says, cutting through my voice like a knife. The apprentices' mirth isn't as loud as before. 'But why did you tell her not to tell me?'

'Because I –' I force myself to look at him, begging him silently to wait until we're alone. 'I thought, if . . . I don't know, I don't *know*, Nick, please don't –'

He looks at me until I feel my throat tighten and my lungs ache. Then he looks round at Margareta and Timo and all the others – I can't see Sophie but she must be there somewhere – and the laughter dies in a final quiet gulp, as if it's been swallowed by something bigger. We wait for Nick to speak. 'How can I lead you when you don't trust me?' he asks, his voice very soft. 'Before, when you had faith . . . you were truthful and innocent . . . How *can* I work miracles when you betray me? You lie, and mock, and fear . . . Oh ye of little faith . . .'

No one answers. Nick turns back to me. 'If you had brought him to me, this boy . . .' He lets the words hang; he doesn't say, *I would have resurrected him*. But everyone knows what he means.

'But –' I say. 'But that's not fair – Nick, no one *else* . . .' I stop. I can't defend myself. There's no point trying.

He's not listening anyway. He takes a deep breath and looks beyond me, talking to everyone. 'We'll conquer Jerusalem. The sea will open before us, and we'll take back the True Cross, and the Holy Land will be Christian again. We *will* conquer Jerusalem. But only if we stay innocent, only if we're holy, only if we're pure. We must stay children, the beloved of God. *Unless ye be as little children* . . .'

Mostly there's silence; a few people cross themselves. But there's a whisper behind me, not quite reverent: 'Hear that, mate? No growing up allowed . . .'

A muscle flickers in Nick's temple, and he turns slowly on his heel, staring at one person after another, until each one looks away. 'We must fight to stay clean. Sin is everywhere; the Devil tempts us with every second that goes by. We must put ourselves in God's hands, trusting completely in his mercy and goodness. We must be fools for God . . . children for God – *idiots* for God. If you can't give yourself totally – if your heart has hooks, and keeps something back – then *go home*. You don't belong here. You belong with the adults, the careful, cowardly adults who might scrape through the needle's eye into heaven – not here. We won't be content with anything but *everything* – not little goodnesses but the whole goodness; we won't give a tithe, but our whole selves. There's no place for wisdom here. If you want wisdom, go home. If you want comfort, go home. If you want safety – *go home*. And if you want God, come with me, and don't be surprised if it's harder than anything you've ever done.'

I've never seen him angry before. He blazes. The light catches the edges of his hair and gives him a halo of sparks.

Margareta drops to her knees, crossing herself over and over. She says, 'Forgive us, Lord. We will be faithful. We will be truthful.'

There's a kind of shuffle as people drop to their knees, uncertain, as if they're scared to move too suddenly. I see Lena, curled over, her hands knotted together. I kneel too, not feeling anything, only wishing this was all over and we were walking again.

Nick doesn't kneel. He waits until everyone is on their knees, and then he bends and draws a cross on Eric's forehead with his index finger. He picks up his T-shaped branch from the ground and walks away, leading the way on his own, putting his weight on the stick. He doesn't wait for anyone to follow; perhaps he knows we'll catch him up in a few minutes, or perhaps he doesn't care. I follow him with my eyes, too tired to move. He trudges towards the edge of the field, leaning on the cross he carries: the cross I broke off a tree for him, without knowing what I was doing.

XIV

But when we do start to walk again there's an odd kind of feeling in the air – the half chastened, half rebellious mood of an apprentice after he's been beaten. There are people praying again – psalms rise around me, high and thin, louder than they've been for days – but there are people shoving and spitting, curses that are unusually crude. Lena takes my hand and won't let go of it. A dark-haired kid bashes into her and then flashes an unconvincing grin of apology at me. I meet his eyes without saying anything and then pull Lena forward, leaving him behind.

But we've only been walking for a few moments when I hear snorts and scuffles and the hissing sound of someone trying not to laugh. When I turn round there's a group of them, looking innocent – all except one, who sees me later than the others and is still imitating Lena's trying-to-be-a-good-girl walk . . .

'What's the matter? Eel swum up your hose, has it?' I say.

He checks and bites his lip, the blood rising in his cheeks, and for a moment I think I've won.

Then one of his friends – the dark-haired one – giggles and says, 'So you're the boy that swans around with no

186

clothes on, flashing your naughty bits . . . What is she, then? Your wife?'

'Tell you what,' I say, keeping my voice level, 'why don't you find a nice clearing in the trees, take down your hose and get your little friend to swive you sideways?'

He whistles, a long mocking note. 'Why, is that something you recommend?'

'Just –' But there are too many of them; if I hit him I'll get massacred. I put my hand over Lena's and squeeze, so that she won't notice that I'm shaking. I say to her quietly, 'Come on. They're not worth bothering with.'

'*Ouch*,' the boy says. 'What a *withering* insult. What knife-sharp, blistering repartee. I bet not even *Mistress* Redhead there could do better.'

I can't stop myself. 'What do you want? Honestly. I'd like to know,' I say. 'Why can't you leave us alone? What are you trying to do?'

He blinks. He licks his lips, ready to speak. I've made him pause, at least.

But it's the other boy that speaks first, the one I caught mimicking Lena. He squares up to me, his eyes steady and malicious. 'You heard the Boss, right? We're supposed to be pure. So you don't belong here, you and your blithering moon-struck sow, you should go ho—'

My breath hiccups and stops. 'You little –' But I don't dare to let myself finish, because the fury's like a great gaping mouth surfacing beneath me, and if I let it it'll swallow me.

I pull Lena sideways, dragging her away from them, until she whines a protest. They laugh and whoop but in the end they carry on walking, leaving us behind. We stand at the side of the path. I count to a hundred to give them time to go further ahead, muttering the numbers

187

under my breath, not meeting anyone's eyes. If only Lena had stayed quiet and pretended to be normal . . . If only she hadn't mentioned *me* . . . I hate myself for thinking that, but I can't help it.

And those little *skites* . . . Even Paul isn't that bad. They really *mean* it.

'Rufus?' Sophie's voice.

'Red?' And Paul's.

'Think of the Devil,' I say, but I can't muster anything but relief. I look up and Sophie's got a soft, concerned expression, and Paul is half-smiling, swinging his hand so that I can see Sophie's fingers laced through his. Sophie catches my eye and detaches herself from him, and I feel a smile grow on my face as Paul's fades.

'Are you all right, Rufus?'

'Yes.'

'You look . . . You've gone very pale.' She brushes my forehead with her fingertips, a hint of a caress. Warmth kindles somewhere in my gut. 'This morning was . . . sad. Poor Hetty.'

'Yes.' There's no need to say anything about Lena, or what's just happened; I know it's stupid, but I can't help feeling ashamed – that those kids could talk to me like that, that I'm the sort of person that sort of thing happens to . . .

Paul says, 'Rather embarrassing for you, I expect. When your . . . when *she* –' he jerks his thumb at Lena – 'started saying she'd found a body and you'd taken off your clothes . . .'

'She did find a body. And the *body* didn't have any . . .' I'm so sick of explaining this.

'You went pretty red, Red. Really – *red* red, Red.'

'Paul,' Sophie says. 'Leave it.' Then she turns to me. 'Come on. At least it's not raining.'

I nod. She's right. At least it's not raining. At least now she's taken my hand, not Paul's. At least Lena seems happy enough, wandering along beside us, humming a high-pitched note that sets my teeth on edge. At least . . .

Lena says suddenly, 'Why don't those boys like me?'

Oh, God . . . I'm too tired to think about how to tell her the truth. 'They do,' I say. 'They were just teasing. They do like you.'

She seems to believe me, because she goes back to her singing. Sophie and Paul seem happy enough too, as if what happened this morning only happened to me. I swallow, trying to get rid of the tightness in my throat, telling myself it's only hunger and fatigue, but I can't. From somewhere in front of me a raucous voice sings, tunelessly, 'In a window there we stood and kiss—' and a chorus joins in and shouts, '*Swived!*' Sophie shoots a glance at me; when I don't smile, she looks at Paul and they both laugh.

I keep Sophie's hand in my left, take Lena's in my right, and we go on walking.

At long last, at the end of the day, we stop. It's nearly sunset. I've made a pyramid of wood, but no one's suggested that we set fire to it yet. There are a few bonfires scattered here and there, under the trees, but it's still light, and we don't need the heat. It's summer again, as if the year is back on the right path.

Paul drops a piece of bony, charred meat in front of me, another one in front of Lena, and then leans over to give one to Sophie. For a moment we don't make any sound apart from the chew and rip of eating. Then, finally, I say, 'Thank you.'

'Yes, Paul,' Sophie says. 'Thank you.'

Paul shrugs. 'You're welcome.'

'You don't have to,' I say. 'I mean –'

'You've got a hidden stash of bread, have you?'

'I just meant –'

'Drop it, will you? I said you're welcome.' He gnaws at the piece in his hand: it's a little larger than mine and Lena's, not as big as the bit he gave to Sophie. I force myself to look away.

It's not enough, but it's better than nothing. I lean back on my elbows, suddenly exhausted. I feel as if I've gone for months without sleeping.

'This is the part I like,' Paul says suddenly. 'The end of the day.'

I watch him. He must be as hungry as I am, but he lets the meat dangle between his fingers and stares at the long shadows creeping across the field.

'Yes,' Sophie says. 'When you can stop walking.'

Paul smiles at her briefly then grimaces, twirling the half-bare bone. 'Yes, but . . . When you've done what you can. It's so simple. To get to God, you just have to keep walking . . .'

I'm not sure I've ever heard him mention God. I look up from his food to his face. He's looking towards the sun, the last copper-coloured light staining his cheeks, glinting on his greasy mouth.

'I know what you mean,' I say.

He looks at me, and there's no hint of anything but interest in his eyes. 'Yes,' he says. 'I thought you would.'

I look away and close my eyes, feeling the fading heat of the day on my eyelids. Vespers-time. The words come to mind effortlessly. *Glory be to the Father, the Son and the Holy Ghost. As it was in the beginning, is now, and ever shall be, world without end . . .* And Paul's voice, unexpectedly clear: *To get to God, you just have to keep walking.* I think, *Jerusalem* . . . Maybe we'll actually get to Jerusalem. And in a flash, brief but clear as lightning, I understand what that means. Not sunlight and spices, riches and fruit and silk, all the things I told Lena stories about – but something greater by far, grander and more glorious, dazzling as the dying sun. It makes me breathless, makes me open my eyes and dig my hands into the grass, hanging on to the earth.

'Are you all right?' Sophie says.

'Yes, I –' I look at Paul. I never thought I'd like him, even for a moment; but I can see now how someone can be transformed, how light can shine through them like water and make them lovely. And . . . I look round at Sophie and Lena. I was stupid to think things had gone wrong. We're thinner and hungrier than we should be, but we're here, aren't we?

Paul suddenly seems to remember his rabbit leg and starts to tear at it noisily. He says, his mouth full, 'Yeah, Red, you look like someone's offered you the Holy Grail for a chamber pot.'

The moment dies like a flame, but the hope is still there, the new unexpected contentment. I flex my feet, wincing as one of my newest blisters brushes the ground. 'It's nothing. Forget it.'

For a while we're silent. Paul sucks at the bone and then throws it into the undergrowth. Lena still hasn't said anything. Every so often she looks over her shoulder, glancing from side to side. She's too still, more alert than usual, like a fish that senses a shadow on the surface.

Sophie says, 'Come for a walk with me, Rufus.'

Lena catches my eye and opens her mouth, but her face is blank and I don't know what she's thinking. I should stay with her. She probably doesn't remember those boys, but I ought to stay. We could pray together. That would calm her down.

I say, 'Lena, you'll be all right here with Paul, won't you?'

Paul says, 'Red –' and then stops, looking from me to Sophie.

Sophie says, 'We won't be long. We'll be back before it's dark.'

Lena frowns and pokes her skirts with a finger, twisting as if she's trying to drill a hole. 'Promise?'

'Promise,' I say.

Sophie says, 'That's all right with you, Paul, isn't it?'

He clenches his jaw and crosses his arms over his chest. 'Of course it is. Just don't be too long. And don't go too far. There could be all sorts of things in the woods.'

'Really? Basilisks? Ghouls?' Sophie smiles at him, as if the joke isn't at his expense. 'The erl-king?'

'Don't worry,' Paul says very quietly, 'the erl-king only likes children. Once he sees what you two are up to . . .' He leans forward and adjusts one of the twigs in the rough pyramid I made for the fire.

Lena says, 'Are you going to *swive*?'

Sophie's smile wavers and she blushes. 'Come on, Rufus.' She grabs my hand and pulls me away before I have time to say anything. In the red light of the sun her cheeks are an impossible scarlet. She drags me, stumbling, deeper into the trees, until we can't see Paul or Lena any more. Then she catches my eye, heaves a deep breath, and we both start to giggle.

I lead her gently through the trees, along a little path that could have been made by people or rabbits or wild pigs. When we glance back the sunlight is horizontal, edging every leaf and twig in red gold, setting the woods alight without consuming them.

'Look,' Sophie says, pointing. The path curves uphill, through a high arch of trees that meet overhead like a cathedral, and just where it goes out of sight there's a dark edge of stone. We take a few hurried steps, hand in hand, until we can see it properly: and it's a little stone hut, on its own on the hill. It has slit windows, a thatched roof that's dark with damp and rot, and a door that's twisted off its hinges, gaping half-open. No one's lived there for a long time.

'We must be near a village,' I say. I feel such a rush of relief and excitement that I want to laugh. We'll get proper food, and alms, and help, and we'll see ordinary grown-ups going about their business . . . something I didn't even realise I missed, until now.

But Sophie isn't listening. She lets go of my hand and runs ahead, her hair flying out behind her in tangled tails that catch the light. She runs as if she's never been tired in her life. 'Come *on*, Rufus!'

I walk after her as fast as I can, swearing to myself as my muscles protest and my blisters come back to life. It's like treading on nails. Sophie gets to the hut, bends her head and slips through the gap between door and doorway before I'm halfway up the hill. When I'm finally there, or nearly, she comes out again, absent-mindedly dragging a cobweb off her face. She's smiling.

'It's a hermitage, Rufus. It's lovely.'

I slide round the door the way she did. For a moment it's too dark to see. Then my eyes adjust to the light and I see an altar stone, a cross set in front of an arched window to the east, where the sky's already darkening, a jumble of logs in the corner. A hermitage that someone's using as a storeroom. It's chilly and smells of wet wood.

From the sound behind me I know Sophie's at my shoulder. She says softly, 'No one knows it's here. It's ours. Our house.'

I take a step sideways and run my hand over the wall. It's bare stone and mortar and I feel it crumbling, leaving grit on my fingertips. We're on our own. I want to stay here for ever.

'There's – look, a candle –' Sophie scrabbles for her tinderbox, laughing. It's a miracle that the candle's here at all, and then it's alight and even more of a miracle, throwing dim watery gold on to the walls and floor. Sophie turns back to me and her shadow slides and dances on the wall.

If this was really a hermitage, it must have heard so many prayers, seen so much sanctity. There must be holiness in its walls, in its smell of damp. I open my mouth but the words don't come.

And then Sophie's there, kissing me, and I forget everything else. It's not the house of God, it's ours.

I'm wrong, of course. It *is* your house. You're there, in the weed growing in the cracks between stones, the humped backs of roots swelling under the foundations, the stench of water that won't go away. You're there, watching and waiting – the things you do best – while Sophie and I satisfy our little human desires. Your eyes follow us through the shadows. When I run my hands down Sophie's back you know how smooth her skin is; when she kisses my mouth, lacing her hands through my hair, you know what I taste like, how my skin smells of grime and woodsmoke, how she closes her eyes and feels the floor tilt under her. You know it all, and feel it all, both of us at once: my pain when she pulls too hard at my hair, her pain when I jerk away and step on her foot by mistake; mine when she bites just too hard on my lip, hers when I shove her back against the wall . . . and the pleasure, too, that rises like water, as we reel against each other like sailors. You see it all, every movement, every scale of sweat blooming on our skin, every tiny shiver. Your eyes are the only still thing in the world, while we grapple and dance in each other's arms. The candle flame wobbles and dips, as if it doesn't know where to look; but your eyes are like glass, unblinking, steady, exact.

But this isn't what you're interested in, not really. This isn't what you came here to watch. So you stay where you are, coiled, out of sight, while we sink to the floor in a mess of clothes. We murmur, and rock, and the blood surges in our ears, but you're listening to something outside. There's the noise of tired feet tramping up the path – we don't notice, of course, we're deafened by our own breathing, clinging to each other like survivors in a storm – and a creak as the door sags and protests. Now you're raising your head and baring your teeth. This is what you've been waiting for; *this* is . . .

Nick.

He pauses for a moment, peering round the edge of the door, blinded by the sudden murk and the glimmer of the candle flame. He says, 'Is someone here?'

We turn to stone. I hear the silence flooding up around us, submerging us until we can't even breathe. Sophie's mouth moves and the world pauses, waiting for me to decipher the shape of her lips. *It's. Nick.*

We can't be found like this. We can't. I stare into

Sophie's eyes without seeing her. Oh God. Oh, sweet Lord of Heaven . . . The moment seems to last for ever.

Then I grab her and roll, pulling her with me, hooking our clothes with my toe, until we're in a huddle just out of sight of the door, behind the logs. I can't move smoothly and we're noisy – there's the thump and scrape of wood, Sophie's gasp of surprise, the swish of material dragged across the floor – but . . . you're on our side. At the same moment Nick hauls the door open and it creaks and scrapes the stones beneath. He grimaces and squints at the hinges, which aren't hinges at all but wide strips of rotting leather, and whistles through his teeth, letting go of the door. He says again, 'Hello?'

I look at Sophie. She's got her eyes squeezed shut, like a child trying to make herself invisible; but all the same I form silent words. *Don't say anything. Don't say anything.*

Nick takes a few steps forward, frowning at the candle flame. It's just dark enough outside, now, for it to shine through the window slits; just dark enough for someone outside to notice it, as long as the shadows fell in the right places. But if you hadn't called him, he'd never have seen the little light; he wouldn't have come looking for the hermit, wondering who was at prayer here. The flame is your bait to lure him . . . He looks round, still frowning, wondering who would light a candle and leave it there, burning on its own. Then he laughs quietly, as if he understands. He kneels, dropping to the floor in a practised, unselfconscious movement, and bows his head.

He says, 'Thank you, my Lord.'

I close my eyes. I don't want to hear this. Nick's voice is too casual, too intimate; it's like overhearing a conversation between lovers.

'Today was . . . really hard. You wanted it to be hard, didn't you? Things are never easy, with you.' There's affection in his voice, and gentle mockery – of you or himself, I don't know which. 'I just have to keep going. You're the Way, right? And when I'm ready to drop, or turn back . . . when I remember I'm only human – yes, my Lord, human, remember what that's like? It's *rubbish* – then you do something like this, for me. Lead me to a church and light a candle for me. Work a little private miracle, so I don't quite forget who you are . . .'

I open my eyes again and Sophie opens hers at exactly the same moment. We stare at each other, frozen. Her hands are pressed against my chest. I can feel her fingernails.

Another low, soft laugh. I've never heard such love in someone's voice; not my mother, or Sophie, or my father . . . Such confidence and contentment, such exasperation. A hot rush of jealousy roars in my ears like the sea.

'Magnificat anima mea Dominum,' Nick murmurs: *my soul doth magnify the Lord* . . .

And you say: *Mine*.

You uncoil so fast the world ripples around you. You surface, raising your terrible head in a swirl of transparency, and gravity lurches from side to side like a ship. There's a split second of stillness. Nick's eyes widen. His irises shrink, swallowed by blackness. Then you're around him, your head to his, dragging him down into the shadows. He gasps and cries out, snatching desperately for breath. The long wet curves of your body wrap round and round him, holding him, drowning him. He grabs for the ground, pressing his fingers helplessly against the stone. Water seems to gurgle in his throat and he retches.

His whole ribcage fights to breathe. His spine is locked. You open your jaws and sway from side to side, rocking him, your grip tightening and tightening. He doesn't dare to struggle; he braces himself, trying to endure, knowing he's at your mercy. You lean nearer, until your teeth are touching his temple and you could strike before he has time to see it coming. He stares at you and tears run down his face.

I can't bear to watch. I look down. Sophie whispers, 'Do something.'

'I can't.' I can hardly hear my own voice.

'Help him. He's ill.'

'No,' I whisper. 'He isn't. Not – ill.'

'Look – he's –'

'Shut up.' I shift my weight so that she couldn't stand up easily, even if she wanted to. 'Leave him alone. He'll be all right.'

'But –'

'Please. *Please*.'

You let him go. I hear the thud as you slip away, slick as satin, letting Nick drop to the ground. You've made your point. He's yours, and he knows it. You've left your marks: the rope of bruises looped on Nick's skin, the blue tinge on his lips. He takes a great rasping gulp and coughs the air out again. The breath claws at his throat, in, out. He's lying on his back, staring at the roof. One side of his face is stained gold from the candle flame. After a long time his hand comes up and scrubs at the other cheek, as if he's trying to wipe the shadow away. He looks bewildered.

Sophie mouths, 'Is he all right? What's happening?'

'I think so. I don't know.'

She squirms and I shuffle backwards and let her sit up.

She cranes her neck to look past the pile of wood. She whispers, 'Can't we help him?'

I whisper back, so low she has to lean towards me to hear, 'If we do, he'll know we were here. And anyway, we can't.'

She gives me a long look. Part of me wants her to ignore me and go to help Nick, but she doesn't. She sinks back down against the logs and reaches for her dress. There's no room to put it on but she drapes it over herself silently. I'm not cold but I get my shirt and cover myself with it. We sit, waiting for Nick to leave, without meeting each other's eyes.

It's dark by the time I hear him get up, and I'm half asleep, cramped and aching from the hard cold floor. I hear him come closer and wonder if he's seen us. Maybe we left something where he could see it – a purse, a girdle, a shoe – and he knows we've been here the whole time. Maybe . . . but I'm too tired to care. It goes dark and I smell hot tallow and wick-smoke. Ah. Suddenly I pity him, this boy who'll blow out a candle so it's still there for the next person.

His footsteps move away and fade. He hasn't tried to open the door this time – just slipped out, as quiet as a fish. Just to be sure, though, we wait and wait, before we know it's safe to come out. We fumble for our clothes by touch and turn away to dress, hunching and cowering, trying not to reveal too much. When we leave the hermitage we don't look at each other. At least, I don't look at Sophie. It's so dark I can't tell whether she's looking at me or not.

And it's so dark we can't find our way back to Paul and Lena. There are a few fires, still not quite dead, but they don't give off much light. I stare into the blackness, trying to work out where we were and where we came from, but the longer I search the darker everything seems. In the end we find a little hollow in the grass where the thistles are fairly thin on the ground, and huddle together, back to back. There's nothing we can do but wait for morning.

And when the morning comes, we're woken by the dawn, and it's easy to tramp across the field in the raw sunlight to the space under the trees where Paul is sleeping. I sit down near him and drink from the gourd of water. It tastes sweet and new. Sophie crouches opposite me, waiting, and takes it from me when I've finished. She drinks, wipes water away from her mouth, and says, 'Where's Lena?'

I glance round. She's not here. I prod Paul in the ribs and he groans and opens his eyes. I say, 'Where's Lena?'

He blinks and rubs his face without answering.

Sophie says, 'Where's Rufus's aunt, Paul?'

He looks from her to me and back again. There's a pause.

'I thought she was with you,' he says. 'She went to find you last night. Didn't she find you?'

'No,' I say. 'Didn't she come back?'

'No,' he says. His face is blank. 'I'm sorry, Red, I thought – she said . . .' Silence. 'No. She didn't come back.'

And the sun keeps on rising.

PART IV

*The confirmation
of the testament*

XV

Suddenly I can feel the breeze on my skin, and smell the new dew-dampened ash of the fire. A blister tingles between my toes and then begins to sting. A bird sings above my head. I realise that there's birdsong everywhere, like a glittering curtain, and I marvel that I didn't notice it earlier. It's a sharp, beautiful sound, like running water. For a few moments I'm so awake – so alive – that I hardly have room for fear.

Sophie says, 'Paul . . . what do you mean, she didn't come back?'

Paul clenches his jaw and shrugs, not looking at her.

'Didn't you . . . Why didn't you stop her?'

'She's a big girl, Sophie. What was I meant to do, tie her up?'

'Did you *try* to stop her?'

'Oh, for God's sake . . .' He shakes his head, reaches for the gourd and washes his mouth out, spitting neatly into the remains of the fire. 'She said she was going to find you two. And I thought –'

'You thought you'd let her find us, because you knew we'd be –' Sophie breaks off, shaking her head, too disdainful to finish her sentence. 'I suppose you thought it would teach us a lesson, if she caught us at it.'

Paul opens his mouth, turns to look at her and closes it again.

I say, 'Where did she go?'

'I don't *know*, Red!' He sounds impatient, but his voice fractures on the next words. 'She went into the woods, the way you two went, and if I *knew* where she was now I'd –'

'Yes? You'd *what*?' Sophie says.

He rubs his forehead. 'I don't know. Go and find her, I suppose.'

Silence. Sophie looks at me. But I can't think. I can't move or breathe properly.

She says, 'Rufus?'

I say, 'I have to find her.'

'Nothing'll have happened to her. She probably got sleepy, or . . .' Paul gets up, drawing his cloak round him, stretching his shoulders. 'She'll be fine.'

I nod. He's right. He has to be. It's just that I can't help thinking about those kids, the venom in their faces when they called her my *sow* . . . They told us, Lena and me, to go home. And if they found her wandering on her own –

I spin on my heel and start to stumble deeper into the trees, swinging my head to look from side to side so quickly that I start to feel sick. 'Lena!' I call, but nothing answers me except the bounce of my own voice, thrown back at me faintly from the trees. Where could she have gone? Surely, if she followed us . . . she would have followed the little path up towards the hermitage, and then . . . '*Lena!*'

There's the noise of someone following me. I hear the crack of twigs, then fabric ripping and Sophie cursing. I don't wait for her.

'Rufus. Rufus! Wait!'

I speed up, driving myself up the hill towards the hermitage. If only I wasn't so tired . . . but Lena must have been tired too. Maybe she didn't go uphill at all – maybe she went along the slope the other way, looking for us. I turn round, my heart pounding in my throat, paralysed with indecision.

Sophie hurries to catch up, smiling at me tentatively as if she thinks I stopped because she asked me to. 'Rufus . . . she won't have gone far. She can't have. It was only a few hours ago that she . . .'

We look at each other, both recognising the lie. If we can make seven leagues in a day, then Lena could be miles away by now. On another path, in other woods. I imagine dark cloisters of trees, wolf-eyes that slide from shadow to shadow, ravens, the gates of the Wild Hunt carved in a cliff-face. I start walking again.

'Wait – *Rufus* –' Sophie says again. I don't wait, but she runs to catch up and carries on talking as if I'm hanging on her words. 'Won't she come back to where we were? If we just *wait* – now it's light –'

'And if she's lost? Or hurt? Or if . . .' If those boys have found her . . . I remember how I once saw Lucas's friends torturing a cat, and swallow hard.

'She's probably gone home, Rufus – she probably changed her mind and didn't come looking for us, just went back the way we came –'

'Then that's one of the directions I'll look in. *Lena!*' I try to keep walking, because when I'm moving the fear and guilt stay a few paces behind, not quite catching up. But my body won't obey me. I stop and take a breath and my knees fold me neatly into a heap on the ground. I say, 'Sophie . . . we have to find her, *I have to find her . . .*'

She puts her arms round me. 'Rufus,' she says very gently, 'are you sure this is the best thing to do?'

'What?'

'Don't you think . . .' She licks her lips: it's such a small sound, I don't know why it sets my teeth on edge. 'Rufus . . . maybe this is for the best.'

I don't say anything. I stay hunched over, squeezing my hands flat against each other.

'They'll be setting off soon,' Sophie says, and I feel from the way her weight shifts that she's crouched down next to me. 'We'll look for her for as long as we can. But we can't look for ever. Sooner or later we'll have to go on, before the others leave us behind.' From the sound of her voice you'd think being left behind was the worst thing in the world; and perhaps it is.

'You don't think we'll find her.'

'I . . .' She sighs, and I smell her breath. It's musty and sweet, like old honey. 'Rufus, we've come this far . . . *you*'ve come this far. Isn't it worth going on?'

'She could be hurt somewhere. Waiting for me to come and look after her.'

'You might never find her. Even if —'

I stand up roughly, not caring if I knock her backwards into the bracken. 'All right, *all right*. Let's stop wasting time.' I stare into the shadows, wishing the sun were a bit higher. It'll be another few hours before I can see clearly through the trees, and then it'll be too late, I'll be on the road again . . . I have to find Lena. It's now or never.

I look around, praying under my breath: *Please, protect her, let her be all right* . . . It's hard to move; wherever I go, she might be somewhere else . . .

'Rufus,' Sophie says, 'you look that way and I'll go up

the hill. Go as far as you can in fifty breaths, and then work your way back. I'll do the same and meet you here.'

I open my mouth to argue, realise she's being sensible, and nod. I start to walk. When I glance over my shoulder Sophie's standing still at the bottom of the hill, shading her eyes to look at the field beyond the trees, where the others are. I can hear the noise of people getting ready to start walking. These days it only takes a few minutes between waking and setting off – now that we're used to it, and no one has much food left over from the night before. It won't be long before they leave us behind, and we'll have a hard morning's march to catch up. After a while Sophie catches my eye and shakes her head, as if she's reminding herself to concentrate. She hurries up the hill, peering into the trees on both sides of the path.

I count my breaths, following the path in the other direction until it curves sideways. In, out, forty-nine, fifty . . . I call, 'Lena! Lena!' and there's no reply but the clapping of birds rising from the trees in alarm. My voice sounds weak and reedy. Around me the leaves drip dew and the bracken rustles. '*Lena!*'

I keep calling, over and over, until the syllables lose their meaning. I make my way slowly back the way I came, pausing for fifty or a hundred heartbeats at a time, listening and waiting, watching for a movement in the trees or a patch of colour, raking the ground with my eyes for a footprint or the mark of fingers dragged through the mud. But there's nothing. She's been swallowed by the forest, lured away by the erl-king or Frau Holle . . . The back of my neck prickles and I whisper a paternoster like a charm.

When I get back to Sophie she's crouched on the ground, playing with something in her hand; but she looks up when she hears twigs cracking under my feet, and I can see from her face – hope, sympathy – that she hasn't found Lena, or anything that might help us find her. She clasps her hands behind her back, like a servant girl trying to be polite, and says, 'No luck?'

'No. I'd better go back. I'd better go further. And you too – count a hundred breaths before you turn round, and then a hundred and fifty, and then two hundred –'

'And if that doesn't work?'

'Then two hundred and fifty,' I say. She doesn't meet my eyes. 'If we work outwards from here . . . we'll keep coming back so we don't lose each other, and if one of us finds her –'

'It's getting late.'

'I know. But . . .' I follow her gaze, down through the trees to the field. All I can see now is flattened grass and patches of ash. It's quiet too. 'We'll catch them up.'

'What if the path forks? You know the way to Jerusalem, do you?'

'Please, Sophie. I can't leave her here . . .' If she *is* here. She could be anywhere: crouching somewhere, naked and keening and bloody, already pregnant; or face-down in a stream, swinging from a branch by her girdle, in purgatory, in heaven.

Sophie stares at me, then looks away. Her face is pale and there are dark crescents under her eyes. 'We don't have time, Rufus. If we don't go soon . . .' She bends her neck as though her head is suddenly too heavy.

I move towards her until her forehead is resting against the front of my shoulder, and I put my hand on her hair.

I can feel the edge of her ear on my lips. 'Please,' I say. 'Please. Just a little bit longer.'

She takes a deep breath and then moves away without looking up. 'Go on, then. A hundred breaths this time.' She trudges up the path.

I watch her go, then I cheat. I run back to where I turned round before, and only then do I start to count. It's counterproductive, because now I'm breathing faster, but I'm glad to be sweating, I'm glad that the air is burning my throat. The pain makes me feel as if I'm doing something useful.

There's nothing. The trees stretch in every direction, endlessly. I shout and shout and no one replies. Then, suddenly, there's something behind me – a cry, an echo, an answer . . .

Lena – ?

I run. This time I don't even notice my blisters.

But it's Sophie. She's waving something, running towards me and speaking before I'm close enough to hear her. 'Over there, I just caught sight of it, the other way . . .'

'You've found her?' Where is she then? Too heavy to lift, too badly hurt to walk? *Oh, God* . . .

'No. Not her. A scrap of her dress,' Sophie says, breathless. 'But in the other direction – she must have gone *ahead*, not back –' She opens her hand and I see a scrap of material, muddy and unrecognisable. I stare at it and she closes her fingers on it and grabs impatiently at my shoulder. 'Rufus! She's gone *ahead*. Do you understand?'

'Of course – I'm not an idiot – of course I –'

'Then let's go.' She swings round and her skirts swirl out in a ragged circle.

'Let me see it.' I hold out my hand for the bit of fabric.

She hisses through her teeth and shoves her hand out. A little knot of worsted, damp from her hand, leaving streaks of mud on her palm. It could be anything. It could be . . . I say, 'And where did you find it?'

'Over there.' She points down towards the field. 'Where the path goes south.'

'How do you know it's Lena's?'

'Because –' She rolls her eyes. 'Because I *know*. I know what her dress is made of. It's this stuff. Trust me, Rufus, please.'

There's nothing else I can do. I nod and reach out to take the fabric, just to roll it in my fingers and check it's really there; but Sophie closes her hand over it and turns away, as if she didn't notice the movement. She starts to walk. She's quicker, now that we're going after the others. I feel the same lightness in my own step – the relief, that we'll catch up with the crusade again, that we're on the right path. And there's no reason why Lena shouldn't have gone that way, after all.

I glance back, one more time, just in case; then I hurry after Sophie, watching her skirt trail raggedly through the mud.

It's hard to walk fast, but the trail's easy to follow. We've always been near the front, so I've never seen the damage we do as we pass, before now. The undergrowth is flattened at the side of the path. On the lowest parts, where the rain still hasn't drained away, the mud is churned up until it's knee-deep, and the effort of getting through it makes the sweat run down between my shoulder blades. When I leave the path to piss I almost step in a little nest of night soil; I know it's human because there are skit-smeared leaves scattered about. It makes me wonder what Jerusalem will be like once we've been there for a few weeks.

We walk until the sun is almost overhead. Sophie is always a few steps in front; when I stop to catch my breath at the top of a slope she doesn't wait for me. I know how she feels – uneasy, breathless with something that isn't quite fatigue – but there's a kind of urgency in her walk that I don't feel in my own. Maybe it's because I can't help looking back over my shoulder, or from side to side, hoping to catch sight of a familiar shape or face. I try to breathe quietly in case I hear a thin, tuneless melody or a cry for help. But there's only the path, going on and on.

Until finally we come out of woodland into a fallow field, and the crusade is spread out in front of us. For a moment I'm looking at them as if I've never seen them before, and I want to laugh. The *crusade*. Hundreds – thousands maybe – of grimy kids, scratching and sucking their thumbs and squabbling. The grown-ups are in little groups, as tired as anyone else. But there's singing, and mock fighting, and every here and there people are grinning, pointing ahead or turning to speak to whoever's behind.

I look up, further, to see what they're pointing at. And my heart lifts.

Just beyond the front of the column, there's a village. The village that the hermitage promised us wordlessly. Roofs, wattle-and-daub walls, smoke from cooking fires. I can smell it from here. I want to join in the singing.

Sophie catches my eye and smiles. The sunlight shines in the tangles of her hair, so she looks like an angel. I know what she's thinking: that we'll get some proper food, firewood that actually burns, blessings in a dialect we only just understand, maybe even alms or a roof over our heads tonight, if we're lucky. I say silently, *Thank God, thank God*, as if some danger's been averted.

Sophie says, 'Come on. Let's run.'

We don't need to run. We don't even need to hurry any more; no one's going any further today. But I roll my eyes, grinning, and say, 'All right.' And we stumble together along the path, hand in hand and giggling, until we're out of breath and my blisters feel like fire. Then we hobble together, wincing and swearing at every step, our curses getting more elaborate every time. It's not until Sophie says, 'Heavy swinging cullions of the Holy swiving Martyrs, *ouch*, my *feet*,' that we reach the lagging back end of the crusade. A toddler looks round and stares up at us solemnly.

'Don't stop,' I say, tugging at her hand. 'If we get to the front we might get the first food.'

'Mmm. They might let us sleep in a house. All right,' Sophie says, and speeds up again. We hurry through the people, moving the littlest kids bodily out of our way by their shoulders, turning sideways to slip between the grown-ups.

We reach the head of the column – behind Nick and Timo and Margareta, who are three body-lengths in front, walking straight-backed, without looking round – just as they reach the first house of the village.

There are men blocking the path. They have heavy staves, and one has a scythe. For a moment I think they're there by chance. Then one of them looks at Nick and tightens his hand on his staff, and I realise they're there on purpose. They edge into a semicircle, weapons at the ready.

Nick stops and looks round at them. He glances at the path in front of him, as if he might ignore the men and their weapons and just keep walking. My chest tightens and I realise I'm holding my breath.

He says, 'Peace be with you.'

One of the men nods. He says, 'And with you, son.' His vowels are pulled out of shape by his accent, like waterlogged wool.

'We come in the name of Christ, our Lord. Will you let us pass?'

The men swap looks. The youngest – with a blond, wispy beard and watery eyes – steps forward, dragging his staff on the ground. 'I'll show you the way round. You're going south, right?'

'You've had news of us,' Nick says. It's almost a question.

'The thing is, son,' the first man says. 'Thing is . . . We're not saying you're right or wrong. But we don't have any food to spare. Nor are we going to let our kids run away with you, no disrespect.'

'God won't let you starve for feeding his chosen,' Nick says.

Another glance, thrown from one man to the next, like a ball. 'That's as may be. But we'd take it as a favour if you went with Ben here. You can sleep in our fallow land if you want.'

Nick nods slowly. He understands what they're saying. No food, no shelter, no alms. He says, 'Let us pray in your church. Please.'

For the first time, the leader clenches his jaw. 'You won't fit. Not all of you.'

'Then –'

'No. All right, sonny? I said *no*. You're not crossing

this line. You think you know what God wants? Well, looks like he wants you to keep out of our village. Or you won't get another damned step closer to the Holy Land than you are now.'

'Just the church,' Nick says. He's leaning on his cross-shaped branch, and his knuckles, his hand, even his wrist are white with tension. 'Let me pray in your church. On my own. I promise I'll –'

'You keep the hell out!' He steps forward, swinging his scythe over his shoulder and down to Nick's eye level. Nick winces, but his feet stay where they are. 'I don't mean you any harm, but I swear, if you try and tempt our kids away –'

'All right, that's enough,' Margareta says. 'We won't come into your village if we're not welcome. We'll take the long way round, and shake the dust off our feet when we've gone past.'

Nick turns to look at her, but she doesn't meet his eyes.

The young man – Ben – picks up his staff and says, 'I'll take you round then. It's not much further. There's a stream . . .'

So they're not even letting us use their well. I daren't look at Sophie, in case she's as angry as I am. I wish I could see Nick's face, but he's still staring straight ahead at the scythe blade. I have a nasty, creeping feeling that he's going to walk right on to it, but he doesn't. He takes a deep breath and turns to follow Ben, with Margareta and Timo.

I don't think the people behind realise what's happening. Not at first, anyway. We hear the mutterings spread backwards like a cloud going over the sun. Ben looks nervous; I can see from the set of his shoulders that he's expecting an arrow in his back at any moment. Once he stumbles and Margareta says, 'Keep walking,' with no warmth in her voice at all.

In the end – after half an hour, perhaps – he stops and points at the field in front of us. 'This is fallow land, so you can stay here. The stream runs through the ditch down there.'

Margareta looks over her shoulder. From here we can still see the village, but obviously they think we're far enough away to be safe. She says, 'You brought us a long way round.'

'The path curves, that's all,' he says, too quickly. 'I've got to go back. Good luck. Hope you get to Jerusalem.'

Nick says, unexpectedly, 'Could you bring us any food at all? Anything. A couple of loaves or a bit of meat. Just for the littlest ones.'

'I –' He falters. 'I'll see what we've got spare . . .' His eyes slide sideways and his right hand tightens on his staff, his left creeping to grasp it lower down.

Nick must know that means *no*, but he nods and says gravely, 'Thank you. God bless you.'

Ben swallows and turns to go. We watch him walk straight back through the field. It hardly takes any time at all before he's gone out of sight behind a house.

Nick says, 'Well, then . . .'

Margareta says, 'We should go on.'

Nick glances back at the people behind us. The murmurs of discontent are louder now; finally someone raises her voice so we can hear the words, and she's saying, 'What's going on? Why didn't they give us anything?'

'We should stop here,' Nick says slowly. 'We should rest. At least it'll be safer here than in the forest. And they may relent and give us *something*.'

Timo says, 'You mean no one'll walk further today, even if you tell them to.' His voice is hoarse and sharp, as if there's something wrong with his throat.

Margareta says, 'I think we should go on.'

Sophie looks at me. There's something odd in her expression. She whispers, 'She's right. We should go on.'

I say, aloud, 'Let's rest here.'

I don't think Nick hears me, but he closes his eyes and leans his forehead against his T-shaped staff. 'We'll stop here. We'll stop here. No arguments.' Then, without waiting for an answer, he turns aside and lowers himself to the ground. He leans back and closes his eyes. In the sun his face looks as white and flat as a saucer of milk.

Timo drops where he is. He lands awkwardly, half on his knees, and keels sideways. It looks uncomfortable, but he lies still, as if he's too tired to care.

Sophie takes my hand and pulls me away from the crowd, towards a patch of shade, where the trees are growing in the ditch, and sits down. I can hear the gurgling of water.

'I'm so hungry,' she says on a kind of helpless breath, like a sigh. 'I'm so *hungry* . . . and those tight-fisted, greedy skites . . .'

I watch the crowd unravel and spread out, dropping to the ground, making little circles and groups. No one's smiling. We ought to be pleased to have an afternoon to rest, but we can't forget the village behind us. I let my eyes slide over them. I notice Paul, huddled in his cloak even though it's a warm day; Lucas, almost unrecognisable, with a beard and his hair falling over his eyes; Hetty, as blank-faced as a sleepwalker, her hand outstretched emptily to the side as if she's still holding on to Eric's wrist.

Dear Lord. I've forgotten about Lena. I've *forgotten*.

I struggle to my feet again, my cheeks blazing, even though no one but me knows what I'm thinking. I say, 'Sophie – Lena must be here somewhere – we didn't pass her on the road, so . . .'

'Oh, God,' Sophie says, under her breath. It sounds like a groan.

'I'm going to look,' I say. 'You don't have to come.'

'I won't,' she says. 'Why don't you do something useful, like find some food?' She glares up at me, then flops forward until her forehead is flat on the ground, between her knees. She looks like a rag doll.

'I have to find her,' I say, trying not to get angry.

' 'Course you do,' she says, the words indistinct. 'Good little Rufus.'

'What's that supposed to mean?'

She sits up, so suddenly she has to brace herself with her arm. 'You're such a *milksop*. I suppose you think it's your duty to go back for her? Well, it isn't. You think you're being virtuous but you're just being cowardly.'

'Cowardly?' I hear myself say, like an echo.

'You want an excuse to go home and leave me here. Why don't you admit it?'

'I want to find Lena. I'm worried about her. If some-one's hurt her –'

'I need you more than she does. She was fine without you. I *need* you . . .' Suddenly she's crying.

I feel the breath catch in my throat. 'Sophie . . . I'm not going to leave you . . .' I kneel down and put my arms round her. The feel of her back under my hand reminds me of something, someone else. 'I won't leave you, I promise.'

She nods, hiccups, giggles weakly, wiping her face over

217

and over. I rock her gently, watching her shadow slide back and forth over her legs, her torn skirt.

And in a flash I know, as clearly as if she'd told me, that the scrap of material she found this morning was from the hem of her own dress, not from Lena's at all. I swallow. 'Sophie . . . when you found that bit of worsted . . .'

I feel her raise her head to look at me, and take a little breath that doesn't have anything to do with crying. I wait for her to explain, or prevaricate, or lie.

She says, 'They would have left us behind. I had to make you come with me.'

I ought to feel angry, but I'm just bewildered. 'How could you?'

'You were ready enough to believe me,' she says quietly. 'You must have known, deep down. You must have known.'

'No. I didn't.'

She snorts. 'Poor, innocent little Rufus.'

I stand up shakily. 'So . . . she didn't come this way. She could be anywhere.' We could have been walking away, all this morning, when I thought . . . I thought I'd find her tonight, when we stopped; that as long as I kept walking, I'd find her eventually . . .

I walk away, circling the field, looking at every face until I'm sure it isn't Lena's. I frown, keeping the sun out of my eyes, squashing the anger down. After a while all the faces look familiar; I don't know if it's me, so tired I can't see straight, or if it's the expressions which are identical. When people notice me staring they glare, or shuffle behind someone else. Paul is the only one who raises his hand and starts to smile. I pretend I haven't noticed and keep my face stony.

Lena isn't here. I wasn't expecting her to be.

But it's only on the second time round the field that I notice that the kids who called her a sow aren't here either.

XVI

I can't stop walking, even though my feet ache and every bump and stone on the ground presses into my soles like a knuckle. If I stop moving I'll have to make a decision. So I keep circling the field, despair growing in my stomach. I avoid the corner near the trees, where Sophie's sitting; I know from the tingle on my neck that she's watching me, waiting for me to go back to her.

Lena went into the woods last night to find me. But she didn't find me.

I'm scared by the things I can see in my head, the things those kids could've done if they'd found her wandering on her own in the dark. Things they could still do, if they haven't yet . . .

I have to go back. I've wasted a day walking in the wrong direction . . . but I might still find her. And no matter what Sophie says, Lena needs me more. The promise I made Sophie a moment ago wasn't a proper promise at all. Not like –

I took the crusader's oath. I told Nick I'd stay . . .

Oh God. I stumble, feeling the little flashes of pain on my feet join up into a hot glow that throbs and slowly subsides. *That* promise matters.

My eyes start to sting. There's a pain in my throat, as

if an invisible noose is tightening round my voice box. I blink, trying not to give the tears room to surface. I can't break my promise to Nick. Not *that* promise.

But it wasn't a promise to Nick, was it? It was a promise to God – the crusader's vow – and God will understand, even if Nick won't. He knows that I have to go back for Lena, that I'm not being cowardly. He knows that I don't *want* to go back. He knows it's much more of a sacrifice than going on . . .

I daren't say goodbye to Sophie. Anyway, she'll know where I've gone when she never sees me again.

I look at the kids all around me, and suddenly I'm not one of them any more. The feeling is so strong I'm surprised no one can see it, staining me a different colour like dye. The cross on my cotte makes my skin prickle and crawl. But I *want* to stay. I want to go to Jerusalem with everyone else. I want to keep my promises.

It takes every scruple of my willpower to move my feet, one after the other, step after step, until I'm following the path that Ben led us along less than an hour ago. My whole body hurts with reluctance, but I keep going.

When we all walked this way, in the other direction, there were so many people and so much noise that now it feels like a different place. The leaves rustle and whisper above my head. I can hear voices, and the clink and thud of someone working. When I peer sideways I realise the village is only a little way away, the kind of distance I could run across before anyone had time to notice me. I crouch and squint through the leaves, watching. Now and then someone speaks in a sharp voice that carries in the afternoon stillness, but the rest of the time there are only the wordless, busy noises of a village going about its everyday life. There's a melody, whistled in time to the thump of someone chopping wood; a splash as someone empties a bucket; a crescendo of banging and joyous gasps and grunts in two voices, followed by silence and soft laughter. I catch sight of something – someone – moving between the houses. It's a woman with a baby in her arms. She rocks it and makes faces at it, and my heart jangles like a purse. She looks so lovely: smiling, shading the baby's face with her hand, walking as if it's something she might choose to do, or not, knowing all the time that she's not really going anywhere. She's not tired, or hungry – or anything else, except unconsciously content. I shut my eyes. I want so much to call out to her that I don't trust myself. I'm so full of longing it could be trickling out through my fingertips. But at the same time I don't understand. These are the people who chose not to come with us. God called them, and they didn't answer. They shouldn't be happy. They shouldn't be innocent.

She turns and wanders back into the shadow of the house, bouncing the baby, and then goes round the corner and disappears. I feel the tension go out of my body in a great harsh rush, like disappointment.

And without meaning to – without wanting to – I get up, push my way through the undergrowth, and run towards the shade of the buildings. The smell catches me unawares: hot mud, the dusty smell of wattle and daub in summer, thatch. I huddle against the uneven wall of the nearest hut, my heart beating fast. I shouldn't be here. That man with a scythe . . . But I can't help myself.

Slowly my breathing deepens and my heart stops pounding in my temples. Maybe all I wanted was this sense of being alone . . . but I stand up, careful not to make any noise, and look sideways at the dried, rutted road. There are houses in both directions. The village is too small to have a forge, so the chipping noise I can hear must be something else – rough ironwork over a make-shift fire, maybe, or just a kid playing with a spoon and an old horseshoe . . . but I can't see anyone. I slip to the far corner of the house and then turn north, away from the sound. I stay on the balls of my feet, ready to run away if anything moves. Nothing does.

There's a gurgle of words from inside a dark doorway, and I swing back against the nearest wall. But it's only a little kid, half singing, half talking to himself. A girl's voice counts to five and I hear the skitter of a stone on a hard blood floor. Then she counts to six and throws it again, and I grin. Hopscotch. Just like the children in Cologne, before Nick came. I wait until she's in the middle of her next go, then inch quietly away along the wall until she's out of earshot.

The next house is empty. I'm careless – I go round the corner without looking, almost through the door-way – but I'm lucky too. There's nothing but the trestle table and hearth and the beds of straw at the other end, splattered with sunlight where the thatch has rotted. There's the hum of a wasps' nest above my head. I step forward, listening to the silence of four walls around me. A long way away that clinking noise is still audible.

There's bread on the table, and sausage, and a pitcher of water. Ready to be taken out to the people working in the fields, probably. My tongue is drowning in saliva. I feel the emptiness in my stomach swell and change until it's the exact shape of the loaf.

But I don't take it for my own sake. I take it for Lena's.

I break off just enough to fill my mouth and hold the rest under my arm, keeping my hands by my sides. As soon as I swallow my whole body aches for more, but I grit my teeth and ignore it. I look both ways and dart back into the street. That way – north – there are more houses and a squat stone church, but there's no more time for looking around. I have to get away. I glance around one more time, because my back is prickling and I feel like a thief.

There's a sudden movement in the shadow of the church. I freeze, panicking. But the figure does the same, and suddenly there's something familiar about it. I whistle gently, then pitch my voice low and call, 'Nick!'

He stands still, poised to run, until I'm safely past the last house before the church, and there's still no sound from anywhere near. Then he says, 'Rufus? You shouldn't be here. What are you –'

'Neither should you,' I say. A few weeks ago Nick would have smiled, conceding the point, but now he narrows his eyes and stares at me like a king looking at a servant.

'Did anyone see you?' he asks.

For a moment I think he's seen the bread under my arm, but he hasn't. 'No. I was careful. Nick – I only wanted – I –'

Finally his face relaxes, although he still doesn't smile. 'You followed me.'

'I . . . Yes.' I've never lied to him before.

'Rufus . . .' He shakes his head. Then he beckons to me and goes into the church. There's a tympanum of Adam and Eve, and the snake grins at me as I walk underneath. Nick says, without looking back at me, 'I think you must be very dear to God.'

'What?'

'He seems to ask as much of you as he does me. Or almost.' He adds, quietly, 'My Saint John . . .'

I don't know what to say. I feel the sweat cool on my forehead. 'Nick . . .'

He laughs and kneels, looking up at the altar. 'Don't worry. It's not blasphemy.'

Right now I don't give a swaying swive about blasphemy – or you, for that matter. I want to kneel beside Nick, lower my voice, lean towards him, as if he's a priest who can give me confession. I want him to put his hand on me and make me into someone new. I clear my throat. 'Nick. Listen. I have to go.'

He glances at me and sighs. 'All right. I'll come with you.'

'No. No – I mean, I have to go back . . . My aunt is – she got lost yesterday. I can't go on. I have to go back.' Nick pauses in the middle of crossing himself, his hand touching his forehead. I say again, 'I have to go back,' as if those are the only words I know.

Nick says, 'What do you mean, *you have to go back*?' I wish he'd move, but he doesn't.

'I can't go on with the crusade. Unless – if I find her, we'll follow – if we don't get left behind, we'll try to catch you up –'

He could be a statue. 'But you promised.'

I try to walk towards him, but my body is made out of stone. 'I know, but – please, Nick, she can't look after herself and I'm scared someone'll hurt her –'

'You made a vow. So help you God.'

'I have to go back,' I say. 'I have to. Please, Nick, don't you understand? I can't leave her behind.'

'No,' Nick says. His hand comes away from his face

225

very, very slowly. 'I don't understand. You can't go back for her. Leave now and you'll turn your back on God for ever.'

I open my mouth but there isn't enough air in the church – in the entire world – to make the right word.

'*Nothing* is more important than the crusade. It's very simple, Rufus. You know what God wants of you. If you refuse now, he might forgive you. But he'll never ask anything of you again.'

'That's not – no, that –'

'Is that what you want? You've turned your back on one father, Rufus. Are you going to reject God too?' Finally he stands up and meets my eyes.

I stare at him. This isn't Nick. Something else has taken over his body, is speaking through his mouth. He's gone as white as bone and his eyes are gleaming.

'I love Lena. That's why I've got to . . . it can't be wrong to love her . . .' My voice cracks like a kid's. I make the word again, silently: *love*.

For a heartbeat Nick's gaze flicks away and he bites his lip. Then he looks back at me. 'At night everyone needs candles,' he says. 'But when the sun comes up, you can blow them out.'

'What?'

He steps forward, and a thin shaft of sunlight catches his hair like a flame. 'Forget her,' he says softly. 'Forget everything. Let the dead bury their dead.'

'But –'

He moves further towards me, until the gap between us is narrower than a hand's breadth. 'Forget Jerusalem, the Holy Land, the True Cross. They're not important either. They're just . . . pictures. Toys. Jerusalem isn't important. It could be anywhere.'

I hear a bubble of disbelief rise in my throat and try to swallow it before it bursts, but I can't. It echoes off the stone walls like a hiccup.

Nick smiles, almost mocking. 'God is in the crusade, Rufus. In the vows, in the journey, in the *trying* . . . the other things are only . . . parables. Symbols. When I was a child, I spake as a child, I understood as a child, I thought as a child. But when I became a man, I put away childish things.'

This is heresy. It has to be. But I can't say it.

'And your mother and father, your aunt . . . All those little loves don't matter now. Forget them. You're here.'

He's so close to me. I don't know whether to step back or step forward. I close my eyes and hear a child's voice calling a long way away, and the clink-clink of metal on metal. What if Nick's right? What if . . . ?

He puts his hand on my shoulder. It's the same hand that brought Eric back to life, and the same hand that couldn't do it again. For a moment I see Hetty's face.

I say, 'I – Nick, please –'

A silence. When I open my eyes he's watching me, waiting. We look at each other for an eternity. His hand seems to burn through my cotte and shirt. He leans in, until he's too close for my eyes to see him properly. In spite of myself I draw back.

He says, '*Judas.*'

I pull away from him, the breath knocked out of me, and he laughs; but not as if he thinks it's funny. 'I should have known from your hair,' he says. 'Everyone says you can't trust a redhead.' He turns on his heel and stares at the altar, his face set in an odd, harsh grimace. I don't recognise him.

I follow his eyes. A shadowy Christ looks back at me from his throne, face blank. Silence.

'I thought God had sent you to me,' Nick says. 'I trusted you. I thought you understood . . . but you can't understand, because if you did, you wouldn't leave.'

I hold the gaze of the stone Christ, trying not to blink first.

'If you go, Rufus . . . if you betray me like this . . . You *can't*. I thought you loved me.' There are tears in his voice but not on his face. 'You know – don't you? – that if you leave now I'll never forgive you. Never. God might, but I won't.'

'Please . . .'

'Why did you come at all? Why didn't you stay at home? You could have looked after your aunt for the rest of your life, and you'd never have known what you were missing. I wish you hadn't come. I wish I'd never set eyes on you.'

Then he turns and looks straight into my eyes and says it again.

It's like someone stamping on the world, breaking its backbone. Suddenly I'm down on my knees, hands spread out on the floor, the dirt standing out starkly on my skin. I'm caught in a strange sort of stillness, like a fly in amber. Even my heart seems to have stopped. Part of me watches, intrigued, as I struggle to breathe.

The air floods back in.

And I say, 'I'm sorry, yes, yes, yes, yes, *yes*, all right, I won't go, I'll do whatever you want, whatever you say . . .' The words spill and run into each other so that even I don't know what I'm saying. 'Yes, Nick, yes, please, I'm sorry, stop . . .'

There are footsteps. He's crouching in front of me, his hands on my elbows. 'It's all right. It's all going to be all right.'

The voice pours out of me, like vomit. 'Please, Nick, I'm sorry, I'll stay, sorry, sorry, I'll do whatever you say –'

'Hush.' He tries to help me up, but he's not strong enough. 'Well done. It's all right.' He touches my face. Then he kisses me.

I stand up, pulling away from his hands, watching him rock back on his heels, off-balance. I'll do whatever he says, but I can't bear to be close to him. I feel sick. My skin crawls. Huge shudders run down my back, like retching. I turn and stumble towards the door, desperate for sunlight, to be alone.

'Is this yours? Wait – Rufus –'

I've left the loaf of bread, but I don't care. Nick's touched it now. He can have it.

I run south down the little road, through the houses, towards the field where everyone else is. I don't care if any of the villagers see me; I feel as if I could keep running for ever. Nick calls out after me but I don't look round. The air scalds my throat.

The clinking noise gets louder. I glance sideways as I run. There's a man, just older than an apprentice, hammering at something beside a glowing charcoal fire. He looks up, his eyes catching the movement, but I'm still running and a house slides smoothly into the space between us.

Nick calls out, 'Rufus! *Wait!* Where did you get this –'

The clinking noise stops. I speed up, glad of the pain in my feet, glad of the tiredness and the stitch that stabs upwards under my heart like a wound. I can see the others now: the field is only a little way away, trampled and dusty, full of sleeping children. Already there are a couple of fires, wrinkling the air with heat. Someone – I'm too far away to see his face – puts his hands on his hips and watches me run.

The field and the people in it get bigger and bigger, until they're on the same scale as me. Then I slow down and stop, panting, the hot summer sweat rolling off me and dripping into the dirt. It's Lucas, standing there watching me. He looks like a grown-up; I take three or four breaths before I recognise him. He says, 'What the hell's going on?'

'Nothing,' I say.

He frowns, staring over my shoulder. I turn to look. Then I understand what he means.

There's a man in front of the nearest house, and he's got hold of Nick, twisting his arm behind his back. It's the man I passed, who was working at a makeshift forge. He calls over his shoulder. Nick's fighting to get away, but he's no good at it; he's wriggling and squirming but he doesn't kick or bite. The man shouts, 'Hey! Ben! Come and help!' and before he's shut his mouth there are villagers at his side, helping to keep Nick under control. I see a woman bend one of Nick's little fingers back until he yelps and stops struggling.

Lucas says again, 'What the hell . . . ?'

I watch them manhandling Nick, their hands dragging and wrenching his clothes, unnecessarily rough now that he's gone limp. One of them turns to look at us and shouts, 'You little skites – we told you to keep away!' Then he wrestles Nick out of the other man's grasp and marches him towards us. Nick stumbles and gasps.

Lucas says, 'Hey – he's not hurting you –'

'We asked you nicely, you little *gits* –'

'What's he done? He hasn't hurt you.'

'He's a thief. He stole bread. So much for being God's chosen!' The man holding Nick is only a few feet away now. He turns to Nick and hisses into his face. 'You disgust me, you little fraud.'

'I —' But Nick sees me and doesn't finish his sentence.

Lucas says, 'Let go of him. He's only a kid.'

'Only a kid?' The man laughs, twisting the fabric of Nick's shirt so that it cuts into his neck. 'I thought he was supposed to be a prophet. But you're right. He's just a selfish, greedy little kid. Think he was going to share that loaf with anyone? I doubt it, somehow.'

'*Let go of him.*'

The man grins, showing his teeth. 'I should cut his thieving little hands off.'

He's not joking. I take a step forward, open my mouth to speak.

'All right, Kit, don't get carried away.' It's the man who spoke to us this morning. He still has his scythe over his shoulder; he might have come straight from the fields. 'They're just hungry kids.'

For a moment the tension relaxes. The man — Kit — shifts his weight, giving Nick more room to breathe. Nick coughs, squeezing his eyes shut.

The man with the scythe gives it casually to one of the women. He takes Nick away from Kit like a grown-up separating two scrapping children. But he doesn't let go of Nick's shoulder. 'We warned you, sonny.' He looks round at us and adds, 'We warned you all. Don't come into the village, we said. We don't have any food spare. And you —' he turns back to Nick — 'you're the leader, right? You should know better.'

My back prickles with foreboding. I glance over my shoulder. Almost everyone is listening. There are rows of faces turned to watch, pale and gaunt and perfectly still. A clear, cool voice says, 'He *is* our leader. He *is* God's chosen. He brought a boy back from the dead.'

The man only presses his lips together and nods tightly. He raises his voice a little. 'If I really thought you were God's chosen . . . well, stealing wouldn't just be wrong, it would be blasphemy. I'd skin you alive . . . But your mate there has got a point. You're just an ordinary, sinful little kid. And *this* is what we do to kids who steal in this village.' He jerks his head at the nearest woman. 'Get the birch, will you?'

Someone – but it isn't Lucas this time – says, 'He belongs to God. Don't you dare lay a *finger* on –'

'I'll do what I damn' well please with him,' he says, and a muscle pulses in his jaw. 'It's about time someone showed you lot what happens to nasty, arrogant, disobedient children. God's chosen, my *armpit*.'

Nick says quietly, 'Please don't hurt me.'

'Shut up.' The man's voice is taut with hostility and something else, like fear . . . He glances away. I think he's looking for the woman who's bringing him the birch, but instead I see two children peering round the corner of a doorway. The smaller one is sucking his little finger. The man's hands tighten on Nick.

Then the woman is coming towards him with a bunch of twigs. I feel sick.

'If you dare to touch him – I'm warning you . . .' The voice could be any one of us.

The man doesn't react. We're only kids, after all; what could we do? He steps back, keeping one hand on Nick's shoulders, looking him in the eye. Then he says, 'And *this* is for the sacrilege.' And he hits him.

His flattened palm hits Nick's cheek with a noise like

something snapping, as loud as anything I've ever heard; but Nick doesn't make a sound.

The man reaches out to take the birch twigs. But his hand doesn't get there.

I don't know who moves first. All I know is that it isn't me.

For a heartbeat – half a heartbeat – there are only a couple of us running forward. The men have time to swap looks, to roll their eyes, for one of them to swing his staff carefully sideways so as not to hit anyone. They reach out, pulling the children away from the man holding Nick, confident enough to be gentle. One of them says, 'Give over, sonny, let's not get carried away . . .'

And then there are more of us, and suddenly they realise that we may be kids, but we outnumber them a hundred to one. And everything changes.

Suddenly there are hands grabbing for weapons. There are panicked curses from the villagers who've been stupid enough to lean their staves against the nearest wall or let children wrest them away. There are men staggering, set on by several kids at once, dragged to their knees and kicked in the face. There are metal blades catching the light, clumps of hair on the ground, shouts, blood.

Nick calls out, 'Don't – stop, *stop* –' but no one's listening. Another man drops to the ground, pressing his hands between his legs, wracked by dry sobs. I think someone's kneed him in the cods, but then I see the blood pooling underneath him and follow his gaze to the red scythe-blade that dances in front of his face. Everyone's shouting. Some people are using words, but most aren't. It's not about Nick any more. It's about the fact that we're hungry, and exhausted, and furious, furiously vicious . . . It's about the fact that they wouldn't give us any food, that they don't believe in the same God as us, the fact that they're grown up.

God, oh God, please . . .

I want to run. I want to throw up. I want to join in.

Something hits me in the small of my back. Then there's a hand on my shoulder like a claw, dragging me sideways. I pull away instinctively, and as I twist a hand swings into my face, just slow enough for me to duck. It still grazes my temple – the skin is like stone, roughened from working on the land – but most of the force has gone out of the punch. I drop to my knees, shielding my head with my forearms. When I look up I realise, with a strange shock, that it's a woman who hit me. Now I'm on the ground, out of her way, she doesn't seem to care that I'm there. She barges into the next knot of kids, driving towards the doorway where those two village children are standing, petrified, their eyes wide. She shouts, 'Go inside! Go *inside* –' but there's so much noise no one hears except me.

A dark-haired, skinny apprentice steps in front of her, deliberately, laughing. He slides his arm out of her grasp and says, 'You stupid peasant *cow*.' Then he smashes his forehead down into her face. She reels backward with her hands over her face, a frantic flower of blood spurting through her fingers. She's saying something but the words gurgle in her throat. The apprentice knees her in the stomach, almost lazily. She staggers, her eyes spilling water over her hands, but she keeps trying to get to her children. I watch her as if I'm not part of any of this and pray for her to make it. But I know she won't. Her arms flail as she tries to stay on her feet.

The scythe-blade swings downward, diagonally, weaving,

out of control. Whoever's holding it isn't big enough to take the weight. The blade could go anywhere; drop on anyone, do anything . . .

Something makes me close my eyes. I squeeze my eyelids together so hard I can feel my pulse thrum behind my skull.

The woman screams. At least someone screams, and I know it has to be her.

The sound cuts through the other noises. When I open my eyes everyone is frozen, or nearly, the violence paused in a kind of tableau. She's bleeding. The front of her dress is stained, a continent of dark spreading slowly down the wool. For a moment I think it's only coming from her face. Then I realise that one whole sleeve is drenched: so much blood that I can smell it, so much that it pours into the dust and sounds like a drunkard pissing. And the kid holding the scythe is open-mouthed, staring, like everyone else. This isn't the kind of blood you get when you're scrapping in the streets, the kind that you wear home as a badge of honour. This is real – the kind of blood you die of. She runs out of breath and her scream gutters, like a candle going out. She's clutching her arm and her whole hand is clotted with red.

Someone says, 'Dear Jesus . . .'

She reels, blinking, as if she's very, very tired. She says, 'Please . . . my children,' and fixes her eyes on the doorway. But her gaze slips clumsily, like a knife that's not sharp enough. She frowns.

The man whose scythe it was – the leader – says, 'Amalie.'

She collapses. She says, 'Don't hurt my children.' The blood spreads out underneath her, stinking of metal.

Silence. The world pauses, balanced on the apex of a triangle, waiting. It can tip either way: we'll stop fighting now, or we won't. I open my mouth but I don't know which words will land on which side.

And a voice answers her – a voice I don't recognise, no one's voice, everyone's voice – calling out from somewhere behind me. 'Don't worry,' it says, and I can hear it smiling. 'Why would we hurt your children? They're coming with us.'

It's like a hand casually dropping on to the scales: it changes everything. The villagers look at him. The silence gathers and breaks, like a wave.

Someone says, very quietly, 'They are *not coming with you.*'

Then the fight explodes again. But it's deadly serious now, desperate and vicious and primitive. There are still grunts and gasps of pain, but now there's no shouting, as if no one has breath to waste. In front of me there are hands, broken faces, bodies suddenly horizontal in the dust, as if the earth is spitting them out. A head rolls sideways on its neck to look at me, and the eyes stare and stare and don't blink. I stare back and drops of red scatter around me like enamel beads. A long way away there's a kid wailing.

A shadow slides over my face and I look up. Two men, almost evenly matched, and the bigger one has his fingers spread in the other's face. I don't recognise either of them. They're cursing at each other but the words are so meaningless they're just noises. They shift their weight, shuffling, and one of them braces his knee against my shoulder. For the first time it occurs to me that I might be in danger. No one's noticed me so far because I'm on the ground, but I can't stay here for ever. I stay still until the man is really leaning on me, using my weight to stay upright, then I move. I slide sideways and roll, aiming for the edge of shade that surrounds the nearest hut. The men stumble and crash into the dust. They both cry out as they hit the ground. The impact forces the smaller man's head up, and I recognise him. It's the man who stopped me hitting Paul, weeks ago. I struggle to my feet and run, before anyone sees me, before I see the end of the fight. I feel dizzy; the world seems to slide underneath me as if it's been greased.

I turn round the corner of the hut and crouch, my back against the wall, trying to get my breathing to slow. It's quieter here. It means I can hear more, and further. That kid is still crying – the full-lung wail that'll go on for hours unless someone stops it – but there's another layer of sound. For a moment I think it's my own breath and heartbeat, rushing in my ears like a river. Then I realise it's the noise of hundreds of kids, not fighting, but . . . kids being *busy*, absorbed, playing at something . . .

Somehow it scares me more than the fight did.

I get up again and run, heavy-footed, to the next hut, and peer round the corner. When I look sideways, back towards the main street, I can see doorways, a broken edge of mud wall, shadows. Everywhere there are children – crusader children, unkempt and grimy, the crosses on their clothes faded almost to invisibility. Here a knot of girls – I recognise one of them, a loud-mouthed little madam from Trier – hovers by a doorway, holding their skirts up by the corners like bulging sacks. A tiny boy is holding a loaf that's bigger than his head. There's a shout and the noise of protesting cattle from the far end of the longhouse. Then a boy, about my age, comes out into the sunlight, blinking. Another girl runs to meet him and starts to juggle with pale eggs. One of them splats into the dirt but she just laughs.

My stomach says, *Eggs. Please, an egg. An egg . . .*

A woman steps into view and stops, her mouth open. Then she shouts, 'Get out of there! You little – you thieving *skites –*'

They all turn and look at her. If they were alone they'd be scared, but there are ten of them – fifteen, as more faces appear in the doorway of the cattle-shed, then twenty, twenty-five – and all they do is laugh. Someone says, 'It's all in a good cause, mistress.' The laughing girl says, 'Sorry, are these eggs yours? Oh, well, in *that* case –' and throws one in a fast, casual arc. The woman flinches and it falls and breaks, and her mouth tightens as if she's trying not to cry. A giggle ripples round the children and I feel my own lips moving, as if I can't control them.

The woman says, 'Look – we don't have enough food for ourselves, honestly, if we did we'd give . . . and there are so many of you –'

' 'Course you would,' the first boy says. 'Sure. Wouldn't chase us out of your village with scythes *then*, would you? Wouldn't smack our prophet across the face. Wouldn't call him a liar. Oh no.'

'He did steal a loaf of –' She stops herself, just too late.

The girl with the eggs isn't laughing any more. She opens her hand and drops another egg, splaying her fingers deliberately. 'Oops. Was that one of yours too? Oh dear. I'll just have to get another one.'

'I'm sorry,' the woman says. 'I didn't mean – please, that's our food . . .'

'Go away and stop bothering us,' the boy says. 'We've got another cow to kill.'

She looks at his hands and her face goes white. 'No – *no*, you didn't – you can't have –'

'Go *away*.'

Someone flicks a bit of mud at her, but she doesn't move. She's still staring at the egg, spread out on the ground in an obscene splash of yellow. Then someone flicks a bit of stone. It catches her above the ear, but she hardly seems to notice.

'Go away. Go. Away. Go. Away.' It turns into a kind of chant. Now everyone has a stone in their hand. 'Go *away*.' A pebble lands in the dust at her feet. A sharp bit of flint smacks into the hollow of her shoulder and spins away, catching the light. She cries out and seems to see us for the first time. She holds up her hands, her mouth moving, but it's too late. The chant goes on. The stones fly through the air. It's like a game. It's not quite real. Another egg hits her across the chest and it's like a joke. She turns to run and a pottery jug soars through the air and hangs in the space above her before it drops, breaking on her head and throwing her forward on to the ground. She lies face down. She doesn't move. We stand and look at her. A couple of panting boys drag a cow carcass through the furthest doorway and glance round, wondering what they've missed.

The girl with the eggs – although she doesn't have any left now – says, 'Oops . . .' and makes a little noise like a hiccup.

The hot summer quiet comes back. Everyone catches their breath, like the pause after a race. After a while someone turns aside and mutters something, and people start to drift away.

The boys hoist the cow carcass on to a stick, grunting and cursing, and tie its feet together. Someone checks the main street and calls back over his shoulder to say that the fight's still going on and they should take the long way back to the field. They swagger past me, singing, and their eyes slide over me as if I don't exist, or as if I'm one of them. Other kids follow, singly and in groups, their arms or hands or skirts full of pilfered food. They can't have left *anything* for the villagers.

I stay where I am until the dirt track is empty again. Seeing all that food should have made me feel hungry, but it only makes me feel sick, gluttonous, as if just seeing it was the same as swallowing it. The sounds of the fight rise and fall in my ears. The dark, skinny apprentice that I noticed before wanders past, panting and grinning and shaking one foot as if he's got cramp. He doesn't notice me. He wipes the sweat off his face with his shirt, spits into the dust. Someone shouts something and he turns and shouts back, 'Just going for a scumber, all right? Back in a moment. You can carry on without me.' They're winning, then. It doesn't come as a surprise.

I don't have to be here. I can go back to the field, where they must be gorging themselves on the villagers' food; I can walk away and wait in the woods until nightfall, and by that time it'll be over. I can pretend I haven't seen any of this.

I wonder where Sophie is, and Paul. I haven't seen them since I left without saying goodbye. It's just as well I *didn't* say goodbye, I suppose, now that I'm not leaving after all.

Nick might still be fighting. He might be dead. I don't care. I refuse to care.

I walk to the edge of the longhouse and turn right up the main track. If I look left I know I'll see the fight, still going on, but I don't. I keep my chin level and my shoulders back and I walk as if I have every right to be here. I'm not part of this. It has nothing to do with me.

I make my way to the only safe place I can think of: the church. I try not to look up as I go in but I can't help catching the eye of the carved snake above the arch. It gives me another unsympathetic grin. *This is all your fault*, it says. *You stole that bread, not Nick. If you hadn't* . . .

I sit down on the floor, my knees up to my chest, and blink at the shadows until they resolve themselves into arched windows and altar and Christ enthroned. I'll stay here until the shouting stops.

There's a kind of snuffling sound. At first I think it's an animal. I raise my head, looking round for a pig, or hedgehog, or dog . . . and then I see a man's back, his head bent so that from this angle it looks as if he hasn't got one. He's kneeling in front of the altar – where Nick knelt, before – and sobbing into his hands. After a long time he snorts and wipes his face and I see the edge of a wispy beard and lank, thin blond hair. Ben, the one who took us to the field . . . I feel a sudden surge of anger. If this wasn't God's house I'd get up and kick him in the kidneys, and run before he had time to turn round. If they'd only *welcomed* us, none of this would have happened. It's their own fault for being stupid and avaricious and hostile. If they'd been decent Christians we'd never have got out of control, and no one would have got hurt, and Ben wouldn't be here, crying and spraying snot everywhere.

I wait. It ought to feel horrible, sitting listening to a grown man weep. But I don't care any more. As far as I'm concerned he can go on for ever.

A new deep note comes into his voice. He rocks forward and back, smacking one hand on the floor. Flecks of spit and tears fly through the air, flashing silver and gold in the sunlight. He says, 'Please . . . don't let this happen. Amalie . . . not Amalie . . .'

Amalie . . . the woman who got hit with the scythe. I'm surprised that I remember her name, but I do. I trace an invisible shape on the stone with my finger, drawing a little family tree. The children were hers, and the leader of the villagers seemed to be her husband, so . . . Ben could be her brother. Or her lover. More than a friend or a cousin, anyway, from the way he's crying.

'Lord, have mercy . . . protect us, protect us all . . . these *devils* . . .' His voice sinks back into a morass of sobs.

It takes me a moment to realise he means us when he says *devils*. But even that doesn't really bother me. He's ignorant. He's a stupid peasant. He's probably a pagan. He –

But something gives way in my mind, like a beam finally snapping under too much weight.

I get up and I'm half running, half stumbling towards him. I drop to my knees beside him and put my hands together and I'm saying, 'I'm sorry, I'm sorry,' before I even realise that I mean it. I don't dare to touch him but I close my eyes and join in his prayer. *Lord, have mercy*. There's moisture on my lips that could be tears or sweat or both. 'I'm sorry, we didn't mean to hurt you, *I* didn't mean to –'

He stops crying. He turns to stare at me, shifting back to look me up and down. He says, 'What?'

'I'm so sorry,' I say, and I don't dare to meet his eyes. I keep my gaze fixed on the impassive Christ-in-judgement

242

on the altar. 'We were only hungry, we . . .' I'm freezing. My damp, sweaty shirt is clinging to me. I start to shake. 'We only . . . Nick . . .'

When I close my eyes I can see the village as it was a few hours ago. A woman and a baby, two kids playing hopscotch, a pair of lovers, a man bodging a ploughshare or an axe over a home-made furnace, and everyone else out in the fields, with food set ready for when they came home. I say, 'We never meant to hurt anyone. It was only – we –'

He shoves himself to his feet. The snot in his nose pops and slurps as he sniffs. He says, 'You're one of them. Of course you are. And do you know what they've – what *you've* done to my Amalie? She's dead. She's – and you dare to come in here to ask God for *mercy* –'

I look up at him. I don't have time to get to my feet. He swings an arm back, and I watch it, unable to move. He's going to hit me. Well, I've been hit before. And I have to admit he's got a point – it's not exactly unprovoked . . . I watch. Here it comes.

It doesn't come. He pauses.

Then his thigh swings forward and up, so I smell dust and the stench of groin-sweaty wool, and I look down at the material getting closer to my face, the smooth hemisphere of his knee, like a club of wool-covered bone, the wrinkles unfolding as the angle changes, the marks on the wool of dirt and dried rust or could-that-be-blood? getting close enough to read, like an alphabet, the kind of marks my father would spot and know I'd been fighting when I was little, yes, that's his knee, even closer, and somehow I know this is bad, definitely, this is going to hurt, but somehow it's all happening so fast that even though I have time to think all this I don't have time to move aside, I don't have time to block –

My jaw snaps shut. I'm knocked backwards.

I have time to wonder if he'll hit me again. Then I'm gone, like a mayfly swallowed by a fish. *Gloop*.

XVII

There are mouths of darkness on both sides of me and they spit me out. I see flowers of purple and green, lapis blue, bright unlikely colours that open and swirl in front of me. I'm in the middle of thinking something, but I can't remember what. The flowers fade and everything goes mostly black. I can smell fire.

Then the pain hits me smack in the middle of my forehead, going right through to the back of my head, and I realise that the darkness isn't my eyes and I'm not dreaming any more. I'm awake and it's night-time. And it feels as if I've got an arrowhead stuck in my brain, just where my spine meets my skull. It takes a couple of deep breaths and quite a lot of thought before I decide that on the whole that's unlikely, mainly because I seem to be still alive. But oh God it *hurts*.

All I want to do is go back to sleep, or back to being dead, or whatever it was. But something makes me lift my head, gingerly, as if it's a brimming bucket and the smallest jolt will spill myself all over the floor. I watch a patch of golden light slide back and forth. No, not gold but copper or bronze – redder, hotter than gold . . . but it's dark. There shouldn't be any light at all. Something catches in the back of my throat and I cough, and for a moment the pain flares up until it's the only thing that exists. Then, as it fades, I realise I can smell smoke.

I ought to get up. I think about it, trying to remember which bits of my body need to move. I feel like a puppet without strings. Slowly, inefficiently, I push myself to my knees. There's another flash of pain. First I notice that there's blood on the edge of the altar stone, where my head must have landed. Then I notice that my ribs and ankle hurt too. I think about this for a while, before I decide that Ben must have kicked me a couple of times after he knocked me out. This doesn't seem entirely fair, but I can't seem to muster much outrage. At least he's gone.

I push at the floor until I realise that won't actually help me stand up. Then I try another tactic and manage to put some weight on my better foot. It's much harder than it ought to be, and I wonder vaguely whether the world – or maybe you – doesn't want me to get up and is subtly sabotaging my attempts. But in the end I'm – somehow – on my feet, swaying gently. The windows are glowing like molten metal. It's like being on the inside of a waterfall at sunset, or inside a lamp, or . . . anyway, it's beautiful. I could watch it for ever.

Except that . . .

Something's burning. I don't know whether the church roof is wood, or thatch, or stone . . . The village is burning.

I should get out.

I cling to this idea because it's nice and clear, and only has four syllables. I make my way to the door, trying not to use my bad foot more than I have to. I have that night-marish walking-through-pottage feeling, but I know I'm awake because everything hurts. The air is thick with smoke. It smells like hell.

The heat hits me as I come out into the open air. I stand and cough, bracing myself against the arch. The stone is warm.

All the houses are burning. The sky is black with smoke, so the flames flicker and blaze against a charcoal-coloured ceiling. The noise is deafening: the roar as the fires suck at the air, the bangs of wood collapsing, the giant, uncanny rustle underneath, like the voice of the fire itself . . . But no screams. That's good, isn't it?

I feel sick. A thick black frame grows at the edges of my vision, but I push it away, breathing slowly. If I faint now I might never wake up. I step forward, and remember just in time not to put my whole weight on my other foot. My mind hovers behind me for a moment and then catches up. If *all* the houses are burning . . . in Cologne, at home, the houses are packed together, so fire spreads easily, scampering across roofs. But here there's more space between them. And there's no wind. Sparks might fly from one to another, but for *all* of them to be burning, all at once . . . Someone set them on fire, on purpose.

I limp down what used to be the main road through the village. Where are the villagers? Shouldn't they be passing buckets of water from hand to hand, sloshing uselessly at the fires? The ground rolls and ripples, as if there are more flames underneath it threatening to break through. I have to flail at the air to keep my balance. I'm not completely sure where I'm going, but I keep hobbling. Maybe I'll go and find everyone else. Yes. Find everyone else. Find Sophie and Nick. They need me. Or do I need them? I can't remember. Either way, I have to find them . . . I hear myself muttering, 'Yes. Find Sophie. Find Nick. I promised. Good . . .'

There are little dark figures running around, outlined against the flames. I think for a moment that they're just in front of me, and try to catch one in my hands like a moth. Then I understand that they're people – children – and quite a long way away. They're watching the furthest longhouse burn. I can hear them shouting in hoarse, high-pitched voices, but I can't hear the words. If they're children they'll be on our side. I'll go and ask where Nick is.

I pass some people who are sleeping on the ground. It's funny that they're sleeping here, in all this noise and smoke, with their eyes open and soot settling on their faces. I walk carefully round them, trying not to wake them. Silly people. They're very careless. They've let their children go to sleep too, in the middle of the path, where someone might trip over them. There's even a puppy curled beside them, a little girl's hand still tight on its fur. The ash falls like snow, into their hair, their mouths, clinging to the membrane of their eyeballs.

They're asleep, I say to myself, only asleep, although I know it's not true.

Oh, God, oh God, oh God.

I keep walking. I'm not sure any more whether or not the pain in my ankle is a bad thing, because at least it gives me something to concentrate on.

The kids are dancing in front of the burning house, shoving and wrestling and giggling as a portion of thatch collapses in a great *whoosh*. It's the house I stole the bread from, I think. Where the wasps' nest was there's a swarm of sparks, skirling upwards between black beams. Someone claps and whistles and my whole head rings.

I was going to ask one of the kids where Nick was, but my body takes me sideways into the shadows. They might not have set the fire – they might not have killed the villagers – but all the same . . . if I speak to them, I'll be one of them. So – no, I'll keep on walking, and in the morning it'll all be over. We'll go on, like we always do, and by the time we get to Jerusalem we'll hardly remember . . .

I stop where I am and stare. Someone is kneeling a few feet away, watching the house burn. In this light his hair blazes red and he could be anyone, but I know it's Nick: a new, dark Nick, black outlined in bronze, sparks dancing around his head like rubies. It doesn't surprise me. Of course he's here. Someone's put him here on purpose, for me to find. I stop where I am and look at him. With a sudden lurch in my gut I see the fires reflected in his eyes, hot tongues of flame licking over his pupils. He could be made of heat, of shadows and embers. One touch of his hand would burn right down to my bones.

He's saying something. I wonder what it is, and like magic it gets louder until I can hear it, even over the noise of the house collapsing. 'O ye Winds of God . . . O ye Fire and Heat, bless ye the Lord: praise him, and magnify him for ever . . .'

I open my mouth to call out, but the taste of smoke settles on my tongue. I don't know what God he's praying to. I'm not sure it's one I recognise.

I'm going to be sick. I swallow frantically, squashing the blackness down, and reel sideways. I want to lie down and go to sleep. I say, 'Nick . . .' but it's too quiet and he doesn't hear me. He keeps praying, his face turned to the flame-filled skeleton of the house. He's smiling. I say again, 'Nick,' already knowing that it's no good. I reach out for something to lean against but there's nothing. Oh God. I have to get to somewhere safe before my knees give way. If I went right up to Nick, collapsed in front of him, he'd *have* to notice me . . . but something stops me. Instead I turn right, wading through darkness that doesn't want to let me through, to the edge of the houses. If I find the path it will take me back to the field without my having to go through the rest of the village. Somewhere in the undergrowth . . . but it's too dark to see anything. I stare at the black web of a tree, outlined against fire, but it leans to the left, more and more, until it spins off and away. I blink and look at my feet and they do the same thing. The sky whirls round and round my head like a pebble in a sling.

The path. I've found the path. Now all I have to do is . . .

I vomit. My skull feels like a wineskin, bulging at the seams, ready to split. I retch and retch, until I'm only bringing up bile. Then I drop to my knees and curl up into a ball. The leaves brush wet fingers against the side of my face. I'm safe here. I'll just rest a moment before I go to find Sophie.

In my dream there's a voice talking to me, and it's a voice I recognise, it's someone I know intimately, but it isn't Nick, or my father, or anyone else I can think of. I'm watching Nick pray to the flames, and nothing's different from how it really was, so I don't know how I know it's a dream, but I do. The voice is a whisper: a very quiet, insinuating sort of whisper that comes from just over my left shoulder. It says, *His eyes were as a flame of fire, and on his head were many crowns, and he had a name written that no man knew but he himself. And he was clothed with a vesture dipped in blood, and his name is called the Word of God.*

And Nick looks up and sees me, and he hasn't got a face.

This time what wakes me is the thirst. Or possibly it's the cold. It's early morning, and the world is green with sunlight filtered through leaves, dripping with dew. My mouth is so dry it's like dust. I brush my hand through the bracken next to me and suck the moisture off my palm. It only makes me thirstier. My head doesn't hurt as much as it did but my bones are too heavy, so that when I move they weigh on my muscles like iron bars. And I'm so cold I'm sweating, which means I've probably got a fever. I get to my feet, shivering. At least now I can stand up without vomiting. The air smells smoky, and there's a black edge to the leaves, but apart from that everything is new, clean.

I have to find the others. It's still early, so they won't have left yet. If I hurry . . . I giggle stupidly. Well, all right then, not *hurry*, but . . . I walk carefully, feeling the earth with my feet as if it's the ground which could give way at any moment and not my legs. There's birdsong, absurdly loud. I walk under the last arch of trees into the field, shading my eyes against the low glare of the sun.

For a moment I think I've got confused. This can't be the right field. There's no one here.

But it *is* the right field. There are dead fires, a cow carcass that's been stripped obscenely of its rump, the ash and debris of a feast. Here and there in the furrows there are bits of food, crusts or bones or fruit-cores. The grass is flattened.

Where is everyone? It's too early for them to have gone . . . unless they feasted and then walked through the night, but why would . . . ? I blink and look around again, wiping the sweat from my face, hoping that by some miracle they'll all appear out of thin air. Sophie . . . Nick . . . Lucas, Margareta, Timo . . . even Paul. *Please* . . .

No one.

I sway and stare. How could this have happened? It's like a curse or a magic spell. Suddenly I'm more alone than I've ever been in my life. Pain flares behind my eyes and I reach out to steady myself on nothing. I've been left behind. I've been, oh God, God . . .

I try to think clearly. All I have to do is follow. That's all. It won't be hard to find the way they went. I raise my head and stare south across the field and I can see the muddy scar where they forded the stream. It'll be easy.

I'm so thirsty. I stagger down to the stream and kneel at the edge, scooping water into my hands to drink. The footprints in the mud have mostly been washed away. They can't have been made this morning . . . and I realise, slowly, that I don't know how long I was asleep. Maybe they've been gone a whole day, or two . . . Never mind. I'll catch them up.

The water in my mouth is icy cold and I'm trembling so hard I'm scared my teeth will fall out. But it's so good; I'm so thirsty . . . I get tired before I quench my thirst, and collapse on to the grass, cradling my head on my arm. Just a little rest before I go after the others . . . After a long time the sun comes over the trees and I feel it starting to dry my shirt. The tentative warmth makes me shiver more. When I'm sick again the vomit is clear and cool and almost tasteless. I shuffle forwards and drink more water. I close my eyes and my body hovers somewhere in the middle of too hot and too cold. I can feel every bone in my body aching.

* * *

I'm asleep. I'm awake. I'm drinking, and the water is running down my front and making me shiver uncontrollably. It's still early morning, but the sun's swapped sides, or I have, and it's getting slowly darker. I'm staggering across the field. I think I'm drunk. I've got a bit of meat in my hand. I take a bite and it's cold and full of dew. I'm lying in the dark and there are hundreds of little fires. I try to get to one but no matter how far I walk it doesn't get any closer. I realise it's a star and I'm walking round in circles. I go knee-deep in something icy-cold that's like very heavy air. I lean forward and drink and then I fall over and lie on wet rocks. I'm so hot I don't mind being covered in water like a blanket. My father comes and looks at me and goes away in disgust. I try to explain. I'm trying to eat again. I'm sick again, but I don't mind. When I'm too tired to be sick any more I go to sleep. I call out to my father but he doesn't answer, even though I know he's there. I'm freezing, I'm boiling. I see a rabbit looking at me. I can see it clearly, every twitch, every brown-furred muscle, and that means it's day and I've got colour again. It's sunset. It goes straight from sunset to sunrise with nothing in between. That worries me a bit, because there's no night in heaven and maybe that means I'm dead. Eventually I can sit up without vomiting. I'm trying to eat again and this time it almost works. I'm drinking and I manage not to spill it all on my shirt. I can get to my feet without shaking. I'm warm. My shirt smells of fever, but I'm not sweating any more.

I realise I've been ill.

It's a blazing, clear-skied afternoon, with a soft breeze that ruffles the grass and tugs at the trees over my head. I take a deep breath and my lungs fill with the smell of summer. Fingers of warmth slide under my shirt, tracing gentle shapes on my skin. I feel newborn. I take off my shirt and rinse it in the stream, watching weeks of grime drift into the water like smoke. My hands are thin and white and miraculous. I'm not absolutely sure I should be alive, but I'm glad I am.

There's a kind of space in my head, as if the fever has cleaned it out. Everything seems a very long time ago, back in my childhood: Nick, the burning village, Sophie, God . . . Here there's only birdsong and the noise of the stream, perfect solitude, perfect freedom. I've been released from my promises, because the choice has been made for me. It's too late to go after the others.

I'm going home.

I spend one more night in the field outside the village. Before it gets dark I steel myself to go and look at the wrecked, burnt-out houses, to see if there's anything left that might be useful. It's horrible. The wood-and-daub walls have collapsed in some places and baked into hills of cracked clay in others. Everything smells bitter and there's dark grey dust in the air that gets between my teeth like grit. The ground still seems to be giving off heat: an unhealthy, feverish kind of heat, as if hell is very close to the surface. It's not quite silent, but the little noises of things cooling or finally dropping to the earth make it seem quieter. They sound like footsteps; I can't help looking round, again and again, even though I know no one's there.

I walk the whole length of the village, holding my breath and turning my face away when I pass the bodies, past the church. I keep going, light-headed, until I'm nearly at the place where the villagers met us. And there, almost out of sight, is a little hut that hasn't been burnt.

I approach it carefully, but there's no sound, and when I go inside there's a whiff of sour milk and a broken jug on the floor. I imagine an old woman, hearing a scream, dropping a jug but not even stopping to clean up the mess before she runs to see what's going on . . . then I close my eyes, blocking out the picture. I start to pray, before I realise I don't know what I'm praying for, or to whom.

I go through her things and take a chaperon and a thick wool mantle, a gourd for water, and all of her little store of food. It makes me laugh that I'm taking all this, just to go home, when I set out with nothing . . . The laughter takes me over, so that I have to sit down on the bench and catch my breath while the world spins around me. I think about lighting a fire in the hearth and trying to make some porridge out of her soggy supply of oats, but the idea of fire makes me flinch. I think about staying the night here, on her bed of straw, under a roof, but I'm squeamish about that too. None of the villagers were shriven before they died; they might walk at night, and if they do I don't want to be here to see them.

So I go back to the field. I eat until I'm full, which isn't very much because I've been ill, but it feels good anyway. When it gets dark I wrap myself in my new clothes and lie looking up at the stars. I try to sleep, but I can't. For the first time I realise how used I've got to the sounds of hundreds of kids, all murmuring or crying or kicking in their sleep. Now I'm alone. I'm tiny and insignificant and the stars are staring at me. If I died now no one would know, ever. My heart stutters and pounds in my chest and I sit up, panicking, breathless. I don't lie down again, but in the end I fall asleep just before dawn, leaning against a tree.

In the morning I sleep late. When I wake up the sun's

over the trees, shining into my face. I leap to my feet automatically, worried that the others will leave me behind; then I relax, because I've already been left behind, and it doesn't matter what time I wake up. It gives me an odd, painful feeling of relief.

I eat a dried apple and a strip of smoked fish, drink from the stream, fill my gourd with water and splash my face. It strikes me that I used to make the triple sign of the cross every morning when I dressed, but I haven't done it for days and I don't do it today either. I tie the food into a bundle with the mantle – it's already too warm to wear more than a shirt and cotte – and find a branch to lean on as I walk, and then I'm ready to go. I don't even glance at the path the others took, south, across the stream; I set my face in the other direction and walk without looking back.

I get tired sooner than I should. I think it's because I've been ill, but my ankle hurts too, and my head. At first I try to go on. Then I realise there's no reason to hurry. It's afternoon, hot and quiet and lonely, and I sit down at the edge of the path and let myself drift. I've got food for several days; then, at Trier, I can beg or run errands or sell the mantle I took . . . It's shocking, somehow, to realise that I'll almost certainly get home before St John's Day. It must be less than two months since I left.

When I feel better I stand up again, but my ankle's stiffened and I hear myself yelp when I try to take a step. I'm glad I've got my stick. I lean on it and hobble forward. I should find somewhere to sleep – somewhere away from the path, in case there are bandits or thieves. My eyes play tricks on me, telling me I'm going round in circles, but I know it's only because I've been here before, walking in the other direction. Sooner or later I'll come to the place where we slept the night Lena disappeared. I can sleep there, out of sight, hidden by the undergrowth. Or –

And just as I think of it, and look up the hill through the trees, I can see it: the hermitage, only just visible from this angle but clear enough when you know it's there. With any luck it still has a pile of wood, ready chopped, and a candle, and what's more it has a roof and walls. I struggle up the hill, going too fast from impatience and fatigue. I have to stop and catch my breath and the forest rustles around me. I'm sure I can feel someone watching me, that tingle on the back of my neck . . . but there's nothing, no one. No one human, anyway.

When I finally get to the doorway the door has sagged even more and it takes all my strength to get it open far enough for me to go in. I step into the cool darkness, smelling the damp, the scent of old stone and prayer. Something else too, but I ignore it. This is where Nick prayed, where Sophie and I –

No. I dig my fingernails into my palms and stay still, riding out the pain. I'm on my own now. I refuse to let myself feel anything.

My eyes adjust to the darkness. There's a dim pile of something in front of the altar, and for a second I think Sophie and I must have forgotten our clothes when we left. That's stupid, of course. But . . . I step forward, a nasty idea uncoiling in my gut like a worm. Please, no, not another body, please . . .

It isn't a body. I crouch and look more closely, my heart skittering with relief. Clothes. Just clothes. A dress – I think – of grimy linsey-woolsey, a cyclas and a linen shift, in a tangled puddle on the floor. As if someone undressed in front of the altar, pulling each layer off over her head before she dropped it casually on the ground. Or . . . no, not quite. My mind slides uncomfortably. As if . . .

There are flowers on the altar. That's the other smell: the perfume of flowers, suddenly so strong that I wonder how I didn't recognise it immediately. It's cloying, so pure I can almost taste it, like damask water or orange-flower oil, imported from somewhere rich and far away. The flowers on the altar are only speedwell, tiny wilting eyes that can't hold my gaze, but I can definitely smell roses. I step over the clothes and go right up to the altar, partly to look more closely at the flowers and partly because I'm dizzy and I need to lean on something. I lean forward and take a deep breath. Just speedwell, smelling of grass and wilted weeds. That's not where the smell's coming from.

I look down and on top of the clothes is a clumsy, cobbled-together wreath of wild flowers; but no roses.

And suddenly I know what's bothering me about the clothes. It's the way that the cyclas is on top, the shift on the bottom. When I take my clothes off, I drop my cotte first, *then* my shirt . . . It's not as if whoever-it-was undressed; more as if she disappeared out of her clothes, leaving them to collapse, empty, on their own . . . As if she ascended cleanly into heaven and left nothing but what she was wearing, and a wreath of flowers dropping to the ground a fraction of a second later.

I go down on my knees and reach for the dress, dragging it towards me, until I can smell the grime, and dust, and a familiar privy-and-sweat scent. There's a smear of bonfire ash on the back, a mucky hand-print, a tallow stain that I've seen a hundred times before. I feel a kind of sob rising in my throat, and even though I'm on my own I try to swallow it.

Lena. They're her clothes. So where is she? And what

the hell was she doing? Did she just *dissolve* in the middle of a prayer? Did she strip, deliberately, in the presence of God? Or did someone else leave her clothes here, posing them in a grubby wreath of fabric, laying the flowers carefully on top?

If it's a miracle, it's a very cruel one. I raise my head and stare at the light coming in over the altar. The cross on it is empty; there's no one to ask.

If I'd only come up here first thing, when I found out she'd run off . . .

The scent of roses comes back stronger than ever; and then it's gone and I don't know whether I really smelt it at all.

I hold the dress in my arms and breathe into the material. I stay like that, curled up, hugging Lena's clothes, until it gets dark. Then I stretch out and lean my head on them, and fall asleep in the smell of home.

XVIII

I walk and walk, day after day, until I have to wrap a rag tightly round my ankle every morning, and by the afternoon I have to loosen it because of the new swelling. I have blisters in the fold of skin between my thumb and my palm from leaning on my stick. I strip to wash in a stream one day and I'm shocked by the way my ribs stick out. When I catch my reflection in a pond later that afternoon I don't realise immediately that the tangled darkness falling over my face is my hair.

I get lost a couple of times, but in the end I realise and make my way back to the right path. Even where there wasn't a path before, you can still spot the way we took from the broken branches and bits of debris. I catch myself shaking my head at how much rubbish we managed to throw away, when we didn't even have anything to eat. But at least it makes it easier: as if we laid this trail on purpose.

Maybe we did. Maybe we always knew we'd be back.

I get into a kind of rhythm, waking at dawn and stopping in the middle of the afternoon. Then I lie in a kind of dream, without thoughts, watching the sun go down and the sky darken. The weather stays fine, and I'm grateful for that.

I lose track of time. After a while I run out of words, even in my head. Days go by. I look at the food I've got left and eat smaller portions. I drink at every stream I pass, and play games when I piss, like a little kid: picking out leaves and spots of sunlight in the undergrowth, trying to improve my aim. My ankle gets more and more painful until the whole of my calf is sore and tender to the touch, but there's something clean about the pain because it fills my head and stops me thinking. I get along all right, as long as I lean on my stick.

At Trier I stay the night in a pilgrim hostel. The monks are suspicious at first, because I look like a beggar, but I write my name and read it back in a passable imitation of my father's voice and they soften and let me in. I'm surprised by the way the pilgrims look at me without contempt, as if I'm grown-up. At dinner someone asks me where I've come from and I say, 'Cologne,' and he nods, impressed. Most people from Cologne, he says, are too snotty about having the Three Kings to bother coming to Trier to look at the Holy Nail. As if the Magi were more important than Christ our Lord! He hits his knife on the table to emphasise his point, and starts to tell me how, in his humble opinion, the Holy Nail outranks the Three Kings and both of them outrank St James, and going to Santiago is nonsense, the only better place than Trier is Jerusalem . . . Then he asks me magnanimously what I thought of St Andrew's Holy Sandal. I tell him I haven't seen it, and I don't intend to, and he shuts up. At night I'm supposed to share a bed with three stinking men, but it's too soft. I lie down on the floor, wrapped in my cloak, and fall asleep there.

When I leave Trier the next morning I fall in with a another group of pilgrims who are going to Cologne.

They invite me to walk with them, because there's safety in numbers, and I can't think of any reason to say no. I don't talk to them much but they don't seem to mind, and a couple of them are old or ill so it's not too hard to keep up. They share their food with me; I don't know why, but I take it anyway. We pass through a little village that looks familiar, and I realise it's the village where Margareta and the others joined us. We hear the priest say Mass, and he gives me a long look as if he's trying to remember where he's seen me before. Later he asks us for news — *the news in Trier*, he says, as if he can't bear to mention the crusade by name. I stay silent, but no one notices. Someone tells him there's none, or only the usual stuff, and he goes away, his shoulders sagging. The village is very quiet. I don't see any kids.

And slowly, day by day, we get closer to Cologne. The boundaries of the world shrink back to where they were a month ago. One afternoon I see the city walls and St Severinus' Gate looming above us, and I wait for the surge of warmth and relief at finally coming home. It doesn't come. It's just Cologne; it's just the place I left. When the guards at the gate ask us our business, I don't bother to say who I am; I let them think I'm a pilgrim like the others.

It's only once we're through the gate, and the air is thick with the smell of the city, that I stop and look around. Everything seems unreal, too vivid, like a dream that's suddenly solidified. Nothing's changed. It's as if I haven't been away at all. I stop and let the others go ahead. One of them — a witty, fiery widow, about Lena's age — hesitates and looks back at me, but I ignore her. I take a deep breath, and memory rises like a tide. The pain in my ankle flashes suddenly into the foreground of my mind and I crouch, hissing through my teeth and squeezing the muscle with both hands to dull the ache. My hair falls into my eyes and I smell the grime and sweat in it. It hardly looks red any more. My nails are black, and my groin crawls and itches. I shut my eyes and for the first time it hits me: I'm home. And I don't want to be.

I can't bear it. I don't want to go back to my father. I *can't* . . . But now there's nowhere else to go.

I pick up my stick and trudge towards my father's house.

It's chance, that's all, that I go past the Bird and Tree; and chance, too, that one of the pilgrims waves at me through the doorway, beckoning me in. I hesitate for a moment, but it's before Nones and there's no reason to go straight home. I make myself smile and nod, and then I'm inside, leaning my staff against the wall, making my way through the press of people to sit down with my new companions. I struggle to remember their names and then give up. They don't really matter, anyway. Someone pats me on the back, says, 'We made it! Time for a drink, before we go and pay our respects to the old cittern-heads in the cathedral.' It takes me a moment to realise he means the Three Kings. Someone else puts a tankard of ale on the trestle in front of me. I thank him awkwardly. But no one's listening to anyone else. Someone starts singing; it could be a psalm or a ballad, I can't tell which.

I sit and drink, not joining in, feeling like a stranger. I let my eyes wander round the room. I watch the hunched shapes blocking the light and smell the stale, on-the-road scent that we all share. My gaze slides over the bench where I sat the day I brought Nick here. It seems so long ago. It's like being an old man coming back to the scene of his youth – except that I don't feel anything: no nostalgia, no pain. My mind remembers Nick but my heart doesn't. My heart doesn't seem to remember anything at all.

Until I glance at a man slumped in the corner of the room, head against the wall, and my pulse sends a shock of heat all the way to the tips of my fingers.

It's Nick's father.

I duck my head in a panicky, instinctive move that threatens to spill my ale. I don't know why I'm so scared that he'll recognise me. The shock brings bile into the back of my throat, and there's a burning, acid sensation in my gut. I try to drink casually, but I can't swallow properly with my head at this angle and I feel a trickle of moisture seep from the corner of my mouth. *Please, don't let him see me. Please . . .*

I wait until my heartbeat slows, and then – keeping my head lowered to hide my face – I look over at him again. Yes. It's Nick's father. I knew – didn't I? – that he didn't come with us when we left Cologne, but I never wondered where he was, or what he was doing. I never asked, never wondered how Nick felt . . . And all the time he was here – doing what? Getting fat on Nick's reputation? I blink, staring through a curtain of grimy hair, struggling to work it out. Why didn't he come with Nick? Didn't he love him enough? How *could* he stay here when he knew his son was going off to Jerusalem, facing every possible danger, leading the world to salvation? I don't understand. How *could* he?

Poor Nick.

I hold on to the edge of the tabletop, trying to keep the feelings at bay. I count my fingers and the planks in the trestle and the wet rings of ale. I listen, anchoring myself in the noise of the tavern and, beyond that, the rest of the city.

And . . . the tavern doesn't sound quite right. It sounds . . . unbalanced, too quiet. Or . . . there's something's missing. But more than that. It sounds . . . angry. Like a hive before it swarms, or the distant grumble of thunder. The noise of misery, building up, collecting in the walls, eating through the beams.

I draw a face on the table, slowly, trying to think. And I remember that I didn't see a single child all the way from St Severinus' Gate to the Bird and Tree.

Then I *want* Nick's father to see me.

I stand up, pick up my ale, and stride over to stand in front of him. I wait there, unmoving, until someone looks up and shifts aside for me to sit down. I down the ale and slam the tankard loudly on the table, so that Nick's father jerks and opens his eyes. I pitch my voice so that it cuts clearly through the noise, and I say, 'Reckon you owe me a drink, mate.'

The man next to me swaps looks with his friend. They think they can hear a fight on its way.

I say, 'Hey. You. Nick's father. Whatever your name is. What is it? *Old* Nick?'

He frowns, blinks, and drags himself into a more upright position. He's got fatter, but up close he looks ill. His eyes are bloodshot, and a muscle in his cheek twitches. He says, 'Who the hell are –'

'I bought you a drink,' I say. 'An ale for an ale. That's the rule. You owe me.'

'I don't know who you are. Go scrape.'

'I bought drinks for you and your son, the day he preached at the cathedral. Don't you remember? The day before he left. The day –'

'All right, all right –' Suddenly he's fumbling for his purse, his jaw clenched. 'You're drunk, sonny, and I don't know what you're talking about, but –'

'Really?' I lean towards him, but I don't lower my voice. 'You don't remember Nick, your son? Or are you saying he's not your son? Was he someone else's little get that you thought you'd make some alms out of?'

Heads are turning now. Nick's father starts to stand up, spilling a couple of coins from a shaking hand. 'You've got the wrong man. I don't know what you're talking about. I'm just a pilgrim, like you.'

'Well, that's funny, because I'm not a pilgrim. I'm a crusader. If I hadn't got ill, I'd still be on my way to the Holy Land. With *your son*.'

Someone says, behind my back, 'Jesus Christ. He's one of the lost kids . . . he's come back . . .' and someone echoes, 'The lost kids . . . so where are the others?'

Nick's father steps awkwardly round the end of the trestle. He gives a swift, furtive glance at the doorway, then keeps his eyes lowered. He mutters, 'Don't get carried away, sonny . . . Let's talk about this somewhere else. Somewhere quiet. Please don't – look, I'll make it worth your while . . .'

I open my mouth to speak but a woman grabs my sleeve. Her eyes are wide and wet. 'You're one of the lost children? My little girl . . . Where are they? Are they coming home? What's happening to them?'

Other voices join in, other hands pull at me, trying to get my attention. I grit my teeth and shake them off. This isn't what I wanted. I say, 'Some of them are still walking. Some of them died. Lots of them.'

'Who? Which ones?' Then they're all talking at once, trying to catch my eye. 'My Alke, is she – ?' 'My Freddie

266

and Elbel, twins, you couldn't miss them –' 'Sighard, a big strong boy, with a birthmark –' 'Ytel, he's nearly twenty but he still acts like a child, playing silly jokes –'

'I don't know – I *don't know*!' I shout, and slowly the noise dies to a simmer. I point at Nick's father. 'Ask *him*. It's his son who took us away. And he's been getting rich on the proceeds, I bet. Look at him. A fat mitching rat with a tankard of ale. Just sitting there, while . . .' My voice creaks and wavers, and I have to swallow. I step sideways, so that Nick's father and I are nose to nose. 'Tell them who you are. Admit it. You brought Nick here so that he could take away their kids.'

'No,' he says. 'No, I didn't. That's not me. That's not me –' He reaches out, a flabby, pleading hand dabbing my shoulder. 'Who is this Nick anyway? I've only been here a day . . .'

If he'd been lucky, it might have worked. But someone calls out, 'Right. You weren't here scrounging drinks yesterday morning, then? You lying shack-rag!'

'Yeah, scrounging drinks because you had to give all your money to your God-touched son!'

Someone grabs him by his arm. Even now, he could probably brazen it out, but he gives a gulp of cowardice and panic, twists away and tries to bolt. Before he's taken a stride he's surrounded. A woman's voice rises above the general noise: she shouts, 'If my Ytel's *dead* – you'll pay for it, I swear you'll – you lying, cheating *skite*!'

'Dead or not,' I hear myself say, 'you'll probably never see him again.'

She looks round at me, her mouth opening, as if I'm God and every word I say is true. Her face crumples. She makes a noise like someone treading on a pig's bladder: half squeak, half sigh. Then she launches herself at

Nick's father, clawing at his eyes, his hair, his ears, anything she can get hold of. 'You evil, you evil, *evil* man, you *evil* –'

I stand and watch, my heart racing. Someone will pull her away from him any moment now. He's shielding his head with his arms, twisting sideways to protect himself, making animal noises of pain and protest. But no one moves, except to hem him in. More words rise around me like debris on a flood: *evil, evil . . . took my son – took my sister's children – my apprentices – never see my Alke again – who's going to look after me when I get old?*

And then someone says, 'We should hang him, the skit-brained waster . . .'

Nick's father lifts his head, his eyes blank with fear, and looks straight at me. I stare back, trying to work out where I've seen that look before.

'Yes! Then no one will steal our kids again in a hurry.'

'Yeah. He deserves it.'

'Yeah, string him up –'

On Nick's face. Of course. The expression Nick had when he was seeing God, helpless in God's hands . . .

I say, 'Wait. Stop. I didn't mean –' These are grown-ups; they'll listen. They're not like kids. '*Wait*.'

'Move aside, mate.' A man elbows me to one side, without malice, and says to someone else, 'Get some rope.'

I stagger and try to push back, fighting to get into the heart of the mob so that they'll listen. This isn't what I wanted – I wanted to humiliate Nick's father, hurt him, make him sorry – but not *kill* him . . . 'Maybe – hey! I might be wrong, it might not be – please, wait –'

Someone hits me across the face with their forearm. I reel back, my face on fire, and feel a trickle of blood ooze from one nostril. A woman gives me a sympathetic look and puts her arm round me, steering me to the nearest bench. 'Careful, love. You just sit here and stop getting in the way.'

I twist, grabbing her shoulders. 'But they're going to – they can't – please, help me stop them –'

'It's all right, love.' She pushes me on to the bench. She's surprisingly strong. 'Let the grown-ups sort him out. Don't you worry, lovey. You just sit there until the bleeding stops, and then go home to your mamma and papa.'

There's no time to answer. They're taking Nick's father outside, through the passageway into the stable-yard. I get up and run after them. I can't let this happen. They're *grown-ups*, for God's sake! Why won't they listen? I stop in the doorway, shaking. The knot of people around Nick's father is too thick, too frenzied, for me to have any hope of getting their attention. And there's a tree by the wall – scrawny and stunted, but strong enough to serve as a makeshift gibbet.

Someone shouts, 'This is for our kids, you thieving skite!'

'And tell the Devil to expect your son!'

Nick's father is begging, sobbing, flailing at the hands holding him. He ought to be praying. Someone ought to get him a priest. I say, under my breath, 'Dear God, help him, help him . . .' and I don't know if I'm praying for his soul or his life.

Someone comes out of the stable with a rope. There are so many people surrounding Nick's father that I can't see how they'll manage to tie it round his neck. But somehow they do. He starts to scream, hoarse and high, like a stuck pig. Then there's a sudden breathless gasp and he stops. A man throws the loose end over the nearest branch of the tree and hangs on to the end, dragging it over. Someone else joins him and together they haul downwards, like bell-ringers. Nick's father gurgles and sways on the tips of his toes, clutching at the rope round his neck. Everyone's shouting. I hear a woman's voice, unexpectedly sorrowful, among the curses: 'What kind of father *are* you?'

And then I close my eyes, and when I open them again Nick's father is a heavy, stained lump on the end of the rope, while the branch above him trembles from his last feeble spasms. A magpie struts along the wall, cocking its head, watching him with interest. His body has purged itself: the dust beneath him is wet, and his hose sag darkly at the back. Someone's tied the rope to a rail. It creaks as the body swings; then there's no sound but the last dregs from his bladder, dripping into silence.

I step aside from the doorway while the mob disperses. Some of them go past me back into the tavern; some hurry out through the side gate of the yard, suddenly subdued. After a long time I'm the only person in the yard. The magpie flicks its tail and hops closer to the knot of the rope, waiting for me to leave.

I walk slowly forward, until his stench catches in my throat and I see the bloody clouds in the whites of his eyes. I say, 'You stupid man. Why didn't you go with Nick?'

The magpie looks at me, steadily, its head on one side.

'You stupid, stupid . . . he's your *son*. Why did you let him – ?' A lump rises in my throat. 'You – damned, stinking –'

But I can't speak. I bite down on my lower lip, tasting the metallic crust of dried blood, but I can't stop the tears coming. I can't help it. I lean forward, my hands on my knees, like an exhausted messenger, and start to cry.

I'm crying because that body, swinging there, should be Nick. They only hanged him because Nick wasn't here . . . And I wish it *had* been Nick. Because he made me leave Lena behind, when I could have found her; because of the village he burnt, the fires in his eyes, the way he kissed me when I agreed not to leave him. Because –

Because I left him. Because he left me.

Because I know now what I could have had.

Someone – God, Nick – offered me the world. He offered me passion, and danger, and glory, and extraordinary love. And now I know . . . Somehow, without my even realising it, there must have been a moment when I chose something else.

PART V

The thief of man

XIX

You like to let us think you've finished with us. You're like a little kid playing with water: after the slosh, the big splash when you smack your palms down on the surface and send water flying everywhere . . . after that you like to wait, unmoving, for as long as it takes to settle down. You stay still until we think the storm's over. You wait until we think we can trust you again, until we think we know what's coming. You let us relax; or almost.

So you watch. You watch now. Slowly the world rolls and washes this way and that, each wave smaller than the last. The ripples subside, die away nearly, until they're just a kind of trembling, a faint quiver that no one except you would notice. We've been bracing ourselves, fighting to keep above water, fighting not to drown; but now – slowly – we find our feet again. You watch our lives re-form themselves from patches of colour, splinters, into something coherent: things that, after all, we can live in. They make sense again, just about. They shiver back into place, smoothing themselves out. They'd look solid to anyone but you. The world is steady again, so still and flat that we can forget you're there. And we do forget, slowly. *I* forget.

Almost.

*   *   *

And if you're watching me now, you can see that for a moment I'm at peace: that the noise and heat of the streets, the stink, the hectic jostling of the people . . . that all these drown out the murmur of unease in my head that's never quite gone away. You watch me lean my head against the stone doorway of a church and stare upwards, my eyes narrowed. The sky is blue, stained with smoke round the edges, focusing heat like a crucible. It's summer again. I cross my arms and let my skull empty itself of everything but the deep, hot blue.

The door creaks behind me. A hand slips into mine, and I look down. Rosa smiles up at me; or not exactly at me, but at the space behind my head, as if she's dazzled by the sunlight after being inside the church. She says, 'I've finished, Papa.'

'Sure? You can stay as long as you like. I don't mind waiting.'

She shakes her head gravely, as if there's only so much prayer it's sensible to do in a day. Then she says, 'Is it really where Jesus was born?'

It takes me a moment to work out what she's talking about. Then I say, 'No, sweetheart, but it looks the same inside. The lady who built this church wanted it to look like the church in the Holy Land where Jesus *was* born, that's all.'

Rosa thinks about this for a while, bending my fingers sideways as if she's forgotten that they're part of some-one else. She says, 'Would Jesus know the difference?'

'Yes,' I say. 'Bethlehem is in another country.'

'But he hasn't been to the Holy Land for ages and ages. Hundreds of years. He might not remember what it's like. If he came here, he might think this *was* Bethlehem. I mean, if someone just plonked him here without telling him.'

'I suspect that the weather's better in Bethlehem,' I say. 'Maybe not today, but . . .'

'All right. But suppose he didn't go outside?'

'Well.' I take a long breath. The smell of damp stone catches me unawares, sliding a cold fingertip over my brain. I shiver and step forward, trying to leave the memory behind. 'I think it's not *quite* the same as the real Church of the Nativity. I think it does look a bit different.'

'Then what's the point?'

I shrug, making a silly face at her, and pull her gently away from the doorway, into the sun.

'*I* don't remember where *I* was born. So Jesus —'

'Jesus is . . .' I try not to laugh. I say, 'I think Jesus is a bit different from you, Rosa. Maybe even a bit cleverer. If that's possible.'

She knows I'm teasing her, but she ignores it. 'Yes, but *no one* remembers where they were born. Do they? *You* don't either. Bet you.' She giggles when I don't answer, and adds, 'Anyway, he wasn't born in a church, he was born in a stable. Everyone knows that. So why didn't they build a stable?'

'I don't know.'

'What was I born in? Was I born at home?'

'I don't —' I stop. The noise and heat rise around me, but now the unease is stronger, irrational but insistent, running through the day like a current. I say, 'You'd better ask your mother about that.'

She rolls her eyes. 'She'll tell me to ask you. She always does. Whenever I ask anything.'

'Well, I . . .' I clear my throat. 'Let's go home, heartling. Come on.'

'But —'

I start to walk without answering, holding her hand so that she doesn't wander off. I pilot her carefully down the street, making a path between the people, shielding her with my body when a drunkard reels out of the tavern and staggers in our direction. People glance at me, their gazes lingering a little longer than they should, noticing how old I am, calculating; then they look at Rosa and smile. I wonder how long it'll be – how many more years of immigration, peasants and pilgrims and traders – before people stop looking at me like that, wondering if I was one of *them*, if I'm the one of *them* who came back, the nearly-only one . . . I squeeze Rosa's hand and she squeezes back without even noticing, gazing up at the rooftops through wisps of silvery-blonde hair.

Now we're at the corner where we turn down a quieter street, and I tug Rosa gently round, careful not to break her reverie. I feel a familiar, ludicrous surge of triumph that I've got her this far safe and sound. It's as if she senses what I'm thinking. She looks up at me and grins, and I feel the same grin – exactly the same – on my own face. It looks out of place on her: like it's too big for her mouth, something she'll grow into, like a hand-me-down shirt. It fills me with a secret, selfish kind of joy, that there's something of me in her. When Sophie sees Rosa grin like that she laughs, and says she'll stop doing it when she meets a boy she wants to impress. Once I asked how come Sophie married me, then, when, after all, it was *my* grin she was insulting? She told me the grin was neither here nor there, because what else was she supposed to do, with Rosa a babe-in-arms and nowhere else to go?

Then we looked at each other and stopped laughing, and I never said it again.

Rosa says, 'So where *was* I born?'

'You weren't born,' I say. 'You hatched from an egg. Your mother had to sit on you for a whole year before you pecked your way out.'

'*Really*, Papa.'

'No, you're right. *Really* you were born in a desert in Africa. Your mother was too ill to suckle you and so the lions hunted for food for you. We raised you on raw meat. After we brought you home you wouldn't sleep unless we roared.'

'*Really*.'

'On a ship,' I say. 'Your mother and I were coming back from England, sailing to Genoa, and there was a storm. The sea –' I pause to step over a puddle of slurry. 'The sea rose up like mountains and the mermaids sat on top of the waves and watched, like people in a gallery. And when you came out they sang.'

'Papa,' she says, warning me, and then ruins the effect by giving me my grin again.

'You were a gift,' I say. 'You dropped into our arms. It was like Jesus ascending into heaven, only the other way round.'

She's trying not to laugh. She raises her eyebrows at me, half amused, half stern, the way she'd look at an animal, something small and sweet and helpless. My heart twists painfully inside me and I look away.

'I don't know, Rosa,' I say. 'I wasn't there. Does it matter?'

The grin fades. She narrows her eyes and then looks sideways, as if she's thinking. She says, 'No-o . . .'

'I'm pretty sure you weren't born in a stable, though.' I try to laugh, but she doesn't seem to notice. 'Rosa . . .'

A pause. Somehow we're not holding hands any more. She brushes her hair out of her eyes, leaving a shadowy smear of something on her forehead. Her face is very serious.

Then she looks up and smiles.

'No, Papa,' she says. 'Don't worry. It doesn't matter.'

'I'm sorry,' I say. I don't know what I'm sorry for. Something cold strokes my back like a hand.

She shakes her head at me, smiling, and somehow it's as if she means it – really means it – and it *doesn't* matter. She says, 'Don't worry, Papa. I'll just ask Mother. Don't *worry*.'

'No, I mean –' I stop.

'Silly sausage,' she says, and laughs; and then runs ahead of me, racing for the house with the unicorn signboard, swinging herself round the doorpost and in, breaking into a tuneless, breathless kind of song. I see the edge of her skirt drag in the dirt and disappear through the doorway.

I stand still, feeling something familiar raise its head in my gut: something old and deep-buried, but never quite forgotten.

I lift my head and stare at the sky, watching for the slightest hint of movement, the smallest ripple. But there's nothing: only blue, and the impersonal, bewitching heat.

A clear sky.

At that moment, you're coming into the city.

You're one of a crowd: unremarkable, underfed, with a staff and a gourd and a burden on your back. You walk lightly – as if you're not quite sure that the ground beneath you is solid – without meeting anyone's gaze. Only your hands, your forehead and the expression in your eyes would give you away, and no one looks at you for long enough to notice those. Most people don't even seem to realise you're there. But there's a man ahead of you who glances over his shoulder, and even though his gaze doesn't linger, you smile as if you know him. It's hard to tell if he's with you or not. He's richly dressed, with a foreign air that's hard to place, and he doesn't look like your companion; but you walk together into the city and when he turns into a side street you follow him, a pace or two behind. He rolls one shoulder uneasily, as if he's trying to dislodge a fly, but after that first glance he doesn't look back.

You follow him all that day: from tavern to cathedral to another tavern, and between times as he walks the streets in a steady, relentless pace that might be purposeful or, on the other hand, might not. He keeps his cloak on even though it's a hot day, and grips it close across his chest with one hand. When people meet his eyes he holds their gaze, and he's never the first to look away. He visits church after church, like a man with an obsession, although he never crosses himself or kneels. Later, just before the curfew, he goes to an inn and gets silently drunk on his own. You sit opposite him, but neither of you speaks, and he stares straight through you like a man not talking to his wife. He drinks until his eyes are blank and soft, and the older servingwoman asks him maternally if he wants a bed for the night. Then he glances up, tells her that if she means *her* bed, yes, he'd like that – as long as she's not in it . . . The people next to him guffaw, and when the woman flounces off, her face the colour of blood, he smiles at them and winks. The soft look has gone from his face, like a cloud that's been burnt off by the sun, and now he's witty and crude and loud, until everyone in the tavern is chuckling and offering him another drink. He accepts gracefully. Suddenly he's the centre of attention; but he doesn't tell anyone his name, or where he's from, even though they ask. Instead he shows a magnanimous, casual interest in this little northern city – a charming place in its own way – and listens patiently to stories of pilgrims and crusades and stolen children. He yawns a little, but politely, behind his hand, and now one of the old men – Matthias, sir, your servant – has got into his stride and won't be stopped. So he sits still, rolling his head on his neck as if he's relieving an old pain, and puts up with the onslaught of information as old Matthias holds forth: ten years ago or more, God's truth, there wasn't a single child left – hey, mate, don't interrupt, all right, hardly *any* children left, only the ones that got locked up, the ones with sensible parents – like a curse, it was, and not one of them came back, either – hey, will you just let me . . . ! Oh, if you must be pernickety . . . well, yes, sir, he's right, *one* came back, Johannes the goldsmith's boy, the redhead, and wasn't *that* a shock for old Johannes, especially when the girl turned up too! First married apprentice in *that* household, I can tell you . . . but he's settled down, the lad, taken over the business now that old Johannes is . . . What was I saying? The curse, or crusade – honestly, call it what you will but crusade my left *buttock* – that was a while ago now . . .

The stranger smiles, nods, leans back in his chair and yawns. No one notices that he's stopped drinking; that ever since someone mentioned the crusade not a single drop of ale has passed his lips. He asks idly, 'So what became of the – was there a – what would you call it? – a prophet? The leader?' He shrugs, one-shouldered. 'Some nobleman's son, maybe? A prodigy of learning?'

There's a general laugh, and he ducks his head to sip his beer.

'A prodigy?' Matthias takes a gulp of his own drink, swilling it round his mouth. 'Ha. Not likely. Prodigy my armpit. He was only a peasant kid.'

'He must have had *something*,' the stranger says pensively. 'For all those children to follow him. Apprentices and grown men and women too, I heard.' People swap looks, and he laughs with an easy amusement. 'Clearly you don't think so . . . What did he do then? Promise them a share of the spoils? Or just make a pact with the Devil?'

Suddenly there's a kind of unease in the air. Someone says, 'Might've done, for all that.'

'Black magic,' an old woman says. 'Must've been. My Ytel . . .'

'Black magic?' the stranger says. 'Do you really think so?'

'Yes, I do,' she says, wiping her mouth. 'That little shifter wanted to lead them to hell.'

'Oh,' the stranger says lightly. 'But your . . . your Ytel, did you say . . . ? Why did you let him go then?'

Silence.

He smiles, as if he hasn't noticed the new feeling in the air. He shakes his head, still smiling, and brushes the rim of his cup with a finger. 'If you knew he was a black magician, this boy . . . maybe you should have stopped your Ytel going . . .'

Another pause. Someone says, 'Are you saying we didn't love our kids? Because *if that's what you're saying –*'

The stranger stretches his legs out in front of him, crossing them at the ankle. The smile is still hovering at the corners of his mouth. 'It was only a question.'

'Well, it's a question you better not ask again, mate, not if you want to walk out of here on your own two feet.'

A slow nod, as if he's considering this. 'So . . . what happened to this boy then, in the end? Or . . . his mother or father . . . ? If he had anyone . . . but I suppose they would have gone with him, on the crusade.'

But no one replies. When the silence goes on the stranger looks round, eyebrows raised, faintly mocking. 'Don't you know? What, no ideas at all?'

The woman who spoke before opens her mouth suddenly, a bleak, harsh look on her face, but old Matthias sees and leans across her, sputtering beer over the table. 'He did, he had a father, if I remember rightly, but no one knows what happened to him. Probably . . . he probably, yes, you're right, probably went with him . . .'

''S'right,' someone else says. 'Probably went with the others. Probably.'

'And . . . suppose he didn't . . . ?' The stranger looks up at the ceiling, following the smoke stains with his eyes. 'Perhaps he stayed here, in Cologne. Or went back to wherever they came from . . . ?'

The cold, draughty silence rises again. At last Matthias says, 'Why're you so interested anyway?'

The stranger tilts his head to look at him. 'Just making conversation,' he says. 'I'm sorry, I'm foreign to these parts.'

'Well, look,' the man next to him says, twisting round to stare at him. 'Look, mate, just keep your nose out, all right? We don't have anything against you, but . . . this is, well, this is our kids we're talking about, and you don't get over it easily. So you'd better drop it, understand?'

'Perfectly. Thank you.' The stranger stands up at last,

stretching one arm behind his back as if it's stiff. 'You've been very hospitable. I'm sorry if I've offended you.'

No one meets his eyes; except you, of course, and he doesn't acknowledge your look even though it's full of compassion. Someone mutters, 'God speed,' and sudden loud conversations spring up everywhere, like weeds.

The stranger takes a last look around, his eyes moving over the faces like a man trying to read when he doesn't know how. Finally he does look at you, and his face wipes itself clean, his eyes clouding over. He moves towards the door.

Old Matthias follows him with his gaze, and tugs at his nose. Then he calls out, 'No hard feelings, sir. Just . . . no hard feelings.'

The stranger gives him a small smile over his shoulder. There's something unexpected about it, something childish.

'Where did you come from anyway? Look, let me buy you another drink. Tell us the news from . . . wherever it was.'

The smile broadens to something that isn't childish at all. 'The Holy Land,' the stranger says. 'No, thank you.'

'You're a crusader, sir? Really, I'd like to get you another –' But he's gone before Matthias can finish his sentence.

And then the stranger is on his own again, in the darkness outside the tavern, with only you for company. You lean against the wall next to him, not quite touching. You watch him and wait. He puts his hand up to cover his eyes and takes a deep breath. Then he laughs silently, uncontrollably, until he's leaning over and struggling for breath. He whispers, 'The Holy Land . . .'

You wait until he's serious again. Then he moves off

into the dark street, making for one of the taverns he was in earlier, where he'll be able to get a bed. You follow him, like a servant or a shadow, and now that he's drunk he almost believes you're there.

XX

The night comes and goes. Now it's early morning, and halfway across the city I'm alone in the workshop, working at a tiny intaglio. The sun is still too low to shine over the roofs, so even though it's going to be a clear summer day I'm working by the light of a candle. The intaglio is fiddly, careful work that makes my temples and forehead ache, but I like being alone, listening to the sounds of the street outside gradually building, feeling the last breaths of cool air wafting through the house. The apprentices are just starting to wake up; I can hear their grunts in the hall, their matter-of-fact curses as they drag themselves up off the floor. Sometimes Symon, the youngest, comes out with a particularly inventive obscenity, and because I'm on my own I can laugh quietly to myself.

When the church bells start to ring for Prime I put the intaglio down and stretch, staring into the candle flame. It's not just my head that hurts. My neck and back are sore, and even though I'm sitting down my ankle is burning. I hobbled down the stairs like an old man, hissing with pain. Normally in the summer, in dry weather, it's not too bad; but I still get nightmares, and I wake feeling as if I've been beaten up. Today it's especially bad, even though I don't remember what I was dreaming about. Sophie shook me awake, told me I was shouting, rolled over and went back to sleep. I lay there for a while and then remembered the intaglio. It's an order for a nobleman, a copy of one of the jewels in the Shrine of the Magi, and I was glad to get the commission. I pick it up and smile, running my fingernail over the pattern, because I never thought I'd be the sort of man to *want* to leave his wife in bed and go downstairs to work.

Slowly the noises of the household multiply and get louder. I bend over the intaglio again, trying to pretend for a little while longer that I'm the only one awake; but I hear Sophie's footsteps on the stairs and her voice next door, chivvying the apprentices and snapping back smart replies to their grumbling. Symon says clearly, 'Hell, the poor old skite, hair like the Devil and a wife to match,' and I laugh out loud. Sophie says, 'Which is why he's apprenticing a little demon like *you*, Symon,' and adds, 'and if you want breakfast at all today you'd better keep a civil tongue in your head.' But she's trying not to laugh, because Symon's her favourite as well as mine. Then a door bangs, and another. I concentrate on the gem in front of me, comparing it to the drawing, wondering if I've overdone the muscles on one of the figures. When I look up Sophie is leaning over the table with a cup of milk and an apple and bit of salted herring. I roll my eyes at her and she smiles and says, 'I know, I know. Breakfast is for children and invalids. So don't eat it.'

'I won't.' I reach for the apple and say, with my mouth full, 'Where's Rosa?'

'In the solar, with your father.'

I nod and take another bite, but I'm not hungry any more. I remember now: my dream – my nightmare – was about Rosa and my father. I chew slowly and the apple tastes of last autumn, dusty and old.

'Are you all right?' Sophie picks up the intaglio and turns it this way and that, as if she's not really expecting me to answer. 'I'm sorry I woke you.'

'Yes. Don't be. I was –' I stop and shrug. 'It's good to do some work before the others are in here, getting in my way.'

'You look like death. Or nearly,' she adds, still playing casually with the gem. 'Like the onset of leprosy. Or a man about to be hanged.'

I see my hands clench and tremble and I slide them under the table, out of sight. We've all seen men hanged; I don't know why the thought of it still makes me flinch. I say, too strongly, 'I'm fine.'

'It was Rosa, wasn't it? I've *told* her not to ask questions all the time. I don't know where she gets it –'

'No, it wasn't Rosa.' I take the intaglio out of her hand and hold it to the flame, checking the depth of the engraving. 'Thank you for the food.'

She watches, her face frowning and unexpectedly beautiful, lit on one side by the candle and on the other by the light from the windows, split between fire and sky . . . 'I want you to be happy,' she says. 'I want you to be happy. Are you?'

I laugh, from surprise more than amusement, but when I look at her she's still watching me, waiting for a reply. 'Sophie . . . the apprentices'll be in here any moment. I should try to finish this before –'

'Do you dream about the crusade?'

I drop the gem on the top of the table and watch my

fingers scrabble for it. The blood rings in my ears. *The crusade*. It's dangerous to talk about it. When we were newly married we'd try, sometimes: but the memories are too sharp, slicing to the bone at the lightest touch. Now we know better, wrapping them in silence, keeping our secrets on high shelves, out of reach. It protects us both. 'Sophie . . .'

'You call out names in your sleep. Did you know? Lena, and Rosa, sometimes, but mostly it's –'

'*Yes*, I'm happy. Yes.' I manage to get hold of the intaglio, and squeeze it between my fingertips till I know it's stamping itself on my skin. *Set me as a seal upon your heart . . .*

She watches me and nods slowly. 'Good,' she says. 'I'm glad.' Then she brushes my face lightly with her fingertips, flicking my hair off my forehead, and goes, leaving me there on my own.

And in a way it's true. I look at the tiny figures in relief on the pad of my index finger, Venus enthroned, Mars in front of her . . . and this *is* happiness, of a kind: making something small and perfect, working quietly on my own. Or not happiness exactly, but something nearly as good. Nearly.

Set me as a seal upon your heart, as a seal upon thine arm, for love is strong as death . . .

I say, 'Stop it,' just as the door creaks and I hear footsteps behind me. *The coals thereof are coals of fire, which hath a most vehement flame . . .*

Symon's voice says, 'Talking to yourself, Master? First sign of madness, you know. Any moment now you'll be putting rushes in your hair and claiming to love your wife.'

It breaks the spell as completely as a dropped jug. I

snort, choking back a sudden laugh, and pretend it was a cough. 'Be quiet, Symon,' I say, without looking up. He mutters a penitent – if unconvincing – apology, because he doesn't realise I'm only just managing to keep a straight face.

And then the workshop is full of people, the other apprentices getting the furnace going, the journeymen scratching and burping and asking not-quite-impertinent questions about whose half-eaten apple is this? and what sissy is having his breakfast at *this* hour of the morning? I grit my teeth and try to assume an air of sombre authority, and I'm so, so glad I don't have time to think.

We work until dinner, and the noise and heat rise until by dinner-time we're all running with sweat and even I'm thankful to go into the hall to eat. It looks as if Rosa and Symon have fought again; she looks haughty and won't speak to him at first. But when Symon prods her and teases her and makes redhead jokes under his breath, glancing at me, she says loftily, 'Symon, that's my *father* you're insul—' and then bursts into giggles and hits him and forgets not to eat. I watch them covertly, half protective and half amused, until he catches my eye and gives me a sly, happy wink that makes him seem disconcertingly grown-up. My father would be furious if he were here; but I grin before I can stop myself, and have to cover my mouth with my hand. Sophie sees it and smiles at me, our eyes meeting across the table.

After dinner, while the apprentices are dismantling the trestle-board, the journeymen and I go back into the workshop and I watch the new man engrave a border on a plate. He seems nervous but today his work isn't too bad, and I let my thoughts drift. I'm standing at his shoulder, staring down at his hands, when Sophie says from behind me, 'Are you busy?'

I look round. 'Not more than usual . . . Why?'

She opens her mouth, closes it again, bites her lip, and finally beckons me over. There's nowhere to talk in private unless we go upstairs to the bedchamber, but she lowers her voice and pretends the journeymen can't hear. 'It's your father. He's . . . he'd like to see you.'

'Tell him I'm in the workshop.' I hear the dismissal in my voice and take a deep breath, because as soon as my father asks for me I start to turn into him. 'Can't you . . . Sophie, I'm working.'

'Yes, I know,' she says. 'But he wants to see you. Rosa took him his dinner and he started asking for you. You know what he's –'

'All right!' The new journeyman raises his head, looking round, surprised; I can tell the others are listening too, because they keep their heads studiously lowered and don't even glance at each other. I lower my voice. 'All right. Now?'

'I think it would be a good idea. Rosa . . . you know she can get upset . . .'

'Christ.' I catch the new journeyman's eye and stare back at him until he blinks, embarrassed. I wonder idly whether I should pretend that was a prayer, not a curse, but I decide it's not worth it. I say, 'I'll be back in a little while. If you want the furnace stoked while the apprentices are still in the hall, you can do it yourselves, all right? Give the little skites time to finish clearing up at least.' The others grin and nod, but there's too much understanding in their eyes and I can't bring myself to grin back.

I make my way upstairs, the old pain in my ankle

tightening like a hand. There's the sound of voices in the solar: my father's, raised to a kind of shout, and Rosa's. I stand outside the door for a moment, take a deep breath, and go in.

My father is in the corner of the room, the window on one side of him and Rosa on the other, hanging on to his arm. She's trying very hard not to cry. I hear her say, 'Grandpapa, it's me, it's Rosa,' but my father shouts, 'I want Rufus! Find *Rufus*!' without even looking at her.

I say, 'It's all right, Rosa. I'll talk to him.'

She makes a noise like a sob and runs past me and out of the door. I look at my father, despising myself for the sudden cold moisture in my palms and armpits.

My father says, 'That child needs some discipline. You spoil her. She's running wild.'

'Father . . .' I waver between resentment and relief that he's lucid. 'You wanted to see me.'

But the relief is short-lived. He frowns. 'I wanted to see Rufus.'

Oh God. I say, 'I *am* Rufus. I'm your son.'

'No . . . Rufus went away. He left us. He . . . one of the lost children . . .' The note of command has gone out of his voice. Now he's an old man. 'My Rufus, my only boy . . . left me . . .'

'I,' I say. 'Am. Rufus. Father, *I am –*'

'And Lena, little Lena, that was a mistake, she should never have . . . I'm sorry, I'm sorry, poor little Lena, it was, she was making so much *noise*, crying so loudly, and then I pushed her and she fell, never had good balance though, it wasn't my fault she fell . . . and then never the same, after that, stupid, not sure she ever even learnt to wipe her own arse . . . I'm sorry . . . Where's Lena? I want to see Lena.'

If he doesn't know who I am, I might as well leave him to it, wailing to an empty room. But something – not love, but not duty either – keeps me there. I say, 'Father. You know that Lena never came back. You know that. I came back, but she didn't. Remember?' But of course he doesn't remember.

'Never came back . . . like all of them. None of them came back. Not Lena, or Rufus . . .'

My mouth is so dry I walk over to the jug Rosa brought and pour myself a cup of ale. It tastes of nothing – of weak, fermented water.

'My Rufus, my boy . . . my son . . .'

I go to the window and stand there, pretending not to listen. I watch the reflection dancing in my cup, the wheel of light breaking up as my hand shakes. A snide, hostile voice in my head says: *O my son, my son! Would God I had died for thee, O my son, my son . . .* I say, 'Father. Was there anything you wanted in particular?'

'Never the same after he left. His mother died of grief . . .'

I turn, hearing the splash of ale as it slops out of the cup. 'My mother did *not* die of grief. She died of a swelling on her breast, as you well know. And what's more, it was after I came back, so if it *was* grief –' I can't help the flippant note that creeps into my voice – 'it was probably grief at my ruined marital prospects, or the fact that I came back at all . . .' But I run out of momentum. He's not listening anyway.

'All the city streets . . . no children anywhere . . . all the men who lost their sons, all the . . .' He starts to mumble.

I can't bear it. I down the rest of the ale in one go, set the cup neatly on the chest beside the window, and walk to the door.

'Don't go. Please don't go –' For the first time he's actually looking at me.

I waver, wanting to be anywhere else but here. Finally I say, as gently as I can manage, 'What brought this on, Father? Has something upset you?'

'Little Rosa. Don't let her out. Don't let her go.' He reaches out and grasps at the air, trying to drag me closer. I stare at him, trying to work out if he knows what he's saying. 'If you let her go, she won't come back. Like Lena, like my boy Rufus.'

The same unforgiving part of me wonders who he thinks Rosa is, if not my daughter, his granddaughter . . . I say, 'Yes, you're right. I'll lock her in the bedchamber.'

He nods, not hearing the sarcasm. 'Yes, good boy. Good boy. Always obedient. Should never have let you go.'

'You didn't let me go, Father.'

'You were a good boy.' He smiles up at me and the air in my lungs turns to something heavy, unbreathable. 'Rufus . . . Knew you'd come back in the end. My son. You were a good boy.'

I bite my lip. In a moment he'll change his mind, and tell me Rufus never came home. I stay where I am, waiting, telling myself it won't last.

'You weren't like most children. My son, I thought, my son, he's like me . . . a chip off the old block, they said in the workshop,' he says, and laughs. 'Quiet, though. Good boy. Shouldn't have let you go.'

It should hurt less, not more, when he knows who I am; but it doesn't. I concentrate on the noise coming from the men downstairs and the draught from the window. 'You didn't let me go. I *chose* to go.'

'That boy, preaching . . . outside, in the street . . .' He

blinks, screwing up his face, and his gaze wanders to the window. 'He's outside . . . Mustn't let Rosa out . . .'

'I've got work to do, Father. If you need anything else, call for Sophie, or –'

'But I *did*, I shouldn't have, I'm sorry, oh, I'm sorry . . .' His voice is suddenly so soft, so miserable that I turn instinctively to see if there's someone else in the room. I say, 'You did what?'

'Let you out. Little Rufus. Shouldn't have. Shouldn't have unlocked the door.'

I stand so still I feel invisible, weightless. I can't remember how to clear my throat or move my mouth.

'Left food. Left you some food, unlocked the door. Shouldn't have.'

'No,' I say. 'No, you didn't, Father. Lena did that.'

'Didn't mean to let her go too . . . but she was never, never . . . not like you. But how was I supposed to . . . ? If God's calling him, I thought, if God really *is* calling him . . .'

'Papa . . .' I clench the toes of my bad foot until the pain flares, sickening, reassuring. 'You didn't let me out. You locked me in, remember? You hit me and took me upstairs and . . .' I laugh, flatly. 'It wasn't *you* that let me out.'

'Didn't think you'd go, though, not really,' he says, staring at me with red-rimmed eyes. 'Good home, good prospects, I thought, no need for that nonsense . . . unless God really *is* –'

'This is utter nonsense – this is *complete b*—' I stop myself and grimace, digging my thumbnail into the gum above my front teeth. 'Please, Father, don't upset yourself. You didn't –'

'I suppose,' he says, very quietly, 'I suppose that means God *did* call you.'

I cover my face with my hands and laugh helplessly. Through it I can still hear my father talking, but I let the words blur and wash through me.

And by the time I'm listening again, he's saying, 'And he never came back, my son, my Rufus, now I'm all on my own . . .' and it's too late to ask him to say it one more time, tell me if he really *did* let me out, if he's sure, quite *sure* it was him, not Lena, not my mother, not Daniel or one of the journeymen . . . and too late to ask if, if he did, if, if, then . . .

I stare unseeingly at the window. My father, my papa . . . I want him back – his old self – so that I can hate him properly, so that I can be angry without this sickening uprush of pity, so that if he said *Good boy* I could let myself believe he meant it. But he's not coming back, is he? He's gone further than I ever did.

I leave the room and slam the door behind me.

I'm planning to go back to work, but my ankle hurts and I can't walk properly. I sit on the top stair and put my head in my hands. Oh, God . . . If he let me out . . . But I don't believe it. He's just confused, making things up. He couldn't have done. I shut my eyes and imagine myself locking Rosa up, then changing my mind and unlocking the door again . . . No. I'd keep her there for days, if I had to – for her own good, to stop her doing something stupid . . . I wouldn't *want* to, but I'd do it – the way I'd beat her for doing something dangerous, because I have to, because I know best . . . I would. Wouldn't I? My ribs contract, pushing the air out of me in a kind of sob. How *could* he? I'd rather die than let Rosa run away. I'd rather she hated me than ended up like me . . .

'Sweetheart, what – ? Was it bad?'

Sophie. I nod and shake my head at the same time, half laughing, without looking up.

'Should I go and keep an eye on him?'

'I don't know. No. He's not dangerous. Just don't let Rosa in there till he's a bit quieter.'

There's a silence that's filled with the rustling of Sophie's skirts as she sits down next to me. She says at last, 'Of all the men to lose their minds, I never thought your father would be the type.'

'He hasn't lost his mind. The leech said that metal-working has unbalanced his humours, that's all. It happens to us all in the end.'

'I hope it doesn't happen to you.'

'I have no doubt,' I say, through my hands, 'that I will end up *exactly* like my father.'

Sophie doesn't react to that. She says, 'What did he say?'

'He told me to lock Rosa up. Told me if I didn't, she'd never come back. The way Lena and Rufus never came back.'

'Oh,' she says. 'One of *those* days.'

There's a little pause, and then she starts to giggle. It's contagious. She leans her head on my shoulder, and I reach up and stroke her hair while we both shake with laughter. We sink deeper and deeper into hysteria, hold-ing hands and squeezing until the bones creak, letting the tears roll off our faces. After a while Rosa comes up the stairs and steps over us, rolling her eyes and trying not to let our giggles infect her. Sophie recovers for long enough to say, 'Rosa, I need your help with the herbs,' and then we both take a couple of deep breaths, wiping our cheeks.

'Yes,' Rosa says. 'Oh, there's a man in the shop, Papa, and he asked for you.'

'I'll go down and see him,' I say, and get to my feet. I feel so tired I could sleep standing up.

'Who is it?' Sophie says. 'The man for that cameo?'

'Intaglio,' I say. 'There's a difference. Possibly. Or someone from the cathedral, about the money they owe us. I don't know yet, do I?'

Rosa says, 'Symon said he thought he was an infidel.'

'I hope he said it quietly,' I say.

'Not quietly enough.' Rosa grins at me. 'But it's all right, the man only laughed. *I* think he's very handsome actually. Although he does have one of those little infidelly beards.'

Sophie catches my eye and says sternly, before I can take a breath, '*Infidelly* is not a word.'

Rosa opens her mouth and then closes it again. She looks up at me, and then reaches out and takes my arm. 'Come on, Papa. Otherwise Symon might say something else. He's so silly.' She leads me down the stairs, talking cheerfully, as if she's the parent and I'm the child.

In the workshop doorway I detach myself and go through. The journeymen are working quietly and the apprentices are bent earnestly over their tasks, pretending they're working quietly. As I go past, Symon whispers, 'Rufus the goldsmith's workshop! Roll up for the reddest gold in Cologne!' and I flick the back of his neck with my forefinger, hard. He yelps and jerks his head up, catches my eye and gives me a laboured, innocent smile. Then, when he thinks I'm not watching any more, he elbows the boy next to him in retaliation. It doesn't even occur to him that it was me.

There's a man standing by the trestle at the other end of the room, next to the door on to the street. I stand still for a moment, watching him. There's something odd about his shape, the way the material of his cloak falls around his shoulders. And he *might* be an infidel, for all that: richly dressed, with a kind of foreign air, skin that could be tanned or naturally dark, and, yes, a little infidelly beard . . . But that's all to the good: someone who knows that Cologne gold is the best, not someone who remembers you when you were in your swaddling clothes and still can't believe you're capable of making a decent fist of anything . . . I run over possibilities in my head: something small, probably, for him to take home – a ring, a clasp, a pendant . . .

He turns round, as if he feels my gaze on him, and says, 'Rufus?'

Something squirms inside me at the sound of his voice. There's something . . . Then Symon hisses, from the back of the shop, 'Look at the hair and take a guess!' and there's a muffled giggle.

I promise myself that I'll strangle him as soon as this man has gone. I say politely, 'Yes, that's right. I'm Rufus. At your service.'

'Oh. I . . .' He lowers his eyes, sweeping his boot across the rushes. 'I see.'

'I was redheaded from the moment I was born, so when it came to baptising me my father didn't have to think too hard . . . And it's still as apt as it ever was.' I smile, inviting him to laugh at me. If he thinks I'm a fool, he won't bargain as hard.

But he doesn't smile back. 'Yes,' he says. 'Yes, I can see that.'

There's a pause, and a trickle of unease runs down my back and blooms across my shoulder blades like cold sweat. I want to stare at him, but his gaze flicks back to my face and I glance away. I swallow and try to muster my politest manner. 'So . . .' I say. 'How can I help you?'

'You have a good workshop,' he says, and even though he doesn't have a foreign accent the words sound stilted. 'A good business. Someone told me that you worked on the shrine in the cathedral.'

I nod, strangely relieved, as if some danger has been averted. 'Yes. Nicholas of Verdun's workshop did most of it, I'm afraid, but the newer, less important work . . . the back panels, the Crucifixion, the . . . not that the Crucifixion isn't important, I mean the position on the shrine . . .'

He gives a small half-smile. 'I understand.'

'Yes. Well, that was ours. It was an honour. And good for business too.' I hear my voice – oily, smug and obsequious at the same time – and take a deep breath. 'Most of the shrine's thirty years old, of course. We were only adding the final touches.'

He nods, turning the corners of his mouth down in a wry, thoughtful way. He's got a scar across his cheek, running down like a crease from temple to jaw. My heart is beating too fast, far too fast: it must be the heat, the furnace and the hot sunlight that's slanting in from the street.

I say, 'Perhaps you'd like something of that kind? A reliquary or a crucifix?' I remember that he might well be an infidel and bite my tongue. Lord, what am I saying? 'Or I have a very fine intaglio, a copy of the Venus gem on the front side of the shrine – if you wanted something more . . . pagan . . .' Dear God. I look up at the ceiling and wish it would collapse, just to put me out of my misery.

'A good business,' he says again, as if it's a password. 'And a good household . . . children, I suppose . . .'

'Only one. A daughter.' I wriggle my shoulders subtly, trying to get rid of the tension. I'm not going to get a quick sale, so I might as well relax. I gesture at the stools next to the table. 'Please, sit down. Let me offer you a cup of wine.' Christ, I hate this. As soon as Symon's old enough I'll make him talk to the customers.

'Thank you.'

'And . . . perhaps you'd like to look at some examples of our work?'

'I . . . yes.' Slowly he sits down, without looking at me.

I call to Symon to bring two cups of wine. I fetch the smallest chest, put it on the table in front of me and unlock it, taking the pieces out one by one, waiting for the stranger to say something. My hands are shaking. It's the heat, the lack of sleep . . .

The jewels shine in a row. I put another one down, and another. They clink on the wood. Some of them are my own work, and some of them are my father's.

Silence. Surely he'll say something, even if it's only to scoff or ask me if we have anything better . . . I wait, staring so hard at the cameo in my hand that I could close my eyes and still see it. He has to say *something* . . .

He says, very softly, 'Rufus. Do you really not recognise me?'

I don't look up. 'No,' I say. 'No, I don't.'

'Don't you?'

I say, 'No, I'm afraid not,' and the cameo vibrates in my hand until it rattles against the edge of the table.

There's a pause, so that in the end I can't help myself and I look at him.

And in a sudden, sickening rush, I understand what my eyes were telling me, three different things at once: that it's Nick; that he's lost his left arm; and that a long time ago, a lifetime ago, he was so beautiful it's no wonder everyone believed he belonged to God.

XXI

I look down at the cameo I'm holding, the sardonyx, pale clasped hands on a deep red background, and I'm fourteen again, fourteen and in my father's workshop. A gust of fetid air blows in from the street and I'm back there, ten years ago, ripened with loneliness till I'm ready to drop into your hand, into Nick's . . .

But I'm here too – this is *my* workshop – I'm both at once, fourteen and twenty-four, split-souled, stretched so tightly in both directions that I can't move. Something vertiginous, something horrible, has happened to time, and I'm seeing double, myself and not myself, sick with being fourteen again, sick with *not* being fourteen. I hear someone make a kind of croak, and even though there aren't any words I know it's a prayer, a *please don't do this to me* kind of prayer, a *please just leave us alone* prayer, and if Nick had any decency he'd be praying the same thing, praying for you to have mercy and shove off out of our lives for ever.

Nick says, 'I'm sorry. Are you all right?'

I watch my fingers going whiter and whiter. There must be a process that will unclench them and put the clasp back on the table before I squeeze so hard it breaks, but I can't remember how to do it.

'I thought you'd recognise me. I know I've changed. But I thought – *you* . . .'

'What do you want, Nick?'

'I . . .' He leans away and then jolts back to upright, as if he's realised just in time that his stool doesn't have a back. 'Perhaps we should . . . talk somewhere else.'

Oh, God, the journeymen, the apprentices . . . I tell myself that if I can pull myself together now, hold myself together for a few minutes, just until we're out of hearing – if I can pretend everything's fine so that at least the apprentices don't realise what's going on – then everything will be all right. I don't believe it, but it helps. I put the cameo on the table, and once I've let go of it my hand is almost steady. I say, 'Yes, of course. Follow me.' I stand up and lead him to the back of the workshop and through the door. Symon is just coming through with two cups of wine; I pluck them fluently out of his hands, pass one to Nick and take a gulp out of the other. Symon blinks and starts to say something, but I've gone past before I have time to hear what it is. Nick says, 'Rufus –' but I ignore him too.

They've dismantled the table in the hall and stacked the benches on top of each other, so I look around foolishly for somewhere to sit. Somehow I don't want Nick to see me like this – unsure, unmanned – so without thinking I sit on the floor against the wall. I know immediately that it's wrong, but it's too late, because Nick smiles and sits beside me, bracing himself against the wall with his elbow as he sits down. I hear him take a sip of his wine, swallow, lick his lips. Every sound is so clear that I could be watching him.

He says, 'I am sorry. I didn't mean to surprise you.'

I wrap my fingers round my cup, wishing I'd got one of

the benches out and sat on it, like a grown-up. I say, 'Don't worry.'

'I was so glad to hear that you were here. Still alive, I mean, but . . . with a good business, a – family . . .'

There's something funny in his voice: I don't believe that he *is* glad. I say, 'And you. I never thought, I mean, I never expected to see you again . . .'

Silence.

I put my cup down on the rushes and press my hands into my face. My palms smell of metal. I say, 'For God's sake, Nick. Tell me what you want, and then get lost. Please.'

He shuffles against the wall, as if to ease an ache in his back. He says, 'Tell me what happened to my father.'

I slide my fingers down to my chin, feeling the grooves of teeth behind my closed mouth. I say, 'I don't . . .'

'I asked in the Bird and Tree. Well, everywhere. But in the Bird and Tree they knew. They wouldn't talk about it. He didn't go home, did he? He stayed here. And then something happened to him.'

'You can't believe everything you hear in the Bird and Tree.'

'I know. They told me I'd made a pact with the Devil. But . . . please. You do know. Please, Rufus, don't lie to me.'

I look at him and instantly wish I hadn't. I say, 'He was hanged.'

A pause so short I might have imagined it. 'For what?'

'For being your father.'

He breathes out. There's a strange sloppy rattling noise; I don't realise what it is until he puts his cup down on the floor and spreads his fingers, deliberately keeping his hand still. 'You saw it, didn't you.' It's not a question, so I don't answer.

Silence. Eventually he says, 'Did he make a good death? Did he have a priest?'

'No.' I lean my head against the wall, feeling the cool stone press on my skull. 'He died cursing and screaming.'

Nick nods very slowly. He says, 'He's probably in hell, then.'

'Probably,' I say.

'Oh well. I suppose that means I might see him again.' I turn to look at him, because it sounded like a joke, but his expression is completely serious. He rubs the side of his face with his hand, as if he's shielding his eyes from mine.

'I'm sorry,' I say, as if I want him to think I don't mean it.

'I always thought it would be me,' Nick says. 'I expected martyrdom for myself. Not for him.'

'It wasn't a martyrdom, for God's sake. It was pathetic.' I keep looking at him, hoping to see him wince. I don't know why I'm so desperate to hurt him. 'He would have said anything just to get away with his life. It wasn't *martyrdom*. He'd just got up a lot of people's noses.'

'Right.' Nick turns his head and stares back at me. 'Rufus . . .'

'What?'

'You're angry with me.' He reaches out, brushes the shoulder of my cotte with his fingertips. 'But it was *you* that broke your promise to *me*.'

I draw my knees up and clasp my hands round them. If I'm going to feel like a kid I might as well let myself sit like one. I say slowly, 'I was ill, Nick. I fell and hit my head the night you burnt the village. When I woke up, everyone had gone. I didn't break my promise.'

I'm not looking at him, but somehow I know he's

306

smiling. As if he *cares*, as if it still, ridiculously, after ten years, after so long, as if it – stupidly, foolishly – it still *matters* to him that I didn't leave him, and it was all a mistake, that I never quite failed in fidelity, that I never *quite* failed in love . . . I clear my throat, reach for my wine, and wonder if in the heat I've managed to get drunk without noticing.

I say, 'I went home. I looked for my aunt but I never found her. I never knew what happened to her. I came back to Cologne because there was nowhere else to go, and the day I got back they hanged your father in the stable-yard of the Bird and Tree. I came back to my father and he apprenticed me, the way he was always going to, and a year later Sophie turned up with a baby and we got married.'

'I'm sorry about your aunt.' He's a better liar than I am; he's almost convincing.

'And my father is losing his mind and tells me, every week or so, that his son Rufus was one of the lost children who never came home. And I'm getting to the stage where I believe him.'

Nick laughs; and somehow the laugh makes the pain go away, just a little. He says, 'Of course – I heard about your father. Johannes the goldsmith. He should've called you Johannes, after him. My Saint John . . .'

'I'm not your Saint John. I never was. Any more than you were Christ.'

'Yes. I know. I didn't mean . . .' He smiles at me sideways. 'I know. Sorry.' It disarms me, almost completely.

There's another silence, but this time it's full of the smell of the rushes on the floor and the quiet banter of the journeymen in the workshop. I let my head rest against the wall and shut my eyes.

'Thank you for telling me the truth,' Nick says.

'How did you find out I was here?'

'I asked,' Nick says, and when I turn to look at him he laughs again. 'I went round the taverns, and everywhere I went people bought me drinks and told me stories about myself. I asked the right questions, you see. Or rather, I didn't ask them. They thought I was a little bit bored, and the more I yawned the more they told me. The most exciting thing that's happened here for a generation, and the foreigner isn't even *interested* . . . They'd all join in, trying to outdo each other. And every so often they gave me information I didn't already know, like that Johannes the goldsmith's boy was the only one to come back, apart from that sluttish wife of his who turned up with a baby a year later . . .' He catches my eye again and shrugs. 'Their words.'

'You make it sound very easy. To make them tell you.'

'You don't beg your way from Cologne to the Holy Land without learning how to get what you want from people.'

I sit up straight. 'The *Holy Land*? You got to the –' The smell of herbs from the garden catches in my throat and makes me cough. I take a breath and cough again, for longer than I have to. 'You went to the Holy Land?'

'That was the idea, Rufus.'

'But – you *got* there? You really – ?' I squeeze my fingers together and dig my fingernails into the spaces between my knuckles: incredulous, and painfully, desperately jealous.

'Yes. I am a real, grown-up, cursing, hard-drinking, unshriven, mostly unrepentant, further-from-God-than-I've-ever-been, *proper* crusader.' Again the voice that says it's a joke, the face that says it isn't. He grimaces. 'Not to mention lacking the full complement of limbs.'

I glance at him and he smiles. I say, 'I'm sorry.'

'Don't be. You should have seen the man who did it.'

'Did you . . . kill him?' The words fill my mouth like a bung, hard to spit out. *Please, no. Not Nick. Please* . . .

He meets my eyes, as if he knows exactly what I'm thinking. He says, 'No. But it made a hell of a stain on his furcoat.'

The laughter cracks out of me, like something spilling from a broken crucible. I shake my head, feeling Nick's shoulder tremble beside me, both of us giggling like kids.

In the quiet afterwards, I say, 'What was it like?'

'Hot. A desert. Horrible. Like hell.' I wait for him to carry on, but he doesn't.

'And Jerusalem? *Jerusalem* must have been . . .'

'I never saw Jerusalem. I was at Acre. Then the siege of Damietta.'

'Where's that?'

'Nowhere near Jerusalem.'

'Oh.' I wait. There must be more. The *Holy Land*, for heaven's sake: there must be something he can say – about what it was like really to be there, the place where God lived for thirty years, or about the glory of fighting to get it back . . . I say, 'Did we win?'

'Well . . . Yes and no. We –' he flashes me a look and puts a tiny, mocking stress on the word – '*we* didn't get Jerusalem, which was what we wanted. Or at least, that was what everyone said we wanted. Damietta surrendered to us, but then we had to give it back. They promised us the True Cross in return, but when I left we still hadn't got it.'

'It sounds very . . . not how I imagined.'

'Oh, Rufus.' He laughs. 'I wish you'd been there.'

'So do I.' He flashes me an odd look – guarded, pleased,

calculating – and I pick up a couple of rush-stalks from the floor, folding them together and frowning hard as if I'm concentrating. I say, 'What about the others?'

'What others?'

'The –' I feel my finger stinging and realise I've cut myself on the edge of the rushes. 'The *others*, Nick. Remember? There were hundreds of us. Thousands.'

'Oh,' he says. 'Those others.' He watches the blood ooze out of my finger, bright and smooth as enamel.

'Yes, those others. What about them?'

'*What* about them?' He reaches over, takes a stalk of lavender out of my hand and crushes it until the scent rises. 'We went through Rome, you know. But I didn't see the Pope. Very disappointing.'

'Yes, but what about –'

There are voices from the garden, and the bang of a door. Rosa says, 'I know, but there's cuckoo spit all over the leaves, and I just think the rosemary is *nicer* . . .' Nick looks at me, enquiring, and I smile and shrug, momentarily distracted.

Then Sophie comes through the door with a basket full of herbs, saying over her shoulder, 'When I tell you to do something, young lady, you don't argue, understand? When you have a house of your own you don't have to grow any lavender at all –' She sees us, and stops. Her eyes go to Nick, and then to me. She says, 'I'm sorry, I thought you and your guest would be in the workshop.' She bobs a little curtsey.

I open my mouth, but before I have time to reply Nick says, 'It's all right, Sophie.'

'Thank you, sir,' she says, smiling, but her forehead creases as she looks from me to him, wondering why I've told him her name, and why we're sitting on the floor like kids. She looks back at him, then back at me. She's still staring at me when her expression changes, as if *I'm* the one she hasn't seen for ten years. She says, 'Dear Holy Mother of Jesus.'

Nick says, 'It's nice to see you.'

'*Nick*,' she says, and the flowers leaning out of her basket start to quiver. 'What do you want?'

'Nothing,' he says, and somehow from the smoothness of his voice I know it's a lie. He hasn't finished with us yet; there's still something he wants.

Rosa calls pensively through the doorway, 'Do really rich people sprinkle their floors with pepper?' She comes into the room and stands there, surprised, a small blue rosemary flower tucked jauntily behind her ear. She looks round at us, sensing that she's not quite welcome. 'Oops. Sorry.' It's not until Nick smiles at her that she remembers her manners. Then she drops a low, elegant curtsey and murmurs, 'Forgive my intrusion, Father.'

Sophie says, 'Rosa. Go upstairs.'

Not even Rosa would disobey her parents in public; but she doesn't exactly obey either. She curtseys again, very slowly, because she knows we won't tell her off for that – or not with Nick there, anyway. Then she glances at him, fluttering her eyelashes so subtly it's hard to be sure she's doing it on purpose.

Nick says, 'This must be your daughter.' He says it to Sophie, with a strange, pointed emphasis.

'Yes,' Sophie says.

'She's very beautiful.'

Rosa grins, and hurriedly turns it into something more demure. Her cheeks have gone very pink. I realise suddenly, clearly, that in five years she could marry someone Nick's age. I say, 'You heard your mother, Rosa.'

'Yes, Father,' she says, taking one small step.

Sophie says, '*Now*,' and her voice is so harsh that Rosa flinches. Then, before Rosa has time to respond, Sophie grabs her by the wrist and drags her to the stairs, so quickly Rosa catches her ankle on the bottom step and yelps. Sophie gives me a hot, helpless look over her shoulder; then they go up the stairs and out of sight.

I say, 'I'm sorry. Sophie is very protective of Rosa. We both are.'

'Naturally,' Nick says, a glint of mockery in his eyes. 'You *should* protect her from me. I'm a stranger. Your apprentice thinks I'm an infidel.'

'Rosa's only a child.'

He glances at me, humour turning to bemusement, and with a great surge of relief I realise that he's not interested in Rosa at all. The thought hasn't even crossed his mind.

I say softly, 'What do you want, Nick? If you haven't come to steal our children away?'

He starts to speak, then brings his knees up to his chest, reaching out with his hand as if, for a moment, he's forgotten that he can't lace his fingers together. He hesitates, rests his wrist on his kneecap.

'All my life,' he says slowly, 'I knew what I was meant to do. I was God's chosen. It was all set out for me. There wasn't room for me to say no, or do anything else, or be anyone, anything except God's messenger . . .' He tails off. He shakes his head and adds, in a different tone, 'Steal your children? Is that what you think of me?'

'It's what Sophie seems to think of you,' I say, and he doesn't seem to notice that I haven't answered the question.

'Yes, I see that.' He nods, and there's another silence, as if it's hard for him to speak. I hear him lick his lips before he goes on. 'I hated it sometimes. Knowing I had no choice. I used to have nightmares about Jerusalem, about dying before I got there . . . I was ill at Brindisi, and I thought I was damned. I thought, God made me for one reason, for only that, and now I'm going to die before I can do it. I could *feel* the fires of hell.' The corner of his mouth quirks up. 'I was feverish, of course.'

I put my forefinger in my mouth, sucking the dried blood away, worrying the split skin with my tongue.

'I was so desperate. I envied you. You have no idea how much I envied you. Everyone except me could go home . . . I wasn't allowed to doubt or wonder. I had my angels, and they were . . .' He hesitates. 'Cruel. They were cruel. To be loved so much without asking for it – that's hard.'

I glance at him but he's looking straight ahead.

'I spent my whole life trying to be a crusader, because that's what God wanted. And then I *was* a crusader, and it didn't seem to make a difference to anything. I mean . . . I couldn't see why God cared if I was there or not. One skinny peasant boy, who could hardly hold a sword. But I kept telling myself there was a reason for it. Everything in my life was leading to something great – I'd play some crucial part when we took Jerusalem, even if it was only to take an arrow meant for someone else, or I'd find the True Cross, God would come to me in a dream and tell me where to look . . . And then . . .' He tilts his chin sharply towards his left shoulder, what's left of it. 'Then *this* happened. For a while I was too ill to know what was going on, and when I came round they told me I could go home, I was no use to anyone any more.'

'That's not . . .' I say, scrabbling for a comforting word. 'Of course you're –'

'Not much use as a crusader, though, am I? They were right about that.' A pause. For the first time he sounds tired. 'And God . . . left me. He abandoned me.'

'He wouldn't do that, Nick.'

'What the hell do you know about it?'

Silence. 'Nothing,' I say. 'You're right. Nothing.'

'You don't know what it's like: to give yourself – utterly, without question – to something worth giving yourself to. And then to have yourself given back.'

I stay quiet, my mouth full of the taste of blood.

'I can't do it, Rufus. I was God's, and now I'm not. I can't bear it.' His breath catches in his throat and he clenches his fist.

I stay absolutely still, as if the slightest movement will betray me. I say, 'So go back to the Holy Land. There must be something you can do. Polish bits of armour or something. Carry water. You're not a cripple.'

'We won't get the Holy Land back. I know that now. Whatever God wanted . . . it wasn't that.'

'Then . . . live like everyone else. Settle down with a wife and kids. Go to Mass every Sunday. Say your prayers at night, make the triple sign of the cross when you wake up. Make a pilgrimage to Compostela . . . Pay someone else to make a pilgrimage to Compostela. Just be *ordinary*, Nick.'

'Like you?'

'I didn't –'

'And you're happy, are you?'

The sudden viciousness of it takes my breath away. I hiss through my teeth as though I've been punched, and don't answer.

Nick watches me for a moment, and then turns his head away again. 'At Damietta . . . there was a funny little man,

314

an Italian. He was mad – a fool – but mad for the love of God, mad like a child. People called him a saint. He crossed into the infidels' camp and tried to convert their leader.' He waits, as if he's expecting me to say something. When I don't, he takes a patient breath and goes on. 'He was extraordinary. He was a friar – he wouldn't take anything, he'd vowed to stay poor for the rest of his life, he put himself entirely in God's hands. He didn't fight, he wasn't a soldier. But there was something so perfect, so – *absolute* – about him. The holiness that comes from trying to do the impossible, day in, day out. That's what we had. That's what we lost. And I thought –'

He's paused on purpose, so that I'll have to speak. I say, 'Go on.'

'That's what I want to do. I want to live like him.'

'You want to be a monk?' I can't keep the scepticism out of my voice.

'A friar. Yes. With nothing, really with *nothing* – no money, no possessions, no home – no rest, no comfort, no self . . . It's inhuman, isn't it?' he adds. 'Inhuman and glorious. But God *is* inhuman. It's all or nothing. This –' he flicks his fingers at the room in front of us, the lozenges of light on the rushes – 'is nothing. What does it mean, really, to say your prayers at night, when you spend the day selling jewels to rich men? It's not enough.'

I pick up another handful of rushes and pick the herbs out, rubbing the leaves between my fingers.

'And if God doesn't want me back . . . if he's abandoned me for good . . . well, then I'll die knowing I loved him more than he loved me. And that,' he adds, his voice flat, 'would be something.'

I'm holding a sprig of rosemary. I pull it apart slowly. I say, 'I don't think God *has* abandoned you, Nick.'

He looks at me and smiles. I smile back. The little woody twig of rosemary digs into my palm and the scent rises in the warm air.

Then Nick says, 'Come with me.'

A pause while I try to make sense of the words.

'Come with me when I go.' He reaches out with his hand. His fingers hover above my handful of herbs, and for a moment I think he's going to take them away from me. Then his forefinger touches my wrist, very lightly: a hardly perceptible pressure between the veins, the perfect place for a wound, a nail. He says, 'You failed him once, Rufus. You don't have to carry on failing him.'

'I can't go with you, Nick.'

'Don't be afraid.'

'I'm not afraid. But I can't go with you. It's too late.'

The finger presses down, dark against my pale, blue-banded skin. Then he takes it away. He says, 'You made the crusader's vow. You remember?'

'Of course I remember. But –'

'It's still binding. It always will be.'

The sunlight glints in his eyes; and for a moment I feel such a sudden, intense pain that I get to my feet, staggering a little, turning away so that he can't see my face. I make an effort to breathe, but the air is swamped in perfume – the herbs from the floor, from the sun-baked garden – and the fragrances settle on my tongue, mercilessly sweet.

Nick says, 'If you die with that vow unfulfilled, you'll be damned.'

I press my back teeth together till the hinge of my jaw starts to ache. Then, in a strange, adult voice, I say, 'That vow is between me and God.'

The rushes scrape over the floor as he struggles to his

feet. I feel the temperature of the air change as he comes close to me, behind me, not touching. He says, 'You don't have anything here to stay for, Rufus.'

I feel the tension in my throat relax, suddenly, until I can laugh. I say, 'Only my life. Only Sophie and Rosa, and the workshop, and the apprentices.'

'You love Sophie, do you?'

'Yes,' I say. 'Enough.'

'And you've forgiven her?' I don't move, and he makes a very small sound, like a sigh. 'Oh, Rufus . . . Is this the penance you've chosen for yourself? Living like this? Bringing up another man's child?'

For a second I don't understand the words properly: I think he means *another child of man, one more human being* . . . Then, slowly, like a schoolboy deciphering a Latin text, I make sense of what he's telling me. I hear a man I don't know say, 'Another man's child?'

'Sophie told you,' Nick says, a sudden crack in his voice. 'She did tell you.'

'Rosa is mine.'

There's such a long silence I wonder if he's slipped away, out through the workshop and back to the Holy Land. Then he says, 'God forgive me.'

'Rosa is mine,' I say, in the matter-of-fact tone I use to tell Symon his work is rubbish. 'Believe me, Nick. I do *know* where babies come from.'

He says, 'I'm sorry. Oh, Christ, I'm sorry.' When I turn to look at him his head is bowed and his hand is dragging at the cloth over his chest. I watch him, wondering how I could have failed to recognise him, even now, even after ten years.

I say, 'Paul.' And once I've said it, it's as if I've always known.

'He was going to settle in Genoa,' Nick says, raising his eyes to mine. 'He kept telling us, rubbing it in our faces, he could mention his father's name and the money-lenders would give him anything he wanted . . . Stuff this for a game of crusaders, he said, he was going to get rich . . . And Sophie agreed to stay too, because by then she didn't have much choice.' A slight pause, as if he's wondering what else to tell me. 'Then . . . he died. Just after we got there. A fever. He'd had boils, like a plague. They joked that his boils were bigger than Sophie's bump. He died.'

'So she . . .' But I don't need to finish the sentence. It's all very clear.

'I thought she'd told you. I'm sorry, Rufus. Believe me.'

I nod. I turn on my heel and walk to the other end of the room, as if I can leave myself behind. I say, 'So you're right, after all. There's nothing to keep me here.'

Nick makes a sudden move towards me, then checks himself.

I turn back and look at him. I concentrate, imagining him three weeks from now, his clothes ragged, mud-stained, his beard spreading over his face and his hair dropping into his eyes. His face will sink back into his skull; the scar on his cheek will tighten like a stitch. Tiredness will destroy the poise he must have fought for, after he lost his arm. I imagine the long days of sunlight and hunger, the vivid dreams, the surrender to something impossible.

I say, 'But I can't come with you.'

'Please.'

'No.'

He opens his mouth and then shuts it again, as if he can feel the way the space between us has solidified. He

318

nods and adjusts his cloak, rolling his shoulder as if it's stiff. He says, 'Goodbye, then.'

'Goodbye.' I almost add, *God bless you*.

'If you change your mind –'

'I won't.'

'Yes, you will. You'll regret it. I promise you.'

I smile, and suddenly I'm a grown-up – properly a grown-up – again. 'Of course I'll regret it. But I won't change my mind.'

He smiles too, wryly, tilting his head as if to concede a point. 'No. But if you do, I'll be at the Bird and Tree. I'll wait.'

'Get lost, Nick.'

He grins and gives me a mock bow, hand over his heart. A hiccup of loss starts in my gut and I swallow hard, trying to keep it there. He moves to the door and pauses; then he turns, with his hand on the lintel, and says, 'I forgive you, Rufus. I forgive you everything.'

I don't say anything.

He laughs softly. 'You don't give a damn whether I forgive you or not, do you?'

'No,' I say slowly. 'No, I don't think I do.'

He drops his hand and goes through the doorway, the last blade of sunshine sliding across his back. I follow him blindly, back into the heat of the workshop. The journeymen glance up as I go past them, and I would make an effort to look normal if I could only remember what it's like. Nick pauses at the table and picks up my father's little cameo. I go over to him, wishing he'd go now, quickly, so I don't have to say anything else.

He waits until I'm near enough to hear him without his having to raise his voice. He weighs the gem thoughtfully in his hand, as if it's told him something he wanted to know. Then he leans close to me. He says, 'I'll swap my crusader vow for yours.'

The look in his eyes . . . It's like a child, offering to swap toys. I say, 'What?'

He smiles. 'An exchange. Your crusader vow –' he draws a little playful cross in the air over my heart – 'for mine.'

'I don't understand.'

'That's all right. You don't have to understand.' His smile dies, and it's as if he's never laughed at anything in his life and never will. 'I'm taking your vow away from you. In the sight of God – here, now – I'm taking it on, in your place. And in exchange, you can have mine. Mine, that I fulfilled. I'm giving you a completed vow for a broken one. That's a good bargain.'

'Nick, what –'

'And whoever gets to heaven first can put in a word for the other one.' He turns, dropping the cameo on the table, and goes to the door.

'*Nick* –'

He doesn't look round. I run after him, ignoring the journeymen's stares, and grab his arm, swinging him to face me. We're half in the workshop, half in the street. Someone shouts, 'Gardy-loo-ooo . . .' and a glittering, sharp-smelling rain falls from a window opposite.

'Thank you,' I say.

'I owed you.' He looks at my hand until I release him. He doesn't smile.

I step back and watch him for as long as I can bear. Then I give him the kiss of peace. After a second I feel him move to kiss me back, but I've already drawn away, short of breath, giddy from the heat. He swallows. 'The Bird and Tree,' he says, 'Don't forget.'

As if I could. As if I'll be able to sleep tonight for thinking about him, what he's said. As if . . .

I go back into the workshop. I stand in the dark, letting
my eyes adjust, and then put the jewels on the table carefully back into the chest, one by one. If I looked through
the window I might see Nick still standing there, but I
turn my back.

Symon says, 'All that time, and the tight git didn't want
anything?'

'Nothing I offered him,' I say.

And then, for what I hope will be the last time today, I
dissolve into laughter, crossing my arms over my ribs and
snorting painfully, joylessly; and the people around me
swap indulgent, fatherly looks, even the apprentices, and
I carry on so long, so loudly, that in the end they join in,
even though they don't know what's funny, and the whole
workshop fills with slightly mad mirth, rings with it, and
no one stops until Sophie comes down to find out what's
going on, and we're swept away, stupidly, ridiculously,
because that's how laughter goes, sometimes, and after
all we're only human.

XXII

At last, when the workshop is quiet again, I settle down and try to work, but I can't. It's as hot as hell – we're all dripping, like meat on a spit – and my hands aren't steady enough; I'm scared I'll make a mess and have to start again, like an apprentice. I can feel the others watching me. In the end I stand up and say, 'I'm going out. If anyone comes in and wants to see me, tell him to come back tomorrow.'

They nod. I crouch by the bucket of water and splash the sweat off my forehead, cooling my face and hands.

Rosa's voice says, 'Where are you going? Can I come?'

I look up, and she's peering round the door. *Another man's child* . . . Suddenly there's grief snarling at me like an animal, waiting to bite; I clench my jaw and stare back at it, daring it to try. I say, 'Eavesdroppers never hear anything good, Rosa.'

She frowns, considering, and says, 'Not good, maybe, but useful. Otherwise I wouldn't have heard you say you were going out, would I?'

I fight to keep my voice steady. 'No, you can't come. Go back to your mother.'

'Are you going to the cathedral? Please. You can show me the shrine.'

I cup water in my hands and stare down at it, trying not to let anything show on my face. My reflection trembles as the grief bares its teeth. Any minute now . . . I say, 'I've shown you the shrine before. Hundreds of times.'

'You can show me again. *Please.*'

'Rosa, *no.*'

'Papa –'

'*No!*' The water spills out of my hands and over the floor, and I close my eyes. When I open them and look up at her she looks ready to cry. I study her face, searching for something that looks like me, but there's nothing. She looks like Sophie: a haughty, snub-nosed angel. I've always been glad she didn't have red hair.

I can't speak. I stand up and walk out into the street, where the sun has slipped behind the roofs opposite and there's an unexpected chill in the air, as if the weather's changing. I take shallow breaths, concentrating on not letting myself feel anything. It doesn't work.

I go to the cathedral and kneel below the crucifix that hangs over Bishop Gero's tomb. I close my eyes. I can't remember any prayers. All I can say is, *Why? Why me, why now? What are you playing at?*

Do you want me to go with Nick?

I could go with him. I could. Abandon Sophie and Rosa and the apprentices, give up everything. I imagine myself walking through the gate with Nick, back on the road to glory, all my failures redeemed. The thought sends a stab of desire through me, so sharp it could almost be despair.

I take a deep breath, weighing the longing against the sadness, the ecstasy against the sacrifice. Something says, *Yes.* And I don't know whether it's myself or you.

I get up, my knees trembling, and turn towards the door.

A grimy hand catches at my arm. A deep male voice says, 'Rufus. Don't see you here much.'

I look up, already twisting out of his grasp. It's a man I know, a carpenter – the same age as me or a little older – who must have been one of Lucas's friends. I can't remember his name. I say, 'No, I don't come here a lot.' I try to push past him, but he steps into my way and gives me the kiss of peace. He smells of sweat and woodshavings, and his mouth is sticky.

I force myself to smile and kiss him back. I want to go – to go *now* – but he kneels, still smiling at me, and nods to the space beside him as if he's going to pray aloud and wants me to join in.

I hesitate; and then, because I've hesitated, I can't do anything but kneel down next to him. I curse myself silently, then I curse him. What am I doing? One paternoster, just *one*, and then I'll leave.

But he doesn't say a paternoster, or an Ave. He doesn't say anything.

I wait in silence. I look up at the crucifix, and for a moment I don't see God, just a man who's been betrayed, whose whole purpose was to be killed in the nastiest possible way to make up for what other people did.

'It's not pretty, that crucifix,' the man beside me says, as if he can read my mind. 'Gets me every time. Crucifixes – well, they're about the victory over death, mostly. But this one . . . the poor lad's *dead*. He doesn't *know* he's victorious. He thinks it's all over.'

There's something funny in his voice: something casual and affectionate, like a father talking to his child. It catches me off-guard, and I reel and shut my eyes, willing the ache in my throat to die down. There's a silence, and I think he hasn't noticed.

Then he says, 'You all right, mate? You look a bit . . .'

I nod, not trusting my voice. I wish he'd go away. I wish he'd shove off and leave me in peace.

He breathes in, the air hissing in his nose, and I hear him sniff again and then snort thickly. For a moment I think he's doing it on purpose, to be tactful; but when I glance sideways at him he's digging up inside his nostril with a finger and inspecting what comes out.

'Bit of a miracle, that cross,' he adds, looking pensively at the scaly shred of snot on his fingernail. ' 'Course, you know the story.'

I still don't trust myself to speak, but he doesn't seem to care.

'You know – Bishop Gero donates it, consecrates it, and then what does he find but it's got a whacking great crack in it. Can't let the workmen loose on it, so he gets a bit of the Eucharist, bit of the True Cross, shoves 'em into the crack, and hey presto! the crack's gone.' He touches his tongue to his snotty finger, then seems to remember that I'm there and wipes it on his cotte. 'Bit dubious, if you ask me.'

I swallow. I'm not interested in his story, but at least now I can say something without my voice breaking. 'From a theological point of view?'

'No,' he says, surprised. 'From a woodworking one.'

'Ah.'

'Nice, though. All this cobbled-up skit-brained nonsense about getting back the True Cross, when it's right there all the time.'

There's a pause, and he beams at me. I take a deep breath, looking into his face, feeling the force of his good humour like sunshine; then I turn away.

'Like a parable,' I say, speaking to the forlorn wooden face above me as much as to the carpenter. 'Splendid. Very profound.' But too easy, I want to say. It's too easy to tell me that what I'm searching for is here, that it's been here all the time. It's too slick. No, I'm sorry. You'll have to come up with something better than that.

He must hear a strange note in my voice, because he coughs and scratches his head. 'Saw your lady wife the other day,' he says, so transparently trying to cheer me up that I could almost laugh. 'And your little girl. She's growing up quick, isn't she? Sweet little thing, she is. Got your dad's smile, hasn't she? You can spot it a mile off. I said to your wife, 'fraid that runs in the family, Johannes and Rufus and now Rosa. Pity she favours her father's side so much, but at least she's not red-hea—' He stops, takes a moment to hear what's he's said, and then laughs. 'No offence. She's a lovely kid.'

'None taken,' I say.

There's a pause. I can feel something inside me slipping away, that blazing certainty dying. It leaves something quiet in its place.

'I'll leave you to it, shall I?' he says, standing up. 'Didn't mean to distract you. You've probably got things to think about.' He pats me on the shoulder, like a kid leaving a puppy on its own for the first time. 'God bless.'

His hand is grimy and calloused and scabbed here and there from woodworking. It's such a human hand, such a kind hand; so different from Nick's. If only I could remember his *name*, but I can't. I say, 'And you.'

He hovers, shifting from foot to foot. Then he jerks his head at the crucifix and says in a quick, jocular rush, 'You know he *didn't* die, right? Not for ever?'

I look into his face, and in spite of myself I'm grinning. 'Yes,' I say. 'Yes, I do know he didn't die.'

'Good. That's the main thing. Right. You look after yourself.' And he strides away. He looks back at me, catches his toe in a crack in the floor and almost falls on his face.

I wait until he's gone. Then I say aloud, 'All right. If this is what you want. I'm here.'

There's no answer.

Unless silence *is* an answer.

You're in the street, waiting for me. I come out of the cathedral as the bells start to ring for Vespers, and you get up from where you've been sitting and follow me. It doesn't matter whether I know you're there or not; you stay three paces behind me, close enough to reach out and steady me if I stumble. But I don't stumble.

The bells ring and ring. I make my way home to the workshop, to Sophie and Rosa, and as we're approaching the Bird and Tree you take a few quick steps to catch me up, so that you're by my side as we go past. I walk under the signboard without pausing or looking up at it, and so do you.

And as we walk I'm thinking about a new commission I got a few days ago, a cup with engraved letters, and about whether I can entrust it to one of the journeymen or whether I should do it myself. I'm thinking about how Symon is actually doing quite well, and whether I should pretend I don't know that he sneaks out to play football when I'm not there. I'm thinking about what we'll have for supper, and how tomorrow I shall lie in bed until Sophie *makes* me get up, and how the linen smells of lavender in summer and damp straw in winter, and how you get used to the smell of damp straw until it's not at all unpleasant. I'm thinking about Rosa, and wondering if I already know the man she'll fall in love with one day, and if so, who it is and whether she'll marry him.

I turn the corner into the goldsmiths' street, and the smell of sweat and metal hits the back of my nose, and the familiarity of it makes something relax inside me, very slightly.

I look sideways at you, meeting your gaze. And even if you're not there I'll pretend that you are, and even if you don't love me I'll make believe that you do.

AFTERWORD

The story of the Children's Crusades is a strange one. The accounts of them are conflicting, obscure, brief and generally written long after the event, which means it's very hard to be sure exactly what happened. This is a pain for historians, but a godsend for writers. In *The Broken Road* I've invented things – the way the crusade begins, for example, and the burning of the village – but as far as I know I haven't had to contradict historical fact directly.

The basic events, as far as they are agreed to have happened at all, are these: in 1212 – after the disastrous Fourth Crusade, when Christian forces sacked Constantinople (modern Istanbul), also a Christian city – two distinct groups of children set off from Northern Europe to reclaim the Holy Land from the Muslims. The better-known of the two armies set out from France, led by a boy named Stephen, and made its way south to Marseilles where – or so one of the accounts tells us – the children were promised safe passage to Jerusalem, loaded aboard a ship, taken across the sea and sold as slaves. The other crusade (*my* crusade, as I can't help thinking of it) can be traced from Cologne to Genoa, and then to Rome. Its exact course, as well as the fate of most of its crusaders, is uncertain; but Nicholas, the leader, reached the Holy Land, fighting in the Fifth Crusade at Acre and the siege of Damietta. Later he returned to Cologne, where his father had met a mysterious 'bad end'.

I chose to write about the German crusade partly because it was less well known, and also because the average age was much higher: these were mostly young adults, apprentices and peasants rather than what we would think of now as children. But, as well as those factors, there was something in the details that intrigued me. The death of Nick's father, for instance, and Nick's return to Cologne: what happened, how did Nick find out about his father's death, what was it like for him to come back from the Holy Land? But it wasn't just Nick that inspired me, it was the progress of the crusade itself, dwindling and slowly petering out in Italy . . . It doesn't have the (almost certainly fictional) melodrama of the French story, but the tale it tells is equally powerful: a dream that fails not because of deliberate human evil, but because of the kind of world we live in, because it's *hard* to go on walking day after day, because the sea doesn't open up for anyone, because, in the end, we're human. As it turned out, Rufus's story didn't go that far, but it has the same kind of feeling about it. We fail. Hopes of glory die. And yet, somehow, we can learn to live with that.

Lots of people have written about the Children's Crusades, and it's not hard to see why. They're a perfect setting for a coming-of-age story: hundreds of kids all leaving home at once, driven by hopes of glory and adventure, only to find that it's not that simple. I feel like I recognise those teenagers, desperate to get away from their parents, to sleep under the stars, have sex away from watchful eyes . . . There's something about it that feels timeless. We've all been there! But in some ways that actually made it harder to write. It was easy to forget that the thirteenth century wasn't the twenty-first, or even the twentieth century – to think of the Middle Ages as just a picturesque background, to write the story as if it was modern, as if freedom and romance and excitement were *all* it was about. The temptation, in a society which is often either intolerant or apathetic in matters of religion, is to downplay (or even ignore) the spiritual aspect. But that felt – well, cowardly, I suppose. It's risky to put God into a novel. But I really wanted to try it.

So God, or at least Rufus's idea of him, is one of the major characters. I wouldn't claim that he's a properly medieval God – any more than Rufus's crisis and final acceptance of his faith are properly medieval, either – but all the same I did try to get a kind of historical flavour in the way the book thinks about Christianity. In the Middle Ages people were much more comfortable mixing ideas of the Divine with earthier, ickier aspects of life, in ways which can seem really weird to us. (For example, there were between eight and eighteen relics venerated as the Foreskin of Jesus – which, by the way, led to obvious questions about credibility, until in the end the contro-versy was solved by the Church threatening to excommunicate anyone who tried to get to the bottom of the mystery.) Medieval people were obsessed with the body – unsurprisingly, given the lack of decent medicine, contraception, drainage, hygiene, and so on – and they didn't separate the spiritual from the physical in the way we do. So Rufus's God exists in the same world, and sometimes in the same sentence, as things like boils and chamber pots and testicles. Sadly, as this is a book for young people, I couldn't use quite the same words that

Chaucer would have used! But the principle's there, and I like to think it's kind of authentic.

But I wasn't trying to write a history essay – and I hope it shows! That's not an excuse for inadvertent inaccuracies or anachronisms (no doubt there are a few I haven't noticed, in spite of my research): it's more about what I was trying to write, and why I was trying to write it. All historical novels should be about the past – but *every* novel should be about the present. So although I loved thinking about the real events and the real people, I wanted to write something which would resonate with modern readers – about faith, and love, and idealism, and loss . . . When historical novels work, it's because they have something universal at the heart of the narrative, so that within all that period detail the reader can see something that they recognise. I loved doing the research for *The Broken Road*, and I suppose it would be nice to think that it's mostly accurate – or even vaguely educational . . . But all that means nothing, unless the story it tells is true *now*.

* * *

For anyone who is interested in reading more about the Children's Crusades, there are three books which I would wholeheartedly recommend.

Out of all the fiction I read on the subject, there was one novel which was overwhelmingly my favourite: George Andrzeyevski's extraordinary *The Gates of Paradise*.

For an analysis of the Children's Crusades in another context – and for a thought-provoking and moving book about childhood and our attitudes to it – I would suggest Blake Morrison's *As If*.

And for a fascinating, authoritative and thorough discussion of the history of the Children's Crusades – what really happened, and what probably didn't – there is no better book on the subject than Gary Dickson's *The Children's Crusade: Medieval History, Modern Mythistory*.

GLOSSARY

Armoire, n. a cupboard

Aqua regia, n. a mixture of nitric and hydrochloric acids, so called because it can dissolve gold, a 'noble' metal

Ave Maria, n. the Hail Mary, the most common prayer to the Virgin. In 1212 the prayer was shorter than the modern version; translated from the Latin it ran, 'Hail, Mary, full of grace, the Lord is with thee; blessed art thou among women, and blessed is the fruit of thy womb, Jesus, Amen.'

Barehide, n. a hide with the hair removed, or one that has not been dressed

Braggett, n. a drink made of honey and ale fermented together, often spelt 'bragget'

Bunghole, n. the hole in a cask, which is closed with the bung; also used to refer to the anus

Cameo, n.   a gemstone on which is carved a figure in relief

Canelle, n.   cinnamon

Capon, n.   a castrated cock, or a small chicken

Chaperon, n.   a hood or cap

Cittern-head, n.   literally the grotesquely carved head of a cittern (a musical instrument not unlike a guitar), used as a term of contempt

Cods, n.   the testicles (more usually 'cod', the scrotum)

Comyn, n.   cumin

Crespine, n.   a net for the hair, sometimes made of lace

Cullions, n.   the testicles

Cyclas, n.   an upper garment, tunic or surcoat, made shorter in front than behind, generally worn by women but also sometimes by men

Damask water, n.   rose-water distilled from damask roses

Dizzard, n.   a fool or idiot

Drawplate, n.   a jeweller's tool for reducing the thickness of wire

Dugs, n.	the breasts
En cabochon, adv.	polished rather than cut, so that the gemstone is smooth and rounded
Erl-king, n.	literally the King of the Elves, a malevolent figure in German mythology reputed to steal children and carry travellers to their deaths
Feast of Misrule, n.	otherwise known as the Feast of Fools, a feast generally held around Twelfth Night or the new year, where the traditional hierarchy was reversed and religious rites were mocked and parodied; associated with the creation of a 'Boy Bishop', who temporarily usurped the authority of the real bishop
Felter, v.	to have sexual intercourse
Frau Holle, n.	in German folklore, a mythological figure associated with witches, winter and the dead; as leader of the Wild Hunt, she is associated with Odin, the Norse god of battle and death
Frumenty, n.	a dish made with hulled wheat and milk, seasoned with cinnamon, sugar and other flavourings.
Get, n.	offspring, child, especially illegitimate; the original form of 'git'

Go scrape, phr. a form of contemptuous dismissal, equivalent to a mild profanity

Hornbook, n. a child's reading aid, on which the writing was protected by a clear sheet of horn; often included the alphabet, the roman numerals I to X, and the Lord's Prayer, mounted on wood

Hose, n. clothing for the legs, similar to leggings or tights, sometimes covering the feet, sometimes reaching only down to the ankle

Hypocras, n. a drink made of wine flavoured with spices

Intaglio, n. an engraved gemstone where the figure is sunken rather than raised, the opposite of a cameo

Jape, v. to have sexual intercourse

Jenny, n. a prefix used to denote a female animal, e.g. jenny-ass; sometimes used on its own

Journeyman, n. an artisan who has served his apprenticeship but is not yet a master of his trade

Lammas, n. the 1st of August, observed as a harvest festival

League, n. a measure of distance, varying

somewhat in length but generally estimated at about 5 kilometres

Leman, n.   a lover or sweetheart

Linsey-woolsey, n.   a textile, made of a mixture of flax and wool

Lorelei, n.   in German legend, a beautiful nymph who haunted the Rhine, luring men to their death with her singing

Mantle, n.   a loose sleeveless cloak

Mercer, n.   a merchant of fabrics, especially silks, velvets and other fine materials

Milksop, n.   a feeble, timid or ineffectual person, especially a cowardly or effeminate boy

Mitching, adj.   thieving, skulking

Mixen, n.   a dunghill, a midden

Moon-struck, adj.   insane, deranged, dazed, idiotic

Night soil, n.   human excrement

Nixie, n.   in German folklore, a water sprite or nymph with a human torso and a fish's tail

Nones, n.   one of the eight services of canonical office celebrated by the church, also used to refer to the hour at which it took place. Roughly speaking, the approximate times of each were: Matins at midnight, Lauds at 3 a.m., Prime at 6 a.m., Terce at 9 a.m., Sext at midday, Nones at 3 p.m., Vespers at 6 p.m. and Compline at 9 p.m.

Nuncheon, n.   a snack

Palfrey, n.   a horse

Paternoster, n.   the Lord's Prayer, especially in Latin (of which the first words are '*Pater noster*', 'Our Father')

Patten, n.   thick-soled footwear, especially clogs or wooden platforms, designed to raise the wearer's feet above the level of the mud

Pottage, n.   a thick soup

Prime, n.   see **Nones**

Quent, n.   the female genitalia

Quim, n.   the female genitalia

Scrip, n.   a small bag or satchel, especially as carried by pilgrims and beggars

Scumber, n. or v.   **n.** the dung of a dog or fox; **v.** or of a dog or fox; to evacuate the faeces, used jocularly to refer to people

Shack-rag, n.   a ragged, disreputable person, a rascal; a variant of shag-rag

Shifter, n.	a trickster, an idler
Shrive, v.	to hear someone's confession and give them absolution
Skit, n.	dirt, faeces
Skite, n.	dirt, faeces
Solar, n.	a room in a medieval household where the family could enjoy some privacy, usually smaller and more comfortable than the hall
Stog, v.	to be stuck in mud, mire, etc.
Stoolball, n.	a medieval ancestor of cricket
Surcotte, n.	a surcoat, an outer coat or garment worn by both sexes
Swive, v.	to have sexual intercourse, to copulate (with someone)
Terce, n.	see **Nones**
Tithe, n.	a payment or tax due to the church, originally a tenth of what was produced
Turnshoe, n.	a thin, flexible shoe made inside out and then turned
Vellum, n.	a fine kind of parchment prepared from the skin of calves

Vespers, n.   see **Nones**

Wattle-and-daub, n.   a rough building material or wall consisting of woven laths covered by mud or clay

Weatherfish, n.   a kind of fish, also known as a thunder-fish

Wimple, n.   a garment of linen or silk worn by women so as to envelop the head, chin, sides of the face and neck, still worn as part of the habit of some orders of nuns

Withy, n.   a willow wand

Wodnek, n.   in German mythology, a male water spirit

Woolsey, n. or adj.   woollen

Worsted, n. or adj.   woollen

ACKNOWLEDGEMENTS

I owe more than I can say to Rosemary Canter, not only for this book but for all my previous novels. She was a brilliant and inspiring agent and I will miss her.

I would also like to thank everyone at United Agents, especially Jodie Marsh; everyone at Bloomsbury, especially Emma Matthewson and Isabel Ford; Kryss Brady, for her help and feedback; Ben Schofield, for sending me his copy of *Medieval German Tales*; and Gary Dickson – for his book *The Children's Crusade: Medieval History, Modern Mythistory*, and also for his personal generosity in responding to my queries. All mistakes and inaccuracies, needless to say, are my own.